Praise for

"Faced with a complex... the very end, Brennan doles out just the right amount of family drama while moving the story effortlessly between cases. This is the beginning of a fabulous new series from the queen of crime fiction."

—**J.T. Ellison,** *New York Times* **bestselling author of** *It's One of Us***, on** *You'll Never Find Me*

"Allison Brennan just raised the bar for private eye fiction! *You'll Never Find Me* is complex, combustible and convincing. Secrets, action, suspense, *You'll Never Find Me* has it all!"

—**Matt Coyle, Shamus Award–winning author of the Rick Cahill private eye series**

"A complex thriller . . . jurisdictional infighting, vendettas, and power plays . . . allows the author the opportunity for some clever sleight-of-hand."

—***Booklist*** **on** *The Missing Witness*

"Set among Louisiana's swamps and brooding atmosphere, *Seven Girls Gone* is a complex mystery whose characters are as intriguing as the storyline."

—*Denver Post*

"An intense, pulse pounding thriller from start to finish. There were so many suspects, not to mention surprises and twists."

—***The Reading Cafe*** **on** *The Wrong Victim*

"Allison Brennan is always good but her latest and most ambitious work ever . . . is downright spectacular . . . A riveting page turner as prescient as it is purposeful."

—***Providence Journal*** **on** *Tell No Lies*

"A lean thriller starring a strong and damaged protagonist who's as compelling as Lisbeth Salander."

—***Kirkus Reviews*** **on** *The Third to Die*

DON'T SAY A WORD

Also by Allison Brennan

Quinn & Costa Thrillers

The Third to Die
Tell No Lies
The Wrong Victim
Seven Girls Gone
The Missing Witness
See How They Hide

Regan Merritt Series

The Sorority Murder
Don't Open the Door

Angelhart Investigations

You'll Never Find Me

Beach Reads and Deadly Deeds

For additional books by Allison Brennan,
visit her website, allisonbrennan.com.

DON'T SAY A WORD

ALLISON BRENNAN

/|| MIRA

/|| MIRA™

Recycling programs for this product may not exist in your area.

ISBN-13: 978-0-7783-6862-5

Don't Say a Word

Copyright © 2025 by Allison Brennan

All rights reserved. No part of this book may be used or reproduced in any manner whatsoever without written permission.

Without limiting the exclusive rights of any author, contributor or the publisher of this publication, any unauthorized use of this publication to train generative artificial intelligence (AI) technologies is expressly prohibited. Harlequin also exercises their rights under Article 4(3) of the Digital Single Market Directive 2019/790 and expressly reserve this publication from the text and data mining exception.

This is a work of fiction. Names, characters, places, and incidents are either the product of the author's imagination or are used fictitiously. Any resemblance to actual persons, living or dead, businesses, companies, events or locales is entirely coincidental.

For questions and comments about the quality of this book, please contact us at CustomerService@Harlequin.com.

TM is a trademark of Harlequin Enterprises ULC.

MIRA
22 Adelaide St. West, 41st Floor
Toronto, Ontario M5H 4E3, Canada
MIRABooks.com

HarperCollins Publishers
Macken House, 39/40 Mayor Street Upper,
Dublin 1, D01 C9W8, Ireland
www.HarperCollins.com

Printed in U.S.A.

For everyone who has lost a loved one to drugs.

Nobody made a greater mistake than he who did nothing because he could do only a little.

—Edmund Burke

PROLOGUE

Phoenix PD Officer Josie Morales stood over the body of a kid who couldn't be over eighteen. She said a silent prayer, but still wanted to punch something. What a waste.

"Where's the damn ME?" her partner, Tyrell Jones, said. "It's already hot as balls out here."

"Detectives are on their way," Josie said. The ME always came after the detectives.

She and Tyrell had just finished their morning briefing when dispatch reported that park rangers had found a dead body in Mountain View Park, only a couple blocks from their precinct. Now they were stuck here until the detectives cleared the scene. Their coffee run would have to wait.

"How long until the dicks get here?" Tyrell said. He wasn't a fan of the detective squad, mostly because of how some of them treated uni's.

She asked dispatch for a status.

"Twenty minutes," she told Tyrell.

"Fuck," he whispered as he took another long look at the deceased. "Drugs," he said, though they couldn't be certain. They couldn't see any blood or external wounds, but that didn't mean that a drug overdose was the cause of death.

Josie had already sectioned off the area with crime scene tape, not because she thought this was a homicide, but because she didn't want people being disrespectful and nosy. A couple joggers slowed as they passed Josie, straining their necks to see what the cops were doing. Tyrell glared at them, then walked back to their patrol car and returned with a tarp. They carefully covered the body.

"Fucking waste," Tyrell muttered.

He'd been a uniformed officer for fifteen years and planned to retire after putting in his twenty, then open a bar. Or a gun range. Or a gym. It changed depending on his mood, but one thing was certain, he'd told Josie more than once, he wanted to work for himself and take orders from no one except his wife.

He was cynical and rough around the edges, but Tyrell was a solid and seasoned cop. He never dodged calls and called out cops who routinely did, which didn't make him a lot of friends. Josie had learned a lot from Tyrell since she'd partnered with him after shifting to days three months ago, and while she wished he would be a bit more diplomatic with their colleagues, she respected and trusted him.

Josie kept her eyes on the people in the area, making sure they stayed beyond the crime scene tape. She glanced at Tyrell and, even though he was wearing sunglasses, she could tell by his tight jaw and the way he stood that he was upset.

He had two kids. To see a dead teen was difficult for her, but had to be harder on a father.

By the time a detective sedan pulled up, they'd drawn a larger audience, but Josie had put the tape far enough away that onlookers couldn't overhear their discussion.

"Well, shit," Tyrell said when he saw Rachel King was the responding detective. "Deal with her, I don't have the patience today." He walked over to the tape to wait for the ME's van.

Good that Tyrell walked away, because Rachel had made few friends during her years on the force, primarily because she was both prickly and hypercritical of uniformed officers. However, the CSI who rolled up behind her was Josie's cousin Nico Angelhart.

Nico smiled when he saw her, but before they could exchange a word, Rachel removed the tarp and motioned for him to take photos.

He was quick, methodical, and efficient as he photographed the body, the surrounding area, and then motioned that Rachel could search the victim. They would want to identify him as soon as possible and notify his parents. Josie was glad she didn't have to do that part of the job.

As she watched, Rachel turned out the teen's pockets. A small baggie of blue pills along with a couple twenties were in one pocket; his other held a thin wallet.

Rachel opened it. "Arizona State Identification Card, no driver's license. Elijah Martinez, seventeen. Lives in an apartment off Nineteenth Avenue. That's more than two miles away. What's he doing here?" She continued flipping through the wallet. "Sun Valley High School," she said. "That's . . ."

"Less than a mile down the road," Josie said. "My alma mater." She was trying to build a rapport, but the detective neither looked at her nor acknowledged her comment.

Rachel handed the wallet, drugs, and cash to Nico, who sealed them in separate evidence bags. Most likely fentanyl. Dammit, this was the sixth fentanyl death Josie handled since moving to day shift. She'd stopped counting the ODs that she and Tyrell reversed with Narcan.

But Elijah Martinez was the youngest.

"No sign of external injuries. Likely drug overdose. Nico, what do you think?"

"The ME will do an exam, but I see no weapon, no biologic matter, no sign of violence or bruising. No external signs of drug use, no needles. Eight likely fentanyl tablets in the bag." He couldn't confirm fentanyl until the pills were tested in the lab. They'd seen fentanyl tainted with xylazine, an animal tranquilizer, as well as stimulants.

"Time of death?"

"You know better than to ask me," Nico said with a half smile.

"But?" Rachel pushed.

"Four to six hours."

Rachel glanced at her watch. "Likely after midnight. Call the ME, they can take the body. Officer . . . Morales?"

"Yes," Josie said.

"Did I see that the park rangers called this in?"

Josie nodded. "They found the body at 5:35 a.m. My partner and I were first on scene at 5:45."

Josie followed Rachel's gaze as the detective looked up and down the park. Martinez lay against a tree west of the small gazebo and playground area. The rest of the park was open space, grass, paths, and a community garden. The body couldn't be seen from the road, but it would have been seen from the main east-west trail before it forked north and south.

If someone was paying attention, Josie thought. She'd encountered runners who put in their earbuds and looked straight ahead. If someone saw the body, they might assume homeless. But the park rangers rousted the homeless from the area early every morning.

Nico said, "The ME will have a van here within forty-five minutes. I'm going to inspect the playground."

Drug addicts often left paraphernalia in the area they partied. The park would be overrun with kids this morning before the heat drove them indoors.

Josie joined Nico. He handed her an extra rake and together they combed through the sand, looking for pills, foil that might contain drug residue, needles, and anything else that might be a danger to little kids.

"How're things?" Josie asked.

"Good. Just lost my intern."

"Theo?" Theo Washington was a nineteen-year-old student going through the forensic science program at Paradise Valley Community College. He worked part-time for Nico's sister—and Josie's best friend—Margo.

"His internship ended yesterday, and he starts classes next week. I tried to get him hired part-time, but it's not in the budget. Fortunately, I'll have first dibs on him in May when he graduates. While he sometimes jumps to conclusions—probably Margo's bad influence—" he added with a smile "—he's detail-orientated and takes direction well. Doesn't mind tedious work."

"Shouldn't you give Margo credit for his positive skills as well?" Josie said lightly, knowing Margo and Nico loved ribbing each other.

"And further enlarge my sister's already big ego?" He laughed. "Anyway, his computer skills could be better—I thought everyone in his generation were tech gurus. He's adding an extra computer class at my suggestion."

"Is he still working for Margo?"

He nodded. "We had dinner last night and she gloated about it."

"You'll be gloating in May."

"Damn straight," he said. "She won't mind. The city can pay Theo far more than she can, and it's a great career. Plus, Theo is motivated."

They found two used condoms—both older than twenty-four hours, per Nico, so he tossed them. One foil that seemed old but had what was likely fentanyl residue, so he bagged it. And a knife, which he also bagged, though it didn't appear to have blood on it. Probably fell out of someone's pocket.

"You think this is an accidental OD?" Josie asked Nico as she tossed a broken beer bottle into the trash can.

"That's up to the ME."

"We've enough of them," she commented.

"Yeah, we do. I wish we could find whoever left him to die, though no one will prosecute."

"Bingo," Josie said. Generally, if an individual left someone to die when that person could have been saved with prompt medical treatment, it would be charged as a misdemeanor, if charged at all. It was a debate they'd had at their grandfather's house on occasion—moral, ethical, and legal ramifications of action versus inaction. Retired Judge Hector Morales loved to play devil's advocate. He could argue any side of any issue effectively, and was brilliant at seeing different angles. He'd been a respected jurist for more than forty years.

"Doesn't make it right," Nico said.

"I'm with you. You know, Sun Valley High School won't have a school resource officer until October. I can probably get permission to talk to the students, especially since the kid went there."

School resource officers worked for a special division of Phoenix PD and, depending on funding levels, would be assigned to high schools in the region. Josie had applied for the program, but hadn't been accepted into one of the limited slots. She'd apply again next year.

How did she explain she felt invested in finding out what had happened to Elijah Martinez? "I've seen dozens of ODs since I've been a cop—six in the last two months alone," Josie said. "But this kid is the youngest. How did he end up here?"

She didn't mean here, physically; she meant dead.

Nico understood and said, "I've worked so many of these cases they're a blur."

He sounded discouraged and sad. Josie didn't want to think of Elijah Martinez as a statistic, one of many, lost and broken. He was a son. Maybe a brother. A friend. A student. And until last night, he'd had a future.

Josie wasn't going to easily get past his death. Maybe she didn't want to. Maybe, if she found out the how and the why, she could do something to help fix this crisis.

"I'll talk to the school," Josie said. "I'll convince the principal to give me a forum."

"Good," Nico said. "I'm not really as cynical as I sound, but I have to stay detached or I can't do the job."

Cops—and apparently CSIs—compartmentalized so they could

handle difficult and tragic cases, then go home to live a relatively normal life with normal relationships.

But sometimes, it was hard. And Josie did care—a lot. If she stopped caring, she'd have to quit being a cop. Make yet another career change after a long line of career changes.

If she could prevent another kid from ending up like Elijah Martinez, she'd talk to every school in Phoenix. Would it help? She didn't know, but it couldn't hurt.

She glanced at the tree behind the crime scene tape, knowing a young man lay dead under the tarp. *I have to do something*, she told herself.

Josie had no idea the can of worms she'd open when she spoke to the student body the following week.

chapter one

MARGO ANGELHART

I love my family. Every single one of them, from my brothers and sisters and parents and grandparents to every aunt, uncle, cousin, and cousin-by-marriage. I love them when they annoy me, argue, or agree. The Morales family and everyone who came from them—the Orozcos, Garcias, Angelharts, and more—put the unconditional love of family above all.

You know Zazu from *The Lion King*? The brightly colored bird who commented that there was "one" problem in every family—and two in his? Yep, the Angelhart-Morales clan had more than two, like my cousin Pedro, who fell down every conspiracy theory rabbit hole he tripped over. If I had a dollar for every time he called wanting me to investigate some wild idea—like the time he put six different news stories together to prove the governor had been replaced by a look-alike—my mortgage would be paid. I love him, but thankfully he lived out of state and I only saw him once in a blue moon.

But Pedro wasn't the wackiest character in our family.

Today, it was my older sister, Tess. As I ate one of the breakfast burritos I'd brought in for the office, I considered hopping in my

Jeep and heading to my grandparents' cabin in Pinetop, cell phone off. Just me and the open road.

Tess was driving me up a wall. Yes, she was planning a wedding. Yes, she had "only" seven months left. Yes, she was nervous because she had two failed engagements before falling for Dr. Gabriel Rubio. But if she changed her mind about the bridesmaid dresses *one more time*, I would stand next to her in jeans and a T-shirt.

"You're my maid of honor," Tess said as I poured myself a cup of coffee and wished I had some whiskey to dump in. Hell, I'd drink the whiskey straight even though it was eight thirty in the morning and I didn't even *like* whiskey.

"Yep," I said. "I promise, you'll have the best bachelorette party ever. In March. Six months from now." Meaning, I didn't want to talk about it because I hadn't thought about it. Because—*six months away.*

I'd looked up all the duties of a maid of honor, and there were a lot, but Mom was taking care of most of them because she wanted to. Thank God. I don't think I would survive until Tess's wedding day if I were responsible for everything that the books told me I was responsible for.

"We're getting married in April!"

"That's what the invitations say." Which were at the printer, so she couldn't change them.

"I can't go with the burgundy I love. It just won't work!"

"Why? Is it against the law?"

"Don't be sarcastic, Margo," Tess said. "It's spring. Burgundy is a fall or winter color. I want something light, something that says spring and birth."

"Are you pregnant?"

Tess's eyes widened and she practically blushed. "Margo!" she snapped.

"What? You're the one that said *birth*."

"Stop."

"If you want burgundy, then we wear burgundy."

"No! If you don't want to help, just say so."

Tess walked into her office and slammed the door before I could respond.

Where was Jack when I needed him? Did my brother know Tess was going to have a meltdown this morning so he stayed away from the office until the last possible minute? Probably. He avoided confrontations whenever possible.

I didn't come into the office every day. My mother would love if I did, but I'd worked solo for eight years. I didn't *need* to be in the office all the time. Sometimes I missed the autonomy of being completely on my own, so I came in only when necessary—like today when Mom called and said Uncle Rafe was coming by to talk about a possible case.

I'll admit, I was a bit hurt that Uncle Rafe didn't call me first. For the last eight years, I'd worked several cases that he'd brought me. Most didn't pay, but that never bothered me. Some people needed help and didn't have the money for an investigator. They paid what they could. My big clients covered what I needed, and it all worked out in the end. Then I join the family firm and Rafe goes right to my mom. Sure, she's his sister, but *still*.

One of the agreements Mom and I made when I joined Angelhart Investigations was that I could bring all my regular clients over. To be honest, I didn't have many clients on retainer because I mostly worked individual cases, but I had both a law firm and a bounty contract I didn't want to give up. Mom didn't like me taking bounty assignments, but they were fun. Some people think I have an odd definition of fun, but there's something wholly satisfying about tracking a fugitive and hauling his ass to court. Jack worked with me on my last case and I think he had just as much fun as I did, though he'd never admit it. So far, our family arrangement was working.

Of course, we'd only been in the same office for three months, so there was still time for me to screw everything up.

I glanced at the clock—past nine. Mom said be here at eight thirty. An early riser by nature, I didn't mind mornings, but sitting around an office was not my idea of fun *or* work. I had background checks to run for Logan Monroe, a new client I'd helped out of a jam back in May. He'd put Angelhart Investigations on retainer. It was a win-win for everyone—we all liked the successful entrepreneur, he paid well, and he valued honesty, even when it stung. He'd also gained a new best friend in Jack, despite them being near polar opposites.

Maybe in part because Jack was dating Logan's sister.

Jack walked in looking angry, which was very unlike my calm, cool, collected big brother.

"Hey, Jack, I brought you a breakfast burrito from Orozco's. It's in the kitchen. Mom's running late." I jerked my finger toward her closed office door.

He turned to me, blinked, as if not expecting to see me. "Thanks," he said, then went into his office and closed the door without getting his food.

Definitely unlike my big brother who never turned down a breakfast burrito from our cousin's Mexican restaurant. And, in the time I'd been working with my family, not once had I seen him close his door.

First Tess panicking about wedding dresses, now Jack being grumpy. With my even-tempered little sister, Luisa, back at college full-time, I couldn't even commiserate with anyone.

I turned to my computer—I'll admit, one of the perks of joining the family business was the new computer. My old machine worked at the speed of molasses. I plotted how I wanted to handle the background checks this week. Tess had already run credit reports, confirmed previous employers and schooling, and my job was to verify references. You'd be shocked at how many people listed fake jobs and references, thinking employers wouldn't check.

I went into the break room to pour more iced coffee into my Yeti. Our office manager, Iris Butler, made the best iced coffee around and always had some chilling in the fridge. I sipped. Perfect.

The break room had once been a giant kitchen when the building was an orphanage. It had since been converted into a comfortable space—the adjacent dining area now had a small table, a couple couches, oversized chairs, and television that was rarely turned on. I could easily have lived here.

When I stepped back out, my mom was escorting a fifty-something man into the conference room. From their body language, they knew each other. Mom saw me, motioned me over.

"Margo, this is Manny Ramos. We served on a charity board together many moons ago."

I knew the name, but we'd never met. Ramos owned a string of convenience stores in Central Phoenix called the Cactus Stop. I frequented the one closest to my house, when sometimes convenience trumped cheap. My first major investigation, more than eight years ago, involved the murder of a clerk at one of the Cactus Stops.

"Nice to meet you," I said.

"Likewise," Ramos said. "I wish it could be under better circumstances."

I glanced at my mom. I wish I knew what the circumstances were.

"We're just waiting for Raphael and Mrs. Martinez," my mom said to Ramos. "Coffee? Water?"

"Don't go to the trouble."

"No trouble. Margo, can you? I'll call in Jack and Tess."

"Sure," I said and went back into the kitchen to grab some water bottles. Iris took them from me. "Your uncle just drove up. I'll bring these in, along with a coffee tray."

"Thanks," I said and went to greet Uncle Rafe.

He wore his cleric's uniform—black short-sleeved shirt, black slacks, and white collar. A simple wood crucifix hung on a leather string around his neck. A woman with a tired, drawn face walked in with him.

"Uncle Rafe," I said. "I heard you were coming in." I extended my hand to the woman. "I'm Margo Angelhart."

She took it, her hand small and shaky. "Alina Martinez. Thank you."

I didn't know what she was thanking me for. I said, "I assume Manny Ramos is here for you?"

Alina gave me a sad smile. "I'm late. I'm so sorry."

"We're not late," Uncle Rafe said, taking her elbow and escorting her into the conference room.

My phone beeped. My cousin Josie had sent a text message.

Hey, do you have time to meet?

I responded immediately

Always for you, Pussycat.

I smiled. Ever since we watched *Josie and the Pussycats* one summer when we were eight, I'd adopted that nickname for her, which she used to hate. Okay, she still hated it, but that didn't stop me. She'd called me worse, trust me. Josie was not only my cousin, but my best friend.

I'm off today, I'll meet you wherever.

I considered, then texted back: **I'm going into a client meeting. I'll text you when I'm done, good?**

Josie responded with a thumbs-up emoji.

I pocketed my phone and followed Rafe and Alina into the conference room.

My mom, Ava Angelhart—the head of Angelhart Investigations after an illustrious career as a prosecutor, county attorney, and in private practice—looked the part. Impeccably dressed, she wore heels and a light gray suit with a pale pink blouse. As always, her hair and makeup was polished and professional. She sat at the head of the table, with Tess to her left taking notes and Jack beside her. To her right, Alina Martinez sat between Uncle Rafe and Ramos, a box of tissues within reach.

I barely refrained from squirming as I sat next to Jack. Emotional scenes always made me uncomfortable.

Tess didn't look at me. We'd have to talk later. Seventeen years of sharing a room while growing up either created friends for life, or enemies. We had been friends. Sure, we butted heads and argued, but I would do anything for my sister, and she'd do anything for me.

Until three years ago when our lives were shaken and stirred and rubbed raw after our dad pled guilty to a murder I was positive he hadn't committed. We barely talked until a few months ago. We were still working through the minefield of emotions and issues, but mostly, I thought, we were okay. I needed to keep it that way.

When we were all seated, Mom said, "Alina, I'm so glad that you came in. We are here to listen, then share our best advice on how to proceed. I am so deeply sorry for your loss."

I was curious and wished Mom had clued us in. By the expressions on Jack's and Tess's faces, they had no idea what was going on either.

"Thank you," Alina said. "I—I don't know where to start." She looked from Ramos to Uncle Rafe.

Uncle Rafe asked her, "Would you mind if I explained how we came to be here?"

She sighed in relief. "Thank you."

Rafe said, "Ten days ago, Alina's only child, Elijah, died at Mountain View Park in Sunnyslope."

I knew the park well. When I was little we had soccer games there, and when I was older I often hiked the North Mountain trails which could be accessed from the park.

"Elijah was a high school senior and honors student. He has never been suspected of doing drugs, yet the ME ruled that he died of an accidental drug overdose."

Silent tears rolled down Alina's face.

"I recognize that teenagers often do things we wish they wouldn't do, and drug use is very common," Uncle Rafe continued. "I don't want you to think I have blinders on. I believe in forgiveness and redemption because there are many things we need to be forgiven for. Catholics, even good Catholics, fall off the path. However, I knew Elijah and I know Alina and their family. On Friday, we had the funeral Mass where I met Mr. Ramos, who owns the Cactus Stop where Elijah worked for the past six months."

"Mr. Ramos was generous in helping with all the arrangements," Alina said. "I don't know what I would have done without him."

Ramos squeezed Alina's hand. "Anyone in my position would have done the same."

Uncle Rafe continued. "I spoke with Elijah's teachers and his friends. It was after that, and after prayer, that I reached out to Alina yesterday and suggested we talk to someone who can look into what happened the night Elijah died."

I had a whole bunch of questions, but Jack spoke up first. "The police would have conducted a death investigation in conjunction with the ME's office."

"They did," Rafe said. "After the funeral, we learned that the police have closed the case. The ME's report was taken at face value. They are no longer investigating how he obtained the drugs or who he was with the night he died."

"No one cares," Alina said, her voice almost too quiet to hear.

Uncle Rafe took her hand, held it. "I called Josie, who was the responding officer that day, to see if she could find out more, because one week doesn't seem long enough to get answers. She said she would do what she could, but indicated that the detective in charge wasn't open to pursuing other angles. That at most, she'd refer the case to the drug unit."

Josie. Was that why she'd texted me? To give me a heads-up?

Jack nodded. "If there is no evidence of homicide, they'd close the case and refer follow-up to the Drug Enforcement Bureau. It could become part of a larger drug investigation. Most drug-related deaths are accidental overdoses."

"Elijah did not do drugs," Alina said. Her voice, though quiet, was emphatic. "He would not. Since his father died in an accident ten years ago, it's been him and me. He has always been a good son. He planned to go to college. He even took night classes at the community college this summer, because he wanted to get ahead. He has straight A's. His teachers like him. His friends are good kids—they know he doesn't do these things. I need someone to find out what happened to him. Someone gave him those drugs. I don't think he knew, and then he died. Alone." Her voice cracked.

Before my mother could speak, I said, "Alina, are you suggesting that someone gave Elijah drugs without his knowledge or consent?"

She nodded. "*Sí*. That is correct. He would not do that to himself."

Mom said, "Are you prepared to share everything about Elijah, his friends, give us access to his room, his property, his life history? Are you prepared to learn the truth, no matter what we find?"

"Yes, yes," she said. "I need the truth. No matter what."

Ramos cleared his throat. "I'll fund your investigation. Alina," he said when she began to protest, "it is the least I can do to help. Elijah was a good young man, and he worked in my store. I want answers, as you do."

Mom said, "We can discuss that later. For now, I need to confer with my partners. Rafe, can you take Alina and Manny out for a moment?"

Rafe didn't want to leave, I could see it in the way his body tensed, but he simply nodded and the three of them left the room, closing the door behind him.

"We need to decide if this is a case we want to take," Mom said.

"Yes, of course we take it," I said without hesitation.

"We have paying clients we need to continue to service in a timely and professional manner," Mom said.

"Ramos said he was paying," Jack countered. "What am I missing?"

"Alina doesn't feel comfortable accepting more money from Manny. He paid for Elijah's burial."

"I managed to juggle paying clients with non-paying clients for eight years all by myself," I said.

"By working eighty hours a week."

"Point?"

"My point is that you and Tess are working the background checks for Logan Monroe's resort, and we have a deadline to complete that work. Jack has several subpoenas for the law firm that has us on retainer that must be served in a timely manner. We also have a criminal case we've been asked to investigate for the defense. I haven't decided whether we'll take it—I'm meeting with the defense attorney later today to go over the facts."

I frowned. "Shouldn't we all vote on whether we take it or not?"

"Mom vets our cases," Tess said. "This isn't a democracy."

I bristled. "I vet my own cases."

"You want to go back to taking sex pics of adulterers?" Tess snapped.

Mom cleared her throat. "Margo, I would not ask any of you to work on a case you didn't want, or stop you from working on a case you had passion for. However, in this instance, I'm pre-vetting the case. Meaning, I need to be comfortable working with the defense before I ask any of you to work on it. And because it's a capital case, I would be very involved with the legal end."

"Capital case?" Jack asked.

"A woman accused of murdering her husband."

"Holy shit," I said. "It's the Madison O'Neill case."

Mom nodded.

I grinned. "Well, either way, I'm all in. That sounds like fun."

Tess wrinkled her nose. "What if she's guilty?"

"Still fun. If she's guilty, we'll prove it and the defense lawyer can work out a plea. If she's innocent, we'll prove it, and she won't go to prison for life. Mostly, it's completely different than the boring crap we've been doing for the last few months, dropping subpoenas and running background checks."

"Which pay our bills," Tess countered.

"Tess," Mom said, sounding sharp and irritated. Was she sensing that Tess was picking on me because of the dress argument? "Let's shelve this discussion for the time being. I'll let you know what I learn on the O'Neill case, and then we can decide—as a group—whether to take it or not."

"Circling back to what you said, Mom," I said, "that you wouldn't stop us from working a case we had a passion for. I want to help Alina. Uncle Rafe asked us to." And he wouldn't ask if it wasn't important to him, which made it important to me.

"It's difficult to say no to my brother," Mom said with a small smile.

Tess glanced at me. "I can handle the background checks solo."

An olive branch? "Thanks, sis. And I can check whatever you need in the field. I can multitask with the best of them."

Tess preferred working in the office, or researching at the court archives, or going down an internet rabbit hole. I much preferred field work.

Jack said, "Uncle Rafe said he talked to Josie."

"I'll talk to Josie this morning," I said.

"I can feel out the case with my contacts at 620," Jack said. Jack had been a Phoenix PD officer, then detective, for more than a decade, until three years ago. By "620" he meant the main police headquarters at 620 Washington, which wasn't far from our office. "I can do that and get the subpoenas served on time."

"So you're all on board," Mom said. "I need to leave to make my meeting, but I'll talk to Manny. He wants to help, but for now we'll respect Alina's wishes and not accept money from him. He may be useful in gaining access to Elijah's coworkers, which will make things easier for us."

"That works for me," I said.

"I'll tell them, then send them back here." Ava rose and left the room.

"Do you think this kid is really the saint his mom made him out to be?" Jack said. "I mean, we were pretty good kids, but we all had our moments of stupidity."

"We won't know until we start asking," I said.

"She deserves to know what happened to her son," Tess added. "It's heartbreaking."

It was, but it happened all the time. Kids made bad decisions. Most of the time they didn't die, but sometimes they did. Sometimes they went to jail. Sometimes they got away with it and did it again . . . and sometimes they had a wake-up call and turned their life around.

But sometimes, a kid was in the wrong place at the wrong time and whatever happened was not his fault.

Where did Elijah Martinez fit in?

Uncle Rafe and Alina walked back in, sat down where they had before. Ramos stood on the threshold and said, "I can't stay, I have a meeting, but I wrote my cell phone number on the back of my card. If you have any questions, or need any access to the Stop where Elijah worked, call me direct and I will make it happen."

He put a couple cards down on the table, then crossed to Alina, bent over and kissed her cheek. "I'll stop by later this week. If you need anything, call. I mean it, Alina." He then shook Uncle Rafe's hand. "Good to see you again, Father," he said, then walked out.

"He's a good man," Alina said. "Is it . . . is it truly a burden to help me without payment? I can pay, but not all at once."

"It's not a burden," Jack said. "If we find this taking longer than we expect, we can revisit the issue."

I had a pretty good grasp of what we needed to do. Talk to Elijah's friends, coworkers, the responding officer, and the detective. Find out where Elijah was the twenty-four hours before he died, and in learning the timeline, we may be able to piece together who he was with and where he obtained the drugs. It seemed pretty cut-and-dried. Of course, people could lie, especially kids who thought they might get in serious trouble if it came out that they left their friend dying of an overdose. But in this day and age, they wouldn't be prosecuted. They might at the most be put on probation or sent to drug rehab. And that could be a wake-up call.

"We have some questions," Tess said kindly, "and the more you can tell us, the better, okay?"

"Of course," Alina said. "Father Rafe says if anyone can find the truth, it's the Angelharts."

Uncle Rafe caught my eye. He smiled that slight smile he had when a situation ended to his satisfaction. Yes, he was a priest, but he could be very manipulative. Fortunately, it was usually on the side of truth, justice, and the American way, so I was okay with it.

Tess took notes, and Jack and I asked most of the questions. What school Elijah attended, who his closest friends were, did he have a girlfriend, a list of his teachers, who attended the funeral, how long he worked at the Cactus Stop and which location, did he own a vehicle or how did he get around. An hour later we had a very good sense of who Elijah was, at least from his mother's perspective, and I had a list of people to talk to first—a teacher, the guidance counselor, three friends, and his supervisor at work. She only had Elijah's work number and the number for one of his friends, Andy Perez. I'd have to track down the others. What they told me would dictate my next steps.

When we were done, I walked Uncle Rafe and Alina to the door. "I'd like to come by your house and look through Elijah's things, if that's okay with you, Alina," I said.

"*Sí*. Anytime."

I wanted to talk to Josie first, so said, "Would this afternoon be good? I'll text you exactly when, but probably between two and four."

She nodded. "I will be home. My supervisor has been very generous with time off, but I need something to do, so I go back part-time tomorrow, then full-time next week. Everyone has been kind. Father Rafe. Mr. Ramos. Elijah's teachers." Alina touched her chest over her heart. "Everyone who met my son liked him."

"I'll see you this afternoon," I said to Alina. Then I hugged Uncle Rafe and said, "We'll talk later."

As soon as they walked out, I went to my office and called Josie. "Uncle Rafe and Alina Martinez just left."

"Damn, I wanted to give you a heads-up. I didn't know they'd go see you, but Uncle Rafe called me yesterday with a hundred questions, and I had a feeling he was going to ask you to look into that kid's death. You're taking it, aren't you?"

"Yep. Have time to meet?"

"It's my day off, so anytime, but I don't want to go downtown."

"I have some research to do here, then I'll come up to your neck of the woods." Josie lived in a small condo in Desert Ridge.

"I'm not going to ask you to come all the way up here."

"Not a problem. I want to go to the wine store and get Uncle Rafe his favorite tequila and my mom her favorite wine."

"Oh, shit!" Josie said. "I totally forgot Aunt Ava's sixtieth birthday party!"

"You didn't, because it's not until Thursday. What are you doing for yours?"

September was a big month of Morales/Angelhart birthdays. Uncle Rafe's was the day after Mom's, and Josie's was two days after Uncle Rafe's.

"My mom's taking me to a spa, then I have a date."

"Who?"

"I'll tell you later. I'll meet you at those tables outside Barnes & Noble at eleven thirty, good?"

"See you then."

chapter two

MARGO ANGELHART

Jack walked into my office eating the breakfast burrito I'd left for him.

"We have a kitchen," I said. The windows in the building didn't open and my office would smell of eggs and chorizo for the rest of the day.

Jack put his paper plate on the corner of my desk and said, "You're meeting with Josie?"

"Yep."

"I texted Rick for info. The lead detective is Rachel King."

Phoenix PD Sergeant Rick Devlin was Jack's closest friend since they met in the police academy fifteen years ago. He was also my ex-boyfriend.

"Don't know King."

"She's not a bad detective."

"That doesn't sound like a compliment."

"She does the job."

"Nothing more, nothing less," I translated.

He nodded. Jack was a good guy, and he wouldn't talk shit about his former colleagues. I always had to pull dirt out of him.

He'd been one of those detectives who went above and beyond, put in more hours than most, and always followed through—even on a case like Elijah Martinez's that was probably a simple accidental overdose, but could be something else.

"So what Rafe said makes sense," I said. "They closed the case because if it looks like a duck, it's a duck."

But Elijah had to have gotten the drugs from somewhere. If I took everything Alina said at face value—that Elijah was a good kid who wouldn't voluntarily use drugs—someone may have forced him to take them.

Or Alina was wrong about her son. Maybe he was experimenting. Maybe he succumbed to peer pressure. Maybe he hid his addiction well.

"You jumped at this," Jack said.

"It's Uncle Rafe. I'd do anything for him."

"So would I, but . . ." His voice trailed off.

"But what?"

"Margo," Jack said after a moment.

"Jack," I said.

I wasn't going to talk about the past. I typed Elijah's name into a paid service that aggregated all news articles and public records. Another nice thing about joining Angelhart Investigations was that I no longer had to pay for all the subscription services on my own, which added up to a hefty sum.

There was little written about Elijah's death. No court cases, but I didn't expect to see anything there because he was a juvenile.

I scanned his obituary. He would have turned eighteen in February. Honors student. Only child. Survived by his mother, three uncles, and eight cousins.

"Margo," Jack said quietly but firmly, "Elijah isn't Bobby."

My stomach twisted and my eyes burned, but I'd long ago cried out my anger about Bobby's death.

"I'm helping Alina Martinez find out what happened to her son. I'm going to find the truth, good or bad. This has nothing to do with what happened to Bobby."

I had known Bobby since the first day of kindergarten, when our teacher sat everyone in alphabetical order—him, Anderson, then me, Angelhart. We went to different high schools, but stayed close. Bobby was one of those give-the-shirt-off-your-back kind of guys. The guy who'd drive his drunk friends home before their parents found out they went to a party. Who walked girls to their car after football games in sketchy parts of Phoenix. Who'd spend an hour helping with a math problem, even if he had to read the entire chapter first.

We'd never dated. Bobby was like a brother. He had been one of my best friends.

Bobby asked me to his senior prom. It wasn't a date, he assured me. His girlfriend had dumped him two weeks earlier, and he didn't want to go alone. I had a hunch he wanted to make her jealous, but agreed to go anyway. I liked his friends; most of them were fun.

At an afterparty, someone spiked his drink. I didn't realize it right away. He started acting weird, off-balance, and slurring like he was drunk. I became angry, mostly because that meant I'd have to call Jack or my dad for a ride. I'd only had two beers—enough to rule out driving. My mom was a prosecutor; I knew the law and risks by heart.

I confronted Bobby. Called him an asshole. Told him I'd take care of everything. Then his eyes rolled back and he collapsed.

I called 911, but he was dead before the ambulance arrived. Later, we learned someone had slipped ketamine into his drink. He died from asphyxia. The cops investigated. Interviewed everyone. More than a hundred people had come and gone from that party.

No one confessed.

I think his ex-girlfriend drugged him. She probably didn't mean to kill him. But intent doesn't matter when someone ends up dead.

Elijah wasn't Bobby. He might not have been the saint his mother portrayed him as. Yet, he may have been drugged without his knowledge. A friend. An enemy. An ex-girlfriend. None of the above. But if he didn't willingly take the fentanyl, then someone killed him, and that person should be held accountable.

Elijah wasn't Bobby, but maybe this time, justice would prevail.

Jack and I were in a staring match. He broke first.

"If you need me, all you have to do is call." He gathered the remains of his breakfast.

"Thanks." And I meant it. While I didn't like talking about Bobby, just knowing Jack understood made me feel better. "The more you learn from your contacts, the better. After I talk to Josie, I'll check out Elijah's room. There could be something there—drugs, a journal, notes, info on his computer. But I think his friends will be my best sources."

"You would have made a great cop."

I rolled my eyes and Jack laughed as he walked out.

When I left the Army, Jack was still a detective and tried to convince me to be a cop. I'd been in the Army for six years, three of which I'd spent as a military police officer, and the last thing I wanted to do was work in another command structure. I liked making my own hours, working cases I wanted, not cases I *had* to work. Most of that I could do as a PI. Sure, I'd taken many cases I didn't like, but they paid for the cases I cared about.

I finished gathering the information I could find online about Elijah (nothing, outside of his obituary), his school (Sun Valley High School, in Sunnyslope—not far from where I lived), and his employer (the Cactus Stop, on Hatcher). I'd check out the Stop before calling Ramos, using him only if I needed to smooth the way with staff.

I debated how to reach out to his friends—through one of the teachers who'd gone to his funeral or by tracking them down off campus. Pros and cons to each approach, so I'd think on it. Josie's insight might help.

On my way out, I stopped by Tess's office. Her door was open and she wore headphones while typing rapidly on her computer. She saw me, took off her headphones. "Need something?"

"I'm meeting Josie up in Desert Ridge. I'm getting Mom that

wine she loves, since you coordinated the big present. Do you need any other beer, wine, or spirits for the party?"

"No, I have it covered. I already ordered alcohol, Uncle Tom and Aunt Rita are handling the food, and Luisa is going over early to decorate."

Most family events were at either our parents' or grandparents' house. Large events—like Pop and Abuela's anniversary—were at Uncle Tom's restaurant. But we didn't want Mom to have to do anything on her birthday, so we usually took her out to dinner or someone else (not me) would host a party. This year, the party was at Gabriel's house.

"I need to track down Elijah's friends."

"I can help," Tess said. "I'll stalk their social media and send you everything I find. Good?"

"Great," I said. "Thanks."

Maybe she was no longer mad at me for my burgundy dress faux pas. But considering her recent mood swings, she'd soon find something else to argue about.

chapter three

MARGO ANGELHART

Desert Ridge is a community in North Phoenix, west of Scottsdale. The outdoor mall was one of my favorites because it was clean, had stores I liked, a few good restaurants, and lots of parking.

I bought Mom's favorite wine, a bottle of Herradura Reposado for Uncle Rafe, and a six-pack of a good IPA for me since I was at a discount liquor store. I left ninety dollars poorer, grateful I didn't drink much—I'd be broke.

I locked the alcohol in the back of my Jeep and made my way to the covered sitting area outside the Barnes & Noble. Kids played on the splash pad in the center of the courtyard. People moved in and out of nearby shops, and a pair of older women in track suits power-walked past me, deep in animated conversation.

At the next table, a woman in shorts and a T-shirt—accessorized with a diamond tennis bracelet and a Scottsdale-sized rock on her left ring finger—chatted on her phone. Her long, manicured red nails drummed the tile as she said, "What a prick. If Ethan ever said that to *me*, I'd take off for the weekend in his Beamer and see if he *ever* criticizes my driving again. Harumph!"

She wore earbuds, so I only heard her end of the conversation.

I spotted Josie a split second before she noticed me. My cousin was tall and lanky, more like Tess and than me. I was your standard mix of average height and weight, while Josie had inherited the striking features of the Morales side of the family—her dad and my mom were siblings, but she got the better deal: shiny dark auburn-brown hair and big golden-brown eyes. In comparison, I felt mousy with dark blond hair and boring hazel eyes.

It had taken Josie a while to figure out what she wanted to do with her life, but once she became a cop nearly two years ago she'd found her calling. It suited her.

"Margo!" Josie leaned over and hugged me, then plopped down on the chair across from me. "It's been weeks."

"Your schedule, my schedule, your boyfriend, my . . . schedule."

The diamond-studded woman gave us a look as if we had interrupted her conversation. I ignored her.

"I already told my boss I have to leave on time Thursday," Josie said.

Josie worked days, which meant 5:30 a.m. to 3:30 p.m. Day shift was usually coveted, but she was on the Thursday through Sunday schedule, and most cops didn't like to give up their weekends. She'd worked nights for a year and said it threw her entire system out of whack.

"I hope you're bringing the boyfriend you haven't introduced to anyone in the family," I said.

"I can't do that to him," Josie whined. "I've only been seeing Ryan for six weeks, and a family party would be like throwing him to the lions."

"Oh, please. We don't bite, and barely scratch."

"I'll see. He works forty-eight on, seventy-two off, and has to be on duty six a.m. Friday morning."

"A firefighter? I thought guns and hoses didn't get along." She practically blushed, and I laughed. "You really like him."

"Sure, well, yeah, I do," she fumbled. "It just happened. We give Fire a ton of shit. Most of them are jerks, anyway. But the ribbing became more fun with Ryan, and then a few weeks ago we ran into each other off-duty at the Apple Store, of all places. We talked, went to lunch, just clicked."

"I can't wait to meet him on Thursday." I grinned.

"On one condition."

"No promises."

"Come on, you have to keep the family off him. He's an only child."

I laughed. The Morales clan could be overwhelming for someone who didn't have a big family, but I didn't make the promise. If Ryan the firefighter couldn't handle good-natured teasing, he wouldn't fit in with our family and was thus unworthy of my cousin.

I changed the subject. "What can you tell me about the Elijah Martinez case?"

"Tragic." Josie retrieved her Hydro Flask from her bag, drank deeply. "My partner and I responded early Saturday morning, nine days ago. Our first call of the day, but because Mountain View Park is down the street, we rolled out right away. Park rangers found a DB. We didn't have any info until we got there, saw that the deceased was a teenage Hispanic male. Secured the scene, covered the body, called for detectives. There was no external sign of injury. Detective Rachel King arrived on scene, retrieved the victim's wallet and a baggie of small blue pills. She determined likely drug overdose. ME confirmed. Fentanyl."

"Shit," I mumbled.

"Yeah."

"Signs of a party?"

"No sign of anything—no beer bottles, no trash, no drug paraphernalia. He was lying against a tree, in a fetal position. As if he laid down and fell asleep. I've seen it before, but never someone so young, so smart—he was in all honors classes."

"How'd he take the drugs? Ingested? Smoked?" I knew fentanyl could be taken in several ways.

"Ingested," she said. "ME stated time of death between one and three a.m. Saturday morning. His body was found after five by the rangers, we rolled up at five thirty-five. Nico was there."

"My brother?" I asked, surprised.

"Yeah, staffing issues at the lab."

The Phoenix Crime Lab handled forensics for multiple police departments, including the Maricopa County Sheriff and Phoenix PD. While there were specialty units, most of the staff moved seamlessly from one department to another. My brother usually worked in toxicology running all the fancy machines, but I wasn't surprised to hear he was picking up the slack in crime scene response.

Josie continued. "He collected trash from the can—the cans are emptied every evening by park rangers because of javelinas and coyotes, so anything in there was deposited after eight p.m. the night before. There was one of those generic thirty-two-ounce soda cups."

"Did the detective try to figure out if it was Elijah's?"

Josie shook her head. "It's listed as evidence, but no tests have been run because the ME determined accidental OD."

"Wouldn't it be important to know if there was fentanyl in the cup? Or if it was even his?"

"If it's accidental, that means he voluntarily ingested the drugs."

"But if it was in the cup, maybe he didn't know."

Josie's face twisted and she didn't look directly at me. I wondered what was going on.

"Jos—" I began.

"I can't get involved," she said, lowering her voice. "Last week, I spoke at a Sun Valley High assembly. Talked about the dangers of drugs, how many ODs can be reversed with Narcan, how if you're in a situation where a friend is unconscious, call 911, the whole nine yards. After, a girl approached me and said she was friends with Elijah. Emphatic that he didn't do drugs. They studied together every day. She absolutely believes he was drugged without his knowledge but shared no evidence. When I tried to explain it only takes once, she stormed off, spouting a few choice words about cops in general, using both middle fingers as emphasis."

I could picture it.

"The guidance counselor—Lena Clark—apologized for the kid, said she saw no signs of drug use, but that Elijah was under a lot of pressure to do well. Competing for scholarships, taking a full load of classes, an outside job."

"Which means?"

"She didn't want to believe he did drugs, but implied it was possible. She wanted us to investigate further. Lena conceded that if Elijah had used drugs, she felt it was important to know the who and where to make sure it didn't come back to the campus."

Not what I wanted to tell his mother, but truth was better than a lie.

"That gives me a place to start," I said. "Though fentanyl is a depressant, and if you're trying to study, you'd be taking a stimulant, right? Like amphetamines." I knew about drugs, didn't do them. When your dad is a doctor and your mom is a prosecutor, you learn pretty quick that even casual drug use could destroy careers and lives. Didn't mean that I was oblivious to what my friends did.

"Sometimes smart kids striving for perfect grades use drugs to alleviate stress," Josie said. "Uppers to study, downers to sleep. Gracie had a problem in high school."

Josie didn't have to remind me. Our cousin Gracie, who was a year younger than us, would have been valedictorian her senior year if she hadn't spiraled into drug use. She ended up postponing college for a year and going through rehab, but it took a family intervention. Now she's married and runs her own small business. If someone really doesn't want to get clean, you can't force them.

Josie continued. "I put the information I learned from Elijah's friends and the guidance counselor as a follow-up to the original police report, then emailed King about what I added and asked her when the final toxicology report would be available."

"Which would tell you if he was a habitual user."

"Exactly. Some drugs pass through the system quickly, and if he was an occasional user, they wouldn't be in the initial screening—which showed only fentanyl. Anyway," Josie continued, "King wasn't happy with me. She threatened to have me suspended."

"What the hell? Because you asked for information? Bitch." I had never met King, but now I didn't like her.

"I went to the funeral on Friday when I heard it was at St. Dominick's. Offered my condolences to the family. Talked to Lena again, who was there with another teacher. The girl was also there, but left before I could talk to her. Lena was upset about the disposition of the case, and I told her that squeaky wheels get the grease."

"Oh." Meaning, Josie couldn't put pressure on the detective, but the school could. *Yep, that would piss off the detective*, I thought.

"Apparently, Lena called the detective and asked why the case was closed, said I was the one who told her. According to my boss, she used some colorful and insulting language. She's a spitfire, as Pop would say. I wouldn't be surprised if she said something to make it seem like King or the police didn't care. That's probably why King is mad at me. My boss told King not to threaten me—he'll always back us up—*but* he told me to let it go. If I found something in the course of my regular duties, he'd run it up the chain. So don't think he's a jerk."

"I don't. He's protecting you."

"Exactly. I'll help you any way I can, unofficially. But if you uncover anything actionable, I'll take it to my boss and *he* will follow-up."

Police rules, procedures, and office politics were three big reasons I never wanted to be a cop. "Do you remember the name of the girl who flipped you off?" I asked.

"No, and I didn't put her name in the report either." She thought, then shook her head. "I heard it, but didn't write it down. I have Lena's contact information."

Josie pulled up her phone and scrolled through. Tapped a couple buttons and said, "Just sent."

"Thanks. I'll follow up with her first. Was the girl named Angie Williams?"

Angie was the only girl Alina Martinez mentioned as a friend of Elijah's.

"Angie sounds right, but I can't swear to it."

"What's your theory?" I asked. Cops had good instincts, but they also saw a lot of crap, which could make them jaded.

"I don't know," Josie admitted. "Let's say King is right and the drug overdose was accidental. Where did he get the drugs? Who was with him? How did he get to the park more than two miles from his home when he doesn't have a car? Where was he before he died? All we know is he worked that afternoon, left at approximately eight that evening, and OD'd in the park between one and three in the morning. That's at least five hours where King has no idea where he was, who he was with. So yeah—I think we should find answers for the family, but Detective King closed the case because there was no sign of foul play."

"That's messed up," I said.

"She *could* have passed it to the DEB, but she didn't."

"Why wouldn't she?" The inspeak was a bit over my head, but I knew DEB was the Drug Enforcement Bureau and I surmised they generally worked drug-related crimes.

"Like I said, no sign of foul play. And besides, they're also understaffed. Still," Josie added, "DEB is better positioned to determine if Elijah's death fits into a pattern. They could launch a larger investigation."

That doesn't help Elijah's mom, I thought.

"If I find something, can you get it to the DEB without getting slapped?" I asked.

"No problem," she said without hesitation. "Like I said, my boss has my back. I just need something tangible—a witness, catch someone in a lie, even a rumor, if it's something we can follow up on. If you have a suspicion about where Elijah got the drugs, I'll get it to the right people."

"That helps," I said. "I don't want you getting in trouble, but if you can send me a copy of the police report that would be great."

"I'll swing by the Desert Horizon station and email it to you."

"But I'm supposed to fill out forms and get the report weeks later, right?" Police reports were public information, but there was a bureaucratic process I usually had to use.

"I'll fill out the form for you. Dot my *i*'s and all that, but there's no reason I can't give it to you as long as I document that you requested it."

"It's nice having friends and family in high places."

Josie laughed. We chatted, but my mind was only half there. I wanted to talk to the guidance counselor and then to Elijah's friends. Find out everything they knew . . . and then retrace Elijah's steps.

Out of everything Josie told me, those five missing hours seemed to be most important. Where had Elijah gone after leaving work?

Someone saw him. Someone talked to him.

Someone had given or sold him the drugs.

Finding out where Elijah had been during those missing hours would tell me if he OD'd accidentally . . . or if someone killed him.

chapter four

JACK ANGELHART

After serving warrants in Peoria near Lake Pleasant, Jack spent the drive back downtown thinking about how to approach Rachel King. They'd worked together a few times back when he was still a detective. As he'd told Margo, Rachel wasn't a bad cop. But she wasn't a good one either, at least in Jack's book.

He needed to tread carefully. Test the waters with King. Or maybe he could just as easily go around her, reach out to his former partner instead. Most of the cops he'd worked with were happy to help him now as a PI, but he couldn't afford to be careless. If anyone got the idea he was going after a cop, they'd shut him out fast.

Not that he was targeting King—she hadn't done anything wrong. Even if he could convince her he was only chasing down leads for a grieving mother, she still might slap him down.

Jack had always been the diplomat of the family. He'd inherited his mother's shrewdness and his father's bedside manner. Honesty, more often than not, had served him well. And it suited him—lying had never come easy.

When his phone rang and Laura's name and photo lit up the screen, Jack grinned, a wave of giddiness washing over him.

Since his divorce three years ago, he'd rarely dated, and when he had, it never progressed beyond a few dinners and polite goodbyes. Whitney had been his one true love until she pulled the rug out from under him.

Then, two and a half months ago, Laura walked into his life. And just like that, he was "smitten" as his Abuela would've said.

Funny how love finds you when you're not even looking.

"Hello," he answered, the sound of her voice dialing his grin up another notch.

"Hi, Jack. Driving back from the Fitzpatrick ranch out in Black Canyon City, thought I'd return your call."

Laura was a veterinarian who co-owned a clinic. She often made house calls because her specialty was farm animals, and her love was for horses.

"Everything okay?" he asked.

"Routine visit. They have eight mares and a stallion, so I go up twice a year to check on them. All healthy, one of the mares is pregnant. They suspected she was—I confirmed and estimate she's three months along. She has a long way to go. Anyway, sorry I missed your call this morning, cell service up there is spotty."

"You're busy."

"What else is new?" she said with a light laugh that always made his heart swell. "You sound better now than your message this morning. Is everything okay?"

"Mostly." He didn't want to dump his problems on her, but she would understand. "Whitney found out that I'm seeing someone. I should have told her, but I knew it would be a ridiculous conversation and I kept putting it off."

"You're *seeing* someone? Who?"

Her voice was light and humorous. His heart lifted.

"Yeah, I am. A beautiful strawberry blonde with the most amazing green eyes I've ever seen. Smart too. Beauty *and* brains."

"You'll have to introduce me sometime," Laura teased.

"I know we had plans tonight, but I have to cancel. I promised Whitney I would have a sit-down. When she started bringing men around Austin, I made her sit down and agree to terms, so I have to live up to the same agreement."

"I understand," Laura said, and he knew she did. "You're a great dad and want what's best for Austin. That means maintaining a good relationship with his mother."

"She barely says more than two words to me if it's not directly related to our son, until she found out I was seeing you. I actually preferred the noncommunication."

"That's not good," Laura said. "You need an open line of communication *because* of Austin. Avoiding her only prolongs the inevitable and makes conversations that much harder."

"You are a wise, wise woman." Laura was right, but conversations with Whitney made him tense and angry—probably because he forced himself to be calm and agreeable when around her. The tension always gave him a pounding headache.

"Call me when you're driving home," Laura said.

"I won't be in a very good mood."

"Be an optimist, Jack. And I don't care if you're in a crappy mood. We all have our moments, right? And before you say I don't, remember when I yelled at you and poked a finger in your chest?"

"You were scared about the safety of your children."

"That's no excuse for my bad behavior. And still, you like me."

"I more than like you," he said quietly.

He could hear the smile in her voice when she said, "I more than like you too, Jack Angelhart."

"I'll call tonight," he said and hung up.

They weren't far enough into their relationship that Jack had told Laura he loved her, though he knew he did. They were cautious not just because they'd both been burned in their first marriages, but because they each had kids. For Jack, Austin would always come first. For Laura, Sydney and Cody were her life. Her devotion to family was one of the reasons that Jack had fallen for her. And though cautious, in the two and a half months they'd been seeing each other, they were exclusive. Jack had never dated around—it was one girlfriend at a time, even in high school. And Laura, though divorced longer than Jack, hadn't started dating until now.

Warts and all, I loved Charlie. Still do, but I see him now for who he is, not who I wanted him to be. After the divorce, I had to think about my kids, and then my job. Dating was the last thing on my mind.

When Jack brought Austin home last night, Whitney had started the argument about why Jack hadn't told her about Laura. It angered and depressed him that she pushed it. Whitney had wanted the divorce; he hadn't. He'd begged her to go to counseling; she'd refused.

You couldn't force someone to love you, even when you had a child together.

Jack wasn't the kind of man who cried. But when Whitney told him to leave—that she wanted more than he could offer, that she couldn't love a man who couldn't give her everything—he did.

He'd given her all he had: mind, body, spirit. But it wasn't enough. The house wasn't big enough or in the right zip code. The clothes she wanted blew past their budget—and why should she have a budget, she asked. The car she coveted was far beyond his means, and the one he could afford she complained about constantly. She compared their life to her friends who had more, did more, traveled farther, spent bigger.

He'd had two parents who loved each other and raised five kids in good times and bad. They worked through problems and came out stronger in the end. He wanted, expected, the same.

For the first time since he signed the divorce papers, he thought he might have found someone who wanted the same things in life as he did: home and hearth, children and family.

It gave him hope.

It was nearly twelve thirty by the time Jack walked into police headquarters.

He had several reasons for leaving the force three years ago.

The primary factor was a shift in morale. The weight of being a cop had taken its toll on Jack. The anti-cop sentiment and push from the top was intense, and with the added pressure of his divorce and his dad's situation, he needed to step back.

Sometimes, he regretted his decision, but he liked being a private investigator. While he didn't make as much money as when he'd been a cop, he could set his own hours, and that meant more time with Austin. Occasionally, he was offered a private security gig for a VIP, which paid well. He liked working with his family, and with his dad in prison, his mom needed him.

Ten minutes later, he learned that Rachel King was in the field, and Jack's old partner Wendy Lopez was on vacation.

Drug crimes were generally the purview of the Drug Enforcement Bureau, though they often worked in tandem with VICE, where Jack had worked for a few years. He headed toward the VICE wing, mentally running through who he knew that was still here. Fortunately, he didn't have to think too hard. As soon as he entered the squad's suite of cubicles, a booming voice said, "Hey, Angelhart!"

Jack turned as his former commanding officer, Lieutenant Hank Thomas, walked toward him. "LT, good to see you." Jack extended his hand. Hank took it and brought Jack in for a slap on the back and hug.

"Damn good to see you. Whatcha doin' in the building?"

"I had to deliver a couple subpoenas, thought I'd come up and see if you and a few of the others were in while I wait for a dead beat down the street to get back from lunch."

The best lies were couched in truths.

Hank motioned for Jack to follow him through the bullpen and into his office. "Sit, tell me all."

Hank had worked VICE most of his plainclothes career. Though Jack had worked under Hank before he was promoted to command, everyone knew Hank was on the fast-track to management. He was smart, a good cop, and didn't play office politics. Hank did the job right: made clean arrests, put bad guys in prison, and stood by his people.

"Not much to tell," Jack said. They chatted about family, he showed off Austin's sixth-grade school picture, and Hank showed off his new family portrait—Hank, his wife Abby, and their six kids, ranging from sixteen to three.

"How's the PI business? I heard you were involved with that arson investigation a few months back, Desert West Financial."

Jack gave him the nuts and bolts about that case. Then he said, "Well, no beating around the bush—I came in partly because I'm working on another case where King is lead detective. She's not in right now, so I just wandered around until someone had time to chat."

"I have a few minutes. What case?"

Jack told him—including that he was hired by the family—then said, "King closed the case, but there are some holes so we're working it."

"Drug related? Those cases usually cross my desk."

"It was ten days ago. Might not have made it up here yet. The kid was a senior at Sun Valley High School in Sunnyslope. Honors student with straight A's, no suspensions, no known drug use."

"Do you have a case number?"

He glanced at his phone—Margo had texted him the information earlier—and he rattled it off for Hank.

Hank typed into his computer, read.

"Hmm. Seems King slapped at a cop—Morales. One of yours?"

"Yeah, my cousin."

"After King closed the case, she got calls from the mother, the school, a friend of the victim. It may end up on my desk eventually if there's a pattern."

"So you have no open investigation," Jack said to confirm.

"On this? No. I don't have anything open that touches the school. Sun Valley has their problems, but no major drug-related issues since my team took down a coach who was dealing."

"I read about that. Football coach, right? His wife was also involved?" It happened around the time Jack left the force so he didn't remember many details.

"I'll print you the file. We did a damn good job taking the bastard down. All the kids involved would have graduated by now, since it was three years ago. Coach is serving ten-to-fifteen. If in the course of your investigation any of these names pop or you see a similar operation in play, let me know."

"I will," Jack agreed.

Hank typed rapidly on the computer, then pulled a large stack of paper off the printer, grabbed a file folder, and put the papers inside. "Enjoy the reading."

"Thanks, Hank."

Jack left. He wasn't certain this closed case would help them, but it wouldn't surprise him if one or more of the low-level dealers had slipped under the radar and avoided arrest.

He sent Margo a text message.

> I have a pile of paperwork about an old case involving drugs at Sun Valley. It's closed, but maybe something here relates to what happened to Elijah. I'll leave it on your desk.

A moment later, Margo responded.

> Come to my house tonight, six? Pizza and paperwork.

Jack winced. Actually better to tell Margo the truth over text than in person.

> Dinner with Whitney.

No response. Maybe Margo was getting over her hatred of his ex.

Seven minutes later he was in his car when a message from Margo popped up.

Why?

Jack wondered how many nasty messages Margo had started and erased.

I'll tell you later.

Almost immediately came a chain of angry emojis, signifying Margo's displeasure with his answer.
He left to serve the rest of the subpoenas.

chapter five

MARGO ANGELHART

Irritated, I shoved my phone into my pocket. Why was Jack having dinner with Whitney? Why couldn't he tell me about it now? If he was getting back together with his bitch of an ex, I'd be furious. Not only because I like his girlfriend, Laura—the first of Jack's girlfriends I'd ever sincerely liked, going all the way back to high school—but because Whitney cheated on him, lied to him, and put him into debt he had only recently climbed out from.

No, he wouldn't even *think* about getting back together with her. Even though the divorce weighed on him and he wanted to spend more time with Austin, I doubted he would rekindle whatever was left of the marriage that woman sent up in flames. But if she did anything to hurt my brother, I would explode.

Deep breath, I told myself. Jack was a grown-up; he could take care of himself. Still, I hurt when he hurt, so I hoped this was just a minor bump.

I wish he would have *told* me what was going on because my mind always went to the worst-case scenario.

After reading the police report Josie had sent me, I'd set up a meeting with Lena Clark, the guidance counselor, who sounded happy to talk to me.

Sun Valley High School consisted of two distinct buildings. The brick "old school" was built around a central courtyard, while the "new school" to the east was a large three-story structure, constructed in the last decade to replace a worn-out building that dated back to the dark ages. I wasn't fond of the modern design of the new building, which seemed more suited to an office complex than a school. The administrative wing occupied the western end of the old school, which is where I headed for my meeting with Lena Clark.

I introduced myself to the receptionist and informed her of my appointment; within minutes, Lena came to the lobby. She was a petite, trim fortysomething with dyed blond hair, dressed in a long black skirt, white blouse, and gray blazer—with more necklaces hanging around her neck than I even owned. She wore platform heels, but still didn't top my very average height. "Ms. Angelhart?"

"That's me."

She extended her hand. "I was surprised to get your call."

"Thank you for making the time to meet."

"Anything I can do for the Martinez family." She motioned for me to follow her through a door she opened with a card key.

She led me down a long wide hall with offices to the right and floor-to-ceiling windows on the left, which looked out to the partly covered courtyard. The office's interior windows would receive natural light without any direct sun, a plus in Arizona. Lena's spacious office had two windows that looked out into the hall, a couch, three chairs across from her uncluttered desk, and a round conference table that could seat six. Two walls were filled with bookshelves neatly crammed with college prep material, college brochures, and labeled binders.

"Full disclosure," I said when she closed the door behind me. "My cousin is Officer Josie Morales, who spoke here last week. She shared some of your conversation with me."

"I like Officer Morales," Lena said with a genuine smile. "She was so good with the students, straightforward and honest. We haven't had a school resource officer for the last several years. We were supposed to have someone at the beginning of the school year, but it hasn't happened yet. Tell her for me that I think she would make an excellent SRO. It's a position not all those in law enforcement can do well."

"I'll tell her," I said. Josie would be embarrassed that Lena was singing her praises, but her parents would be thrilled. What parents don't love hearing great things about their children, even when they're all grown-up? I tucked away the info to share with the family on Thursday.

Lena sat at the table and motioned for me to sit across from her.

"As I mentioned on the phone, Alina Martinez hired me to find out exactly how Elijah obtained the drugs and where he was during the hours before the fatal overdose."

She nodded solemnly. "It's heartbreaking."

"You told police that you knew Elijah well, and saw no sign of drug use. Would you recognize signs?" I assumed she would, but wanted to start with an easy question.

"Absolutely. I have more than twenty years' experience in the public education system, the last eleven as a guidance counselor. Sadly, drug use is not rare, though I've seen some pushback among young people in the last few years. Still, we're an urban, Title I school with nearly two thousand students. Many of our youth struggle with drug and mental health issues. And, there are unfortunately high achievers who use drugs as a study aid. Students have been known to share or sell their ADHD medication—there is a large market for it."

That wasn't new. When I graduated fifteen years ago kids were selling their meds.

"Do you have knowledge or suspicion that Elijah was taking such medication?"

"He wasn't prescribed anything that we were aware of, and like I told Josie, I didn't see any signs that Elijah was a habitual drug user, but he did put a lot of pressure on himself to excel."

"So you're thinking it's possible."

"Again, I never saw or heard anything, but teens handle pressure in different ways, and Elijah wanted to be valedictorian."

"Could he have been?"

She hesitated, then said, "Probably not, but he was a contender. I'd say he was one of five or six students who are in the running."

"Is there a lot of competition for the position? Rivalries?"

"Some," Lena said. "But the valedictorian is selected by a teacher committee and in addition to grades and difficulty of classes, they look at extracurricular activities, contributions to the school, things like that."

I glanced at my notes. "Alina mentioned three friends Elijah was particularly close to. Peter Barilla, Andy Perez, and Angie Williams. Do you know them?"

"I know Angie well, she's in the honors program with Elijah. Peter and Andy I don't know well, but they have never been in serious trouble." She went to her computer, typed, then swiveled in her chair towards me. "Peter is only on campus in the mornings because of a school-work program. Andy was in Honors Math with Elijah. I don't think any of them are involved with drugs. Certainly not Peter, who had to submit to drug testing for the work program."

"Is Angie Elijah's girlfriend? His mother said no, but . . ." I left it open.

Lena shook her head. "They were friends and in most of the same classes, but I didn't see anything that made me think they were involved in that way." Lena paused, then added, "Angie was particularly angry about the police investigation."

"How so?"

"Angie has a difficult home life. She's channeled her anger toward this tragedy. Elijah's death, the police investigation, the closed case. She cut school several days last week. I told her on Friday that I would try to get her absences excused since she had lost one of her closest friends, but I expected her here today."

"And she's not," I guessed.

"I've done everything I can to find answers for her and, frankly, for myself. I called the detective. Spoke to the principal and the entire administrative team. If the school puts pressure on the police, that might open things up. I even sent an email to the school board. But Angie thinks nothing is enough because everyone believes—her words—Elijah's death was his fault. She thinks no one cares."

"What do *you* think?"

"I think the police closed the case too quickly and we have a lot of questions and no answers," Lena said. "But the idea that someone drugged him on purpose seems like grasping at straws. He had a part-time job, was in advanced classes, applying to colleges—some kids think that a little bit of something will take the edge off. I'm not saying that's what happened, just that it does happen. When I suggested that to Angie, she walked away angry. However, the police should have done more to find out what happened the night he died."

"I have Angie's address," I said. "But if I can't track her down, would you be willing to ask her to call me? You can even be in the meeting if that would make you or Angie more comfortable." I would much rather talk to Angie in private—she might open up more without a parent or teacher in the room.

Lena nodded. "It may help her to know that someone is looking for answers. But please don't get her hopes up. She is focused on one theory and won't even consider a different answer. Sometimes, people we think we know disappoint us."

"Just so you know, I'll be talking to Elijah's other friends too."

"That's more than the police did," Lena said. "I thought if one of Elijah's friends knew something, the police would get it from them. Detective King claimed to have spoken to his friends and family, but she didn't speak to Angie. She closed the case too quickly, in my opinion."

It was now obvious to me why Josie had butted heads with King, and why Josie's boss had told her to lay low. Likely, Lena had mentioned options to King that perhaps Josie had planted in her head.

"What about bullies? Was Elijah considered a bully? Was anyone harassing him?"

"Elijah was one of the nicest kids in the school, and I never heard that he had been bullied. We take the issue very seriously."

Maybe, but there were different levels of bullying, and subtle harassment might not be on anyone's radar. Especially if it happened off-campus.

There was a knock on the door and Lena called, "Come in."

A man a couple years older than Lena entered.

"Am I interrupting?" he asked.

"Of course not," Lena said. "Margo, this is Dwight Parsons, history teacher and Elijah's advisor. Dwight, Margo Angelhart is a private investigator looking into Elijah's death."

He glanced at Lena. "I didn't realize you were going to hire a private investigator."

"Elijah's family did," Lena said.

Lena touched Dwight's hand, a subtle but intimate gesture. Okay, a little love on campus. Who was I to judge?

"I'm glad you can help Alina find some closure," he said, "but sadly, it won't bring Elijah back."

"You knew Elijah well?" I asked Dwight.

"I think so. He's been in two of my honors classes, and I agreed to write him a college recommendation." He shook his head and frowned. "Such a tragedy. He was a bright boy."

"Too much pressure?"

"Only what he put on himself," Dwight said. "Which was quite a bit. Because of his socioeconomic situation, and the fact that his father died when he was young, he was already eligible for several grants, and with his grades I was helping him forge a path for free tuition and housing. But you have to apply and do the work, which can be overwhelming."

"Are you aware of any of Elijah's peers who may have been

adding to that pressure?" I asked. "Or," I continued when he didn't immediately answer, "maybe sharing Adderall or similar meds. Overachieving teens sometimes do that."

Dwight shook his head. "Not Elijah or his friends. I know a few kids who may be using stimulants for such purposes, but they don't move in the same circles."

"Several years ago one of our teachers was arrested for running a drug ring on campus," Lena said. "After, the administration made sure we all had extra training and support."

"It was very informative," Dwight said. "I think our school has done a stellar job reducing drug-related problems on campus."

"Absolutely," Lena concurred. "And anything we can do to help you find out what happened to Elijah, we will. Is there anything else?"

Before I could respond—or ask more questions about the former drug ring—a tall, stately woman stepped into the doorway. Lena glanced at the clock. "Melissa—I forgot about the staff meeting. We're just wrapping up here."

"Did I hear right?" Melissa looked at me. "You're conducting an investigation on school property?"

"No," Lena said quickly before I could answer. "This is, um, Ms. Angelhart. Elijah's mother hired her, I was just answering a few questions."

"Confidentiality still applies, Lena," the woman said.

This was awkward. I would have slipped out, but the woman blocked the exit.

"Of course, I would not violate any student's privacy, but—"

"There are no buts," Melissa said.

Principal or vice principal, I thought. It was in the attitude.

"I'll be leaving," I said and made a move toward the door. Melissa didn't budge.

"Ms. Angelhart," she said, "I'm Melissa Webb, the vice principal of Sun Valley. If you wish to speak to any student or staff member, contact my office first. Understood?"

I bristled. She spoke as if *I* were one of her students or staff.

"I can speak to anyone I want," I said though I should have kept my mouth shut.

Her eyes flashed. "Not on my campus."

"I'm outta here." I brushed past her.

What had been a productive conversation had gone south real fast.

I was now on my own to find Angie.

chapter six

LENA CLARK

"Melissa," Dwight said, "there's no need to blow this out of proportion."

Dwight, dear man, was trying to mediate the situation. He'd been here far longer than she had, longer than Melissa, but Lena didn't want to cause waves with the administration. Melissa was already difficult to work with as it was.

"You were talking about *students* with a private investigator," Melissa said. "You both know better. Dammit, our school has been run through the wringer over the last five years. The student who attacked Ms. Lorenz, who is now suing us for millions. The planning commission delays over our new building. A school board that is demanding weekly reports because our test scores have dropped. Not to mention the scandal with Coach Bradford! And now we have a private investigator asking questions about a simple overdose."

Lena was well aware that the administration had been under a lot of pressure. "I understand, but—"

"Kids do drugs," Melissa interrupted. "It's unfortunate, and I'm sorry it happened to one of our students, but Elijah Martinez is not the first or last teenager who made a poor decision and paid for it with his life. The officer I brought in to speak to the assembly did a good job. I've also been pushing the school board to give us the resource officer they promised. But just this morning I had an irate call from the school board president who claims faculty and students are harassing a police detective. Was that you?"

Lena cringed. "I didn't—"

"You didn't call Detective King and criticize how she investigated the Martinez kid's OD?"

Lena's face heated. "That was not my intent. She took my questions the wrong way."

"It ends here. The police did their job, you do yours. Stay out of it." She turned to leave, then glanced back at them. "The staff meeting is postponed until tomorrow."

Lena watched her leave, listening to her crisp footsteps fade along with the jingle of her keys.

She closed the door, jaw clenched. "That woman!"

Dwight put his hands on her shoulders, gave her a light kiss. "You're shaking."

"She makes me both nervous and mad."

"Don't let her make you nervous."

"Easy for you to say," she mumbled.

Dwight pulled her into a hug, which relaxed her. She had never expected to fall in love again after her failed marriage, but then came Dwight: comfortable, kind, with many shared interests. It had been eight months and they spent most weekends together, and she'd introduced him to her daughters when they were home from college this summer.

Lena stepped away from Dwight. "I'm worried about Angie."

They sat down at the table, holding hands. "So am I," Dwight said. "Do you think she might have been with Elijah when he died? Maybe they got high together and she panicked?"

Lena vehemently shook her head. "Angie is the last person who'd do drugs."

"She comes from a troubled home, she's angry and cutting classes."

"Angie has been angry for years," Lena said. "And her troubled home stems from her mother's drug use—I don't see Angie following that path."

"Cutting classes is new. She's a straight-A student, but if she keeps cutting, her grades are going to slip."

"It's only been the last week." Lena had always felt protective of Angie. She'd achieved so much academically even with no support at home. "If Ms. Angelhart finds something, the police may reopen the case."

"Do you think that's likely?"

"I don't know," she said honestly. "At least someone is looking for answers. Angie needs to know that we support her, that we're here for her."

"She's lucky to have you on her side," Dwight said.

"I'll connect Angie with the PI," Lena said, "And we really need to push the school to implement the Silent Witness program."

"I thought you were trying to avoid getting on Melissa's bad side," Dwight said.

He had a point, but on this subject Lena was willing to fight for what she knew was right.

Dwight kissed her lightly. "You're not going to let this go, are you?"

"Do you really think I should?"

"If it's important to you, I'll back you with the faculty."

"Thank you," she said. "I really appreciate it."

"You can make me dinner as a thank-you," he said with a mischievous gleam in his eye.

She laughed. "I have some work to finish up. Do you want to wait? Or we can meet at my house around—" she glanced at the clock "—five-ish?"

"I'll wait. There's a volleyball game," Dwight said. "I haven't been to one this year, and I hear the team is play-off bound."

Dwight touched her cheek. The warm affection always made her grateful for this man and what they had together. "I know you care about Angie, but remember, she has to meet you halfway. At least *part* of the way. You can't fix everyone. I know, I know—I do the same thing with some of the kids who need that extra push. But if she doesn't refocus on what's important, she's going to lose opportunities. Text me when you're wrapping up."

"Enjoy the game," Lena said and closed the door behind him.

Lena responded to dozens of emails, which took nearly an hour. Then she proofread her proposal about the Silent Witness program. It wasn't the same program that law enforcement had, but instead was modeled after several successful school programs in major cities to provide a portal for students to report on serious campus crime. Before she could change her mind, she sent the proposal to the administration.

They needed to be proactive.

Lena sent the email and hoped the idea took hold. For all her issues with Melissa Webb—and Lena had many—the vice principal was an effective administrator. Thus, Lena focused her argument on how the program would save time and money, plus reduce disciplinary actions. The principal deferred everything to his three VPs, so Lena had to convince them before Principal Borel would sign off.

Lena didn't enjoy school politics, but she understood how they worked.

Her cell phone rang; it was Dwight.

She hit Speaker as she started filing reports. "Fifteen minutes. Maybe I can catch the last match."

"Angie's here in the gym," he said.

She slammed shut her file cabinet. "I'll be there in five."

chapter seven

MARGO ANGELHART

I drove by Angie's apartment on Nineteenth Avenue south of Dunlap. Since she'd cut school, maybe she'd stayed home.

Central Phoenix had its fair share of run-down apartment complexes, especially near the freeway, and Angie's was no exception. While it wasn't the worst, it was definitely sketchy. The complex consisted of clusters of two-story white rectangle buildings, each crammed with tiny apartments and small windows—no balconies, no patios. There was some grass, a few trees, and rows upon rows of identical buildings, all enclosed behind fencing that resembled a prison more than a place to call home. Half the gates were broken or wide open, and any window large enough for someone to crawl through had bars.

I didn't leave my gun locked in my Jeep; I concealed it with a lightweight jacket that covered my holster. First, I wasn't confident that my car was safe here even during the day, and second, the police call log showed sixty-nine calls for service to the complex in just the last two months—averaging more than one a day. I didn't want to be one of those calls.

Angie's apartment was on the ground floor of Building D. The doors were painted black, half had missing numbers, but I figured out D-10 was the second door from the east. Downstairs were even numbers, upstairs odd.

I smelled an excessive amount of chlorine, but couldn't see a pool. After knocking on the door, I stepped back. The street traffic masked any sound coming from the apartment.

Suddenly, the door opened and I was assaulted with the sweet, foul stench of marijuana smoke. A man stood there, his red eyes flashing with irritation.

"What?"

"Mr. Williams?" I guessed.

He snorted. "Nope."

Not-Mr. Williams wore sagging shorts, his beer belly hanging over the waistband. No shirt on his hairy chest. Unshaven face, and not the good kind of five o'clock shadow. He had large doughy biceps, as if he'd once regularly worked out but had slacked off.

"This *is* Angie Williams's apartment," I stated.

"Kid's at school. Or walking home. Text her fucking phone, I'm not her secretary."

I decided not to tell this guy who I doubted was her father that she had cut school today.

"Is her mom home?"

"Working."

"When does Angie usually come home?"

"You deaf? *Call her.* Jeez." He shut the door and I stood there a moment, not quite sure what I had expected or where I should look next.

A few seconds later I walked away.

I went back to my Jeep and considered waiting for Angie to come home, though I didn't know when that would be. I rarely minded surveillance gigs—stake outs were a good time to clear my mind—but I'd told Alina I would come by this afternoon. The Martinez apartment was only three blocks away.

If I wasn't able to track down Angie tonight, then I'd tap my part-time assistant Theo Washington to sit on her place tomorrow.

The apartment complex where Alina lived, though just across Nineteenth Avenue and down two blocks from Angie's, was far better maintained. There were a dozen four-apartment buildings situated on the deep lot. Each building was a cube, two apartments upstairs, two down. The lower units had patios, and the upper units had balconies. A lot of trees, trimmed bushes lining pathways, and a partly covered kids play area. It was just after four in the afternoon and several moms were talking at a picnic table while watching their young children play. No graffiti or trash anywhere. Security cameras on the corners of each building.

Having residents and management who kept the property clean made a huge difference in the crime rate.

Alina Martinez lived in a downstairs unit. I knocked and she answered immediately.

She looked even more exhausted than she had this morning.

"Thank you for letting me come by," I said.

Alina smiled thinly and opened the door for me to enter.

The open sliding glass door let in a soft breeze through the too-warm home. Cluttered but tidy, with a spacious living-dining area and a functional kitchen in the front. A short hallway, likely leading to the bedrooms. Framed photographs covered almost every inch of wall space—mostly older black-and-white pictures of family that reminded me of my grandparents' long hallway Pop called "Ancestor Alley." Many pictures of Elijah everywhere. A prominent wedding portrait of a young Alina, no older than twenty, and her equally young husband, stood out in the living room.

When Alina saw me staring, she said, "My husband, Marcus. He was a very good man. Worked so hard. We had a good life, Marcus and me. A better life after Elijah. Now, they're both gone."

I felt for the woman, but emotions always made me feel uncomfortable, and I never had the right words to help. Tess was so much better at this than me; I preferred *doing* something. In the weeks after Iris's husband died, Tess sat with her for hours and let her talk and cry. I cleaned her house and cooked, then took her teenagers to the movies so they'd be distracted for a few hours.

"You were a lovely couple," I said because it was the first thing that came to mind and it was true. "Would you mind if I looked through Elijah's things? I'll put everything back the way I found it."

She led me down the hall. Elijah's room was also neat, and not as cluttered as the living area. His walls were decorated with music posters of bands I hadn't heard of, and an Arizona Cardinals pennant. A neatly made double bed. A short bookshelf overflowing with books, papers, binders. Laptop computer centered on his desk.

Alina was hovering, and I asked, "Would you mind if I went through his room alone?"

"Oh, yes, of course. Please. I'm sorry."

"Don't apologize, Alina," I said.

She smiled nervously, then left, closing the door behind her.

I went first to his computer. Password-protected. Alina might know the password, but I didn't want to call her back in right away.

Nothing of interest in his drawers—no drugs, no drug paraphernalia, no weapons, no wads of cash. I found a file folder with pay stubs from the Cactus Stop. He had direct deposit and these were pay summaries he'd likely printed from his computer. After taxes, he took home just under $550 every two weeks, though during the summer it went up to $800. That was working roughly twenty hours a week during the school year, and about thirty hours during the summer. A decent job for a teenager.

His closet was messier than his room, but it was mostly stuffed with clothes, sports equipment that hadn't been used in years, worn shoes, an empty laundry basket.

On his dresser were LEGO figurines—maybe a remnant of his childhood. Sticky notes from his mother about chores, reminders of family events. No pictures, but I'd bet he had some on his phone.

I looked around but didn't see a cell phone. A charger sat next to his computer, but no phone *and* no backpack. I couldn't imagine a studious kid not having one. He'd gone to school Friday, then went to work directly from school. His backpack would likely be either at work or wherever he went after.

I pulled up the police report on my phone and skimmed through it. No backpack found in the park.

And no phone logged into evidence.

I was about to leave, frustrated that there seemed to be nothing of import in his room—other than the missing phone and backpack—when I spotted a bright green sticky note in the small wastebasket.

Wastebasket. Private Investigation 101: Always Check the Trash.

I had failed. Well, did I actually fail because I thought of it last minute? I'd give myself a pass this time.

I picked up the small plastic bin and put it on the desk. The sticky note was from his mom.

> Going with Aunt Nina to Kelsey's baby shower, leftover chicken in the blue container.

No date.

There wasn't a lot of trash—a few other sticky notes from his mother, a couple pieces of crumpled binder and graph paper, a flyer for a job fair in the courtyard of the Central Library. The fair had been held on the Saturday his body had been found.

Had he been looking for another job? Or tossed it because he liked his job?

I put it aside and smoothed out the other papers. Math. Just looking at the numbers and letters brought on the beginning of a headache. Some of the letters didn't look right, and I had a flash of my brother Nico doing calculus homework. Greek letters, or something like that. There was something disturbing not only in mixing numbers and letters together, but throwing around Greek symbols to really confuse someone.

I left his room and found Alina in the kitchen slowly washing a pot.

"I'm done," I said.

She turned off the water and dried her hands, leaving the pot in the sink.

"Did you find anything that helps you?"

"Do you have Elijah's computer password?"

"I never thought to ask him."

"Would you mind if I borrowed his computer? My sister may be able to get in."

"You think there's something there? Something about what happened?"

"I won't know until I look. I might be able to check his calendar, maybe emails he sent to a friend. Did Elijah have a cell phone?"

"Of course."

"Did the police tell you if they had it?"

She frowned, shook her head. "They didn't say. I didn't ask. I should have asked."

"It wasn't on his body," I said, then inwardly winced, hoping I didn't sound too callous. "He could have lost it or left it somewhere."

The police should have asked her about it, since it was unusual *not* to find a phone on a teenager.

"Would you do me a big favor?" I asked.

"Yes?"

"I would like a printout of all Elijah's calls for at least the last thirty days. Three months would be great."

"I call the phone company and ask?"

"You should be able to log into your account and print out the bill."

She shook her head. "I don't have a computer."

"Do you get a paper bill?"

She brightened. "Yes. I can get that for you."

"Before you do, one more question. What color is Elijah's backpack?"

"Dark gray. It has a football patch, the Arizona Cardinals, that he ironed on the front pocket. His uncle took Elijah and his cousin to a game for their sixteenth birthdays last year. So expensive, those tickets. I told Donny it was too much money, but he said you're only sixteen once. Ever since, Elijah loved the team, even when they lose."

Which lately was often, I thought. They seemed to either start strong, then fall apart, or start poorly, only to win when it didn't matter anymore.

"I don't know where it is," she said.

"Maybe I can track it down." Work, school, a friend's house—all possible. The contents could be enlightening.

"I'll get the phone records for you."

I waited in the kitchen and looked out the window at the small park in the center of the complex. A couple of the moms were trying to wrestle their kids inside. Did the squeals of laughter comfort Alina? I hoped so.

She brought me a folder. "Here," she said. "These are everything for the year. His number ends in 1719, the other number is mine."

I looked through the file. It cut off ten days before he was killed.

"I need you to do one thing that may help me piece together Elijah's last few days. I need his phone records up until the day he died."

"They will be on the next bill, won't they?"

"Yes, but according to this, we'd have to wait another eight or nine days. The sooner I get it, the better. If you call, as the account owner, they'll send it to you."

"I can do that."

She looked out the window and observed the children. "I don't know what I will do without Elijah," she said quietly, more to herself than me. "I miss him so much."

The pain in her voice tore at my heart.

I would find out exactly what happened. It wouldn't bring Elijah back, but maybe I could give his mother some peace.

It was after five by the time I was back in my car. I called Luisa, my youngest sister, the computer whiz. Like me, she'd done six years in the military after high school—she picked the Marines—and now she was starting her second year of college on the GI bill.

Luisa didn't answer, so I left a message to call me.

I wished I could just go home and analyze these phone records, but Jack left files at the office—the opposite direction from my house.

I was going to be stuck in traffic. I considered waiting until tomorrow to grab the files, but what else was I going to do tonight?

I headed toward Seventh Avenue for the long drive back downtown.

chapter eight

ANGIE WILLIAMS

Angie had spent the day at her favorite place—the downtown Central Library.

She'd planned to go to class, but when she started walking toward campus, the southbound bus pulled up and, on impulse, she boarded it. There was a closer library to her apartment, but it was small and the librarian was a bitch. Central was different—massive, quiet, anonymous. No one bothered you there. She could sit for hours and do homework or nothing at all. No creeps asking for money, no one hitting on her, no judgmental glances from librarians.

Today, she'd buried herself in research, reading everything she could find about fentanyl to try and figure out how Elijah had been drugged. Why hadn't he called for help? Why hadn't he called *her*?

She read about the risks, the symptoms. How to smoke, ingest, or even use liquid fentanyl in nasal or eye drops. Fentanyl was in everything now—cut into pills, powder, dusted on marijuana.

Sometimes people didn't even realize they were overdosing. They just stopped breathing.

She pictured that happening to Elijah and wanted to scream, cry, demand justice.

Depressed and exhausted, she stayed at the library until three, then hopped a bus back to campus for the volleyball game.

Angie hadn't missed any of her friend Gina's volleyball games, even though she technically shouldn't be on school grounds because she'd skipped class today. But she didn't want to go home either. Bruce wasn't the worst of her mother's long line of boyfriends—he hadn't tried to get into her pants, for example—but he was a lazy jerk who watched television 24/7 and worked sporadically.

Gina had been her best friend since forever. In fact, she spent more time at Gina's house than at her own. She loved the large happy Martinelli family. Their house was loud, messy, and full of life. Gina was the oldest of six, including four-year-old twins, but her parents were chill and always invited Angie to stay for dinner. Home-cooked meals beat microwaved pizza or drive-thru burgers any day.

If one of her teachers spotted her, she might get in trouble. But really, what would they do? Give her detention? Make her sit in the library and do homework? She did that for *fun*.

At least she had until Elijah died.

Now, school felt empty. She didn't have a homework buddy or anyone to sit with in class. Most of the honors students were uptight, pretentious, or awkward. She didn't fit in with any of them.

She sat high in the bleachers, as far from the noisy crowd as possible. Most of the kids weren't even watching, they were just killing time. Maybe some, like her, didn't want to go home.

Teachers rarely showed up at games anyway. Even if they did, she was good at being invisible.

If you believed you couldn't be seen, most people didn't see you.

Volleyball was best-of-five. Gina's mom had come to the first game, cheering with the twins louder than the pep squad. Gina pretended to be embarrassed, but Angie knew she loved it.

They won the first game. As Mrs. Martinelli gathered up the twins, she waved at Angie. She smiled and waved back, blinking away tears.

Why couldn't *she* have a family like the Martinellis? Why couldn't *she* have a mom who cared where she was and what she did? Gina sometimes bitched about chores and curfew, but she was never *actually* mad that she had responsibilities. Angie wanted to feel more loved than tolerated.

They lost the second game 25–22. During the short break, Angie spotted Mr. Parsons enter the gym and look around. She ducked behind a group of students, hoping he wouldn't notice her.

Normally, she loved school. Even the classes she didn't like were better than being at home. After school she and Elijah used to study together in the library until he had to go to work.

But Elijah was gone and no one cared. The police closed the case like it was nothing. *Sorry, not sorry, your friend is dead. Don't do drugs or you might be dead too.*

But Elijah *didn't* do drugs. She *knew* that. No one listened.

His funeral shredded her. His mom cried quietly the whole time. His uncle gave a beautiful, heartbreaking eulogy. His cousins looked stunned, as if waiting for someone to say it was all a mistake.

She had no idea what to do when the game was over. She'd already spent the weekend at Gina's and sleepovers weren't allowed on school nights.

Angie *hated* going home, but that was really the only option. She wasn't about to sleep on the street.

Once, during a massive fight with her mom, her mom locked her out of the apartment. Gina was out of town so she slept on Elijah's patio until his mom found out and let her crash on their couch.

She'd turn eighteen in April, graduate in May, and then she'd be gone.

Maybe college—ASU was an option thanks to her grades and

her mom's total lack of money. But she had no idea what she wanted to do.

Until she figured it out, she'd keep doing what she did best: ignore her mother, avoid whatever asshole she was currently screwing, and hide in the library.

Sun Valley won game three and Angie got up to use the bathroom. She waved to Gina and motioned that she'd be back. Gina gave her a thumbs-up, and Angie stepped outside of the gym to the restrooms.

When she was done, Mrs. Clark was there waiting for her outside the door.

"Angie, a minute please."

A demand, even though she said please.

"What?" Angie snapped. She liked Mrs. Clark, but she didn't want this conversation.

"Why don't we go to my office?"

"I'm watching the game."

"You know the rules."

Angie glared at her. Who the fuck cared about the stupid rules. No going to school events the day you have an absence. Blah, blah, blah.

"Angie," Mrs. Clark said, her voice low, "you promised not to skip school again. I know you're upset about Elijah—"

"No shit," Angie said. She was *so* tired of being placated. It was why she didn't want to come to school. Her friends, her teachers, everyone talking about Elijah. He was a statistic, so sad. Don't do drugs, you'll end up dead like Elijah. Laughter because Elijah was a teacher's pet and ha, ha, he was a druggie. People looked at her as if she had been there, as if she had left him to die.

"Angie—"

"Just stop already! Of *course* I'm upset. He's dead and buried and no one gives a shit."

"That's not true."

"You think the police care? Sure, they care a whole lot, because they closed the case. He took drugs, he deserved to die."

"No one thinks that, and your call to Detective King on Friday was unproductive."

"How do you know about that?" Was her teacher now conspiring with the police against her?

"I talked to the detective just like I told you I would. I asked why they closed his case and if there was anything we could do to refocus their attention. She told me."

"They think it's his fault, and it wasn't. *Someone poisoned him.* I know he didn't do it on purpose. Someone gave him those drugs and I swear to God that he didn't know. He *didn't know!*" She was screaming and tears burned her cheeks. What if she was wrong? What if he *had* known?

She wasn't wrong. She *knew* her friend. Even if he had been avoiding her the last couple weeks.

A parent frowned at them as she left the bathroom, then scurried by. Angie wiped her face. She would not cry. She *didn't* cry.

"I haven't given up," Mrs. Clark said. "I want to find out what happened as much as you. I know you're under a lot of pressure with college applications and—"

Angie interrupted. "Do you have a point you're trying to make or can I go watch the game?"

Mrs. Clark bristled. Angie felt bad because the counselor had always been nice to her, but Angie suppressed the feelings. She *couldn't* care.

"Mrs. Martinez hired a private investigator. She would like to talk to you."

"What the fuck can a PI do that the police can't?" Angie demanded. "She can't arrest anyone, she can't do anything."

"If she finds something, she can go the authorities with the information."

Angie threw her hands into the air. "If, if, *if.* Why would the police even listen to her? What about *they don't give a fuck* do you not understand?"

"Do not swear at me, Angie," Mrs. Clark said calmly.

Angie felt bad, her face heated, but she couldn't stop herself.

"This is all just bullshit!"

"Come to school tomorrow. I'll have the private investigator stop by during lunch and you can talk to her in my office. Okay?"

"You're unbelievable. Holding this over my head to force me to come to school?"

"Mr. Parsons told me about the test on Friday, and I'm sure you have a lot of work to catch up on in your other classes. You're capable, but you need to be present."

Parsons. "Your boyfriend told you I was here, didn't he?"

Mrs. Clark blushed and looked surprised.

"Oh, please, everyone knows. It's *obvious*."

"We are concerned about you cutting school and missing classes. It can't continue."

"What are you going to do about it?" Angie said. She had never been this disrespectful to a teacher, especially a teacher she liked. But she was so *done* with the bullshit adults fed her. Her mother. The police. Mrs. Clark. It was like, oh, be a good girl, we'll handle everything. They did *nothing*.

"I'm going to watch the game," she said and walked away.

Mrs. Clark didn't stop her.

By the time she got back, the fourth game was over and Sun Valley won the match, which meant no fifth game. Gina was talking with her team and the coach, so Angie left.

She headed for the side exit, which was the fastest way home, but then she thought, if Mrs. Clark had talked to the PI, she must have her name.

Angie didn't think that the PI would be able to do anything, but she didn't need Mrs. Clark to talk to her. Angie would find the woman herself, talk to her alone, tell her exactly what the police did—nothing.

But she needed the PI's name.

She saw Mrs. Clark and Mr. Parsons talking outside the gym. She didn't have a lot of time.

Head up, not looking anyone in the eye, she walked straight to the administrative building. All the doors were locked—you needed a key or a pass card to get in, except through the lobby.

She went in through the student entrance.

"I thought I locked the door," Mrs. Villines, the school secretary, said. "We're closed." She already had her large purse over her shoulder.

"I just saw Mrs. Clark at the volleyball game. She said she wanted to talk to me and to wait in her office."

"She didn't come in with you?"

"She was talking to Mr. Parsons."

"Oh," Mrs. Villines said with a little smile. Yeah, if Mrs. Clark and Mr. Parsons thought that they were being all discreet about their relationship, they were both idiots. *Everyone* knew. "All right, go ahead."

"Thanks," Angie said as Mrs. Villines buzzed her into the main part of the building.

Angie ran down the hall and into Mrs. Clark's office. She was obviously expecting to return because her door was open, her briefcase on the table, and the computer was still on.

She stared at the perfectly neat desk. Yes, predictable *and* organized.

A business card was perfectly positioned under her monitor.

Angelhart Investigations
Margo Angelhart

Two phone numbers and an email were listed in small print on the bottom of the card. This was easier than she'd thought.

She pulled out her phone to take a photo, but heard a voice so she quickly pocketed the card just as a someone said, "Can I help you?"

It was the principal, Mr. Borel. "Um, hi, Mr. Borel."

"You're not supposed to be in here without a teacher," he said.

Angie didn't think she'd said more than two words to him in the three years she'd been here.

"Um . . ." She saw an SAT study guide on the table. "I just saw Mrs. Clark at the volleyball game. She told me I could pick up this study guide." She grabbed it.

He might not believe her, but it wasn't like she needed to hack in and change her grades or anything. Though she *would* like to erase all the absences.

Before he could question her, she pushed past him and said, "See you tomorrow!" Without looking back, she headed toward the side door, but heard a jingling of keys and voices just outside. She didn't want to explain herself to anyone, so she turned and headed toward the main exit before anyone else could ask her any questions, stuffing the thick SAT book into her already crowded backpack.

Two minutes later, Angie stood on the street outside the school and knew she didn't want to go home. Her mother worked until six, and she didn't want to be alone with Bruce. When her mother was home, they ignored her. When she wasn't, Bruce thought Angie was his personal slave to clean up after him and fetch him beer because he was too lazy to walk ten feet to the fridge.

Besides, she was hungry, and she doubted her mother would have anything good to eat—even though she was a cashier at a grocery store and got a discount on food. Every night, she brought home frozen pizza or chicken nuggets. You'd think just once in a while she'd get apples or milk. So Angie headed toward the Cactus Stop. She'd walked this route many times with Elijah after he started working there last March. He'd been so thrilled because most places didn't hire teenagers anymore and the Cactus Stop paid fifteen dollars an hour *and* he was guaranteed twenty hours a week. He worked five to nine, Tuesday through Saturday. Angie would stop by sometimes to chat or pick up snacks. They always had fruit, even if sometimes it was overripe.

In the summer, Elijah worked longer hours and Angie hadn't

seen him for weeks. When she ran into him the week before school started, he looked miserable and tired. He'd also lost weight.

She'd asked him about it, but he hadn't talked. She'd pushed; he told her it was nothing.

Was his weight loss about his job? School?

Drugs . . .

She pushed the thought out of her mind.

Now he was dead and she couldn't push him, *make* him tell her what had him so preoccupied.

She had wanted to tell the detective about these changes over the last few weeks, but the cop hadn't called her back and Angie left *three messages*. The detective hadn't listened, hadn't cared; Mrs. Clark listened, but couldn't do anything. Angie was so frustrated that everything in her life was out of her control that she wanted to scream.

But she didn't. She focused on trying not to feel so alone and angry.

Angie entered the convenience store. Though the tall, narrow aisles and abundance of merchandise made the place seem crowded, it was clean. She really didn't know what she was doing, except she'd spent so much time here talking to Elijah. Maybe she just wanted to feel close to him. Maybe she wanted to know if anyone worked with him the day he died.

Walking down the aisle of chips, she grabbed a bag of spicy Doritos and a bottle of water. She put the cold bottle on the nape of her neck and felt better. She grabbed an apple from the bowl on the counter; it wasn't bruised, a plus. She put her items down, then realized she knew the kid behind the counter. "Benny?" she said.

"Hey, Angie! How are you?"

Benny grinned ear to ear and walked around from behind the counter to give her a hug. She hugged him back. It felt so good she didn't want to let go.

Benny Vallejo was Angie's ex-boyfriend's little brother. Not so little—he was six inches taller. But she'd known him since she started dating Chris back when she was a freshman and Chris was a sophomore. The three of them used to do things together all the time before Chris went to college.

Tears burned, but she didn't let them fall. She missed Chris, but he was in college and she wasn't. She didn't want to be needy or use him as a crutch or pressure him to visit or anything. He had his life, she had hers, and that was that.

But she missed him, and she realized she missed Benny too. They didn't have it any easier than she did—their mom was long gone and their dad was an asshole who smacked them around. But Chris and Benny had always been a unit, a team, and looked out for each other.

And her, when she was Chris's girl.

"When did you start working here?" she asked, blinking to push back those damn emotions.

"I started on Thursday. Couldn't believe it, I applied months ago, then they called me up Monday and said they had an opening. Totally sweet. My dad is thrilled, you know? And, well, not being home has its advantages."

"I hear ya," Angie said.

He laughed, squeezed her arm because he knew about her screwed-up homelife and she knew about his. There was a camaraderie when you shared something like that. "And I love getting a paycheck. Or I will, when I get my first one on Friday."

Elijah was killed ten days ago. Benny had filled his spot.

"You okay?" he asked. Then his face fell. "Oh. Oh, God. I'm sorry. I didn't think. I'm so sorry about Elijah. Did you talk to Chris?"

She shook her head.

"Why not? Jeez, Ange, he would totally have come up. It's, like, a thirty-minute drive."

She should have. Chris had also been friends with Elijah.

"I know, but he's busy and I didn't want to dump on him."

Benny frowned and was about to say something when another guy, older by a few years, came out of the storage room and walked behind the counter, giving Benny a scowl.

"Sorry, Tony, Angie's a friend."

Benny hurried back around the counter. Angie paid for her items and Benny made change.

She glanced at Tony, who was staring at her. She'd seen him almost every day she came in to chat with Elijah.

"You're friends with Elijah," he said.

She nodded. Tony had always watched her, which sort of creeped her out, though he hadn't made any weird moves on her. Did he know what happened to Elijah? She wanted to ask him what he knew, but deep down she was scared and realized she was way, way over her head. Maybe Elijah's odd behavior these last few weeks had nothing to do with work. Maybe it *was* the pressure of school and college applications, like Mrs. Clark suggested. Maybe he had decided to pop pills. What did she know? People were rarely what they seemed to be.

But he wouldn't do drugs, especially hard drugs, she told herself. No one changed that much over one summer. Did they?

She pocketed her change and mumbled thanks. She wanted to ask Tony questions, or maybe just talk about Elijah because she missed him so damn much, but she didn't. She walked out, feeling as if Tony were watching her the whole time.

Creepy. Definitely creepy.

Benny ran out after her. "Angie, wait up."

She stopped. "I don't want to get you in trouble."

He put a hand on her shoulder, turned her to face him. "You won't. What's wrong?"

She looked up into Benny's warm brown eyes.

"I'm okay," she said. "I miss Elijah, and I shouldn't have come here."

"You ever want to talk, call me, okay? Seriously. You're practically my sister."

He smiled, but that comment made her want to cry even more.

"Okay," she said and gave him a hug, before turning and speed walking south, toward the school and her apartment beyond.

She was glad that Chris had a whole new life away from his abusive dad. She wanted the best for him, and for Benny. The Vallejo brothers didn't need to be dragged down by her innate pessimism.

Her cell phone rang. She answered it without looking, regretting it immediately when she heard Bruce's nasty voice. "Are you in trouble?"

"No. What do you want?"

"There's a woman looking for you. Interrupted my game."

Was it the PI? "What was her name?"

"How the hell am I supposed to remember? Did you skip school today? Maybe it was a truant officer."

She didn't answer. She heard sirens in the distance, not an unusual sound, but still she walked faster.

"Your ma is on her way home. She got a call from the school. I bet you cut. If you're cutting school, just quit and get a fucking job and start contributing to the family."

"You get a fucking job and start contributing!" she snapped and instantly regretted it.

"You little bitch. Don't you talk to me like that. When your mother gets home, she'll wash your mouth out with soap!"

She hung up, pocketed her phone, and headed back to the school where she hoped to catch a bus that went anywhere but home.

She stood at the corner about to press the crosswalk button, but stopped. A half dozen police cars were in the parking lot, lights whirling.

She didn't cross the street. Instead, she headed west, heart thudding, wondering what had happened. She called Gina.

"Yo, Ange! You ran off so fast after the game."

"There's something going on at the school. Police cars everywhere."

"Really? I left, like, thirty minutes ago—it was quiet."

"I have a bad feeling."

"Want to come over for dinner? I can pick you up."

"I can't ask you to do that." Gina drove a beat-up car that her dad, a mechanic, kept running.

"You didn't. I'll take you home after dinner. Are you at the school now?"

"No. Um, I'm almost to the Starbucks on Dunlap near Nineteenth."

"You okay?"

"Yeah. Thanks, Gina. I mean it."

Angie glanced over her shoulder and wished she knew what was going on.

chapter nine

MARGO ANGELHART

I was stuck at a long light at Camelback and Seventh Avenue when my cell phone rang with an unfamiliar number.

"Margo Angelhart," I answered.

"Hi, it's Lena Clark at Sun Valley High. I talked to Angie this afternoon and I'm hoping she'll be here during lunch tomorrow to talk to you."

"You *hope* she'll be there?"

"She didn't promise. We had a bit of an argument. I think she came into my office and took your business card off my desk."

Sneaky kid. I kind of liked that.

"If she calls me," I said, "I'll let you know."

"Please tell her to come to school. It's important for her future. I know Elijah's death has hit her especially hard, but she can't keep doing this."

I agreed with Lena, but didn't agree to tell Angie anything. Honestly, I didn't know what I would say or do, because I didn't know Angie. So far, my sense was she would do whatever the hell she wanted and anything I said, anything anyone told her, would factor in only if Angie wanted it to.

"I'll see what I can do," I said vaguely.

"Margo, I didn't tell you everything this afternoon."

Bingo, I thought. I knew she had been holding back.

"On Friday after the funeral, Angie called Detective King and left a very nasty phone message about the police closing the case. When I called Detective King later that afternoon, I got an earful about it. So I would really appreciate if you can help me get her back on the right track."

I remembered what the vice principal said earlier. "Is it going to be a problem if I come to campus? I can meet after school, if that would be easier for you."

"I'll handle the administration," Lena said. "I have to go. I'll see you tomorrow."

I called Theo Washington and gave him a heads-up that I might need his help in the morning.

"So don't stay up all night playing video games," I added.

"As long as the check clears, you'll have me bright-eyed and bushy-tailed anytime in the a.m., Sugar."

I rolled my eyes and hung up without saying goodbye. Theo had a dozen nicknames for me. I didn't particularly like or dislike them, but he seemed to enjoy trying to irritate me.

I did sort of like when he called me Boss.

Theo had worked for me part-time for the last two years, and now he worked part-time for Angelhart Investigations. He took classes at Paradise Valley Community College two days a week, but he was free tomorrow and I'd use him all day if I needed him.

I wanted to help Alina Martinez, but pro bono cases didn't pay the bills, so the faster I found answers, the faster I could go back to cases that paid.

When Theo was seventeen, I'd gotten him out of a jam. Now he wanted to work at the crime lab. He'd just finished a summer internship with my brother Nico, had two more semesters at PVCC, then he'd be certificated for a job in the lab. It was a great program for kids who either couldn't afford or didn't want to go to a four-year college. Theo was a smart kid and determined to do something productive with his life.

Driving downtown during rush hour was not my idea of fun. Even though I was driving opposite most of the traffic, cross-traffic slowed everyone down. Thirty minutes later I let myself into the office and disabled the alarm system. I suppose I was more upset that Jack had left the files on my desk because he was having dinner with his bitch of an ex-wife. Jack was a big boy; he knew what he was doing—and he wouldn't go down that road again. I hoped.

Whitney had hurt my brother deeply. I would never forgive her.

I decided to go through the files Jack left me now, instead of sitting in traffic going home. I grabbed some cheese and crackers and sat at my desk. The first file was the Elijah Martinez death investigation, which Josie had already sent me. Jack had summarized it on a sticky note. He'd learned nothing new.

The second, thicker file was a DEB bust from nearly three years ago. It made for fascinating reading, and I planned to ask Lena Clark about it tomorrow; she'd already mentioned it in passing.

Sun Valley's head football coach, Ben Bradford, and his wife, Cecilia—a stay-at-home mother of three—had run a drug distribution network using several of his players. The kids recruited others in a pyramid-like scheme, and only one—backup quarterback Eric McMahon who never played in a single down—knew the coach was at the top of the pyramid.

An anonymous tip to Phoenix PD kicked off a deep investigation using *21 Jump Street*-style infiltration. That would have been fun, I thought. I used to love reruns of that old Johnny Depp show. Josie and I both had huge crushes on young Johnny.

The sting lasted three months and culminated in multiple arrests. All the teens involved got probation except for Scott Jimenez, who was sent to juvie for attempted murder. Coach Bradford pled guilty and cut his sentence to fifteen years. Cecilia lied to police. Forensic auditors found she'd been laundering money through an in-home daycare, claiming nine thousand a month in income on their taxes.

Investigators estimated the Bradfords were pulling in more than thirty grand a month, but no cash was ever recovered, and there was no sign they spent the money on luxuries or travel. Police suspected a third party. Neither Ben nor Cecilia ratted on their supplier. Ben claimed he made monthly runs to Mexico, but there was no evidence of border crossings. Later, he stated he met a contact in Yuma, but wouldn't name them.

Cecilia was offered WITSEC if she flipped, but she refused. They offered probation. She still refused. Thus, she got six years in federal prison, and her three kids were sent to live with their paternal grandparents in South Dakota.

I read the report twice, noted all the names, including the officers. The Bradfords lived in the 900 precinct and my ex-boyfriend, Sergeant Rick Devlin, had executed the search warrant on their home. I wondered if he might have insight.

Was I thinking about calling him because I thought he could help or because I missed him? And even if he did have something useful to share, would it matter now, three years later, with the involved kids out of school and the Bradfords behind bars?

I shelved that thought for now.

Scanning my notes, I wondered if something similar might be happening again at Sun Valley. Lena had worked there at the time, she might know more. I tried calling her, but her cell went to voicemail. I left a message for her to call me back.

While the Bradford bust might shed light on how a school-based drug operation could work, it seemed only marginally relevant to what happened to Elijah. Still . . . the police suspected a third party, and Elijah had been a freshman at the time. Maybe there *was* a connection I wasn't seeing.

Angie likely knew more—about Elijah, his friends, his job. Maybe she knew if someone was harassing him or if anything had been weighing on him. And maybe, just maybe, she knew whether anyone from the Bradford drug ring had ties to Elijah.

For five seconds, I debated trying to catch Angie at home tonight, then dismissed the idea. The jerk who wasn't her dad was probably there, plus maybe her mother, and I didn't know how much Angie would talk around them, if at all.

Tomorrow morning was soon enough.

I wrote up a memo for Tess to pull the files from the courthouse about the Bradford case, then decided to print out the memo and stop by her house on the way home. I probably owed her an apology for the burgundy dress argument, though it wouldn't be sincere because the conversation had been silly. Still, it mattered to Tess, and therefore I needed it to matter to me.

Three years ago I walked away from the family business I helped create, angry and upset. I expected Angelhart Investigations' first case to be proving my father, Cooper Angelhart, innocent of the murder he pled guilty to—a crime he refused to explain. I couldn't imagine my kind, intelligent, responsible dad killing anyone in cold blood. But my mother had other plans. Her reason for starting the business, like everything else she'd done—from prosecutor to defense lawyer—was to help those with no one else to turn to. I agreed with the mission, but why couldn't we do both?

Initially, my brothers and sisters had sided with me, but one by one, my mom convinced them to stand down, that we had to listen to what Dad wanted. Everyone complied—except me. I stood alone.

I had never felt so betrayed in my life, so I walked away.

Today, three years later, I had reclaimed my family, but I would never forget how I felt. I had forgiven my mother—mostly—thanks to Uncle Rafe's constant support and wisdom, mostly as an uncle, but also as a priest. I had completely forgiven my siblings because they were doing what mom and dad wanted.

Even though we'd been so close growing up, Tess was the last of my siblings I'd reconnected with. Jack, Nico, Lu—I saw them regularly even when I didn't talk to my mom. But I'd only talked to Tess at family events, and it had been uncomfortable and awkward. There was still this space between us that I didn't know how to fix.

Tess owned a small condo not far from Angelhart Investigations, and being fairly traditional, she wouldn't move into Gabriel's house until they were married. But it was a not-so-well-kept secret that she stayed with Gabriel most nights.

Still, I called Tess to make sure she was where I thought she was.

"Hey, I have something to drop off. Your place or Gabe's?"

She hesitated just a fraction and I almost laughed.

"Tess . . ."

"I'm at Gabriel's. We just had a late dinner and—"

"No need to justify anything to me. I'll be there in ten minutes." I ended the call.

chapter ten

MARGO ANGELHART

Gabriel lived in one of the oldest neighborhoods in central Phoenix, the Alvarado Historic District. Roughly four square blocks of discreet wealth, with about thirty large homes and tree-lined streets.

I didn't fault Gabriel for having money. He was a pediatric surgeon at the nearby Phoenix Children's Hospital and worked long hours. But he also had family money, otherwise even he couldn't afford to live in this neighborhood. Not to mention that these houses rarely went up for sale. They tended to stay in the family.

His house was as subtly wealthy as Gabriel himself. Set back from the street, the two-story Spanish-style brick and adobe home looked modest, but it was spacious and the grounds impeccably maintained. I wouldn't be surprised if it was the largest lot in the district.

Tess opened the door before I even knocked.

"You didn't have to come," Tess said.

"Yeah, I did. Do you have a few minutes?"

Did Tess not want to let me in? Maybe they were in the middle of a romantic interlude and I had interrupted.

"Of course."

I stepped inside. I'd been here a couple times, but since Tess and Gabriel started dating after my split with the family, I hadn't visited often, and only for family events that Gabriel hosted.

The house had been updated since it was first built in the 1930s, but maintained an historic feel. The living room and dining room were stuffy and super formal, filled with antique furniture that was a bit too . . . perfect. A lot like Gabriel himself, though I'd never say that.

"Let's go to the den," Tess said. Maybe she too was a bit uncomfortable in the stately house. Our mom called our home a "working house." Five kids all close in age necessitated durable, comfortable furniture to accommodate our rough-and-tumble childhood. Mom learned quickly to put anything valuable and breakable in hers or dad's offices, which were mostly off-limits.

Gabriel's den wasn't exactly a cozy nook for reading or watching TV—it was nearly the size of my house. Built-in bookshelves lined the walls, a large-screen TV dominated one side, and a video game system sat beneath it. Surprising, given Gabriel's straight-laced demeanor. But the real showstopper was the backyard view: Lush trees framed a vibrant lawn, with a blue pool at the center edged in Spanish tile. White lights twinkled over the yard, casting a fairy-tale glow. Cliché, but true.

I sighed without realizing it until Tess said, "It's lovely, isn't it?"

"You'd better invite me over for a pool party before it gets too cold."

Yes, it gets cold in Phoenix. People forget that winter exists in the desert when summer temps soar over one-hundred degrees for months.

"I'll ask Gabriel about having a family barbecue. It would be fun."

I sank into the buttery-soft leather couch and imagined I could live happily in just this room. Tess sat across from me on a matching sofa.

"First," I said, needing to get my apology out of the way, "I'm sorry I snapped at you this morning about the dresses."

Tess shook her head. "It was me, not you. Well, you were wrong—I can't have bridesmaids wear burgundy in the spring—but I took out my frustration on you. I know you're not comfortable with the trimmings of a big wedding." She bit her lip and didn't look me in the eye.

"What? You're not telling me something."

She glanced toward the door, which she'd closed, and then said quietly, "We have only six and a half months and I'm nervous."

"About?"

"Everything."

"Tess," I said, a warning in my voice to spill it or else.

"You *know*."

I did know. "Say it."

She shook her head.

"Gabriel is not an asshole," I said. "That's all you need to know."

"You didn't like him when you first met him," she said quickly and quietly. "Maybe you sensed something no one else does."

Two broken engagements had really messed with Tess's self-confidence.

"I don't like most people when I first meet them," I said. "Tess, you trust everyone until they prove they're *untrustworthy*; I trust no one *until* they prove they're trustworthy. Two sides, same coin."

Tess laughed. "And to think we were raised by the same parents."

It was odd that I had always been closest to our dad, who was more like Tess in personality and temperament, while Tess had always been closest to our mom who, I was loath to admit, was a lot like me.

Maybe that was why Mom and I butted heads so often. It was like arguing with myself.

Tess sat there as if waiting for something.

"You're going to make me say it, aren't you?"

"I want to know why," she said. "Please."

"Because I love you," I said simply. "Gabriel just seemed . . . too smooth, too handsome, too *perfect*. He's a pediatric surgeon who saves little kids. I thought there had to be something in his past, something he was hiding, because no one is that . . . *good.*" I couldn't think of another word. "Just an all-around good guy."

"Pop and Abuela are great."

"They are rare," I said.

Our grandparents—mom's parents—were two of the most remarkable people I've ever known. Pop is a retired judge, a true patriarch, whose wisdom is unmatched. Abuela raised seven kids while running her own business, often with one or more kids by her side. Her sharp business acumen was a key factor in their substantial wealth, which was build more on her entrepreneurial skill than Pop's steady income.

"Gabriel loves you," I said. "He shows it. I think he's arrogant and has a stick up his ass sometimes, but he makes you happy. That's all I care about, Tess. You deserve to be happy."

Tess's face melted into a warm, sappy smile. "Aw, Margo, thank you. And so do you."

"I'm happy."

"You know what I mean."

I shrugged. "Let's get you married first, then we'll worry about me."

"I have something to show you. I want your gut impression—just give it to me."

Before I could object, she jumped up and ran from the room. A minute later she came back with a thick binder that was decorated with lace and roses. I had seen that binder too many times to count and wanted to bolt.

Her wedding planner.

Tess put the book down on the table and had her finger in the middle, marking a page. "I'm going to show you two colors. Tell me which one for the dresses. Your gut."

I didn't want to be put in this spot, because what if I picked wrong and Tess hated it?

Tess said, "Get that look off your face. Mom and I narrowed it down this morning to these two colors. I love them both. Mom loves them both. And I know you'll be honest. You've always been honest with me."

I breathed in deeply, slowly let it out. "Okay."

She opened the book. One side of the page was red—true red, vibrant and bold. The photos she'd included were of weddings with men in black tuxes with bold red cummerbunds and the bridesmaids in long satiny red dresses. The flowers were mostly white with red rose accents. One photo had bouquets of white roses, lots of greenery, and a few red roses and yellow daisy accents. It was stunning.

The other side was subdued and no less beautiful. Sage green dresses, the men in dark gray tuxes with sage green cummerbunds. The bouquets were mostly white flowers with a few bursts of color and eucalyptus leaves. I loved it. Green is my favorite color and I could envision myself wearing the dress.

Yet . . . red. Tess was red.

Tess was tall, elegant, and graceful, with lush, shiny brown hair. Luisa and I had inherited hazel-green eyes—greener than our mom's golden hue, but not blue like our dad. Tess on the other hand had large, striking chocolate-brown eyes. With her natural beauty and height, she could have easily been a model, and being surrounded by red on her wedding day would make her stand out in all the best ways.

I pointed to the red page. "This is you. Vibrant. Bold. Classy. You will stand out in your gorgeous white dress, and isn't that the point? To shine a light on the bride." Tears were running down Tess's face and I swore out loud. "Well shit, Tess! You told me go with my gut. Okay, do green! I love green. It's my favorite color."

"No, no, it's that—you're right. And I love the red. I didn't think I could get away with it because it *is* so bold, but mom said . . . And then I thought . . . And it's going to be perfect."

She threw her arms around my neck and squeezed.

"Okay, okay," I said and patted her on the back. "Jeez, Tess."

"Thank you, Margo. I mean it."

I didn't know why she could do red but not burgundy, but decided not to say anything because Tess wasn't mad at me anymore.

She stared at her book, head tilted. "Do you like the yellow accent? Or blue? Like a deep royal blue."

"I think you can decide on that later."

"I have to have the flowers ordered by next month."

"Ask Gabriel."

"He's so busy."

"I'm sure he'd like to make a small decision," I said.

"I'll talk to Mom tomorrow," she said and closed the binder. "So, why did you come over? I know it wasn't for wedding planning."

"Shift gears to Elijah Martinez."

"I was thinking . . ." Tess said, then bit her lip.

"What?"

"You don't think he killed himself, do you?"

"Honestly, I don't think so, but that's because I don't know *him*. On the surface he appears to be exactly what his mom said—good student, lots of friends—but Lena Clark admitted he was under pressure because of college and the honors program, plus he had a part-time job. Teens sometimes don't think about the consequences of their actions. Until I know what was going on in his life in the days leading up to his death, I can't rule anything out. I'm not running with that premise, but if I learn anything that steers me in that direction, I'll follow. Until I talk to his friends I won't have a clear picture."

Friends often knew things that parents and teachers didn't.

"Mom says that it's not uncommon for someone to die because they were partying with people who didn't want to get in trouble."

It was true, but it disturbed me. When your friend had a medical emergency, you got help, period. Any consequences were nothing compared to death.

"That could have happened, which is the primary reason I want to talk face-to-face with Elijah's friends." I was good at weeding through bullshit. "If someone *intentionally* let him die, or someone gave him the drugs without his knowledge, then you're looking at manslaughter or homicide. Because the case is closed, no one is looking beyond the obvious. Anyway, Jack left me a file about a Sun Valley High coach arrested for using students to sell drugs. His wife was laundering the money. A little bit *Breaking Bad* but with oxy, pot, and fentanyl instead of cooking meth."

"And you think they're back at it?" Tess asked.

"No, they're both in prison, but I have a list of the students who were involved."

"They were minors—how did you get the list?"

"Jack has a friend on the force. But let's keep that information in-house. I was hoping you could run them, see where they are, what they're doing. Maybe one of them connects with Elijah or his circle of friends. Especially two people involved—Eric McMahon, who was the backup quarterback, and Scott Jimenez, who was arrested for attempting to kill McMahon."

"Send everything to me." She sounded excited, and probably was—Tess loved research. She took my hand. "Margo, I'm so glad you're working with us."

"You've told me," I said.

"But I've never said I was sorry. I treated you like crap when you left the firm. I became a PI because of you. So did mom, though I doubt she'd admit it," Tess added with a small laugh. "I was so angry at you and Mom, but mostly you. And I'm sorry. You're my sister, and I love you."

"All these feelings are going to make me squirm," I said with a smile. "I love you too, and honestly, I gave back worse than I got. It was my choice to walk away because I couldn't live under mom's rules. But I'm back, and I think we have an understanding."

The understanding was that I would still look into Dad's case, and Mom would ignore it. Probably not the best agreement in the world because when I found a thread, I would pull hard on it. Unfortunately, I had been stuck for months.

Gabriel walked in and smiled warmly at us. He wore casual gray slacks and a white polo shirt. "Hello, Margo. How are you?"

"Good, thanks. Just dropping off a research project for my brilliant sister."

He smiled and stood by Tess. She looked up at him with such overwhelming love and affection that I was almost embarrassed. He leaned over and kissed her lightly on the lips.

"Stay for a glass of wine?" Gabriel said. "Or, you prefer beer, don't you?"

"I do," I said, "but I have an early morning, so I should go." I stood up.

"Did Margo pick a color?" he asked Tess.

"Red," she said with a smile.

"Good. That's settled, and we're one step closer."

"Don't remind me," Tess said. "There's so much to do."

"Honestly," Gabriel said, "once you say I do in front of God and family, the rest is icing on the cake."

It was getting sappy. I mean, I was all for a happily-ever-after, especially for my sister, but I now felt like a third wheel.

"I'll leave the file here," I said and motioned to the sealed manila folder. "Email me if you have questions."

Both Gabriel and Tess walked me to the door and, arms around each other's waist, watched as I drove off.

As long as my sister was happy, I was happy.

But if Gabriel hurt her, he would pay.

chapter eleven

MARGO ANGELHART

After debating with myself about whether I wanted to talk to Rick Devlin about the Bradford case, I decided his insight could help so I called him as I drove home from Tess's.

"Devlin," he answered.

He must be on duty.

"It's Margo."

"You okay?"

"Why wouldn't I be?"

"Because you never call me."

"You don't call me either," I snapped.

"I'm sorry, I'm preoccupied."

"You're working."

"On my way to a major accident at Bell and Thirty-Fifth. Likely DUI, injuries, the whole nine yards."

It had to be serious, because as a sergeant, Rick was generally only called out when they needed someone in command to manage the scene.

"I have some questions about an old case you worked. Do you have time tonight? Tomorrow?"

"Not tonight—I don't know how long I'll be at the scene, and I don't like getting home after midnight. Lunch tomorrow?"

It felt so easy. Maybe because I was still basking in the affection of Gabriel and Tess, but I couldn't help but think what would have happened between Rick and me if both of us were less stubborn and more forgiving.

"Name the time and place."

"Twelve thirty, Lenny's or Orozco's?"

"You're making me hungry already," I said, thinking of Lenny's delicious and cheap(ish) cheeseburgers. And 12:30 should be doable—if I didn't track down Angie in the morning, I had the standing appointment with Lena at 11:20. "Lenny's," I said. My cousins owned Orozco's, and while I loved the food, I wanted privacy.

"Bet you haven't had dinner yet."

"I had cheese and crackers," I said.

He snorted. "I'm rolling up to the scene now, see you tomorrow." He ended the call without asking me specifically what I wanted to talk about.

My love life had never been as turbulent as my sister's. In high school, I'd had one boyfriend. We weren't really in love (though we thought we were), and when we graduated, we went our separate ways.

In the Army, I never dated anyone in my unit, which would have been awkward. But meeting civilians wasn't easy, and honestly, I didn't have the energy to maintain a relationship. I dated a firefighter for a while, but he was more serious than I was. Then a construction worker for more than a year. We had fun, but it wasn't going anywhere.

Growing up in my family, casual relationships weren't the norm. Dating was about finding your soulmate. It was hard to shake that mindset, and I didn't want to. Too many of my friends had gone from person to person, never landing anywhere, and none of them seemed happy.

I firmly believe you had to be happy with yourself first before you could be happy with someone else. And for the most part, I was. My dad once called me an "optimistic pessimist," and that pretty much fit.

I left the Army at twenty-four. While bartending and starting my PI business, I met and fell in love with Charlie Endicott. I thought he was *The One*. He made me feel special in a way no one else had. The flutter in my stomach when I saw him, how hearing his voice lifted my mood, how I looked forward to the time we spent together. Sex was deeper, more passionate. Love does that. I hadn't known until I *knew*.

And once I knew, I couldn't go back.

Charlie was the first man I truly loved. He left me for the first woman *he* had ever loved. I never doubted that he loved me when we were together, but when his high school sweetheart returned to Phoenix, he realized he still had feelings for her and thus, we parted ways.

Rick was my friend before we became lovers. Rick needed a date to a wedding and practically begged me to come. I didn't have plans, so I said yes. We had a fantastic time, the chemistry was obvious, and things just continued.

He was exactly my type—fit, active, spontaneous. He liked hiking and hot air balloon rides, but also lazy mornings in bed and soaking in hot tubs. We took it slow, mostly because of his daughter, Sam. We were comfortable.

But Rick and I are both stubborn and set in our ways. He didn't mind that I was a PI, but he hated how close I came to crossing legal lines. So I stopped telling him everything. We'd argue, break up, get back together, and have fantastic make-up sex. Rick also had some baggage. A divorce after his wife left him for France, leaving him with their six-year-old daughter. An abusive, alcoholic father. Certain cases got under his skin, bringing back memories he didn't like to talk about. He never crossed any hard lines, but it was enough to affect his future with the department. I could handle it, but he wouldn't let me in.

Ultimately, those problems we could have overcome because I

loved him and we had a comfortable relationship. I grew close to Sam, more like a big sister than a mother figure. When she confided in me about something and asked me not to tell her dad, I agreed. He found out anyway and exploded.

That moment made things clear. He didn't see me in his life for the long haul. Because if I was going to love—and maybe marry—Rick Devlin, I was all-in, and that meant being Sam's stepmother. But he didn't trust me, and that hurt.

It hurt way more than I expected.

Our four-year on-again, off-again relationship ended in January. I don't see us rekindling it. I understand, Rick is Sam's father. Maybe I should have told him about the online bullying after her first kiss, even though she swore me to secrecy. But I helped her, I was there for her, and Rick cut me out of her life. And damn, I missed it.

I miss Rick, I miss Sam, I miss what I thought we had.

It was dark when I walked into my house. I opened the refrigerator and stared, as if willing food to magically appear. Sighing, I grabbed the bread and jelly that were pretty much the only edible things I had, closed the door, took the peanut butter from the cabinet and made a sandwich. Not the best meal because I didn't have milk to go with it, but it filled the void.

I was halfway done eating at my counter when my cell phone rang. It was Josie.

"Hey, Pussycat," I said.

"Margo, I just got an email from command. There was a stabbing at Sun Valley High School."

"That's awful. A student?"

"No. The guidance counselor, Lena Clark. She's dead. Didn't you talk to her today?"

"Yes," I said, my stomach churning. I tossed the rest of my sandwich in the trash and drank water. "What happened? Do they have a suspect?"

"I don't know, I'm not on duty. It's not public yet—I mean, the name of the victim hasn't been released."

"Can you send it to me?"

"Yeah, don't share it."

"What time? I saw her this afternoon, before school let out for the day."

"Um, it says she left a volleyball game at 5:05 p.m. and was found dead in her office at 5:25 p.m."

"Twenty minutes—that's a narrow window." Then I remembered something else. "Shit, Josie, I talked to her this afternoon." I scrolled through my phone. "She called me at 5:14." My stomach twisted and I felt lightheaded. She was dead ten minutes after we talked.

"What did you talk about?" Josie asked.

"We scheduled a meeting with Angie Williams for tomorrow."

"I'll see if I can learn more."

"I'll call Jack," I said. "Thanks, Josie."

I ended the call and two screenshots popped up into my messages of a memo headed: *NOT FOR PUBLIC DISTRIBUTION*. There wasn't much more than what Josie told me. I brought up Phoenix PD on social media, but the public information officer hadn't issued a statement yet.

I forwarded the info to Jack with a **call me** in bold. Ten minutes later he did.

"Still at Whitney's?" I asked. Did I sound snide? Mean? I hoped not. But I couldn't say his ex-wife's name without an edge of disgust.

I was working on it.

"No, I'm home. Is this the same counselor you talked to today?"

"Yep. The thing is, I'm expecting the police to talk to me tomorrow."

"Why?"

"She called me at 5:14 this evening."

"That's specific."

"I just looked it up. We talked for two minutes."

"About?"

"Something I don't really want to tell the police."

"You can't withhold information in a homicide investigation."

"I know, so I'm going to avoid them as long as I can."

"What's going on?" Jack demanded. He sounded kind of angry.

"Bad dinner?"

"I'm not talking about Whitney," he snapped. "What was your conversation with Lena about?"

"To arrange a meeting with Elijah's friend Angie. She also told me Angie has my business card and may call me herself."

"Okay, so? Why don't you want to tell the police?"

"It's not that I don't want to tell them about the conversation, but I don't want it getting back to Detective King that I'm working on Elijah Martinez's death investigation. Lena said that Angie left an angry message on King's voicemail Friday. I'd like to talk to the kid first, get her side of the story."

"I don't think you need to avoid the police, but I understand the need to have as much information as possible before talking to them."

"I'm only answering their direct and relevant questions," I said.

Jack and I had a slightly different style when it came to working with law enforcement. Jack was always on their side, which I understood since he'd been a cop. I wasn't. Not because cops were generally bad—I knew many and that wasn't true—but because they didn't always have my client's best interests at heart. I didn't want to jam Angie or anyone else.

"Let me find out who's investigating the homicide. King isn't the only detective in Violent Crimes."

"And maybe find out if they have a suspect?"

"I'll see what I can learn. Don't avoid giving your statement for too long."

"I won't, but I'm not saying a word until they track me down. By the way, thanks for the file on the Bradfords. Tomorrow, I'm meeting with Rick about it."

"Why Rick?"

"He led the team that executed the search warrant. Lenny's at twelve thirty, if you want to join us."

Jack snorted. "You don't want to be alone with him?"

"Knock it off." He was partly right, and I didn't want to talk about it. "Let me know what you learn and if the police show up at the office to talk to me."

"Don't avoid them for too long."

"Roger that." I ended the call and considered what Lena Clark's murder meant. While I couldn't see *how* her murder was connected to a teenager's overdose, what were the odds that she'd end up dead only hours after I met with her about Elijah?

Had she learned something she hadn't shared with me over the phone? Did she suspect where he got the drugs? Had she confronted one of his friends at the volleyball game? What did she know that was so dangerous someone killed her on campus? It was risky and reckless.

I needed to talk to Angie Williams as soon as possible. I called Theo. "I'm going to send you an address and a photo of a teenager. She lives in an apartment on Nineteenth, south of Dunlap. Be discreet."

"Always am."

"Get there by six thirty—I suspect she'll leave between seven and seven-thirty for school, but earlier is better." If they didn't cancel classes, which was a definite possibility after a campus murder. But if I had a home life like I suspected she did, I might leave just to get out of the apartment.

"I'm on it, Boss."

I smiled. "Thanks, Theo."

chapter twelve

ANGIE WILLIAMS

Angie and Gina sat in Gina's car on the street outside Angie's apartment building. It was 9:10 p.m. and Gina was past her school-night curfew, but they stared at their phones in disbelief.

Mrs. Clark had been murdered.

There was nothing on the news, other than "a faculty member" had been found dead at Sun Valley High School, but everyone knew.

Andy Perez had texted Angie shortly after they finished dinner.

omg, just heard it's Miz Clark

Then Peter Barilla texted both of them in a group chat.

wtf? is this true?

Gina's volleyball group chat hadn't stopped pinging for the last hour. Everyone was talking about it. Rumors were flying.

Mr. Parsons found her body . . .

They were at our game today! I'm crying, I love Mrs. Clark.

Parsons was sleeping with her.

My mom won't let me go to school tomorrow.

Do we even have school?

Joey heard from Debbie who heard from Coach that there was blood everywhere.

I can't believe this.

Gina, my mom saw your friend Angie yelling at Mrs. Clark during the game. What happened?

Angie had told Gina about her argument with Mrs. Clark, but she hadn't realized other people saw it.
"What do you want me to say?" Gina asked.
"Nothing," Angie said. "It's no one's business."
Gina's phone rang and they both yelped.
"It's my mom," Gina said as she answered. "Hi, Mom."
"Gina, you need to come home now."
"I'm on my way."
"I can see where you are, you're parked by Angie's apartment. And if you *were* driving, you wouldn't answer your phone, would you?"
"I'm sorry, Mom. I meant, I'll leave right now."
"Tell Angie to be careful."
"Do you know what happened to Mrs. Clark?"
"All I know for certain is that she was killed sometime after the volleyball game and the police are investigating."
"Do we have school tomorrow?"

"It hasn't been canceled. But if you want to stay home—"

"No, I'm okay, I just want to know what happened."

"Please come home, Gina. It won't take you longer than ten minutes. Eleven minutes and you're grounded."

"Yes, Mom."

"I love you," she said and hung up.

Gina turned to Angie. "I gotta—"

"I know." Angie hugged her best friend and got out of the car. Gina drove away, and Angie glanced down at her phone when it vibrated.

It was Andy again, in their group chat with Peter.

A, you didn't go to school today but my little sister said she saw you.

Angie told him she went to the volleyball game. Then said, I talked to Mrs. Clark right before I left. A PI is investigating Elijah's death.

Andy said: Really?

She responded. Yeah. I'm going to talk to her.

Andy: Elijah was acting weird the last couple weeks.

Angie didn't want to get into this conversation, especially over text. We'll talk tomorrow.

She pocketed her phone and walked slowly to her door. She didn't want to go home, but where could she go? After a long minute, she unlocked the door and stepped inside. Her mom and Bruce were slouched on the couch in front of the television, the stench of marijuana heavy in the small dark apartment.

"You're not supposed to smoke in the apartment," Angie said.

"Fuck you," Bruce said.

Her mother hit him. "Don't swear at my daughter. Angie, where were you so late?"

"Gina's."

"You could have called."

"You don't usually care."

"I always care! Oh, my God, you think I don't care about my own daughter?"

Clearly, her mother was stoned *and* drunk. If she was just stoned, she would just say hey and Angie would go to her room and that would be that. But Lori was an emotional drunk. Everything was over-the-top when Lori had been drinking. As if to confirm the fact, Angie saw a near-empty bottle of vodka on the counter.

"You made your mother cry," Bruce said. "Apologize."

Bruce was a mean drunk. Not to Lori though. He draped his arm around Lori's thin shoulders as she started to cry.

Angie quickly weighed her options. Bruce had never hit her, but he did break things, and her mom would blame her. She didn't want drama tonight.

"Sorry," she said. She walked to her room and closed the door.

Her room smelled of residual pot, so she opened the small barred window to air out the space, relieved that the temperatures had fallen and there was a light breeze. She lit a lavender candle and sat at her desk.

She heard Bruce and Lori talking, but not what they said. Then they were walking down the hall together, bumping into the walls, and her mother giggled. Their bedroom door closed, but Angie could hear everything—the groaning and giggling and loud sex talk, as if Bruce wanted her to hear everything.

She put on her headphones and turned up her music loud enough to drown them out.

The last time she talked to Mrs. Clark, Angie had been mean and yelled at her. Why had she been so angry? It wasn't Mrs. Clark's fault that the police were useless. Mrs. Clark was trying to help, and Angie took her frustration and anger out on her.

Now she couldn't even apologize.

Her cell phone vibrated. It was Chris.

They hadn't talked in three months. She didn't want to talk to him now.

Scratch that. She absolutely wanted to talk to Chris, but didn't want to dump this on him. If she answered, he'd get her to talk. He was good at that.

Benny must have told him about seeing her today.

She declined the call, then texted him.

Going to sleep, call you later.

He immediately texted back.

Call me now. We need to talk.

She responded with *later* and then silenced her phone and turned it facedown so she wouldn't see any other texts from Chris.

Angie looked at the card she'd taken from Mrs. Clark's desk, flipped it over and over in her fingers. It was getting late, and she didn't want the PI to come here while her mom and Bruce were wasted. And Angie wasn't an idiot—she wasn't going out at night to meet someone she didn't know.

She'd call Margo Angelhart tomorrow.

chapter thirteen

MARGO ANGELHART

I left my house before six thirty in the morning, drove to Black Rock Coffee and turned into the miserably long drive-through lane.

I'd gone to bed late and woke early. I'd sent a spreadsheet of Elijah's calls to Luisa to reverse identify. He didn't have many, which suggested he conversed primarily through apps or via text message. I'd show the numbers to Angie when I found her since they likely had common friends. It wasn't just the investigation that had me tossing and turning; memories of Rick refused to stay buried.

As I waited in line, Josie texted me:

Clark was stabbed with a letter opener that appears to be part of her personal desk set, it was left at the crime scene. Three deep jabs. Body found by teacher Parsons. Autopsy this afternoon.

Brutal and personal, I thought. Lena Clark was petite and could easily be overpowered by someone taller and stronger—man or woman. Who stood there and let themselves be stabbed without fighting back? Someone who knew and trusted their killer, that's who. But even if you knew your killer, wouldn't you try to get away or scream for help?

I rolled my Jeep up a car length, then braked and texted.

> Can you get me more deets? Where exactly in her office? Do the police have a suspect? Surveillance? Please and thank you!

I checked in with Theo—so far, no Angie—but he had a good view of the most logical exit from her end of the complex. I hoped Lena was right and Angie would call me, but she hadn't called last night so I wasn't holding my breath.

One drug overdose off campus and one homicide on campus, less than two weeks apart. Would the police think they were connected? I doubted they'd make that assumption, but I did.

I still couldn't reconcile how Elijah ended up at Mountain View Park more than two miles from his home. My guess was a friend with a car. Which meant someone likely knew he was dead before his body was found.

Speculating with minimal information wouldn't give me insight. I needed to talk to Angie.

After getting iced coffee, I drove by the school to see if it was open; it was. There were two police cars parked outside the administration building, and an officer stood by the main door. Cars were parked in the employee lot, and at least two dozen cars were already in the student lot. The flag had been lowered to half-mast.

As I passed the school, Theo called.

"Yep."

"Your girl is leaving the building."

"Heading?"

"Hmm . . . She just crossed Nineteenth heading east down Butler."

"That's the back way to the school. Thanks, I'm not far." I made a U-turn at the next light, then turned right into the neighborhood and drove down to Butler. She'd pass me in a few minutes.

"That's it? You got me up early to sit on the street for an hour?"

"Call Tess and see if she needs help with research."

"Aw, man, that's boring shit."

"You want to be paid for more than an hour's work, call Tess. Or you can call my mom and see what she needs."

"I'll call your sister," he said and hung up.

I grinned. Theo was terrified of my mother. He towered over her even when she wore heels (which was always), but he once told me when she looked at him, he wanted to confess to crimes he hadn't committed.

My mom *was* intimidating and almost always knew if someone was lying. It could be unnerving.

Angie walked on the opposite sidewalk heading in my direction. She was alone, her head up, her shoulders curved in. She was about my height with dark hair that had once been dyed pink—she had three inches of roots and the rest of her hair was a faded pinkish-beige color that was pulled back into a sloppy bun. She wore torn jeans and a retro black Pink Floyd shirt. I'd seen the thin shirts—made to look old and faded—selling for fifty bucks in the mall. If I wanted to wear Pink Floyd or any other classic band, all I had to do was rummage through my dad's closet.

I waited until Angie was directly across from where I had parked, then I got out of my Jeep and crossed the street. I didn't want to scare her by following in my vehicle.

"Angie, hold up," I said.

She stopped walking and looked at me with narrowed eyes. Her gaze darted around, either looking for help or a place to run.

"I'm Margo Angelhart," I said when I was ten feet from her. "Lena Clark said you wanted to talk to me."

"She's dead." The words came out quickly. "Last night. Everyone's talking about it."

"I heard," I said. "I'd like to talk to you, then I'll take you to school."

She looked skeptical.

"Yeah, I wouldn't want to get into a car with a stranger. I'll buy you breakfast."

"I'm not getting in your car."

I didn't blame her. I'd go to Orozco's, but that was too far to walk from here. "There's a bakery on the corner of Dunlap and Fifteenth, know it?"

She nodded. It was only a few blocks away.

"I'll meet you there."

"Why are you doing this?"

I assessed her. Teens had an uncanny way of knowing when adults were lying, so I was straightforward.

"You were at Elijah's funeral, right?"

She nodded.

"Father Rafe—the priest who presided over the funeral Mass—is my uncle. He brought Elijah's mom to my office and asked if I could find out what happened leading up to his death. I agreed."

"Why?"

"Why did I agree to help?"

"I *know* she doesn't have money to pay you." It was like an accusation, as if I had some nefarious motive.

"I have clients who pay. That gives me flexibility to work for those who can't."

"You didn't even *know* him."

Lena was right. Angie had a lot of anger.

"True," I conceded, "but his mother deserves to know what happened to her son, don't you agree?"

Angie stared, suspicious but curious at the same time.

"Meet me, or don't. I'm going to find the truth with or without your help."

I walked back to my Jeep, climbed in, and drove to the bakery.

I ordered a couple of muffins and sat at one of the tiny tables along the window.

Ten minutes later I had just finished my muffin when Angie walked in. She took her backpack off, sat down across from me, and protectively put her bag in her lap.

I slid over the second muffin.

"Thanks," she muttered and picked at it.

I'd already decided to talk to her like an adult. From what Lena had told me, Angie was no stranger to a tough life—her posture, attitude, and anger all confirmed that.

She was also loyal. Her steadfast belief in her friend hadn't wavered. But I needed to test it, test her.

"You don't think Elijah did drugs."

"I know he didn't. If you think it's a possibility, I'm leaving."

"He could have hid it from you. He could have been experimenting."

"See? You're just like everyone else, you want to believe the worst."

Patience, Margo, I told myself. "I'm trying to figure out how he ended up in a park more than two miles from his house, dead of fentanyl poisoning. I want to know why you are positive he didn't use drugs, why you have no doubts about Elijah."

Angie put her chin up. "Lori—my mother," she said *mother* as if it were a curse, "has done drugs most of my life. Her boyfriends are users and losers. Lori has a job, she gets by, hasn't completely gone off the rails, but I *know* when people are addicts. I can see it in their eyes, in the way they move, in what they say and do. A lot of people ignore the signs, or don't really watch what's going on around them. Elijah had a plan, goals, he thought about the future. He loved his mom. Until recently, I've seen Elijah nearly every day for four years. He did not use drugs. *Ever.*"

A little bell went off in my head.

"Okay," I said. "What happened recently? Did you have a falling out?"

"No, why?"

"You said until recently, you saw Elijah nearly every day. What happened?"

She looked confused, then just rolled her eyes. "He got a job in March, worked full-time over the summer. He was busy."

She sounded defensive.

"And since school started?"

"What are you getting at?"

How did I say it without making her mad? "Well," I said, "you and Elijah were good friends. But he was busy and you really didn't see him much over the last few months. Maybe things changed."

"Someone drugged him," she insisted.

"We don't know that."

"*I* do."

"You didn't answer my question, Angie."

She bit her lip. "He was preoccupied, okay? I saw him in class and we talked and stuff, and after school we almost always studied in the library before he had to go to work. But . . ." she hesitated, then said ". . . lately, he's been quiet."

"Did he tell you anything specific? Trouble at work? With a friend? A bully? A teacher? Something going on at home, with family?"

"No. He *wouldn't* tell me, so I asked. He just said he had a lot on his mind and didn't want to drag me into it." She paused again, as if thinking about what to tell me.

"Be honest," I said. "If you hold back, I can't help."

"I'm not. I just don't know. Elijah was a really good guy"

"Good guys sometimes make mistakes."

"You think I don't know that? You think him dying is his fault?"

"I didn't say that." Damn, this girl was jumpy. "Elijah was under a lot of pressure. I want to know everything about him. If he was preoccupied, why? Worried about his grades? College? Money?"

"He wanted to go to U of A and would most certainly get a full scholarship. Mrs. Clark—" She stopped, frowned. "Anyway, she was really good at helping us with all the paperwork and stuff for scholarships and financial aid. It's not like my mom would know what to do. And his mom had a good job; he told me she changed jobs over the summer, that she liked it and it paid more. He was competitive about grades, but why would he worry about school when he had straight A's?"

"You and I both know kids sometimes take stimulants to stay up all night to study for a test or write a paper."

"So? That doesn't kill anyone."

"It's a pattern."

She frowned. "You don't believe me."

"I don't disbelieve you. But you still haven't given me any reason as to why Elijah was preoccupied. What about people he had problems with, at work or school or at his apartment complex?"

She shrugged. "I don't—" She halted and bit her lip.

"What did you just think of?" I pushed.

"It doesn't make any sense."

"Let me be the judge."

"It was last year. I mean, in May, at the end of the school year."

"Tell me."

She bit her lip and looked torn, but finally it came out. "Elijah reported someone for cheating."

That was interesting.

"What's the penalty?"

"Zero on the test, automatic two-day suspension. But it was the final."

"Who?"

"Danielle Duran. Honors English. The final was a series of questions about the three books we read that semester, then an essay. We were told the prompt and allowed one index card for quotes and citations. She had her entire essay written and accessed it on her smartwatch. Elijah sat behind her and told her to take off her watch. She told him to mind his own business. After the exam he told Mrs. Porter."

"And what happened?"

"Danielle said it was only her citations that she was allowed, but refused to show Mrs. Porter her watch, said she deleted the document after the final. She was given a zero and ended up with a C in the class. I heard her parents threw a fit, but I don't think Mrs. Porter backed down. And because she got a C, she wasn't accepted into Honors English this year. It really screws with your GPA."

I considered what a kid might do. Drugging Elijah seemed to be a stretch, but what if, in retribution, Danielle had drugged him without the intention of killing him? How would she get away with that? Fentanyl was fairly fast acting—he'd start feeling the effects within a few minutes with the dose that was in his system.

"Did Elijah go to parties?"

"I doubt it, he never talked about parties, but don't know for sure. Pete and Andy would."

A party would give someone the opportunity to drug him, or could be where he might buy drugs himself.

"Is there anything else? Anything that he said or did that was out of character?"

She shrugged and shook her head. "All I know is that he didn't do drugs. Not on purpose. He just wouldn't."

Maybe Angie was projecting. Because I absolutely believed, based on what she told me, that Angie herself was clean as a whistle. She was belligerent and had a suspicious nature, but at her core she was a good and moral person. No drugs, no cheating, intensely loyal.

"What about his work?"

"He worked at the Cactus Stop on Hatcher."

"And?"

"I sometimes walked with him after school—at least I did in the spring. But once school got out, I rarely had a reason to go there."

"Did he have problems with anyone at work?"

"If he did, he didn't tell me. How does any of this help?"

"It gives me a place to start, and gives me a sense of who Elijah was."

"Do you really think you'll be able to find out what happened to him?" she asked.

"I think so," I said. "Someone saw him between the time he left work on Friday and when he died. It's like looking for a missing person—you start with the last known sighting and work from there. Do you mind giving me your number? I might have more questions."

Angie held out her hand for my phone, which I handed to her. She typed in her number, gave it back to me.

"Do you know what happened to Mrs. Clark?" she asked. "I've heard so many stories I don't know what's true. Someone said the police think Mr. Parsons killed her because he found her body. That's totally fucked. They were all into each other, and he's a really great teacher."

It was nice to have my suspicion of their romantic entanglement confirmed.

"Do you know for a fact that they were involved?" I asked Angie.

She rolled her eyes. "*Everyone* knew. I mean they didn't announce it or make out in the bleachers or anything, but it was obvious. So," Angie continued, "what happened to her? I feel bad—I said some mean things to her at the volleyball game. I wish I could take it back."

"I'm sure she didn't take it personally," I said. I didn't want Angie to feel guilty, and I believed Lena wasn't the type of teacher who held grudges with students.

I decided to tell her what little I knew to help build trust.

"She was stabbed. My cousin Josie—who spoke to your school last week—said the murder weapon was likely a letter opener. Could have been premeditated or spontaneous."

I'd thought letter openers had gone the way of the dodo bird, but my dad had one on his desk at home. It was engraved, a gift from one of his nurses.

"Don't you think it's weird that Mrs. Clark was killed right after Elijah?"

"I think it's suspicious that she was killed the same day she was asking questions about Elijah's death," I said cautiously, still trying to work things out in my own head. "The police will conduct a thorough investigation. Talk to her friends, colleagues, Mr. Parsons, any exes, even students. They'll collect evidence from the crime scene and look at security cameras."

"Meaning, they'll do their job. Unlike with Elijah."

Still bitter, and I wasn't going to be able to fix that.

"I know people who'll give me a heads-up if something comes up in Lena's murder investigation that will help me find out what happened to Elijah."

"Thank you," she whispered. "I really didn't think anyone cared but me."

"Angie, you need to be very careful," I said.

"I know," she said in a dismissive tone.

"I'm serious. Lena is dead and we don't know who killed her or why. I don't want you to get hurt."

Angie stared at me. "I said I'll be careful."

I didn't know Angie well enough to know if she was being straight with me or not.

"If you find yourself in trouble or you're worried that someone is following you or, I don't know, looking at you funny, trust your instincts. And if you're suspicious of anyone, call me. I don't live far from here, I'll come. And don't start asking questions. Until we know why Lena Clark was killed, keep a low profile."

"Okay," she said.

"Let me take you to school. Even the way I drive, you're going to be late."

I was pleased she didn't argue.

chapter fourteen

MARGO ANGELHART

After dropping Angie off, I headed to the Cactus Stop where Elijah used to work, just to get a feel of the place. I could have called Manny Ramos and had him smooth the way, but I wanted to observe staff without the weight of corporate HQ hanging over them.

My phone rang; it was my mom. I sent her to voicemail, then texted that I was working. I didn't want to talk to her until I had more information. Besides, she'd tell me to reach out to the cops about Lena Clark before they found me, and I didn't plan to do that.

The Hatcher location of the Cactus Stop was smaller than the Stop closer to my house, on the short end of an L-shaped strip mall. I didn't know what I would find, but since Elijah had worked Friday afternoon—and no one claimed to have seen him after he left—this was the best place to start. Since the police hadn't recovered Elijah's backpack or cell phone, I reasoned that he might have left the items at work.

I sat in my car for a few minutes to get the feel of the place. While most of the Cactus Stops were open until midnight, this location closed at 10:00 p.m. It wasn't a well-traveled section of

DON'T SAY A WORD

Hatcher and was located in one of the sketchier neighborhoods. Advertisements papered the windows, which were both dirty and covered with security bars. The front walk however was clean with no trash on the ground.

Teens went in and out. Either cutting school or running late. Maybe, like my senior year, they didn't have a first-period class. An old guy went in, then came back out with a pack of smokes that he'd already opened and lit as soon as he cleared the door. Two lean guys in mechanics overalls entered, then a young teen, then a minute later a weary mother with two young kids walking close to her legs while she pushed a stroller.

After five minutes I entered. The interior itself was clean-ish. Not as tidy as the store closer to my house, but not as crappy as other locations. Anything that was easily grabbed, in demand, or cost more than ten bucks was behind the counter in locked glass cabinets. Only one person appeared to be working. Angled mirrors along the top of the walls allowed him to have a clear view of everyone in the store and what they were doing.

The mechanics were at the counter buying energy drinks, cigarettes and premade sandwiches. They spoke Spanish to the clerk, which I understood, but they weren't talking about anything important.

I walked over to the drinks along the far wall as if deciding what I wanted. The shelves were all stocked with the traditional overpriced snacks and necessities.

I grabbed a water bottle and then went to the chip aisle.

The mom and kids were now at the counter. They had a gallon of milk, cereal, and several cans. She used her EBT card—Arizona electronic benefits. That really sucked. She could get so much more for the money if she went to a real grocery store, but maybe she didn't have a car.

The teen who came in before her was loitering in the corner on his phone, but the clerk didn't seem to pay him much attention. I thought he was acting suspicious. I went to the counter with water and Doritos.

"Hey," I said. The clerk had a badge. Tony, Assistant Manager.

"Hey," he repeated and rang up my items. I paid cash, then handed him my business card. "I'm a PI hired by Elijah Martinez's family." I sounded important and formal, hoping the authority in my voice prompted him to spill anything he might know. "Did you work here two Fridays ago when Elijah was working?"

He stared at my card, blinked several times. "What?"

"According to the police report, Elijah worked here Friday from four in the afternoon until eight. I'd like to talk to whoever was on shift with him that night."

"Why?"

Was he intentionally acting dense?

"I'm retracing Elijah's steps," I said clearly. "He worked here Friday, correct?"

"Um, yeah?"

"You don't remember?"

"I don't work Fridays."

"Who worked here Friday with him?"

"Desi, she's the manager."

"When does she come in next?"

"Friday. She only works weekends."

"Did Elijah leave his backpack here?"

"Backpack?"

Why did he answer a question with a question?

"Yes," I said.

"I don't think so. I haven't seen it."

"Okay, thanks," I said, though he hadn't been all that helpful. "I'll come back on Friday and talk to Desi."

"Okay."

I stepped outside, paused, and angled myself near the door, casually opening my water while discreetly watching the teen through the glass. I'd talk to Desi, sure, but if she was as helpful as Tony, I might need Manny Ramos to make a call. And I wasn't waiting until Friday.

I pulled out my phone, called Theo, then put it to my ear.

The teen immediately went to the counter and said something to Tony. I was a more than decent lip reader, but he wasn't facing me.

Tony glanced out the door, saw me. Theo answered and I laughed, then said, "Ignore me, don't hang up. Just play along."

"Anything you want, sweetheart," he said in his best Humphrey Bogart impression.

I laughed again. I had learned the hard way the first year I was a PI that having a blank smartphone to your ear was obvious. So unless you were talking on a flip phone without a lit screen, you needed to actually call someone, even if it was just to leave a message on your own answering machine.

Tony must not have been suspicious of me, because he rang up whatever the kid was purchasing. He was likely selling cigarettes, nicotine pouches, or alcohol to underage kids because the teen hadn't put anything on the counter to buy. A crime, but it happened all the time. And would that be a reason to kill someone? I didn't see it.

An accident? A dark joke that went very wrong? I could see someone drugging Elijah, just like what happened to Bobby.

The teen put an EBT card into the card reader. I could tell based on the color; it was the same type of card the mom had used earlier. That really pissed me off. EBT cards were for food and necessities, not for cigarettes and alcohol. That was certainly a crime, if the store was selling unauthorized goods and ringing them up as authorized.

Yet, the teen left without any merchandise, and I hadn't seen him pocket anything but his receipt, though I may have missed it. He looked too young to buy cigarettes, but I wasn't ATF, and I didn't care if the store was selling to minors. It was the EBT card that had my hackles raised. I detested people who gamed the system at the expense of others.

But I had no proof.

I waited to see if Tony called anyone about my visit; he didn't. Either he didn't care, or he expected me to return Friday and talk to Desi.

I said, "Thanks, Theo," hung up, and walked to my car. I drank my water and munched on my Doritos, watching the store. Several people, mostly under twenty, entered and left without bags, but that didn't necessarily mean anything. It just seemed . . . unusual. Could be nothing, but I'd run it by Rick during lunch, see if he knew if there might be a scam in play.

The Cactus Stop was ground zero in my investigation. No one had come forward to tell police or his mother where Elijah had gone after work Friday night. Had the police even talked to this Desi?

I glanced at my watch. I had three hours until lunch. I pulled out of my parking spot and drove home so I could track down Danielle Duran and find out if she still held a grudge against Elijah for ratting her out to the teacher.

Angie had been compelling in advocating for her friend. From what little I knew about Elijah, it seemed out of character that he would take something like fentanyl. Maybe his death was an accident, revenge, or prank gone wrong. Maybe he thought he was taking something else.

Someone knew. The more I thought about it, the more I believed that someone had been with Elijah when he died. Was that person guilty of indifference? Or murder?

chapter fifteen

JACK ANGELHART

Jack stayed out of his mom's way.

More than an hour had passed since Margo declined Ava Angelhart's call, and she hadn't called back. Ava grew angrier with each passing minute. He told himself he wasn't hiding in his office; after all, he'd left the door open.

Tess had texted the family chat that she was working from home this morning, so Jack didn't have a buffer with their mom. Still, he was surprised that it took Ava an hour before she stepped into his doorway to vent. "You *know* Margo called you about Lena Clark's murder so she didn't have to talk to me."

"I know," Jack said.

"You should have told me last night. *She* should have called me. I can't protect her if she doesn't keep me in the loop."

"Margo doesn't need protecting, not on this," he said.

"That's not what I meant."

"It's what you said," Jack countered.

Mom and Margo approached the same job differently. Ava was smart and methodical, a linear thinker who relied on tangible evidence. Margo was just as sharp, but trusted her instincts. Like a bloodhound, she followed her nose, shifting course easily when the trail changed. She cared about evidence, but focused more on context and how people acted and reacted.

They both knew what Mom would've said last night if Margo told her about her conversation with Lena: Contact the detective, give her information. Ava believed in full transparency. Margo wasn't dishonest, but she preferred to hold her cards and let others show theirs first. It was an effective way to get people talking.

"I'm concerned," Ava said. "I know you and Margo are capable, but perhaps it would be better to let the police handle it."

"We're not investigating Clark's murder," Jack said.

"Yet, Margo has found herself in the middle of the investigation simply because she spoke to the victim minutes before she was killed. I don't know what the conversation was about, or if Margo has any suspicions about why someone would kill that poor woman."

"We need to debrief," Jack concurred, "but Margo's in the field and I think we let her do what she needs to do."

Ava sighed. "Very well. I just want to make sure that we're covered, but she hasn't returned my call."

Aw, the crux of the problem. Jack and Tess had worked with their mom for three years. He knew her pet peeves—she wanted to be in the loop with all the details of every case. It wasn't that she micromanaged—she didn't tell them how to do the job unless they asked for advice—but she didn't like being in the dark.

Margo had worked with them for three months, and his sister would not share info until she was good and ready.

"What *is* Margo doing?" Ava asked.

"I haven't talked to her this morning. She intended to find Elijah's friends before school and go from there."

"Where's Theo? He's supposed to be working Tuesdays and Fridays, correct?"

"He's helping Tess with research. Mom, Margo has been a PI for eight years, she knows what she's doing."

Iris called over. "Ava, Rita's on the phone."

"Tell Auntie I said hi," Jack said as his mom walked down to her office.

He had talked his mom down. Yes, she worried about all of them, but everything around Margo was still a bit prickly. He hoped things smoothed out over time, because he liked working with his sister. He needed to help restore the balance so Margo didn't walk away.

Jack went back to researching the subject of the last subpoena he had to serve today.

The office doors opened and in walked Detectives Rachel King and Jerry Chavez. *Oh, shit*, Jack thought. Did King have the Lena Clark homicide?

Iris approached the detectives. "Hello, may I help you?"

King showed her badge and introduced herself and her partner. "We need to speak with whoever is in charge."

She made it sound far more confrontational than it needed to be. His mother's door was closed, so Jack rose and as soon as he stepped from his office, Jerry grinned. "Hey, Jack, it's been awhile."

"How's it going?"

"Good, good. Melanie is expecting again."

"Number four?" Jack said.

Jerry grinned, shook his head. "Four *and* five."

Jack laughed. "Holy shit, that's fantastic. Congrats. You good Rachel? How're your boys? Isn't the oldest in college by now?"

She seemed irritated with the small talk. "Yeah, he's up at NAU. Starting his second year, engineering."

"Smart kid."

"Tell me about it," she muttered, then said, "Look we're here investigating a homicide at Sun Valley High School. The victim called your sister Margaret's cell phone ten minutes before she was killed. I tried calling her, but she hasn't answered."

"Margo," Jack said. "You call her Margaret and you'll have two strikes against you." He was trying to keep the conversation light and friendly; Rachel scowled.

"Jack," Rachel said, "we know that *Margo* met with the victim, Lena Clark, yesterday afternoon, and then Clark called your sister a couple hours later. Is she a client? Did she hire Angelhart Investigations? Was she worried about something? Did she have a stalker or other trouble? It's important to our investigation."

"She's not a client," Jack said.

Rachel waited for more.

"And?" Rachel finally said.

"And what?"

"Why was Margo there?"

"You'll have to ask her."

"For shit's sake, Jack."

Jerry put up his hands in a sign of peace. "Hey, Jack, how can we reach her? We just need to get some info, nothing major here."

"Her cell phone," Jack said.

"She's not answering," Rachel snapped.

"She's working in the field. I'll let her know you stopped by."

His mom stepped out of her office and approached them. Iris must have called or texted her about the conversation.

"May I help you?" Ava said in her most professional lawyer tone.

"Mrs. Angelhart, I'm Detective King." She nodded to Jerry. "My partner, Detective Chavez. We're trying to find your daughter Margo. We have questions about her conversation with a murder victim, Lena Clark."

"I heard. It's awful. Do you have any suspects?"

Jack had to force himself not to smile. His mom could be very passive-aggressive when she wanted to be.

"We have had this case for less than twenty-four hours and Margo may have been the last person to speak to the victim. I need to talk to her as soon as possible."

Rachel was definitely irritated.

"We'll let Margo know, of course," Ava said.

"Is Mrs. Clark a client?"

"I can't answer that." Ava said.

"I just told you she isn't," Jack said.

"Just making sure," Rachel said with a slight smirk. "Mrs. Angelhart, you *can't* tell me or you *won't* tell me?"

"Can't," Ava repeated. "Margo often works on a handshake. You'll have to ask Margo if Mrs. Clark retained her."

"Why do I feel that you're being deliberately unhelpful?"

"I don't know why you would feel that way," Ava said, her eyes firmly on Rachel. "Is there anything else we can help you with?"

"When will Margo be in?" Jerry asked.

"She makes her own hours, so your best bet is to call her directly," Ava said.

"She hasn't answered," Rachel said with obvious frustration, "and I prefer in-person interviews."

"Then arrange that with Margo. I don't schedule her appointments."

Rachel's jaw clenched, and Jack wondered what his mother's intention was. This wasn't what he expected after their conversation earlier this morning.

Rachel handed Ava her card. "Please ask Margo to call me when she comes in."

"I will."

Rachel and Jerry left, and Jack turned to his mother. "What was that all about? I thought you wanted to tell them everything."

"I don't know everything that's going on, and I won't speculate with law enforcement. Plus, I didn't like her confrontational attitude."

God, he loved his mother.

"That said, if you or Margo or Tess learn anything that will aid the police in finding and apprehending Lena Clark's killer, I expect you to be forthcoming."

"Roger that," Jack said.

Ava went back to her office, but didn't close the door.

He glanced at his watch, considered heading to Lenny's for burgers with Rick and Margo, then decided against it. He didn't need to mediate between his best friend and sister.

Besides, he had a subpoena to serve.

He texted Margo that King was the lead detective on the Lena Clark case and that she'd come in looking for her.

King wants you to call her. She knows you met with Lena and that she called you.

A minute later, Margo responded.

I'm busy, I'll talk to her later. You coming to lunch?

He responded that he was not going to make it, then added a laughing emoji because it would annoy her.

She sent him an eye roll emoji, then: I'm going to bounce something off Rick, but I might need your two cents. Have a hot date with Laura tonight?

Jack shook his head. Typical Margo.

Barbecuing at her place. You're welcome to join us. Six-ish.

She responded that she'd let him know.
Jack wondered what Margo was up to.

chapter sixteen

ANGIE WILLIAMS

Angie wished she hadn't gone to school today. All anyone talked about was Mrs. Clark's murder.

Two girls from Gina's volleyball team gave Angie the side-eye during break, reminding her that a mom had seen her arguing with Mrs. Clark outside the gym. In every class, all people wanted to do was talk about Mrs. Clark. Everyone wanted to tell a story. Angie hated talking in groups, so kept her mouth shut. It was unnerving when everyone stared at her.

Then the kicker: Right after lunch, Angie was called out of class. Mrs. Webb, the vice-principal, was waiting for her.

Cutting classes had caught up with her, Angie thought. Whatever, she'd take detention. She'd rather be in detention than go home.

"I need you to come to the office," Mrs. Webb said. "I'll clear it with your teachers." She started walking toward the administration building, the keys she wore around her wrist rattling with each step. Angie followed.

"Why?" she asked. "What did I do?" Never volunteer information. There was a chance this had nothing to do with cutting classes.

"The police are here to talk to you about Mrs. Clark."

Her stomach fell and she felt sick.

"Oh. Why me?"

Maybe there were notes in Mrs. Clark's files about all the times Angie came in to talk to her about Elijah's murder. Maybe they wanted to know what they talked about. Maybe Margo Angelhart was right, and Mrs. Clark was killed because she learned something about Elijah.

Maybe the police would finally do something. It just sucked that Mrs. Clark had to die first.

"Mr. Borel and I will be in the room with you," Mrs. Webb continued. "The police are speaking to several students and teachers who saw Mrs. Clark in the hours before . . . what happened."

Why couldn't she just say *murdered*? Angie didn't know why adults always couched hard truths. She was seventeen. She'd seen a lot of shit.

"If you would prefer to have your mother in the room, I can make that happen."

"No," Angie said quickly. The last person she wanted was her mother in a room with cops. Totally embarrassing. "She works today, and she'll be pissed if she gets called to the school."

"If you feel uncomfortable, you can end the interview. But it would benefit you to be completely honest about everything, understand?"

Angie nodded. This was all beginning to sound very formal.

Mrs. Webb used her card key to enter the administrative building. Angie glanced down the hall and saw yellow crime scene tape blocking Mrs. Clark's door. Her stomach dropped. This felt surreal.

Mrs. Webb led her to the conference room. There were no external windows, and the blinds on the windows that looked out into the hall were closed. The dark oblong table had eight oversized chairs. Water bottles, note pads, and pencils were neatly arranged on top of the credenza. A stack of folders with the Sun Valley High School emblem were to one side.

Mr. Borel was there, and he motioned for Angie to sit across from the two detectives. She dropped her backpack to her feet and sat; Mrs. Webb sat next to her.

Mr. Borel said, "Angie, this is Detective King and Detective Chavez. They're investigating Mrs. Clark's murder and talking to everyone who saw her yesterday."

"Okay," Angie said.

Mrs. Webb said, "Would you like a water?" Angie nodded, and Mrs. Webb reached behind her for a bottle. It would give her something to do with her hands.

King, the woman detective, had been in charge of Elijah's investigation. Angie hadn't met her before, but Mrs. Clark had talked about her, and Angie had left a message on her voicemail asking why she'd closed the case. Of course the detective never called her back.

"Angela Williams?" King asked.

"Angie," she said.

"You weren't at school yesterday, but came to campus in the afternoon, correct?"

"Yeah. To watch the volleyball game." Great, now she would probably get in trouble for cutting.

"A witness says that they saw you and Mrs. Clark arguing outside the gym. What were you arguing about?"

Angie shrugged.

"You don't remember?" King said.

"I do. I promised Mrs. Clark I wouldn't cut any more school."

"That's all you were arguing about?"

"Mostly."

"And?"

What was she supposed to say? That no one cares about what happened to Elijah? That she didn't do her job?

"Angie," Mrs. Webb said, "if it's personal, you can say that. We're simply trying to figure out what happened."

"Someone killed her," Angie said. "Just like someone killed Elijah, but you don't care about *him*."

King frowned. "Is that why you left an irate voicemail on my phone, because you think I don't care about your friend?"

"You *don't* care. You still think it was his fault he died."

She tried to control her temper. It wasn't going to help anyone if she yelled at cops.

"Did you talk to Mrs. Clark about the police investigation?" King asked.

"Yeah. I said it sucked that you closed the case. And she said that a private investigator was—" Angie cut herself off. Maybe she shouldn't say anything about Margo Angelhart.

"A private investigator is looking into Elijah's death?" Chavez, the other cop, asked. He didn't look like he was surprised, and he sounded much nicer than the woman.

"Yeah," Angie said, glancing up at Chavez before averting her gaze back to her unopened water bottle. "Elijah's mom hired someone. The PI talked to Mrs. Clark, and Mrs. Clark said she wanted to talk to me and asked if I would come to her office during lunch today. But obviously . . . well . . . that's not going to happen now."

She didn't tell the cops that she spoke to Margo this morning. Maybe she should. But it wasn't relevant, was it? And what would they do? Could they tell the PI to stop investigating Elijah's death? That it was a police matter? Angie had no idea what the rules were, and she didn't want to get Margo in trouble. She was the first person who actually sounded like she wanted the truth as much as Angie.

King was writing, and Chavez said, "Two people reported that the argument between you and Mrs. Clark was heated."

What was she supposed to say? "Maybe. I was just . . . I don't know, mad about the whole thing."

Mrs. Webb said, "Angie, there's no need for you to be upset."

She hadn't thought she sounded upset. She tried to temper her tone, but the anger came out. She looked at Mrs. Webb and said, "They don't care. They don't care about Elijah, and when

Mrs. Clark's murder gets hard, they're not going to care about her either."

"That's not true," Chavez said. "I can assure you, we will find out who killed Lena Clark."

"Whatever," she mumbled.

"After you left the game, where did you go?" Chavez asked.

Angie shot a glance at Mr. Borel. Both the principal and the school secretary knew she'd gone to Mrs. Clark's office, so she couldn't lie about that.

"I went to her office—she said I could pick up some college stuff she left for me."

"You told Mrs. Villines, the secretary, that you were meeting with Mrs. Clark."

Angie shrugged. "I don't remember. She said I could borrow her SAT book. I ran into Mr. Borel outside her office."

He nodded. "Yes, I remember."

"What time was that?" Chavez asked.

"I don't know," Angie said. "It was right after the last volleyball game."

Mr. Borel said, "I couldn't say the exact time, to be honest. I'd been working in my office and left to make a copy, saw Angie in Mrs. Clark's office. Around five, take or leave a few minutes, is my guess."

King wrote it down.

"Anyone else?"

"I heard a couple people talking outside the doors, and I didn't want to talk to anyone so went out the front."

"Why?" King asked.

"Because I cut school and didn't want to be lectured."

Mrs. Webb frowned but didn't say anything. Angie probably shouldn't have mentioned cutting school. But they already knew, so what was the big deal?

"Who did you hear talking?" King asked.

She shrugged. "I don't know, I wasn't really paying attention."

She thought back, trying to remember. There had been a jingle or something, maybe jewelry. Mrs. Clark always wore a lot of jewelry.

"You and Mrs. Clark had an argument and then you went to her office because she left material for you, but you told the receptionist that you were meeting with her."

"So what?"

She was being defensive, but did they—they couldn't think that *she* had killed Mrs. Clark.

"I think you're an angry teenager," King said. "You lash out when you don't get your way, without considering the repercussions."

Detective King thought that Angie was a killer; she could hear it in her tone. She almost couldn't breathe.

Chavez immediately cut in, his voice soothing and calm, "Angie, we need to piece together an exact timeline, which includes knowing *exactly* where you went after you left. We're not just talking to you. We spoke to several staff members and students. Your cooperation will help us pinpoint exactly what happened and when it happened."

"I didn't kill her," Angie blurted.

"We're not implying you did," Chavez said.

Angie glared at King. "She did."

"We want the truth," King said. "You said that you left the campus just before five. Where did you go?"

"To the Cactus Stop."

"Which one?"

"On Hatcher."

"What did you buy?"

She told them, not knowing why this was important.

"And then?"

"I started walking home. I had to pass the school. I saw police cars, so I called my friend Gina. She picked me up and I went to her house for dinner. She took me home around eight. We sat in the car for a while talking."

"Gina Martinelli," Mrs. Webb told the two detectives.

Great, the police were going to talk to Gina, and then her mom and dad, and maybe they wouldn't let Angie come over anymore. This day, this *year*, couldn't get any worse. Chris went to college, Elijah was killed, and her last remaining friend would be forbidden to see her.

King said, "Did you see anyone when you were leaving Mrs. Clark's office?"

"I told you. Mr. Borel. And there were some kids hanging around in the courtyard, but I don't know who. And the people coming in when I was leaving, I didn't see them. One might have been Mrs. Clark—I heard the jingle of jewelry or something, she always wears a lot of necklaces and bracelets and stuff. But I didn't talk to her."

King and Chavez exchanged a look, then King said, "We may have more questions, but you can go now."

Angie grabbed her backpack and left as fast as she could without running. Had she just made everything worse?

She didn't want to go back to class. She walked out, ignoring Mrs. Villines calling after her. She walked down the street to the bus stop.

They thought she killed Mrs. Clark. King didn't like her, that was totally obvious.

Well, she didn't care. Angie wasn't going to take back anything she'd said.

She didn't know what to do. Maybe she shouldn't have talked to the police at all, but she didn't think she'd had a choice. Could she have refused? Asked for a lawyer or something? She almost laughed. With what money? They hadn't arrested her or read her any rights. That had to mean something.

She didn't know. She didn't like crime shows; they were depressing. She liked to read, but mostly fantasy. Nothing real.

Nothing *felt* real right now.

The bus came—it wasn't the one that went straight down to the Central Library, but Angie got on it anyway. It was too hot to wait for the right bus, so she'd have to transfer, but that would give her time to think.

Angie pulled out her phone and saw a series of text messages from Chris that she had ignored last night.

Call me.

You're being stubborn. I know you don't want to be my girlfriend anymore, I get it even if I disagree with all your reasons and think you're wrong. But I'll always be your friend. Call me, tell me what happened to Elijah.

Then, late last night, he texted:

omg I just heard about Mrs. Clark. Angie, are you awake? Please call.

An hour later he sent a final message.

I still love you—even though you are totally stubborn and impossible to communicate with. I hate when you ignore me. If you don't want to talk to me, call Benny—he's your friend too.

She leaned back in the corner of the bus and thought about Chris, Benny, Elijah, and how everything fell apart.

She'd do anything to go back six months to when she thought her life was nearly perfect. Before her mother brought home yet another asshole to live with them. Before Elijah started working. Before she told Chris they had to break up.

Before Elijah died and Mrs. Clark was murdered.

chapter seventeen

MARGO ANGELHART

Lenny's has a classic diner vibe with lots of stainless steel, clean black-and-white-checkered floors, and red vinyl seats. They only did one thing: burgers. And they did them really, really well.

I arrived first and ordered for both Rick and me—one thing about Rick was that he was predictable about his food. We'd eaten here together dozens of times over the years and he always got the Cowboy Burger.

I liked to change things up. I've eaten every burger on the menu except the meatless burger. Today I was sticking with the basics: cheeseburger and fries.

Rick walked in a few minutes after me. He was attractive—short neat brown hair, tan skin from both the outdoors and his mixed heritage. Clean lines, well-built muscles, a chiseled jaw, and a flat stomach. At six feet, he was the perfect height for my five-foot-five frame. But since we weren't dating anymore, I tried to ignore his demi-god physique.

"You order?" he asked as he sat down across from me.

"For both of us."

"How's working with your family?" Rick asked.

"Not as bad as I thought," I said. Rick was one of the few people who knew and understood why I walked away from Angelhart Investigations three years ago. He'd supported me and I would never forget that. When I really needed him, he had been a rock.

Until he reminded me that I wasn't Sam's mother and had no rights or authority over his daughter.

"Jack's happy," Rick said.

"Well, he's falling in love."

"No, I mean that you're back in the firm. But yeah, he's fallen for Laura big-time."

"Have you met her?"

"Jack brought her to one of Sam's softball games a few weeks ago."

My gut twisted. I used to go to Sam's softball games whenever I wasn't working. I hadn't been since Rick and I split at the beginning of the year.

"Her team's playing at Rose Moffatt this weekend, if you want to come."

Rose Moffatt was a large softball complex adjacent to Highway 17, only a few miles from my house.

"Maybe." It would be awkward. The last time I'd seen Sam was at her eighth-grade graduation party at the end of May. She'd wanted me there, Rick asked me to come, so I went. But I didn't stay, because I didn't know how to make it not awkward.

The cook called my number from the counter and Rick jumped up to fetch the burgers and fries served in paper-lined plastic bowls.

We dug in and ate, the silence not uncomfortable. Made some more small talk, which was also not uncomfortable.

Maybe I could go to the softball game—at least one of them—and not find it super awkward. Maybe I'd bring Jack. That'd make it easier.

I shouldn't use my brother as a crutch, but I would.

When we were done eating and had wiped our fingers with a dozen napkins each, I said, "The Bradfords."

"I reread the reports to refresh myself," Rick said.

"You executed the warrant, right?"

"I was part of the team," he said. "The prosecutor's office was in charge, but I supervised the officers. They seized computers, bank statements, files, things like that. Forensics came in and took samples of chemicals, powders, tools. But ultimately, they didn't find any sign that the couple was prepping the drugs at their house. No trace whatsoever."

"What was their house like?"

"Nice, in a little gated community near 101 and 17. Clean, well-maintained neighborhood with a park, lots of trees. The kids were well cared for. Neighbors said the Bradfords were good parents, helped organize neighborhood barbecues, no one said a bad word about them."

"Even nice people are assholes," I said.

Rick cracked a smile. "Apparently the forensic auditor had a field day with Mrs. Bradford's records." He pulled out his small notepad. "She laundered nine thousand a month through her licensed day care that didn't actually exist—meaning, she had a license, declared the money, paid taxes, but never had kids on site."

"Wow, great way to launder money," I said.

He nodded. "Thirty thou in cash in a dresser in their closet. She paid cash for all living expenses, including electricity, gas, groceries, cable, clothing. They had state-of-the-art computers, televisions, gaming systems, and no record any of it had been purchased with credit. The only regular expense that came out automatically from their joint account was for their mortgage."

"I haven't read the entire report yet. I focused on the teenagers who were part of Bradford's operation."

Rick scowled. "That's what really pisses me off. There's a lot of kids who would do nearly anything for money, kids who have miserable home lives. And to have a teacher—a *coach*, someone in a position of authority recruit them into selling drugs? He didn't get enough time as far as I'm concerned. At least he'll never be allowed to work with kids again."

"Was there anything else that you found interesting?"

Rick thought. "I don't remember most of the details, but one thing really bugged me, I never forgot it. Their kids were there when the warrant was served. Bradford was in jail—he'd just been arrested. Cecilia Bradford sat with the kids on the back patio throughout the entire search. I told her she could leave, or take the kids to a neighbor's house, but she said she wanted to watch us destroy her life. That's exactly what she said, in front of the kids. I hope the kids are okay."

"According to the court records, they're living with their grandparents in South Dakota."

"What mother doesn't plead to avoid jail time?" Rick said. "She had a three-year-old. All she had to do was give up their supplier and she would have gotten probation, never had to lose years with her kids. That's what I have a hard time wrapping my head around. I know parents who don't give a shit about their kids, but that wasn't the Bradfords. Everything I saw said they loved and cared for their children."

"Fear?" I suggested. "Maybe loyalty."

"To a drug supplier?"

"Fear," I repeated.

People always had a reason for their actions. The reason might be bullshit or stupid or completely selfish, but there was a reason why Cecilia Bradford hadn't ratted out her supplier. It could be fear—fear that her husband would be killed in prison, or that she would be on the run the rest of her life.

Or it could be calculation. She'd been given six years. Maybe that didn't seem too much to give in order to gain more at the end.

Maybe she'd been bribed. Threatened. Both.

Whatever it was, whatever she did, it reeked of selfishness. Too often people didn't consider that their actions had serious ramifications for others—even their own family.

"Earth to Margo," Rick said.

"Just thinking about choices."

"You think there's something going on at the school like the Bradford operation?" he asked.

I didn't commit. "Maybe, but I have a few other leads. No one involved with the Bradford drug scam is still on campus. I just wanted to understand the operation so that if I see something similar, I'd recognize it. But, to change the subject, what's crime like around Cactus Stop locations?"

He chuckled. "Big change of subject."

"I'm curious. I like the location near my house, it's clean and the employees are nice. I've never seen overt drug dealing, homeless encampments. I've never felt unsafe."

"You pack a gun and a knife," he said with a smirk.

"So do you," I countered. "So my local Cactus Stop seems fine, but the location off Nineteenth and Camelback has had repeat problems. I'm curious about the other locations."

"Hit or miss. Most have decent security. There's only one store in the 900, and we'll get calls for service for loitering, trespassing, I think a robbery once this year, though they didn't get much. The managers do a good job keeping the facilities clean and the owner is willing to trespass the homeless so they don't camp out on the property or panhandle customers."

"What do you know about EBT fraud?"

"Why?"

"Curious."

He raised his eyebrows and waited for a better answer. Clearly he knew me well.

I told him about Elijah's overdose and the subsequent murder at Sun Valley High School.

"Now I'm confused. What does any of that have to do with the Bradfords or EBT fraud?"

"Probably nothing. Though the EBT fraud might—Elijah worked at the Cactus Stop on Hatcher. I checked it out and saw people going in, using an EBT card, leaving without a bag. Could have pocketed something, but at least two people didn't. So it had me a bit suspicious."

"You're thinking maybe his death wasn't an overdose?"

"I'm not thinking anything until I find out what happened the day leading up to his death."

"Financial crime isn't my area," Rick said. "We have an entire team that works those cases. Most EBT fraud that we investigate is where stores let those on welfare use the cards for ineligible items." Rick paused. "I'm not going to jam up people for buying smokes. I don't like it, they're supposed to use their money for food, but we have far worse crimes to worry about."

"It's just a thread I'm tugging."

"If it was common, like they did it regularly and not just for a few friends and family, then they would have to cook the books—meaning, ring up an eligible item, but sell them an ineligible item. The manager would definitely know about it though, because they would be responsible for inventory. If it's a big enough scam, then the financial manager for the business would eventually figure it out. You want me to reach out to one of my buddies in financial crimes?"

"If you have time. Just so I can get a handle on how these scams work."

"I'll send her your name and number."

"I appreciate it."

Rick finished his last couple fries. "That particular Cactus Stop is in a sketchy neighborhood. Think something else might have been going on? Something that could have put the kid in danger? That area gets a lot of calls."

In cop-speak, that meant PPD had an active presence.

"Possible," I said. "He walked home every night, between eight and nine. He could have witnessed a crime, or was in the wrong place, wrong time. But that still doesn't explain how he ended up at a park more than a mile away dead of a drug overdose. There's a five-hour window that's unaccounted for."

"But the police didn't find anything."

"The police did shit." I winced. I was blunt by nature. Sometimes it was a good thing. Not so much when I was talking to a friend who was a cop.

I tempered my tone and said, "I think Detective King was premature in writing off Elijah's death as an accidental overdose."

"That would be the ME's determination."

"Elijah died of an overdose, that's not in dispute. There were no signs that he was suicidal, hence accidental overdose. But what if it wasn't?"

"You mean if someone killed him."

I hedged, just a bit. "I haven't gone that far yet. But considering that Lena Clark, the counselor at the school, *was* stabbed to death less than two weeks after Elijah died, and she was asking questions about his death, I need to consider the possibility. The police didn't retrace his steps. They don't know where he was the hours before he died."

"Margo, while I have a lot of issues with some detectives down at headquarters, I don't think they would have closed the case if there were signs that something was amiss."

"I do," I said. "I'm not ready to say he was murdered, but *someone* has to know what he was doing for those five hours. Josie thinks there's something there, but she's not in a position to investigate—and she got slapped by King for adding information to the report after the case was closed. Plus, King blames Josie for Lena Clark's complaint about the investigation. Both Josie and I talked to one of Elijah's friends, a girl named Angie. She's adamant there was something going on with him that wasn't drugs."

"Your cousin has a soft spot."

"Then I guess so do I."

Rick snorted. "You don't believe that, Margo. You can smell bullshit a mile away, but when you believe in someone, you fight for them. You believe in this teenager."

I considered. "To a point. I met her this morning. She's street smart, but she's also book-smart. I definitely think *she* believes that Elijah was as clean as Mother Teresa, but I also got it out of her that he had been preoccupied and aloof the last few weeks. Uncle Rafe brought Elijah's mother to me. He was her only son. Her husband died ten years ago. I want to find the answers, good or bad."

"I get it." He thought a moment. "If something is going on at the Cactus Stop, if it's a white-collar or fraud crime, I may not have paid attention. We get dozens of bulletins a day."

"The joys of paperwork."

Rick grinned, rose. He took out his wallet and I pushed his hand back. "Nope, you helped me, my treat."

"I don't know what I did, but I won't say no to a free lunch."

We walked out together and as I unlocked my Jeep, Rick said, "I mean it about Sam's games. She'd like to see you."

What about you? I thought but didn't say.

I couldn't even say that I wanted to get back together with Rick, even if he wanted to. What he said back in January hurt, and if he didn't trust me to always do right by Sam, I didn't know if I could live under those conditions. I don't know if I would go back even if he apologized. Which he hadn't.

"Send me the game times," I said. "I'll see if I can make one. But don't tell Sam, in case I don't."

"Roger that." Rick waved and drove off in his truck.

I sat there a few minutes, sipping my iced coffee and wondering if I should just forgive Rick and see if we still had something. I didn't see it happening unless he apologized. If he didn't see how he had overreacted, then he'd do it again, and the next time would be worse. Right now, we could be friends. And maybe that was all we could be.

Checking my phone, I saw I had a message from Josie with the home address of Danielle Duran, and the comment: You're welcome.

I sent her a thumbs-up and mapped the address. Danielle lived only a few blocks from my parents' house—I used to have a friend who lived on the same street. I was heading there when my phone started vibrating. I recognized the number only because this was the third time she had called—Detective King. I was about to answer it, when I saw another call come in. It was an unfamiliar local number, so I declined King's call and picked up the second.

"Margo Angelhart," I answered.

"Margo? It's Angie. I need help."

Her voice was quiet and strained, but I heard noise in the background, possibly traffic.

"Where are you?"

"On the bus. I'm going to the Central Library. I'll be there in, like, maybe forty minutes."

"What happened?" I asked.

"They think I killed Mrs. Clark. Please come, I don't know what to do."

"I'll text you when I get there."

I would call King after I found out what had got Angie so spooked.

chapter eighteen

MARGO ANGELHART

In a private study room in the Central Library, Angie told me about her interview with Detectives King and Chavez. It angered me that they'd talked to her without an advocate, even if the vice-principal thought *she* was Angie's advocate. It was a dicey legal area that I wasn't well-versed in, but it was probably allowed because Angie wasn't a suspect or detained. At least, that's how it started. Based on Angie's description, Detective King was suspicious of her.

"What aren't you telling me?"

"I lied."

"To the police?"

"No—to Mrs. Villines. In the office yesterday. I told her I had a meeting with Mrs. Clark, but I didn't. She let me in. Then I told Mr. Borel that I was picking up something she left me."

"But he saw you leave."

"He saw me leave her office. What if they think I, like, I don't know, hid? The way they were talking to me—I know they think I killed her. I didn't, I swear to God."

"They can't arrest you without evidence. They can, however,

ask you more questions. Do you have the receipt from the Cactus Stop?"

She shook her head. "I didn't even take it."

"Still, they could have security cameras somewhere between the Cactus Stop and the school."

"Benny!" Angie exclaimed. "He saw me there."

"Who's Benny?"

"Benny Vallejo, he's a junior at Sun Valley. And, um, he's my ex-boyfriend's brother. He started working at the Cactus Stop last week, after Elijah . . ." Her voice trailed off.

"Good," I said. "He can give you an alibi. But listen to me—do not talk to the police without a lawyer."

She snorted. "Yeah. Right."

"I'm serious. If they want to talk to you again, call me. I have friends, and my Aunt Rita has a whole team of lawyers who often work pro bono. It won't be a problem."

She didn't look like she believed me.

"Why'd you leave campus in the middle of the day?" I asked. "It's not a good look."

"Because I don't like Detective King, and they were acting all *don't leave town*."

"They said that?"

She shrugged. "Attitude. You know. Disapproving and stern."

I was trying to understand what the cops were thinking, but realized that the only way I could ferret out their theory would be to talk to Rachel King myself.

"Angie, keep your head down, go to school, and do not talk to the police without a representative." I pulled out my business card and wrote *Rita Garcia* and her number on the back. "If you need her, call. Tell her I referred you, but I'll also send her a message to give her the heads-up."

"She'd really help for, like, no money?" Angie shook her head in disbelief.

"She will," I said.

With teens like Angie, actions spoke louder than words, so

I pulled out my phone and called Aunt Rita. After a minute of pleasantries, I said, "I'm sitting here with a seventeen-year-old high school student who was questioned by police at her school about the murder of one of her teachers. They claimed it was perfunctory, but said they might want to talk to her again because she had an argument with said teacher shortly before she was killed. Should she have council with her?"

"I would advise so."

"What if she can't afford it? Her mom can't pay, and she doesn't have her own job."

"Margo, are you trying to make a point with this young lady?"

"Yes."

"Let me speak to her."

I handed my phone to Angie. "Rita Garcia, my aunt."

Angie hesitated, then took the phone. "Hello?" she said nervously, then she listened. She answered a few questions either "Yes," "No," or "I don't know," then said, "Thank you," and handed the phone back to me.

"Thanks, Aunt Rita."

"You don't know what I said."

"You told her why she needs an advocate, that you'd make sure someone was with her should the police want to talk to her again, and that under no circumstances should she answer any more questions from the police related to this crime, even if she's innocent and just wants to help."

Aunt Rita laughed. "Still a brat, Margo."

"Love you, Auntie," I said and ended the call.

"It's for your protection," I told Angie. "The police aren't generally the bad guys, but they can make your life difficult, and I don't want that for you. Lawyers protect the innocent as well as defend the guilty."

"Do you really, honestly believe that Mrs. Clark was killed because she was asking questions about Elijah?"

"I don't know," I said. "It's suspicious that she was killed less than two weeks after Elijah died, and that she had been vocal in trying to find out what happened to him. Which is why I think you should lay low and not ask questions."

"What am I supposed to do?"

"Stop cutting school. Don't put yourself in a position where you're cornered—just in case Lena's murder is somehow related to Elijah. And call me anytime."

"What are you going to do?"

"Investigate. It's in my job description."

She didn't find my joke funny. I continued, "I've been avoiding Detective King all day, so I'll reach out to her and see what she's thinking. You should go home."

"Not now," Angie said. "I'm going to hang here for a while."

I remembered that I wanted her to help me identify the phone numbers on Elijah's bill.

"I have Elijah's phone records, up until ten days before he died. Do you recognize these numbers? I already identified his mom's and yours."

I pulled out my phone and showed her the screenshot of the numbers I'd consolidated from his records.

"Why don't you just call them?" she asked as she scanned the list.

"Because if one of these people is involved in his death, I don't want them to know I'm looking for them—at least not yet. So I have to go to my office and use a private line that won't share my number, which they will likely decline, and then I'll cross my fingers that they identify themselves in their voicemail."

"There's not a lot here."

"I figure he texted more than he called people."

She smiled just a bit. "Yeah. I don't think he called me more than a couple times over the last year. Why don't you just look at his texts? His passcode is his mom's birthday."

"His phone is missing."

"That's weird."

"Yep."

"Didn't the police think it was weird?"

"I don't know."

She frowned, looked at the six numbers I hadn't yet identified. "This one—ends in 1455? That's Gina Martinelli's cell phone. And this one is Andy, and this one is Peter." She pulled out her phone and typed in the other numbers.

"Don't save those," I said.

"I won't do anything, just looking to see if I have a contact. Yeah—this one, that ends in 2239? That's Mr. Parsons. Mr. Parsons was helping Elijah with college applications. I don't know the others."

I wrote down the contact information. "This is good. Do you know when Benny works?"

"I assume after school every day, like Elijah."

I stood, looked at her again. "Do what I say, Angie. Okay?"

"I will," Angie assured me.

I walked out, drove my car out of the parking garage, and called Detective King on the number she left for me.

"Rachel King," she answered gruffly.

"Hi, Rachel, it's Margo Angelhart. You left a message for me to call."

"I left a message this morning," she snapped. "And I've called you multiple times."

"Sounds important, how can I help you?"

She didn't say anything for a second. "You know I need to talk to you about the Lena Clark homicide."

"Now I do."

"Your brother must have called you."

It wasn't a question so I didn't comment.

"I'm at police headquarters," Rachel said, "if you'd like to come in."

"What do you need to discuss?"

I was playing dumb and she knew it and it irritated her. I smiled, enjoying the conversation.

"I have questions about your relationship with Lena Clark."

"I don't have a relationship."

"You know what I mean."

"You should be more specific. What do you want to know?"

"I'd like to talk face-to-face. I'll be here until four."

"If you're going to insist on speaking to me in person, I'll be at my office in ten minutes. I don't know how long I'll be there, but I'm happy to answer any questions you have."

"It would be better if you came here."

"Not going to happen. It's your case, I'm willing to help, but I'm not going to jump through hoops and pay for overpriced parking to make it easier for you."

"Fine," she said, more than a little irritated now. "I'll be there at three thirty."

"Great," I said, but she'd already hung up.

Yes, I definitely knew how to make friends and influence people.

Unfortunately, meeting with Rachel King would delay me tracking down Danielle Duran.

When I arrived at the office, no one was there except Iris.

"Where is everyone?" I asked.

"Tess and Theo went to the courthouse to pull files, and Jack is serving a subpoena. Your mom is meeting with Carmen de la Rosa about a retainer contract with her firm."

Carmen de la Rosa was a shark of an attorney. I had worked for her a few times over the years. I didn't have retainers with anyone, but my mom was a better business manager than me. Retainers meant steady income, but once you were on retainer, you couldn't turn down work because you didn't like the assignment—which is why I didn't accept retainers.

I hope my mom knew what she was getting into with Carmen. I also wondered where she was with the potential capitol case we might be working.

"Aren't you supposed to be out of here by now?" I asked. Iris generally left by 2:30 p.m. because two of her kids—a freshman and senior at the same Catholic school we had all gone to—got out at three. They were in a bunch of activities. Her oldest was in college.

"Maddie is auditioning for the Christmas musical, so JJ will drive her home after football practice. But I'm on my way out—it'll be nice to go to the grocery store without having to rush."

She left, and I sat at my desk and looked through our shared drive at the background reports for pending employees at Logan Monroe's resort. Tess had already confirmed all information that could be confirmed by phone or online, but left a note that one of us needed to drive up to Prescott to talk to a reference who hadn't been reachable. Maybe I'd have time tomorrow or Thursday. It had to be done by Friday. It was a nice drive, but would take me half the day to get there and back. But since Tess had done everything else and was hosting mom's birthday party, I sent her a note that I'd go to Prescott.

At quarter to four, Detective King walked in, solo. I had considered leaving at 3:31 p.m., but figured that was petty.

I walked out of my office and said, "Detective King?" I had no intention of bringing her into my office so she could snoop, so I offered, "Water? Soda?"

"I'm fine," she said brusquely. "I just have a few questions."

I plopped down on one of the waiting area couches. "Shoot."

She hesitated, then sat across from me. Made a point to take out her notepad, flip through the pages.

King was in her forties with wide hips and what appeared to be a perpetual sour expression. Highlights in her brown hair had grown out well past the point that she needed a touch-up because her gray hair was obvious. I wasn't being judgy—okay, maybe a little—but she looked tired and preoccupied, and she definitely didn't want to be here.

"How do you know Lena Clark?"

"I don't, I met her yesterday."

"Where did you meet her?"

"In her office."

"Did she hire you?"
"No."
"Who hired you?"
"For what?"
She frowned. "Why did you meet with Clark?"
"To get her opinion about Elijah Martinez."
King did a double take. "What?"
"To get her opinion about Elijah Martinez," I repeated.
"I heard you. Who are you working for?"
"I have a lot of clients."
"Why are you being evasive?"
"I'm not. I do have a lot of clients." Right now, only two—three if I counted Mrs. Martinez—but I *have* had a lot of clients in the past, and anticipate having a lot in the future. She didn't need to know any of that.

"Who hired you to investigate anything surrounding Elijah Martinez's death?"

I flirted with the idea of telling her it was confidential because I didn't like her attitude, but then decided she'd probably find out anyway since it wasn't a secret.

"Alina Martinez."

She blinked, surprised. This woman would never be able to play poker with an Angelhart.

"His mother?"
"Yes."
"Why?"

I wanted to say, *To do your job*, but I didn't, no matter what I thought of her half-assed investigation.

I also didn't want to give her so much information that she might pull the you're-interfering-with-a-police-investigation card. So I said, "Alina doesn't know where Elijah was after he left work Friday night until he died in the park. His phone and backpack are missing. I'm retracing his steps."

Which is what you should have done, I thought.

She opened her mouth, then closed it. What was she going to say? There was nothing in the police report that indicated she had investigated that angle.

Then she said something that surprised me. "We believe that someone in the homeless community came across his body and took his possessions. This has happened in the past in similar situations. He died between one and three a.m., and wasn't discovered until after five in the morning."

"That wasn't in the report."

"An oversight, but ultimately unimportant. The chances of recovery are slim to none. We added the cell phone serial number to the list of stolen items we regularly provide to pawn shops and secondhand stores. If it shows up, we'll know."

It wasn't unimportant if Elijah was murdered, but I didn't say that.

Rachel changed gears. "Lena Clark called you yesterday at 5:14 and you spoke for three minutes."

"Yes."

"What did you speak about?"

I knew Angie had told them I planned to meet with her today, so there was no harm in sharing that information—and it might help Angie. "Lena offered to facilitate a meeting between myself and another student who had insight into Elijah's state of mind in the days leading up to his death."

"Why?"

"Like I said, I'm looking into his last days in order to give his mother closure. You closed the investigation and she still has questions."

We were getting into the repetitive phase of the interview, and I was ready to send her packing.

"He died of an accidental drug overdose," King snapped. "You can request the autopsy report. I explained it to Mrs. Martinez." She cleared her throat, softened her tone just a bit. "It's a tragedy, and I understand why she might find it sudden and unexpected, but

I don't know what you might be able to learn that will give her peace. Her son is still dead."

"Sometimes," I said, "filling in blanks helps the survivors."

Defensively, she said, "If I had found any information about where he obtained the drugs or who he had been partying with, I would have included it in the report and forwarded the case to the Drug Enforcement Bureau for further investigation."

"Why didn't you?" I asked bluntly.

"Because there were no leads and I couldn't investigate indefinitely. I'm sure you know, considering your brother used to be a cop, that we're severely understaffed. I don't have the luxury to pursue investigations when there are no signs of foul play."

"Sure."

"What's with the attitude?"

Her overreaction was unexpected and made me curious. "I don't have an attitude."

"I have been getting shit about this case. A cop who spoke to the student body created untold problems for me—I've had to field dozens of calls from school administrators, students, teachers, parents. I've finally had to send them to the PIO because I can't do my job if I'm explaining over and over that an accidental drug overdose doesn't warrant further investigation. And that's probably why Mrs. Martinez is spending her hard-earned money on you."

I didn't correct her that I was working for free. I doubt she would care.

"Why do you care if a PI is trying to find out where a teenage honor student obtained drugs that resulted in his death? Whether he took them voluntarily or not, that's a dealer on the street who's going to sell more drugs to more kids who are going to end up dead."

"I don't care," King said in a tone that belied her words. "Do whatever you want, Margo. But Lena Clark was murdered. It was after-hours, most students and faculty were gone. Her ex-husband lives out-of-state. Her boyfriend, a colleague, found her body at 5:25—only minutes after she talked to you."

"Have you looked at her boyfriend?"

"We are. We are looking at several people. This investigation is less than twenty-four hours old. And I don't understand why you are so closemouthed about what you and Lena Clark talked about."

"I told you what's relevant."

"I doubt that."

I bristled. "Not my problem."

Tess and Theo walked in laughing. Theo was carrying a box. Tess looked surprised to see the detective, her eyebrows raised in curiosity.

"Is there anything else?" I asked King as I stood.

"I hope you'll make yourself available if I have follow-up questions," she said.

I didn't say anything because she didn't phrase it as a question. She left, and I rolled my eyes. "Wow."

"You were rude," Tess said.

"She was rude first," I said. "I don't like her."

"You think she's dirty?"

"No," I said and meant it. She didn't have the vibe of a dirty cop. "Overworked, angry, hates her job, and doesn't like anyone questioning her decisions. But not corrupt. I told her what she needs to know."

"Remember, Margo—more flies with honey," Tess said, and Theo laughed. I shot him a dirty look.

"Generally, I would agree with you," I said, "but with her, no. Did you learn anything about the Bradford case?"

"A lot, but I don't know how it'll help. We just picked up the files from the court. It'll take all night to go through it."

"I can do that," I said.

"No, I want to," Tess said.

Tess loved research and paperwork. I didn't, so I certainly didn't offer twice.

I followed Tess and Theo to her office. Theo put the box down on the corner of her desk. Her office was tidy, like mine, but where mine was functional, hers had a charming, almost too-cute vibe. A thriving plant sat on the windowsill, artwork adorned the walls, and bookshelves were neatly organized. A framed photo of Tess's college graduation and several pictures of Tess and Gabriel decorated her desk. A file cabinet doubled as a display for more photos, fresh flowers, and whimsical Hobby Lobby knickknacks. Instead of a lone office chair like me, she had comfy guest seating, and a table draped with a frilly cloth held a stack of artfully arranged books about old-time private investigators, both fictional like Sherlock Holmes and real like the Pinkertons.

Tess sat down and pulled out handwritten notes from her research. "I'll type this up for you," she said, "but here's the gist. And Theo, if you ever decide you don't want to work in the crime lab, you would be a whiz in the research department."

He grinned widely, eating up the praise, and leaned back to stretch his long legs.

"You know the basics, right?" Tess asked me.

I nodded. "I met with Rick today, he served the warrant on the family, so I have his insight as well."

"It started local, they brought in the feds after they started investigating. The wife is in federal prison, Bradford is in state prison. Eyman," she added.

The same prison our dad was in. We locked eyes for a moment, both thinking the same thing, but we didn't say anything about it.

"The investigation started after an anonymous call on September seventh, and culminated in an arrest on January thirteenth. A four-month-long investigation, which included four undercover cops, two on staff with the school and two posing as students. They gathered extensive circumstantial evidence, but no smoking gun—until Eric McMahon asked the undercover female out.

"Law enforcement suspected that McMahon was the primary go-between for Bradford," Tess continued. "The undercover female—her name isn't in the records, she's known as UC3 in the files—had access to McMahon's car, home, and locker. She gathered extensive evidence. McMahon was smart, and he didn't talk about his illegal activities, but had money to flash, took her on expensive dates, and multiple times brought her when he delivered packages of what they later learned were drugs.

"She set up a sting where law enforcement swooped down on McMahon and offered him a plea arrangement—give up Bradford and he'd get probation. He took it without hesitation—provided his girlfriend got the same deal. I don't think he even knows now that she was an undercover cop."

I was impressed. It wasn't easy going undercover. I don't know that I could do it. As a PI, I sometimes pretended to be who I wasn't, but I didn't have to fake it for long so wasn't worried about getting caught up in a lie.

"What happened to the kid who got juvie? Jimenez, I think. Attempted murder, right?"

Tess flipped through her legal notepad. "Scott Jimenez. I don't have much yet, it's probably in the records we pulled, but what I deduced was that Bradford became suspicious that McMahon was talking to the police and paid Jimenez to kill him. Bradford denied it, and Jimenez said no one paid him to, quote, 'kill a rat.' But when police raided Jimenez's house and searched his car, they found a large sum of cash and McMahon's home address written on a sticky note that only had Jimenez's prints."

Theo said, "I think someone higher up than Bradford, someone in the know, realized McMahon was working with the cops, and Jimenez was tagged to kill him."

Maybe, but that seemed a bit too cinematic to be real.

"Is Jimenez still in juvie?" I asked.

Tess shook her head. "He was released a year later and given three years' probation. I have his last known address."

"Send it to me?"

Tess nodded and made a note.

"What happened to McMahon?" I asked. "Jimenez got attempted murder, did the plea deal hold with McMahon?"

"Jimenez pled down to aggravated assault," Tess said. "According to the report, Jimenez shot McMahon when he was leaving his house. One of three bullets hit, but McMahon wasn't seriously hurt. He was with UC3, who identified Jimenez as the shooter. The gun was found in his locker at school."

"Dumbass," Theo muttered.

"They don't have lockers at Sun Valley," I said.

"Not for the general school population, but athletes use lockers in the gym. Jimenez played for Coach Bradford as well."

"I read that his wife got six years, Bradford fifteen?" I questioned.

"Bradford got fifteen to twenty," Tess said. "He pled guilty to multiple counts of drug dealing, child endangerment—because the kids were minors—and money laundering."

I frowned.

"What?" Tess asked.

"I'm just working through a few things . . . Both Bradfords pled, the police believed they were protecting their supplier, but they don't know who that person is."

"They don't even have a suspect," Tess said. "There are two opposing theories. One is that the supplier was local and Bradford used someone else, possibly his wife who wasn't under surveillance, as the go-between because Bradford never met with anyone suspicious. Second theory was that of the lead investigator, DEB Detective Mike Hitchner, who thought that Bradford's semi-regular trips to the border was him meeting with his supplier. But they followed him and never came back with any suspects and never witnessed any exchange. After Jimenez shot McMahon, they didn't have a choice but to shut down the operation even though they didn't have evidence to nail the supplier."

"The Bradfords were scared shitless," Theo said. "You don't give up your supplier if you know the supplier will whack you."

Blunt, but accurate.

"Is there a transcript of the anonymous call?"

Tess grinned. "I can do you one better."

She typed on her computer and a moment later a staticky recording started.

"I'm calling because, um . . ." The voice—young, female—trailed off. "I don't know who to call. I don't want anybody to know I called. It says Silent Witness and I don't have to give my name. But. Um. My, um, Mr. Bradford at Sun Valley High School is dealing drugs. I don't know what to do. I saw him do it last year, and then again yesterday and I can't sleep and I don't want anyone to get hurt again. I hope you can stop it."

The call ended.

Tess said, "The Silent Witness program is usually when law enforcement asks citizens for help in solving a crime and offer a reward. They promise anonymity. This call, however, went to Phoenix PD. Maybe the girl didn't understand how the program worked. The file says the call came from Sun Valley High School, but that's it."

"Play it again," I said, and listened very carefully, eyes closed. When it was over, I said, "My . . . she said *my* before Mr. Bradford."

"Hitchner believes the witness is a softball player. Bradford coached football in the fall, and softball in the spring. There were sixteen girls on the team that spring, six graduated, which leaves ten girls who were still at the school in the fall."

"So she was going to say my coach," Theo deduced.

"What day?" I asked.

"The call came in on a Friday morning, 7:15 a.m."

"Before school," I said. "So maybe she saw something on Thursday and put it together with what she saw before. She said I don't want anyone hurt *again*. It sounds like she or a friend had trouble with drugs."

"That is going to be next to impossible to determine," Tess said. "But I ran a list of all Sun Valley students whose deaths were drug-related in the last five years." She slid over a printout for me.

"You are amazing."

Tess smiled proudly. "I know."

It was an unfortunately long list. Twenty-seven students died from a drug overdose—six of those were determined to be suicides. Nine more died in DUI-related accidents.

"However," Tess continued, "I can't get complete information about kids who survived a drug overdose or kids who are addicts—which a student might consider being *hurt*. The school could possibly provide a list of dropouts, but I don't know that they will. It would be considered confidential."

"This all helps." Even if we don't know where it fit yet. Investigation was about gathering as much information as possible and figuring out how to put the pieces together to see the whole picture.

"How do you see the Bradford case connecting to Elijah Martinez's overdose?" Tess asked.

"I don't," I admitted. "It was a major investigation and Elijah was a freshman at the time, so I need to keep it on my radar. But Lena Clark was killed because she was looking into Elijah's death, of that I'm nearly positive. Could be someone picked up where Bradford left off. Someone who worked at the school then . . . and now. Or Elijah stumbled onto a different criminal conspiracy." I felt like the more I learned, the less I knew . . . because nothing that I had learned told me where Elijah was those five hours before he died.

Tess said, "I'll get started on what I have." She looked hopefully at Theo.

He sighed. "I have classes tomorrow morning, but I can be here after lunch to help."

She smiled. "Thank you." To me, she said, "If I find anything, I'll ping you."

"Thanks, sis."

I went into my office and closed the door.

Eyman State Penitentiary was an hour south of Phoenix, in

Florence. I had been there dozens of times over the last three years to visit my father, and because I was preapproved, I didn't have to jump through hoops to visit.

I was hoping I could finagle my way into seeing Ben Bradford. Because I had that little tingle in my gut that said there was unfinished business there.

Fortunately, the guards liked the Angelhart family. I gave my mother credit for that good will. Not only had she been the county attorney, but she had a good relationship for decades with the Department of Corrections because she'd first been a prosecutor. So the Angelhart name had certain clout with the Bureau of Prisons. I called the assistant warden directly. This wasn't proper protocol, but sometimes there was a good reason to circumvent the rules.

While on hold, I logged into the prison portal and scheduled a visit with my father tomorrow in the ten-to-noon window. As soon as I hit Submit, Assistant Warden Chuck Boxer picked up the line.

"Hi, Mr. Boxer, it's Margo Angelhart."

"How are you, Margo? Your family?"

"Good, thank you. I'm visiting my dad tomorrow late morning, and I would like to speak with another prisoner if possible."

"You know how to request visitation."

"Of course, but it takes time. I was hoping because I'm already going to be there, that there might be a way to cut through some of the paperwork?"

"Who, and what is the purpose?"

"Ben Bradford," I said and opened the file Jack had given me. I read off his prisoner number. "I'd like to ask him about something related to Sun Valley High School." I was trying to keep it as vague as possible. "I don't know if you know much about his case, but he pled on a drug case—using high school students to distribute for him. I have a different case I'm working on for the family of a victim of an overdose, and I wanted his insight."

"Will he cry for his lawyer?"

"No. And if he doesn't want to talk to me, that's fine. I get it.

But it would help me, and I'm looking at his file and he doesn't appear to have any visitation restrictions."

"Let's see . . ." I heard clicking on a keyboard. "Well, he's been a model prisoner, no dings, appears to be doing his time, and keeping his head down. It won't be a problem to visit. I'll put you on the list and when you're done visiting with Dr. Angelhart, just tell the guard on duty."

chapter nineteen

ANGIE WILLIAMS

Angie didn't want to go home, so she decided to stop by Mrs. Martinez's apartment and see how she was doing. Angie didn't really *want* to because she felt uncomfortable around all the sadness. But she missed Elijah, and Mrs. Martinez had always been nice to her, and she figured Elijah would want her to make sure his mom was okay.

Angie was about to knock on the door when she saw Mrs. Martinez and a man sitting on the small patio.

"Oh. Hi. I'm sorry." She held out the small bouquet of flowers she'd bought from a street vendor near the library. They were a little wilted from her long bus ride.

"Angie, dear!" Mrs. Martinez stood, hugged her, took the flowers. "You are a such sweet girl."

"I just, um, wanted to see how you were doing. I can go if you're busy."

"No, no, no, please stay. It is always good to have Elijah's friends over. Mr. Ramos, this is Angie Williams, one of Elijah's closest friends."

The man stood and extended his hand to her; she took it, feeling awkward. He was dressed in a crisp suit with a faint scent of aftershave around him.

"Angie, Angie, so good to meet you. I saw you at the funeral last week." He looked her in the eyes as he held her hand, somber and serious. "It was good of you to come."

"Oh. Yeah, you're Elijah's boss," Angie said.

He nodded and dropped her hand. "I own the Cactus Stop. I also went to Sun Valley High School, many, many years ago."

"Oh." What should she say? "I just wanted to see how you were, Mrs. Martinez, and see if you, um, needed anything."

"I need to go." Mr. Ramos smiled at Angie, then gave Mrs. Martinez a hug. "Again, Alina, please, anything you need at all, you call. I mean it."

"You have already done more than I would ever expect."

"I wish you would let me pay for the investigator you hired."

Mrs. Martinez shook her head. "No, I cannot accept anything more from you. But thank you for all you've done, Mr. Ramos."

"Manny, I've told you, please." He kissed her cheek. "If you change your mind, Alina, please let me know. You have my direct number."

"Of course," she said.

He left, walking down the path toward the street.

"Such a kind, kind man," Mrs. Martinez said. "Let's get these lovely flowers in water." She motioned for Angie to follow her inside. She rummaged for a vase under the sink, then filled it with water. She sighed heavily and Angie saw how tired she was.

"Are you okay?" Angie asked her.

She shrugged. "Nights are hard. I go to daily Mass. Father Rafe is very kind, lets me sit all morning, all day, if I need to. But I've gone back to work part-time. I think that's best. Work will keep my mind occupied."

"Do you have my phone number? I'm happy to help with anything you need. I can go to the store for you." She'd have to walk or take the bus since she didn't have her license, but there was a store not too far.

"You are so kind. You were a good friend to Elijah. I would like your number, because someday, not now, but someday—I'll go through Elijah's room. There may be something you want that would help you remember him."

Angie blinked rapidly. She had never known anyone who'd died. Not someone her age. Not her friend.

But she wouldn't cry in front of Mrs. Martinez.

She wrote her number down on a pad on the refrigerator.

"Do you have enough food and stuff?" Angie asked. "I can cook maybe if you want."

"I have so much food people have brought by, my freezer is packed." To illustrate, she opened the freezer door. Inside were dozens of single-serve frozen meals, some homemade, some store bought. "Sit, you have time?"

Angie had no place to be, so she sat at the small kitchen table. Mrs. Martinez pulled a can of 7UP from the refrigerator and poured it into a glass for Angie. "I remember this is your favorite, like Elijah."

Angie took a sip. "I talked to Margo Angelhart today about Elijah."

"Oh, thank you." She sat across from Angie, her eyes warm and sad and hopeful. "You helped some?"

"I don't know, but I answered all her questions."

"Father Rafe speaks so highly of his family."

"She was nice. She listened."

Mrs. Martinez stared over Angie's shoulder, and for a moment, Angie thought she was going to cry. Then Angie would cry, and she didn't want to do that.

"He was so tired all the time," Mrs. Martinez said quietly. "He worked long hours all summer, took a class at the community college, it was too much. I didn't see him enough. I told him I loved him the night before. He hugged me. Kissed me. I hold on to that."

Angie hadn't known that Elijah was taking classes over the summer. They'd talked about doing it together, but when they were going to sign up, he said he didn't have time because of his job. Had he not wanted to do it with her? Had she made him mad? She couldn't think of anything she'd done.

She wasn't going to hold it against him, because she didn't know what he had been thinking. She tried not to be hurt.

Angie drank her 7UP and listened to Mrs. Martinez talk about Elijah. It was nice to hear happy stories about him.

Then suddenly Mrs. Martinez started to cry. "I'm sorry," the woman said. "I'm sorry."

"It's okay," Angie said, got up, and hugged her.

"I need—I need to go lie down."

"I'll come by in a few days?"

"Yes. Please, that would be nice."

Angie let herself out, then finally let herself cry as she slowly walked home.

chapter twenty

MARGO ANGELHART

I texted Jack that I would be a little late to dinner at Laura's, then drove to Danielle Duran's house.

The Durans lived on a tree-lined street famous because every house had a wagon wheel in their front yard. Most had entwined lights, some were surrounded by flowers, some were left unadorned. Next to the Duran wheel was a whimsical metal cactus wearing a cowboy hat. I never understood why anyone in Arizona had fake cacti on display when it would be so easy to grow a real one.

One of the girls I'd played softball with lived on this street and sometimes her mom would drive me home after practice.

I wasn't exactly sure how to approach Danielle, and I would have preferred to do it without any parents around, but getting back on campus after Lena's murder would be more difficult, so this was my best option.

Sometimes, lying was the most effective approach to getting information. This wasn't something I talked about with my Uncle Rafe, the priest. I understood his point of view, but deception often uncovered truth. Thus, if I needed to fib to get Danielle to talk to me, I would. But I'd start with honesty and see where it went.

Winging it was an important rule in the unwritten PI handbook.

An older SUV and a newer, practical Honda Civic were in the carport. Both had public safety license plates, and the SUV had a Proud Parents of a Marine sticker on the back window. The yard was neatly trimmed with potted flowers on the narrow porch, which was framed by two flags: an American flag on one side, an Arizona Cardinals flag on the other.

When I knocked, a dog barked twice, then stopped. I heard him sniffing around the door. A woman said, "Back, Curly, back."

She opened the door. Through the decorative security screen I saw the distorted image of a tall, slender women in her fifties and a brown labradoodle who stood nearly to her waist, his tongue hanging out in excitement for a visitor.

"May I help you?" the woman said.

"Mrs. Duran?"

"Yes?"

"I'm Margo Angelhart, a private investigator, hoping to ask your daughter some questions about a fellow student of hers who died of a drug overdose. She was in some of his classes, and I'm helping his mother fill in some blanks during his last week, to give her peace of mind." A mom would have empathy with Mrs. Martinez.

"A student died? That's awful. I heard the counselor was murdered yesterday, right on campus!"

"The student died two weekends ago. Is Danielle here?"

"Dani is babysitting until eight," she said.

"Can I ask you a few questions?"

"I don't know how I can help," she said. "Who died?"

"Elijah Martinez."

At first, nothing. Then recognition lit her eyes.

"Oh, I *have* met him. He didn't seem like a drug addict to me."

"It may have been an accident. That's why it's so important for me to retrace his last day. May I come in?"

I was banking on the fact that the house seemed to support law enforcement based on their public display. I was hoping she'd talk to me—and give me access to her daughter. If I walked away now, she might be more wary of me approaching her daughter.

I pulled out a business card and pressed it against the security screen. "It won't take long," I assured her.

"I don't know how I can help, but please come in." She unlocked the screen and opened it. "Curly is friendly," she said as the labradoodle immediately started sniffing my jeans.

I scratched the dog behind the ears, which he liked, and followed Mrs. Duran to the dining table, where she motioned for me to sit. She sat across from me. The dog plopped down next to her.

The house hadn't been remodeled like so many others had been in the neighborhood—including my parents'—but it was tidy with pictures of family everywhere, reminding me of my grandparents' home. The Durans had three kids, if I followed the progression of photos correctly, and Danielle was in the middle.

"One of my friends lived on this street when I was in high school. The Millers, where the street curves." I made a vague motion east.

She smiled. "John and Jackie, yes. They moved to Prescott two years ago when John retired. He and my husband manned the barbecue for our annual neighborhood party."

I grinned. Close-knit neighborhoods in Sunnyslope loved their street parties. I'd been to many.

"Shelley and I played softball together," I said to make Mrs. Duran comfortable. "I haven't seen her much since we graduated. I enlisted in the Army, and she went off to U of A, and I think stayed in Tucson."

"She did. Teaches high school down there. My oldest son is in the Marines, out of Camp Pendleton."

"That's where my little sister was stationed," I said. "I don't want to take too much of your time. Dani and Elijah were in Honors English last year, and according to my sources, Elijah reported your daughter for cheating. I don't want to bring up any bad feelings, but I know it was a bone of contention with your family, and I wanted to ask Dani if there were still hard feelings, or if she knew of anyone else Elijah had issues with."

Mrs. Duran blinked rapidly, surprised, then said, "Oh—*that* Elijah. Yes, I remember. At first I was angry at the teacher for believing anyone over my daughter, who has always been a straight-A student. It seemed unbelievable to me that she would cheat, but Dani admitted it. I had hoped the school would give her grace, but their rules are strict. It turned out to be a blessing in disguise."

"How so?" I asked.

"Dani has always pushed herself, and we didn't realize she was putting so much pressure on herself to get scholarships and good grades. She was having migraines and anxiety attacks, but keeping them from us because she thought they were signs of weakness. She panicked about the final and wrote the paper the night before, saved it to her watch."

"Another student indicated that Dani and Elijah had words afterward because she wasn't allowed into the Honors English class this year."

"I don't know about that, maybe . . . Dani was angry and embarrassed. But she doesn't hold a grudge. Since then, she's found balance in her life. Still has good grades, but isn't under the same pressure. She applied early acceptance to a small college in Colorado and was already admitted. I don't see why she would blame Elijah for being honest. And he died of drugs?"

I nodded. "We're still trying to learn the circumstances of his overdose."

"So tragic." Mrs. Duran shook her head, looked down at my card. "I'll have Dani call you when she gets home, if you'd like."

"That would be great, thank you. She might be able to give me additional insight."

I rose, and Mrs. Duran walked me to the door. She had been forthcoming, yet her daughter may not be as forgiving as her mother believes.

I drove north on the Black Mountain Highway to Desert Hills, a North Phoenix community known for horse properties nestled in a small valley between Anthem and Norterra.

Laura Monroe Barrett lived in a house owned by her brother Logan on five acres off a dead-end street north of West Joy Ranch Road. She'd lived there since her divorce, and I knew from my work with Logan that he'd bought the house for her, but she insisted on paying him a mortgage. Logan had told me once that he had enough money to help his sister so she didn't stress, especially since her ex-husband never had two coins to rub together—but Laura didn't want to take handouts from her brother. Which I understood.

Laura had horses, as well as three rescue dogs. The two Labs stood back from the gate as it opened, their tails wagging as they ran alongside my Jeep as I drove slowly down the driveway and parked behind Jack's truck. The Barretts also had a very old beagle who was probably sleeping, which is pretty much all I'd seen him do.

Laura's son Cody opened the door. "Hi, Margo! Jack said you're coming for dinner."

"And here I am," I said.

At the end of June Logan had hired Angelhart Investigations to protect his sister from an unknown threat and find her missing ex-husband. We'd gotten to know Laura and her kids, thirteen-year-old Sydney and ten-year-old Cody. I wish Austin were here; I missed my nephew and I loved seeing Jack and Austin with the Barrett family. They fit. While Jack had liberal visitation rights with his son—he could see Austin whenever he wanted—he could only have him two weekends a month unless Whitney agreed to more. Which was rare, unless *she* made plans.

"Where's Jack?" I asked the kid. Cody was on the short side for his age. He had dimples and he kept swiping his dark blond hair out of his eyes.

"He and Mom are on the patio. Sydney's taking care of the horses. Want to help?"

"Don't you remember what happened the last time I tried to help with the horses?"

Cody laughed. "You'll get the hang of it."

"Nope, horses and I don't mix." Jack however was a natural, which was another reason I was so happy that he and Laura had hit it off. Fate or divine intervention, I didn't know, but Jack deserved to be happy.

I went into the kitchen and helped myself to a beer—Jack had bought a six-pack of my favorite IPA, I noted. Heading out to the patio, I caught Jack and Laura mid-kiss.

"Want me to take over the grill so you two can have some alone time?" I asked with a grin.

Laura laughed lightly, and Jack frowned and gave me *that look* only a brother can give a sister. I wrinkled my nose at him and sipped my beer.

Laura said to Cody, "Tell Sydney dinner will be ready in thirty minutes. And help her with the horses like you promised, or I'll dock your allowance."

Cody ran off, the two Labs following. Bagel the beagle reclined on his outdoor dog bed.

"We never got an allowance," I said as I squatted to give the old dog a scratch behind the ears.

"It's a daily responsibility tending to the animals," Laura said, "and they both make sacrifices to do their chores. By the way, the kittens are fully weaned, and I'm spaying and neutering them at the end of the month, then they're ready to go to a good home."

When Jack and I were working to protect Laura and her irresponsible ex-husband, a stray cat made a home in the barn and gave birth to six kittens. Cody had declared that the cat was now his.

"I thought you were keeping the whole litter," I said.

"I told Cody he could keep two. It's always good to have cats around. But I'd love to find homes for the others."

"I've never had a cat," I said. We had a dog most of my childhood. We put Barney to sleep when I was fifteen and it was one of the worst memories of my youth. My parents never got another dog. Barney had been part of the family. I'd thought about getting a dog, but not with my current erratic schedule.

"They're great pets. There's one kitten who wouldn't do well being a barn cat—he's the runt of the litter."

"The gray one?" I asked, and wished I hadn't. Laura would take the inquiry as a sign of interest.

She smiled and nodded. "Think about it. He could go home with you tonight. He's still a little on the small side, so I might wait to neuter him. We like them to be at least two pounds. You can bring him back when he's ready."

"I don't need a cat," I said.

"You haven't said no," Jack pointed out with a sly smile.

"What about you? You taking one?"

"Nope. But I think Mom should have one. She had cats growing up—she'd like the company."

Pops and Abuela still had cats—four of them. At one point they had seven.

"You give it to her," I said. "You're the favorite."

Jack laughed. "I don't know about that. I think Lu wins that contest."

Jack was everyone's favorite, but I didn't harbor any ill will.

I sipped my beer and watched as my brother kept glancing over at Laura with a goofy half smile on his face, as if he couldn't believe she was his girlfriend. I liked that. I liked that my brother was happy, that he had found love a second time around when he had been so devastated by the collapse of his marriage.

Thirty minutes later, we were eating amazing barbecue steaks, homemade potato salad, and grilled zucchini. In my thirty-three years, I'd never had grilled zucchini before.

It was after eight when Laura told the kids to finish their homework and we all cleared the plates. I watched as Laura and Jack did the dishes together—the whispers and smiles and genuine affection.

Jack offered me another beer; I declined. Two was my limit. He brought me over a water bottle and we sat in the family room while Laura went out to the barn.

"You're happy," I said.

"I am."

"And everything went okay last night?"

He hesitated a fraction with a glance toward where Laura had gone.

"What?" I pushed.

"It was fine. It didn't start fine, but by the end of the evening, we had an understanding." He paused. "I said things I wish I hadn't, but they got through."

"You mean, you told the truth and felt bad."

"I don't like hurting anyone, even with words. But they had to be said. A reminder of everything I did to save our marriage. I don't think she realized every step I took to prevent what ultimately happened. But there is no going back."

If I had been drinking, I would have spit out my beer. "What? She wants to get back together?"

"God, no. I think—" He paused, assessed what he wanted to say and how he wanted to say it. "I'm not a shrink, but I think Whitney liked having me on-call. She liked knowing I would always come—and I still will. She will always be Austin's mother. But I saw last night—I saw it before, but I knew in my heart last night—that she never wanted to be married to me. I should have seen it fifteen years ago when I first proposed. But we can't go back, and we have Austin. He alone is worth everything."

"Amen," I said and toasted with my water bottle.

Jack was going to be fine.

"Changing subjects because I should be going home soon," I said, "but do you think you can get me a one-on-one with Mike Hitchner?"

His mouth dropped open. "From DEB?"

"Yep. He was lead in the Bradford investigation and I have some questions."

"He's a commander now. I don't know that he would have the time or desire to talk to a PI. Why?"

"I can't find any connection between the drug bust three years ago and what happened these last two weeks with Elijah's overdose and Lena's murder, but I think it would help if I better understood how the Bradford operation ran."

"As in, if it happened once, maybe someone else is running it?"

"Something like that."

"I don't think you can assume that these events are connected. Drugs are a parasite; they're everywhere."

I didn't know how to explain to Jack that little tickle in the back of my mind that told me there was something more here than meets the eye. "It's . . . a triangle," I said lamely.

Jack's lips twitched. "A triangle."

"Yeah, Elijah and Lena are connected through Sun Valley—time and place. They're now both dead—killed less than two weeks apart."

"Whoa—there is no evidence that Elijah was murdered."

"Okay, maybe not *killed*, but Detective King didn't conduct a thorough investigation. She took the autopsy report as the *only* evidence, and there are a lot of unanswered questions. Did you read the police reports?"

"I skimmed them."

"Did you notice that his backpack and phone weren't recovered?"

Jack shook his head and asked, "What did they conclude?"

"They deduced that the phone was in the backpack and someone took it after Elijah passed out or died in the park."

"Logical."

"It's a guess, based on no actual evidence. They haven't found it, and if someone did, no one connected it to Elijah? I don't buy it. I think they dismissed possible evidence of foul play because it doesn't fit with the accidental overdose assumption.

"Now, my triangle theory—Lena Clark has been at Sun Valley for more than five years. She was there when Bradford was dealing drugs, a crime he got away with for apparently years. Hitchner's report is very detailed, and they shut down the operation, but the only two people who went to prison were Bradford and his wife and one student to juvie. I couldn't find any documents about how it started, when it started. Maybe the info will be in the court records Tess is going through. Did he use other kids, kids who graduated before the sting? Plus, no one knows who his supplier was. Neither he nor his wife would talk."

"You think someone picked up where Bradford left off."

"It's an idea that's rattling around in my head. The other point of the triangle is that Lena and Bradford worked at the school at the same time. I could be way off, but Hitchner might have more info there. Was Lena involved in the arrest at all? Did she give a statement? Were there any grudges? Other players who weren't caught up in the sting?"

"Triangles have three points."

"I haven't connected Elijah to Bradford, but Elijah was a freshman when Bradford was arrested—yes, a small insignificant connection. He could have known someone who was involved. If I'm wrong, I can close it off and focus on something else, like Elijah's workplace or his friends. I've talked to one, reached out to the others, but so far I'm ending up dry. No one knows where Elijah was after he left work until he ended up dead in the park. Five hours unaccounted for."

Jack didn't say anything, and I worried that I was way off base. I didn't know how to put all these pieces together. Some were solid, but some depended on me fully believing Elijah's shiny reputation, a kid I had never met.

And there were far too many things I didn't know.

"I'll reach out to Hitchner tomorrow morning, but no promises," Jack finally said. "I didn't know him well when I was on the job, don't have any favors I can call in."

"That's all I can ask. Thanks."

When I left Laura's house thirty minutes later, my rearview mirror framed Jack and Laura standing on the wide porch, his arm around her waist. I had an overwhelming sense of longing that I couldn't explain.

Rick only lived a few minutes away, two exits up the freeway. But he worked swing shift and was probably still at work; even if he wasn't, could I just stop by his house and pick up where we left off?

He'd given me no sign that he wanted to rekindle our relationship. Inviting me to Sam's game? Maybe it was an olive branch. Yet, he didn't think he'd done anything wrong when he lectured me about how to handle Sam. And even *if* I thought he was right—and he was, to a point, since Sam was his daughter—it hurt.

Because I wanted Sam to be *my* daughter too. And Rick didn't trust me.

I headed home. Still torn, still unsure where I stood in Rick's life. And that was a feeling I didn't want.

chapter twenty-one

MARGO ANGELHART

Wednesday morning I woke up before dawn and found two text messages on my phone.

Danielle Duran texted at 11:03 p.m.: **My mom told me to call you about Elijah. I don't really have anything to say, but tomorrow's late start and I have first free, so you can call before 9:45.**

I wanted to assess her in person. It was much easier to lie over the phone, and impossible for me to read body language.

The second text came from Elijah's friend Andy: **We have late start Wednesday. 8 okay?**

I assumed by *we* Andy meant him and Peter. I had left both of them messages yesterday.

How was I going to fit in all of these interviews and get to Eyman Prison before noon? I didn't want to put them off as they might have information. I was mostly fishing with Bradford as I had nothing solid to connect him to anything that had recently happened on campus, but since I put myself on the list to visit my dad, I didn't want to disappoint him and not show up.

To Andy, I responded that I would meet them at Black Rock Coffee on Seventh Avenue at 7:30 a.m. Black Rock was far enough from the school that we shouldn't see anyone they might know, but close enough that I wouldn't feel guilty making them walk if they didn't have a car. To Danielle I said I could meet her anywhere near the school or her house around 8:30 a.m. That should leave me plenty of time to get down to Eyman.

After showering, eating a piece of toast, and a slightly overripe banana, I jumped into my Jeep. Luisa called before I had backed down the driveway.

"I'm on my way to class," she said, "but I got into Elijah's computer last night, removed his password protections, and left it on your desk. Sorry it took so long."

"Long? You had it for a day."

"It actually only took me thirty minutes," Luisa said. "I just couldn't get to it until last night."

Damn, how did the bulk of the Angelhart brains end up in the youngest kid? "Thanks. Did you see anything wonky?"

"Nothing specific, but I downloaded his search history for you. Good news, bad news there—his history is auto-wiped every fourteen days, so there's only three days available."

"What, you can't undelete his old history?" I teased.

"Well, yes, *I* can, but it'll take more time."

"I'm kidding! I'll go through it, see if anything pops."

"He has a cloud account, which you should be able to access simply by being on his computer. I didn't have time to see what he had saved up there."

"Seriously, you're amazing."

"If you need me, call. I can come by this afternoon."

All the praise seemed to roll off her. Did she not know she was amazing? Or did she know and was tired of hearing it?

Who got tired of hearing how brilliant they were?

"Thanks, Lu," I said. "I'll let you know what I find."

I was grinning when I hung up. Computers were not my superpower. I could navigate around a desktop and cyberspace, and I never wanted to throw my smartphone against the wall, but that was the extent of my skills. My little sister? Absolutely incredible.

Black Rock catered to the drive-through coffee crowd, and was my usual go-to for iced coffee when I was in a hurry. Today I parked and went inside. Not a lot of seating, but I got my coffee and sat at a tiny table with three chairs, eyes on the door.

They were a few minutes late and easy to identify. One was tall, gangly with long limbs and shaggy blond hair. The other was not much taller than me, with short dark hair and glasses.

They looked at me, then at each other, and I said, "Andy?"

The short kid nodded. I knew only a little about each kid from Tess's review of their social media. Andy had three sisters and a large extended family they traveled around the state to visit regularly; his dad had been in the military and now worked security for a convention center. Peter had little on his social media but appeared to have an older brother, and his dad didn't seem to be in the picture.

I started to get up. "Go get something to eat, I got you."

"No, that's okay," Andy said. He glanced at Peter and they silently communicated, then sat down across from me.

"Angie called last night," Andy said. "She said you were hired by Elijah's mom."

"Correct," I said.

"So, um, what do you want to know?"

They looked stiff and awkward, so I gave them each my business card and asked them to tell me how they knew Elijah. Andy did most of the talking, explaining that he and Elijah had known each other since first grade and their moms were sort of friends from church. They met Peter when they were freshmen because they were in PE together and none of them were athletic. Peter began his internship right after school started this fall, and Andy worked for his mom on the weekends; she had her own housecleaning business. But the three of them usually hung out together when they were free. Recently Elijah started bailing on them, saying he was working extra hours.

"Except," Andy said, then stopped as if wondering if he should keep talking.

"Except what?" I pushed.

They glanced at each other, and then Andy said, "So Elijah *said* he was working extra hours, but we went by there, like, a week before he died and he wasn't working, even though he said he would be."

That was interesting.

"Did you ask him about it?"

"Yeah, and he said he left early to help his mom, but it was a lie."

"He's not a good liar," Peter said. He tapped Andy and said "Tell her about your mom."

"Well, he talked to my mom a couple weeks before he died."

"About?"

"Working for her. She said yes. She couldn't promise how many hours, but he said anything would help, that he was going to be quitting his job."

That was also news. "Do you know if he *actually* quit?"

They shrugged in unison, and Andy said, "He just said he was *going* to quit."

"Did he say why?"

They shook their heads, then Peter added, "Everyone wants a job at the Cactus Stop. Hatcher is closest to the school, but they hire high school students at all the Stops. It's really hard to get a job when you're under eighteen, unless you know someone. That's why I'm doing the school-to-work program at the corporate office. I'll have a good job right when I graduate."

It was a good program for kids who didn't want to go to college. I asked Andy, "When did he talk to your mom about working for her?" I asked.

"Labor Day weekend," he said confidently. "It was my little sister's birthday and he came to the party."

I did the math. That would have been less than two weeks before he died.

"Did we help?" Andy asked hopefully.

"It all helps," I said, but I wasn't quite sure how it fit. If Elijah was having problems at work and wanted to quit, that steered me toward his work being the source of potential trouble, not school. "Have you ever done drugs with Elijah? Or saw him use? I'm not going to jam you up, but it's important that I have the truth."

"He wouldn't," Andy said. "He's never even smoked pot. I've known him practically my entire life."

I glanced at Peter. "You agree?"

He shrugged. "I never saw him do anything like that. But he was being all, um, well, secretive the last few weeks."

Which confirmed what Angie said. "One more question. Elijah's backpack and cell phone are missing. Have you seen them? Did he give you anything for safekeeping?"

They both shook their heads.

"If either of you remembers anything that he said or did that seemed out of character, or if you hear anything, call me, okay?"

They both nodded.

"Do you want a ride to school?" I asked.

"I have a car," Peter said. They walked out and I looked down at my phone. Danielle had responded to my message.

> My mom leaves for work at 8. Come anytime between then and 930.

At 8:20 a.m., I arrived at the Duran house. Only the Honda was in the carport.

Danielle opened the door before I knocked.

"Danielle Duran?" I asked.

"Dani," she said. She glanced around the street as she let me in.

"Why are you nervous?" I asked.

"I'm not," she said unconvincingly. "My mom was running late, and half the time she forgets something and comes back."

"You don't want your mom to be part of this conversation," I guessed.

"I don't care, but sometimes she gets mama bear protective when I don't need it."

"I can relate," I said.

Instead of the dining table, Dani plopped down on the couch. I sat in the chair across from her. "What do you want to know?" Dani said.

I got straight to the point. "Elijah Martinez turned you in for cheating. You got in trouble, and according to your mother, you don't hold a grudge. Is that true?"

"It is now."

When she didn't elaborate, I said, "Then?"

"I was furious. At Elijah for being a snitch, at myself for being so stupid, at Mrs. Porter for hating me. I mean, I was wrong, I fully take responsibility for my actions. No one *made* me cheat. But Mrs. Porter hated me for no reason, it was so obvious. I mean, I'm sure she had a reason, but whatever it was didn't justify her always marking me down, nit-picking everything, never calling on me in class, being dismissive when I asked questions. I love English. I *love* writing. I wanted to impress the teacher who hated me, and I worked myself up to the point that I had such anxiety about the class that I convinced myself the only option was to cheat."

I was impressed that this seventeen-year-old had such keen insight into her own psyche.

"The day after the final, you had a public argument with Elijah."

"I took everything out on him. But really, he was just the messenger, you know? My parents went to bat for me, and then . . . that's when I just fell apart. I couldn't let them believe the lie. I admitted it, asked for forgiveness, got a zero. That sucked. But this summer I took a couple classes at community college and they were *so* much better than Mrs. Porter's English." Dani looked me in the eye. "Are you here because you think Elijah did drugs because I was mean to him?" She wrinkled her nose. "That would be dumb."

"I'm talking to people who knew him to find out exactly what was going on with him before he died."

"Elijah and I were cool. We were never friends or anything, but we were friendly. And I didn't blame him. He is—was—a pretty straight arrow, and I wasn't being all that discreet when I cheated."

"When was the last time you talked to him?"

She considered. "First week of school? Maybe even the first day. We have Honors Government together with Mr. Parsons. I said hey, he said how was summer, I said I took classes at PV. He said he'd talk to me later about it, because he was thinking of taking some classes at night, but didn't want to be overwhelmed. We never ended up talking about it, though."

"Did he mention the class he took over the summer?" I asked, remembering what Alina had told me about working and school over the summer.

"At PV?"

"I don't know."

"He didn't say anything to me."

"What do you know about his friends? Peter and Andy and Angie."

"I don't really know Peter, Andy is kind of a dork—I mean, nice guy, and we were partners in science our sophomore year, so I say hi and stuff, but—" she shrugged "—we didn't have much in common."

"And Angie?"

"Kind of a bitch. I know, not a nice thing to say, but truth."

"How so?"

"Chip on her shoulder. Always assumes anything you say is an insult. I know she was close to Elijah, and I knew her boyfriend, Chris—"

"Chris . . . ?" I questioned.

"Chris Vallejo. He graduated, goes to ASU. Lives in the neighborhood, so I've known him for years. Don't know what he saw in Angie, but they were pretty tight for, like, two years. Maybe they're still dating, I don't know."

I considered Dani's impression of Angie, as well as my own. Yeah, I could see how Angie might come off as being a bitch. Her default reaction to everything was defensive. But I knew about her home life, thanks to Lena Clark, and I'd met her mother's pot-smoking boyfriend. Those weren't things a teenager would share with just anyone. I saw Angie as doing what she needed to do to make it to adulthood, then I expected her to bolt. I hoped she bolted to college or the military, both viable options for kids who didn't have a good home life.

I said, "Did you know Elijah outside of school?"

She shook her head.

"Did you ever run into him at parties?"

She laughed. "I definitely would *not* have. My dad is a cop. He would skin me alive if I went out and partied. It's really not my thing, anyway."

"Is there anyone else Elijah socialized with? Maybe someone who did party?"

"I wouldn't know. Andy was his best friend, so if Elijah was doing drugs or drinking, Andy would know."

"Did he have a girlfriend?"

"No—but—" She stopped, considered. "I don't know," she said after a moment, "but right before finals, a girl picked him up in front of the school. I barely caught a glimpse of her, just enough to know that she was probably in college. At least nineteen, maybe twenty."

That was the first I heard about a college-aged girlfriend.

"Do you remember her car? If you saw her again?"

"I never saw her again, or if I did, I didn't make the connection. And cars? It was a car. Not new, not a truck, but that's all I can tell you. The only reason I remembered it is because you asked."

I asked about Lena Clark and Dani had nothing to add. She knew her, but hadn't worked with the guidance counselor because her mom was hands-on. I asked about Mr. Parsons, and confirmed that most of the students knew they were dating. I asked about who on campus dealt drugs, and she just shook her head. "If I knew, I'd tell my dad. People don't tell me things, they think I'm a Goody Two-shoes or something. I think that's why the cheating was a big eye-opener for me and my parents. I've never done anything like it before, and I'll always regret it."

She walked me to the door, and at the last moment, I said, "Would you mind giving me Chris Vallejo's phone number?" I could have Tess get it for me, but she was already working on the court records.

She shrugged, pulled out her phone. "Chris is a good guy. Really smart. Maybe that's why he liked Angie. *I* think she's a bitch, but she's a smart bitch."

I thanked her and drove off.

I had time to stop by the office before heading to the prison. I just wanted to check out Elijah's computer now that Lu had broken the passcode. Chris Vallejo's phone went straight to voicemail; I left him a brief message with my number as I walked into the office.

Iris was there and I asked, "Mom and Jack aren't in yet?" They'd met Logan Monroe for a late breakfast.

She shook her head. "Ava will be here by ten."

Good to know. I wanted to be gone before she arrived so I didn't have to fib about my plans for the day. If Mom or Jack knew I planned to visit Dad, they might want to join me. Jack and I often drove down together, but I didn't want Jack with me while I was chatting with Ben Bradford. He looked and acted too much like a cop. I figured if I could learn anything from Bradford, it would be because I *wasn't* a cop.

Luisa had left Elijah's laptop on my desk with a note explaining how to access his browsing history, what email program he used, the user names for his accounts, including social media, and the last time he accessed the computer—Friday morning before he went to school.

"Thanks, Lu," I mumbled with a smile and got to work with one eye on the clock.

Most of Elijah's emails were to and from teachers about assignments, from his mom who sent him a daily inspirational poem or

Bible verse, and a few from other family members. This was par for the course for this generation—they didn't communicate as much by email as they did by text. There were no emails from his three closest friends, except Andy had forwarded a birthday invitation his mother had sent out for his sister Labor Day weekend.

He had taken an online community college class over the summer and there was a chunk of emails, mostly automated, from the class.

Online class? Hadn't his mother said he went to a *night class* after work? Was she mistaken?

Maybe I misunderstood what she said. I would double-check.

Then I thought back to Angie's surprise that Elijah had taken a course, and his question to Dani about the classes she had taken. It made more sense that his mother assumed an in-person class . . . Maybe Elijah spent those evenings at the library.

Every two weeks Elijah received an automated email from an accountant that, upon further research, was the firm hired to process the Cactus Stop payroll. He had filed all of those, along with any other financial information such as his monthly bank statement, into a special folder called Tax Info.

I looked at his sent messages and most of them were about school, college, and a few general inquiries that didn't seem to have anything to do with his work or school.

I skimmed the three days of browser history that Luisa had archived for me. She'd saved it by link and the time and date the site had been accessed.

He accessed Sun Valley High's web portal daily—where he submitted homework and accessed documents related to his classes. He'd visited social media sites mostly in the evening, and Google Maps on Thursday night where he looked up an address in Paradise Valley. I wrote it down and would drive by later. He'd gone to the Cactus Stop corporate page also on Thursday, which had a login for employees where I assumed he could access pay stubs, withholding information, benefits, and the like.

One of the extensions on the Cactus Stop page was *contact*. The night before Elijah died, he'd gone to the contact page. Had he looked up information? A phone number or address? Had he submitted a web form? If so, whatever he'd written hadn't been copied to his email. Could it have been anonymous?

I made a note to follow up and also ask Luisa if she could find the information somewhere on Elijah's hard drive.

Then something jumped out at me.

Elijah had gone to the Phoenix PD Silent Witness information page twice—on Tuesday and Thursday evenings. He'd googled the site on Tuesday, clicked through a bunch of Phoenix PD pages, but Silent Witness was the last one he went to. Then on Thursday he went right to that page.

Had he reached out and called?

I made another note. Rick or Josie would know who was responsible for monitoring the Silent Witness program website and phone.

I couldn't help but think about the Bradford case. The Silent Witness program wouldn't release any recordings without a court order, but there *was* a public recording about Ben Bradford because it came through the 911 system or directly to Phoenix PD.

Had Elijah reported a crime through Silent Witness? Did it have anything to do with his job . . . or something he witnessed at school? If he had used the Silent Witness program, not even Rick could access the information without jumping through hoops, and then he'd only receive non-identifying details.

I considered the original Bradford call. The investigators at the time said they suspected it came from a softball player because Bradford coached softball as well as football. The call came in September, which would suggest that the student had been there both the spring before—during softball season—and the current year. That would make her at least a sophomore when she phoned in, and based on her voice, I couldn't imagine she was much older.

I doubted I'd learn much, but it wouldn't hurt to grab the yearbook for those two years. Elijah would have one; I wanted both.

I texted Angie.

> Can you get me two yearbooks? Your freshman year and the year before that?

She didn't answer immediately, but she was likely in class. *Hopefully* in class.

I then looked through Elijah's photos on his cloud account. There were thousands.

The settings indicated that his phone uploaded photos to the cloud, and I sorted them by most recent first.

Immediately, I saw something very weird. There were no pictures from Friday, the day he died, but there were several pictures that week of people exiting the Cactus Shop at night. I looked at the times, and they all had been taken after 8:00 p.m. on Tuesday, Wednesday, and Thursday. I needed to go back to the store to figure out where he had been standing when he took the pictures. There were dozens of photos, but I didn't recognize anyone. The youngest person looked fourteen, the oldest sixty. Men and women, all ethnicities. Almost all solo. Many of the people were repeat customers—one attractive, clean-cut Hispanic male in his mid-twenties was at the store at least twice a week. Over the six weeks Elijah had been taking these photos, starting the second week of July, there were nineteen pictures of this same person.

No one he photographed left the store with bags. It was something I noted on Tuesday when I stopped by, but I hadn't really thought much about it after talking to Rick.

The Friday a week before Elijah died, he took a photo of a license plate and the Tesla it was attached to.

Some of the pictures were taken outside a different Cactus Stop. I looked at geolocation—he hadn't turned it off—and they were taken at the store off Nineteenth and Camelback, the same store that had been involved in my first big PI investigation eight years ago.

Before July, there were only pictures of friends and family. Hundreds of pictures from what appeared to be a family reunion, then end-of-school-year pictures, the occasional screenshot of something he felt was important to save—confirmation of submitting college applications, a confirmation of a payment made, things like that.

When he was a junior, most of his photos were selfies. I didn't recognize most of the kids but there were several with Elijah, Angie, and a tall boy I didn't recognize but—based on his arm over Angie's shoulder—suspected was Chris Vallejo. These were taken outside a movie theater, on campus, in the stands of the gym. A couple videos of a girl with a wicked volleyball serve, possibly Angie's friend Gina. Dozens of Elijah with Andy and Peter. Pictures of Elijah and his mom, or just his mom while she cooked or was reading or on her birthday when she blew out a candle.

Alina Martinez would want these. But first, I would find out what happened to her son.

My cell phone rang. I grabbed it.

"Hello."

"It's Rick. Jessica Oliver is the lead on financial crimes, said she'd be willing to meet after shift today."

"Great, where? When?"

"She can be at Flannigan's between 4:45 and 5:00?"

"I'll be there." I had been a bartender at Flannigan's nine years ago while working to get my PI business off the ground; it was convenient for cops who lived north of downtown because it was on the way to all major freeways. "Give her my number if she needs to cancel. You going to be there?"

"Working," he said. "Let me know how it goes."

"Thanks, Rick."

I looked at my watch. I was now running late, but if I left in the next fifteen minutes I'd be at the prison before 11:30 a.m. I wanted to know who owned that Tesla. It was the only vehicle Elijah had photographed, which told me it was important.

I called my friend Harry Jorgenson. Harry was sixty and the definition of a crotchety old man. He reminded me of Mr. Wilson in the old comic strips—or in the movie played by Walter Matthau.

Harry worked at a Motor Vehicles Department annex. There were dozens of semi-private MVD's where drivers could get their license, change title, and register their vehicle, among other things. They charged more for convenience and speed, because getting an appointment in the MVD took forever, and there were always lines. I'd met Harry shortly after I separated from the Army while in line at the VA. He had given thirty years to the Army. Over the years he had helped me with some sensitive situations. Like me, Harry was willing to bend—or break—the law if it helped someone in dire need.

He didn't answer. I could ask Rick or Josie, but Phoenix PD tracked everything done on their computers, and if there ended up being a criminal investigation, it could jeopardize the case. Better to go through the back door.

I left Harry a message. "Hey, it's Margo. Call me."

As I walked out of the office five minutes later, my phone buzzed. I hoped it was Harry; it wasn't. Angie had responded to my text.

k

Such was communication with teenagers.

chapter twenty-two

MARGO ANGELHART

My dad was one of the best people I knew.

And he was in prison for murder.

I knew he was innocent, but it was an off-limit subject. He had confessed. He'd told me he was willing to serve "his time."

Yes, he confessed. But he never once told me why he confessed to a crime he didn't commit, or even given me a *reason* why he'd killed Dr. Devin Klein.

It had been nearly impossible to put it all aside. Okay, I hadn't really put it aside. I had looked for information, clues, evidence of my dad's innocence. But every time I thought I was close—like when I talked to Klein's research assistant earlier this year, a woman who took more than a year to track down—I had more questions than answers.

And dad wouldn't answer my questions.

So the choice was to never visit and turn my back on the man who loved and raised me—which would have hurt both of us—or see him and not talk about Klein. I opted for the latter.

There would be a time I would come here with some of the

answers I sought, and I would ask him for the truth. But until then, I had tabled the subject.

Eyman was a medium-security prison and had regular visiting hours, so there were other people meeting friends and family in the visitor's center, but being Wednesday morning, there weren't many. I generally avoided crowded weekend visits.

We hugged—touching wasn't allowed, but the guards generally didn't comment if the moment was brief—then sat across from each other at one of the many stainless steel tables. There was a small outdoor play area through barred windows for families with young kids. A man sat with a woman, side by side on a bench, watching a little boy play. They weren't talking, but I could see the bittersweet happiness in their expressions.

Dad saw where I was looking. "That's Tim. He's a good man, in here for attempted murder. Pled it down to aggravated assault to get five years. His son is four and he's halfway through his time. I often see him in the chapel. He'll make it, I think. He talks about his wife a lot, and she's stuck by him."

Too often felons who were incarcerated for years couldn't function on the outside. Many were repeat offenders who didn't care to even try. Prison became a revolving door. And some tried, but got dragged back into the bad decisions that landed them behind bars in the first place.

But some did their time and moved on—and having a supportive family was the number one factor in them turning a new leaf.

"That's good," I said, though I wasn't really paying attention.

"What's on your mind, Margo?" he asked.

"What, I can't just spontaneously come to visit?"

"You can, but you don't. It's a long drive."

I could lie to everyone except my parents.

Dad waited for me to talk. He didn't ask questions to try and get information, and he didn't push or act irritated or annoyed. He looked content. Neither happy nor sad. He'd been inside for three years and promised all of us he would stay healthy—he worked out as much as he could, walked around the yard daily, and read to keep his mind sharp. A few months ago when I visited, he told me he was tutoring some of the younger men who wanted to get their GED. He said it was fulfilling to help them.

"I was told you were on the list next week."

I smiled. "Caught me. I asked to come today because there's another prisoner I want to talk to and I didn't want to come here without seeing you too."

"I don't think I would have known either way."

"*I* would have known."

I looked at him—really looked. Dad was tall, over six one. He gave his height to Jack and Tess. He had dark blond hair that had gone mostly gray, but it looked good on him, mostly white instead of silver, distinguished. He hadn't lost much, if any, a fact that seemed to relieve my brothers. He had never had a beard or mustache, and remained clean-shaven while in prison as well. His blue eyes were clear and bright. He seemed as well as anyone could be while behind bars.

But I missed him. I missed stopping by the house and talking to him about whatever was on my mind. Laughing over dinner, rewatching our favorite movies, relaxing on the porch in the evening.

"Why are you sad?" he asked.

Because you're in here, I thought.

I said, "The same reason."

He didn't comment.

Then I changed the subject. We talked about family and what Tess had planned for mom's birthday tomorrow. Dad told me he asked Aunt Rita to pick up a specific gift from him, but didn't tell me what it was. Then I told him about my case and why I wanted to talk to Ben Bradford.

My dad had always had a good poker face, but I could tell he didn't agree with my plan.

"Tell me what you're thinking," I said.

"People make decisions—big and small—for a multitude of reasons. Why do you think this man will share information with you when he chose not to share it with the police when it may have helped him reduce his sentence?"

"Fear," I said.

Dad was right. I'd already considered that Bradford wouldn't tell me anything of value, but I was good at reading between the lines.

"I don't have any reason to believe that Elijah was or is connected to Bradford's drug operation," I said. "I want to understand how it worked, because then maybe I can make sense of what information I do have."

"Do you think that this kid was involved in dealing drugs?"

I shook my head. "I think he may have stumbled on a crime and was unsure what to do with the information he had." I told him what I found on Elijah's computer. "I think Elijah was suspicious of someone he worked with. There were photos of people coming out of the store, and there's no reason I can think about why he would take those pictures, except that he was looking for someone or watching someone. And none of that may have anything to do with how and why he died."

Dad looked me in the eye. "Why don't you turn the information over to the police?"

"Because they closed the case. They're not going to reopen based on my gut telling me something weird is going on. Elijah's mom deserves to know if her son was killed, if he died trying to do the right thing."

Dad slowly nodded. "I understand why you care, Margo. But put yourself in Bradford's shoes. Consider his motivation for remaining silent, and what you can offer that would make him want to share anything."

"I'm not going to rat him out."

"How does he know that?"

Okay, good point. I didn't have an answer.

"He's a father," Dad continued. "Fathers will do anything to protect their family."

The sentence hung in the air between us, and I knew he was

talking about more than Ben Bradford. I held my breath, willing my dad to say more.

He didn't. "Be careful," he finally said. "Both with Bradford and in your investigation. Drugs destroy everyone they touch—addicts, their friends and family, society as a whole. And people dealing them don't respect or revere life. If they see you as an obstacle, your life will be in danger."

"I'll be careful, Dad. I promise."

Dad left and ten minutes later Ben Bradford walked into the visitors' room. He looked around, clearly uncertain about the unknown visitor he was called to meet.

I raised my hand. I'd done my research and knew what he looked like.

Like my dad, Bradford had lost weight while in prison, but still looked fit. He'd been overweight but muscular as a football coach; now he was lean and muscular. Though younger than my dad, he'd lost most of his hair and his eyes were tired and wary.

Cautious, he approached.

"You're not a reporter, are you?"

"No."

Still skeptical, he stood and looked me over.

"My name is Margo Angelhart. I'm a private investigator and just want a conversation, you and me. No strings."

Slowly, he sat across from me, keeping his eyes on mine. Skittish, as if he would bolt if I said *boo*. Odd, for a man who appeared as if he could defend himself.

I'd been thinking about what my dad said, that Bradford had no reason to talk to me about anything. Certainly it wouldn't be the first time I'd made a mistake, or went down an investigatory road that ended in a brick wall.

But I was here, and I had to try. Because Lena Clark's death nagged at me almost as much as Elijah's—and Bradford must have known her. I decided to focus on Bradford's connection to the school, with my goal to have him explain how his drug operation worked. If I understood, maybe I could find a parallel in Elijah's life—or Lena's circumstances.

"Do you remember Lena Clark? She was the guidance counselor at Sun Valley."

He nodded once. "So?"

"She was killed in her office on Monday."

"What does that have to do with me? I knew her to say *hi*. We weren't friends."

"Lena was helping me find out what happened to a student who died of a drug overdose under suspicious circumstances."

"I don't care."

But he didn't walk away or ask the guard to be taken back to his cell or the yard. He stared at me, and that gave me hope that maybe I could get something from him.

"I'm trying to understand how your operation worked. Because an honors student with no history of drug use died of a drug overdose, then his guidance counselor was killed not two weeks later."

"Not my problem," he said with a quick glance at the guard.

"Did the kids you used know what they were doing, or were they ignorant, just following coach's orders? From my understanding, only one student knew that you were in charge, but I think we both know that secrets in an operation as large as yours have a way of getting out."

"I don't have to talk to you," Bradford said, sounding angry. "Anything going on at SVH has nothing to do with me, not anymore."

"A woman was murdered on campus, and the only thing she was doing that might put her in danger was asking questions about a student's death. So I started thinking . . . Elijah died of a drug overdose. There had once been a very extensive and long-running drug operation at SVH. The police believed you had a partner—your supplier you didn't turn on."

He laughed.

"Or," I continued, "maybe another teacher took over for you."

That was my sticking point. Sun Valley had had an extensive drug operation going on for years. What if it had just gone dormant?

Angie didn't kill Lena, and unless the police tied her boyfriend Parsons to the crime, someone else found out she was asking questions and, maybe, they feared she would uncover another illegal operation. Maybe I really was grasping at straws, but why else would Lena be killed in her office? It was extremely risky, even though it was after-hours. People were still on campus. It was risky, violent, and spontaneous.

Bradford sat stone-faced.

I continued, remembering what Tess had learned. "You had Eric McMahon recruit dozens of students to help sell drugs for you. You, or your partner, found out he was turning state's evidence and tried to have him killed. When that failed, everything came tumbling down. Maybe you don't believe in redemption. I do. You just have to ask for it."

"I don't need or want anything from *you*," he said, his voice low and angry.

"Whoever you're protecting is laughing all the way to the bank," I said. "They're free and you're in here, your wife is in prison, your kids don't have their parents. You won't be out of prison before your youngest graduates. For what? Because it could just as easily have been one of your kids who ended up dead of a drug overdose."

Bradford got up, slammed his fist on the table, and walked toward the guarded door.

Okay, I went too far. I shouldn't have mentioned his kids.

I sat at the table and watched him leave, thinking.

His anger could just be that—anger at the fact that he's in prison. Or he could be angry because he did have a partner and I reminded him that his partner is free and happily continuing their operation.

But it wouldn't be done in the same way. Because the police had that figured out . . . The school administrators would know what to look for.

Sun Valley High School had over two thousand students. Hundreds of teachers and staff and coaches. Same operation . . . but different?

I may have jumped the gun with Bradford. Bradford never gave up his supplier. He claimed *he* was the supplier, that *he* brought in the drugs from Mexico and distributed them through his network of kids. The police hadn't believed him, but he hadn't budged.

If the police were right, who was his partner? Someone on campus? Were his regular trips to Yuma important or a smoke screen? Would his partner recruit a new Ben Bradford to run his operation, run it himself?

If it *was* on campus, that might be motive to kill Lena Clark if she suspected something. What if Elijah told someone he trusted about his suspicions? Someone who then betrayed him?

Where did the Cactus Stop photos fit in?

Too many what-ifs and half-assed theories. I needed more information, and that meant talking to as many people as possible. Shake the hornet's nest. But unlike Lena Clark, I knew what I was doing was dangerous.

Something was here, just outside my grasp. I had to figure it out before someone else died.

chapter twenty-three

CAL RAFFERTY

DEA Agent Cal Rafferty sorted through the files on his desk and pulled out the one he needed.

He hated paperwork. Most cops did. But Cal liked to think that he detested that part of the job more than anyone.

He turned to his computer and painstakingly input the information from his last interview with a potential witness to a midlevel drug trafficking ring. It wasn't even his case—he was assisting his colleagues in the field by following up on the information they learned. He loved his job in the DEA; he hated the bureaucracy.

Cal itched to be out in the field, but he'd recently finished a major undercover operation with the ASU Police Department and helped take down an Ecstasy manufacturing ring running out of a Chemistry lab. It was a majorly satisfying bust. But George Franks, his boss, had strict rules about spacing undercover assignments. He'd been at ASU for four months, so he had a month of what his boss called "office time." It wasn't that he wasn't working—there was plenty to do. Fielding calls. Consulting with local police. Tracking tips. Following up on interviews. Reviewing cold cases and online chatter. But most of their cases were built over time, and there was no greater satisfaction than having a righteous bust after months of tightening the noose.

There was nothing Cal wanted to do more in his life than stop the scourge of drugs, especially fentanyl. The surge in the use of this deadly drug was faster than anything he or his colleagues had ever witnessed.

He had professional reasons for wanting it off the street, of course. He had personal reasons as well.

Cal's cell phone rang.

"Rafferty," he answered.

"Cal, this is Officer Dave Blair down at Eyman."

"Dave, yeah, how're you doing?"

"Good, thanks. One of your prisoners had a visitor today."

He straightened. He had a guard at every prison where he'd flagged a criminal. Cal didn't flag everyone he'd put away—he'd be getting calls all day and night—but there were a few felons Cal knew who hadn't forked over information in an ongoing case. He had two of them at Eyman.

"Who?" Cal asked.

"Bradford."

That surprised him. Bradford had been arrested nearly three years ago and sentenced after his subsequent plea agreement. Cal could count on one hand the people who visited him—Bradford's parents brought his kids every few months, his brother visited monthly, and a couple friends, who Cal had vetted, visited periodically, until last year. It felt as if everyone who knew him back when he was a popular coach had abandoned him.

Serves him right, Cal thought. He'd exploited teens, ruined lives, and showed no remorse.

His wife was just as bad. Cal wished she'd been put away longer than the six years she'd got in her plea deal. Cecilia Bradford had lied during the investigation and interviews. Cal had no patience for her, and though he objected to the plea, the AUSA went ahead with it.

"Ben Bradford," Cal said with a whistle. "Who visited?"

"A private investigator, Margo Angelhart. Her father is incarcerated here and she visits regularly. She has an in with the visitors' office and got her name put on Bradford's list."

"What did they talk about?"

"I don't know."

"How long was she there?"

"She was here over an hour, but only spoke to Bradford for six or seven minutes."

"What was her demeanor when she left?"

"She was hard to read. I'd say frustrated, not as friendly as when she first entered. I've seen her often, because of her father, and she's always been very polite, chats with guards. I've talked to her a few times, but not today."

"And Bradford?"

"He was angry, cut their conversation short and asked to be escorted back to the yard."

Cal wrote down her name, and then typed it into his computer. First person to visit Bradford in the last year who wasn't family was a private investigator. Very interesting. He needed to know why.

"Can you let me know if he calls anyone in the next forty-eight?"

"Sure."

"Thanks for the heads-up, Dave. I appreciate it."

"Not a problem. Stay safe out there."

"Stay safe in there," Cal said and ended the call.

Cal immediately pulled up Margo's contact information and printed her sheet. She was a licensed private investigator for nearly nine years. Had been an MP in the US Army, stationed in Fort Hood, with one eighteen-month deployment overseas. Left with an honorable discharge nine years ago. Had a concealed carry permit even though it wasn't necessary in Arizona. However, if she took cases out of state, it was easier to get a temporary reciprocal permit if she already had a CCW.

She had no criminal record, which wasn't a surprise since she would have to be clean to get licensed as a PI and to get the CCW. Small social media footprint, but big enough that he was able to piece together her connections. Worked with her family. Grandpa a retired state judge—Cal recognized the Morales name. Her dad had been arrested for killing a fellow doctor at the VA three years ago. Lots of cousins all over Maricopa County, including a Phoenix PD officer, and her brother worked at the crime lab.

Why was she talking to Bradford?

Had she taken a case that was connected to him? Maybe to his supplier?

He had a tingle, that little excited twist in his gut. He'd been waiting for something like this.

Every DEA agent with more than a decade of experience had a case that haunted them, and a case that irritated them. This was Cal's irritation case.

The AUSA offered the entire family witness protection if they gave up their supplier. They both refused. Insisted there was no supplier.

Cal would bet his pension they were both lying.

What did Margo Angelhart know? And why would she go to Bradford instead of the police?

Cal strode down the hall to his boss's office and waited impatiently for him to get off the phone.

"What has you all riled up?" George asked.

"Bradford. He had a visitor."

George raised an eyebrow. "Oh?"

"Local PI. I want to see what she knows."

"Just going to ask her?"

"Not yet. Can I have a couple days to follow her around? See what she's working on before I talk to her? Make sure that she's on the up and up and not working for the bad guys?"

George looked down at a chart on his desk, which gave him a one-page visual of every active case and who was assigned. He made a small notation. "I know you hate riding a desk more than most," George said. "It's all yours. But if you get a line on Bradford's supplier, do not go after him alone, understood?"

"Understood."

Cal ran back to his office, grabbed his gun, and left the building.

chapter twenty-four

MARGO ANGELHART

Angie texted me that she had the yearbooks and would be out after her last class. I arrived early, so parked down the street from the high school.

As kids started to trickle out of the building, my cell phone rang with a blocked number. I answered.

"Angelhart."

"This is Chris Vallejo. You left a message for me."

"Thanks for calling me back," I said. I kept an eye on the exit because I didn't know how Angie would feel about me talking to her ex-boyfriend.

I gave him the basics about what I was working on, and said, "You graduated, but you knew Elijah pretty well, correct?"

"Yeah. We hung out sometimes with my girlfriend."

"Angie Williams."

He didn't say anything.

"Am I wrong?"

"You're right. Have you talked to Angie?"

"Yes," I said. No use lying. If Chris and Angie talked later, I didn't want either of them to think I was being deceptive. "She's given me her impressions. I'd like yours."

"Elijah was a nice guy. I wasn't close to him, we didn't have any classes together or anything. He was Angie's friend. But we hung out."

"No jealousy on his part? Yours?"

He laughed. "Nothing like that. He had a crush on Gina—Angie's best friend—but Gina only thinks about volleyball. She plays year-round. There's no weird love triangle going on. Elijah was a good guy, and I had a job so I was glad Angie had someone else to hang with."

Very Zen of a teenage boy about his girlfriend and another guy. Men and women could of course be friends, but in high school that acceptance seemed mature.

"Did you ever see Elijah on drugs? Or talk about drugs? Most of the people I've spoken to said no, but he died of a drug overdose, so I need to be certain."

"I never saw him take anything. Angie wouldn't put up with that shit. Um—well, her mom is an addict. Not like a major addict, she has a job and everything, but she is pretty much drunk or stoned when she's not working. And probably stoned when she is working."

"That must be hard on Angie. And on you, dating her."

"Hey, we're not our parents. My dad is a prick. Sure, he works his ass off but he makes sure we know it." He paused, as if realizing he hadn't wanted to say so much. I read between the lines. "Anyway," Chris continued, "Angie doesn't remember a time when her mom was sober. So yeah, it bothered her. She wouldn't put up with a friend getting high. Once I got drunk with some friends of mine, just the guys, but I don't drink a lot and I was wasted. I called her, she knew I was drunk, and she didn't speak to me for a week. I apologized. She forgave me, but I knew it was a onetime free pass. She doesn't want to be around that."

"But you're not seeing each other now."

"She—we thought it would be best if we broke up before I went to college."

I wondered whose idea it really was.

"She didn't tell me that Elijah died, I heard it from someone else. I tried to call her—but anyway . . ." He cut himself off.

"Your brother works at the Cactus Stop?" I said, changing subjects. "Did he know Elijah?"

"Sure, through Angie and me. What does that have to do with anything?"

"I'm trying to figure out how everyone is connected and who might have known where Elijah went when he got off work the night he died."

I thought about mentioning the pictures Elijah took of people going in and out of the Cactus Stop, but didn't really know what to make of it yet. And if I did figure it out, I'd want to talk directly to Benny.

"Benny wasn't working there at the time," Chris said. "He felt like shit when he realized that he probably got the job because Elijah died. He even thought about quitting, but I talked him out of it. Like I said, our dad is an asshole, and even though he has plenty of money to help out, he won't give us a dime for college or trade school. Benny needs the job."

I saw Angie exit the school and walk slowly toward my car. I had maybe a minute.

"I don't want to jam up your brother, I'm just asking questions. Do you remember Coach Bradford?"

"Sure."

"Did you know any of the students who worked for him?"

"Probably, but I don't remember anyone specifically."

"Could you name someone on campus who deals drugs?"

"Now? No. I never bought drugs. I mean—we all kind of knew Scott Jimenez was the go-to guy if you wanted something, but that was three years ago and he went to jail. No one knew Coach Bradford was involved until he was arrested."

"If you think of anyone, call me, okay?"

"But you're just trying to find out where Elijah got the drugs, right?"

"That, among other things."

"I don't really talk to anyone from high school anymore."

"Maybe you should touch bases with Angie sometime."

"I've tried," he said, sounding irritated.

I wanted to follow up, but Angie was approaching my Jeep.

"Thanks for your help," I said and ended the call just as Angie opened the passenger door.

She put her backpack on the floor and pulled out two yearbooks. "I checked them out of the library," she said.

"Thanks," I said.

"Why do you want them?"

"I'm looking into the arrest of a coach your freshman year."

"Coach Bradford," she said.

"Yep." I flipped through pages. "Know him?"

"Not really. I remember when he was arrested though, because Gina knew him. Because of volleyball."

"He coached volleyball too?"

"No, but he would go to the games sometimes."

There were a lot of photos of the football team, and some of the faces were small. "I need to borrow this," I said. "I promise I'll get them back in good condition."

She shrugged. "It's fine."

"Do you need a ride anywhere?"

"I'm going to the volleyball game. It starts in a few minutes. Have you found out what happened to Elijah?"

I hesitated to bring Angie into the investigation. She was seventeen and had already overstepped with Detective King. I didn't want her to get into trouble—and I didn't want to put her in danger.

"I'm working on it."

"Did you talk to Danielle? She hated him."

"I did. She isn't involved, and she isn't holding a grudge."

"How do you know?" she asked, belligerent.

"Because I sat down with her. I know what I'm doing." Mostly. I'd made a misstep talking to Ben Bradford today without more information, but the conversation did get me thinking about a wide range of possibilities.

"Whatever," she said and was about to get out.

I put my hand on her arm. I didn't want to tell her everything I'd learned because I didn't know where it would take me, but she could help with one thing.

"What?" she snapped.

I dropped my hand and said, "You need to be careful okay? I'm asking questions, I'm getting answers, and even when I don't get answers, that's okay because then I know where to go next." I wasn't explaining this well. "What I mean to say, I want you to be extra careful. Lena Clark was asking questions and I don't know if her murder is connected to what happened to Elijah, but I'm assuming it is until I learn different. Just think about that, okay?"

She didn't say anything, but she didn't get out of the Jeep either.

I said, "I have some photos Elijah took over the summer." I wasn't confident I was making the right call asking her to look at them, but I didn't know who else to approach who might know these people.

"You found his phone?" she asked.

"His cloud account. They may have nothing to do with his death, but he took pictures of customers at the Cactus Stop. Tell me if you know any of them."

"Okay." She leaned forward in anticipation.

"You have to promise me you won't say anything to anyone—if you see one of these people, don't talk to them, confront them, give any indication that Elijah took their photo. I don't know *why* he took the pictures. Understand?"

"Yes," she said, exasperated. "I *understand*. I'll be careful. I won't talk to anyone." She looked at my phone.

I had already sorted the photos on my phone based on estimated age. I only showed Angie those I figured were under nineteen.

There were fifteen photos of four girls and eleven boys. Angie only recognized one.

"That's Benny Vallejo," she said of the second to last picture.

"The kid who was just hired?"

"Yeah."

"But none of the others?"

She shook her head. "A couple look familiar, but I can't be sure. SVH is a huge school."

I looked at Benny. He was a clean-cut kid, tall and gangly, just waiting to grow into his long limbs. This photo was taken a month before Elijah died. Maybe he'd gone in and dropped off his application, though most applications were managed online. Still, I filed the information away to consider later.

"I went to visit Mrs. Martinez last night," Angie said.

"I'm sure she appreciated that." I renamed the photo of Benny with his name.

"Elijah's boss was there. Mr. Ramos."

"I met him. He owns the Cactus Stops."

"They were talking. He offered to pay you."

"Mrs. Martinez didn't want to accept his money. He already helped with the funeral."

"Really?"

"He's a philanthropist." But now that Angie had mentioned him, it reminded me that I needed to reach out. I didn't want to wait until Friday to talk to Desi, and Manny Ramos could compel her to talk to me. "How is Mrs. Martinez?"

"Sad," Angie said. "One minute she was telling me a story about Elijah when he was little, and the next minute she was crying. I didn't know what to say."

I caught Angie's eye. "Just being there meant a lot to her. I think she would like to see his friends every once in a while."

"Yeah." She cleared her throat, then asked, "What are you going to do now?"

"Talk to more people."

"Is that all PIs do? Talk?"

"Actually, we ask questions. Over and over until we get answers."

She looked skeptical.

"I have a plan. Go to the game, Angie. And remember what I said."

"Yeah, yeah, yeah," Angie said as she climbed out of my Jeep. "Be careful, don't ask questions."

I'd copped an attitude as a teenager, but had I been this rude and dismissive to the adults in my life?

"Angie," I snapped.

She turned to me, surprised with my tone.

"I'm serious. Keep a low profile. And call me, day or night, if you have questions or get a bad vibe. Understand?"

She nodded, and I think she now took me seriously.

chapter twenty-five

MARGO ANGELHART

At four that afternoon, I pulled into the small parking lot outside the Cactus Stop on Hatcher. I had part of a plan, and started by calling Manny Ramos's cell phone number, which he'd written on the back of his business card.

"Ramos," he answered.

"Mr. Ramos, this is Margo Angelhart."

He remembered me. "Do you have news?" he asked.

"A request. I spoke to Elijah's coworkers yesterday, and the manager who worked with him on Friday, Desi, wasn't in. I'd like her contact information so I can reach out."

"Why do you need to speak with her?"

"She worked with Elijah on Friday and he may have said something to her about his plans. I still haven't figured out where he went after work."

"I see. I very much want to help—I went to visit Alina yesterday, she is holding on, but it's hard for her. I want her to have answers to give her some peace. But I have privacy concerns, so don't feel comfortable sharing Desi's contact information. However, I will have my assistant call her and instruct her to reach out to you within the next twenty-four hours. Is that sufficient?"

"Yes, thank you," I said. "I appreciate it."

"Is there anything else I can do?"

Rather than being snide and saying *give me her full name and number*, I said, "It would help if I had Elijah's actual schedule—I assume there's some sort of time card system? From his mother, I have his assigned schedule, but I don't know if he worked late or took a day off, things like that."

"It will help?"

"I'm retracing his steps." I didn't know if it would help until I looked at it. Maybe he left early every Thursday. Maybe he worked late every Wednesday. Until I could figure out what Elijah did when he wasn't working and he wasn't in school, I wouldn't know where he was Friday night.

"I'll ask the accounting department to email you his last three months, is that sufficient?"

"Yes, thank you." I rattled off my email address, thanked him, and ended the call.

I sat in my Jeep and considered why Elijah was taking photos of people leaving the Cactus Stop. It had started mid-July and continued up until the week he died. Based on the time stamps, he left work and watched the door.

I assessed the area around the store and determined—based on the angle and the slight distortion from zooming in—that he had taken the photos from across the side street. A short block wall would provide some cover, and the business on that corner, a veterinary practice, closed at 6:00 p.m., so no one there would have noticed him. But directly south of the vet, on the other side of the wall, the duplex would have full visibility of anyone standing or sitting there.

I made a U-Turn and parked in front of the residence that bordered the clinic. When I stood on the sidewalk I realized that whoever was in this house would have a very clear view of Elijah behind that half wall.

The duplex was a boxy house with two front doors that shared a covered porch. A small table with a sand-filled coffee can that served as an ashtray stood lopsided in one corner. A metal chair with a faded cushion provided the only place to sit. The stale scent of cigarettes filled the narrow space.

I'd smoked for a few years in the Army—three years, to be exact. When I changed my MOS from the Field Artillery Division to Military Police, the stress and boredom of being an MP on base had me take my very occasional cigarette to daily use. I quit cold turkey when I came home.

The smell made me cringe. I didn't crave it anymore—not like I did for the first couple of years after the Army. Instead, my stomach felt queasy.

I knocked on the door.

At first I didn't think anyone was home. Then suddenly the door opened almost before I could register the rattling of a security chain.

A very short, very old black woman stood behind the security screen. She wore large glasses that made her eyes seem unusually big. "You selling something?"

"No, ma'am, I am not. I'm a private investigator."

"A private investigator?" she repeated.

"Yes, ma'am. Margo Angelhart."

"Angelhart?"

"Yes."

I couldn't tell if she was repeating me because she was hard of hearing or ornery. Maybe a little of both, I decided, as she pursed her lips and narrowed her eyes.

"I have some questions about the Cactus Stop if you have a minute?"

"You're not coming in," she said firmly.

"Okay. We can talk out here."

"Hmph."

She closed the door and I thought she wasn't going to talk to me at all. I considered leaving when a full minute later she opened the door again, unlocked the screen, and came outside. She shuffled over to the chair, sat down, and pulled a pack of cigarettes and lighter from the pocket of her apron. She lit up.

She waved her hand with the cigarette and said, "Questions! You going to stand there all day or ask?"

"Thank you," I said, holding back a smile. "Like I said, I'm Margo. And you are?"

"Edith Ann Mackey."

"Mrs. Mackey, I—"

She harumphed again and said, "Call me Edith. My dead husband was a bastard."

"Edith." This woman was a hoot. "Did you notice over the last couple of months a young man standing or sitting behind that wall." I gestured toward the wall separating the vet clinic from the street. It turned and traversed the property line between Edith's half of the duplex and the rear of the vet. It was only three feet high, but when it reached the mid-point of the duplex, it had been built up to six feet to offer privacy to the residence.

"Yes, I did. I demanded to know why he was sneaking around, then when I got closer, I recognized him as the nice boy from the Cactus Stop."

"You know Elijah?"

"Yes, I stop there on my walk every day. Two blocks, every day, even with this bad leg."

"Did he tell you why he was hiding there?"

"He *said* he was just taking a break. I didn't believe him. Told him he was a liar, and good boys don't lie."

"Did he tell you the truth?"

She shrugged, took a deep drag on the cigarette. Slowly let out the smoke.

"Don't know, maybe. Not all, but maybe."

"Which was?"

She stared at me with her magnified eyes. "Why you want to know?"

"Elijah died two weeks ago," I said. "His mother hired me to find out what happened."

She froze, the cigarette halfway to her lips. "I was wondering why I hadn't seen him around."

She thought, took a drag, stared at the store.

"How'd he die?" she asked me.

"The police say he died of a drug overdose. His mother is skeptical. I found pictures Elijah took from that spot behind the wall—people going in and out of the store. Based on the time stamps, he went there when he got off work, stayed for several hours."

She was nodding as I spoke, but didn't look at me.

"Edith, I'm stuck," I said. "Do you know why Elijah was taking pictures of people leaving the store?"

"I don't know," she said, "but I saw him many times. Confronted him. When I caught him lying, he asked *me* questions. He said, 'Miz Edith, you ever notice that when I'm not working, store traffic picks up?' I told him I didn't pay no attention to it, but then I started. Told him so. Told him mornings and nights were busy. Then he said a damn funny thing, made no sense to me, maybe it will to you."

I waited as she finished her cigarette and stubbed it out in the sand. "He said, 'Now I know why they never let me work nights.'"

I didn't know what to make of it.

"One more question," I said. "No one can find Elijah's backpack. Could he have left it by the wall? Did you see it at some point in the last two weeks?"

Edith laughed. "If he left it, it's long gone. So many people in and out of my neighborhood. I've lived here for nineteen years, ever since I retired. See down the street?"

I looked where she pointed, away from the Cactus Stop.

"This was a nice little street. Still is, mostly. People keep to themselves, help when they can. But it's become a pathway from there—" she pointed toward the busier Hatcher "—down to Dunlap. And the people walking don't live here. They don't care about the neighborhood. They *litter.*" She pushed up from her seat and shuffled to the door.

"You know," she said, holding on to the screen door, "there was a dead girl behind the vet a few months back. Younger than you, maybe twenty, not much older. Whole life ahead of her. Died of a drug overdose, I heard. That's what the police said when they came." Edith shook her head. "I saw her there out my window. A Sunday. Thought she was homeless, had that look about her. My granddaughter picked me up for church as she does every Sunday at eight a.m. Mimi is a good girl, has been taking me to church since she got her driver's license, when my eyes got so bad I couldn't pass the damn test. That morning there was a line at my favorite diner after church, so I told Mimi I'd make her pancakes. We got back at ten thirty, and that girl was still there. I called the police, because she hadn't moved."

"I'm sorry," I said. "That must have been upsetting."

Edith didn't respond, but there really was nothing to say. The girl had died, and the old woman felt helpless.

I knew that feeling.

Edith stepped inside the house and said, "Maybe that dead girl upset Elijah as much as she upset me."

Then she closed the door, and I stood there a moment, considering.

I walked over to the vet clinic. They were open, and I considered talking to the vet, but through the window I saw two people with animals in the waiting room. I would come back. Maybe they had cameras I could look at, but they likely didn't keep video for long. Most businesses wiped recordings every few days because of data storage limits.

I stood in the spot where I suspected Elijah had been taking pictures. He could sit behind the wall and not be seen, easily take photos through a section of wall that had crumbled. I looked around and, not seeing anything dangerous like used needles or broken glass, sat. Bingo. This was the exact angle. This was where Elijah sat damn near every night for two months.

He'd told his mom he was going to a night class, but he had taken the class online. Instead, he'd sat on asphalt looking through a hole in the wall. Why?

That was the million-dollar question, but I had that tingle. The tingle that said this was important.

During the drive to Flannigan's to meet Jessica Oliver, I called Josie.

"Hey," Josie answered.

"You working?"

"Yep. What do you need?"

"There was a dead woman on the corner of Hatcher across from the Cactus Stop, behind the veterinary clinic," I said. "She died of a possible OD on a Sunday morning over the summer. A neighbor called it in about ten thirty. Can you look up the case for me? Pretty please?"

"Is this related to Elijah Martinez?"

"Maybe."

"Not a problem, but I'm heading to a call right now. Is an hour or two okay?"

"Absolutely, go save the world, Pussycat."

I heard a deep laugh coming from the car—a laugh that wasn't Josie.

"Pussycat?" I heard faintly and realized that Josie's partner was in the car. Sometimes day shift rode together, sometimes they rode single, but how was I supposed to know Josie wasn't alone?

"I will kill you," Josie said and hung up.

Whoops.

I thought back to what Angie had told me. Elijah loved his job when he was hired in March. They hadn't seen each other much over the summer, and when they started school the second week of August, he had changed, was preoccupied. Angie didn't know why. Elijah asked Andy's mother if she had an opening in her house-cleaning business. He was looking to quit, I deduced . . . but he hadn't quit.

What had changed? Why hadn't he quit if he was miserable at his job?

Could this girl's death have been the catalyst? Had he known her?

I hoped Josie got back to me sooner rather than later.

chapter twenty-six

MARGO ANGELHART

Detective Jessica Oliver was younger than I expected—under thirty—with a petite build, short dark hair and large blue eyes. Cherub cute. Definitely didn't look like a cop.

She walked straight toward me and said, "Margo?"

"That's me. Thanks for coming, Jessica."

"Call me Jessie," she said and slid into the booth across from me. "I remember your brother. I had my shield for about a year when he left the force."

"You made detective young."

She laughed. "Maybe, but I became a cop when I was nineteen. My grandpa was a deputy sheriff in Pima County, my dad was a US marshal and my mom worked in the Secret Service, financial crimes. Which is what I was interested in after hearing some of her stories. My sister is currently in the DEA training academy, and it's my brother who betrayed the family," she added lightly.

"What did he decide to do?"

"Owns a business. Installs and repairs HVAC systems. He's going to make a shit-ton more money than all of us put together, but that's Jimmy. Barely graduated from high school, but he can fix anything." She leaned forward. "Fortunately, he recognizes his limitations and hired a good accountant who happens to be my husband."

"You have an interesting family."

"I wouldn't trade them."

I liked her. Her family reminded me of my own.

Scotty, the bartender, came over to our table. He'd worked here eight years ago when I did, and he hadn't changed, except maybe a little more gray threaded through his dark hair.

"Usual, Margo?"

"Yep," I said. To Jessica I said, "On me, beer, food, both."

"My husband's cooking, so I'll just take a beer. Harp?"

Scotty nodded, went back to the bar.

"Come here a lot I take it?" Jessica said.

"I used to work here while getting my PI business off the ground."

"My husband and I used to come in here all the time when we lived nearby, but we bought a house in Anthem a couple years ago."

"You commute all the way downtown?" Forty-five minutes— longer if she worked regular business hours.

"Sacrifices," she said. "We're trying to start a family and Anthem is a nice community, good schools. My husband works from home, likes the quiet. And I can work out of the Black Mountain precinct half the time." Black Mountain was the northernmost substation for Phoenix PD.

Scotty came back with Jessie's Harp and my Guinness.

"So," Jessie said after taking a sip, "Rick says you want to pick my brain about EBT fraud and scams. Pick away. I'm yours for the next thirty minutes."

"What types of cases do you investigate?"

"I primarily investigate criminal fraud of city and state resources. The last major case I wrapped up was working with the AG's office on a Medicaid fraud scam."

"How does that work?"

She laughed lightly. "In a nutshell? An individual buys or steals a list of Medicaid recipients and then charges Medicaid for services not provided."

"A doctor?"

"Not always. In this case, it started with a receptionist in a provider's office. She copied all the Medicaid patients' records, then with her mother, opened a mental health clinic. It started during COVID when there was far less oversight. They were so profitable they kept it going for years before we shut them down."

"I don't understand. They were ambulance chasers for mental health services?"

"No. There was no actual clinic. They filed false Medicaid claims for patients they never saw for services they never provided."

"How do you catch things like that?"

"It's not easy. Nearly ten percent of payments a year—over one hundred *billion* dollars—are for improper payments. People who don't qualify. Paying more benefits than allowed. Double payments. Paying landlords directly *and* sending the same benefit to the recipient. I could go on and on. For me, I get frustrated because there are people who need help, so when I can stop someone from committing *actual* fraud, it feels good."

"How'd you catch the mother-daughter team?"

"They got greedy. If you keep your scams on the down-low, it's next to impossible to catch you—especially since audits are limited and rare. But they added more patients to their fictional list, and one of those individuals was getting real psychiatric services. That doc ran the patient's records, saw something hinky, and alerted the AG's office. My team was brought in, and it took us six months of interviews and legwork to wrap up those women with a pretty bow for the prosecution."

"Neither was even a doctor?"

"Nope. There are cases like this all over the country. Recently in California, a husband and wife applied for housing benefits using stolen identities and pocketed more than half a million dollars. In Louisiana, a guy ran a similar scam as my mother-daughter team, buying instead of stealing a Medicaid list and charging for services never provided. There are doctors who pad all services for every Medicaid patient, or charge for tests and procedures never done."

Jessie leaned back. "Does that help?"

I nodded. "I knew fraud was out there, but other than a couple civil insurance scams, I haven't worked fraud cases. Last year a private insurer hired me to determine if a loss was legit. Someone claimed a bunch of jewelry was stolen from their house, insured for over two million bucks. But the insurance company was skeptical, hired me to investigate. The wife really thought it had been stolen, but the husband actually sold the jewels to pay off gambling debts he didn't want his wife to find out about, then filed the fraudulent report."

"And he probably didn't even go to prison," Jessie said.

"Nope. But he didn't get the insurance money, and his wife divorced and sued him. I testified for her, she ended up with a nice settlement. In the end, justice was mostly served."

I sipped my Guinness, considered my approach, decided on straightforward. Jessie was knowledgeable and had so far been open.

"Have you investigated EBT fraud?"

"Sure. Lots of scams out there, both to game the system and to steal benefits from those who are eligible."

"What are the most common?"

"Fraudulently applying for benefits, usually under a false identity. Nearly a third of all SNAP fraud is because of false identities. I nailed one guy who ran a scam filing for dead people—literally they die, he applies for benefits, and the system is so behind no one knows the person is dead. He gets the EBT cards, sells them for cash. A lot of people fraudulently apply when they aren't eligible, and many apply under multiple names and socials. There's also skimmers out there who pull the money off EBT cards like people do with credit card readers. That's about twenty percent of the fraud, and it pisses me off because these people are literally stealing from people who can't afford to lose those benefits. They get the benefits back, but that costs the system. It's a mess. I do what I can." Jessie sipped her Harp and munched on the complimentary peanuts.

"What about using an EBT card to pay for ineligible goods?"

"Like alcohol and cigarettes? Happens all the time. The store has to be in on it—they have a UPC code for an eligible item like canned food and ring that up, but sell them a pint of vodka. It's more common for someone to sell their card for cash, use the cash to buy, but I've fined a couple stores. Usually it's just one employee, but management needs to be more diligent."

"What about drugs?" I said. It had been running around in my head why Elijah was taking pictures of people coming out of the Cactus Stop without bags. A few people, sure. Cigarettes get stuffed in pockets. Lottery tickets in wallets. But the numbers seemed high.

"Our DEB unit has caught scammers buying up EBT cards from the homeless, who use the money for drugs and alcohol, then file for a new card saying it was lost, and the process starts all over again."

"What about a store who, like ringing up food for an alcohol purchase, rings up food for an illegal drug purchase?"

Jessie stared at me, all serious, and said, "What do you know?"

"I don't know anything. Just throwing ideas out."

"Very specific ideas," she said pointedly. I kept my poker face. I had no problem sharing my theory with her, but I also didn't want the police to jump in before I had answers about Elijah's death.

"Did you see something that made you suspicious?" Jessie asked.

"Yes," I said. "And, if over the course of my investigation I can find hard proof, I'll turn it over to you. But for now, it's just a gut feeling, so I don't want to blow my own case."

"Which is?"

Carefully, I said, "A teenager died of a drug overdose. I'm tracking his last days, and I think he may have seen something illegal where he worked, which may have led to his death. It's just a theory based on limited information, but I need to prove or disprove before I can move on."

"Well," Jessie said after a moment, "I'll say this. I have heard of instances where a business was involved in fraudulent EBT use. I have even heard isolated cases where an employee was dealing drugs out of a business. A few years back at one of the major grocery stores, a cashier ran the scam, but her manager caught on pretty quick. We put her under surveillance, built a case, arrested her. I haven't seen this sort of operation on a large scale."

"Have you or your team ever investigated the Cactus Stop?"

Her eyes widened. "Not even close. In fact, the owner contacts law enforcement on a regular basis about crime in and around his businesses."

"Ramos," I said.

"Yes, Manny Ramos. He opened the first Cactus Stop more than twenty-five years ago, built one store into more than a dozen. If you know of any of his employees who may be involved in a crime, you need to let me know. He'll help us take bad staff down. He's done it before."

"All right," I said, having no intention of sharing the information yet, "if I uncover anything specific, I'll let you know. I don't want to bring down the hammer on anyone who's innocent."

"Ramos doesn't want drugs on his property any more than we do."

"How would like a scam like that work?" I asked. "I understand ringing up food and giving them drugs or alcohol, but wouldn't there be an inventory discrepancy?"

"On a small scale, it's easy to make disappear. A good auditor—like my husband—could find it if he had access to all the books and receipts, but a good scammer can falsify books. On a large scale? Quarterly records would be off, the bookkeeper would notice large discrepancies and likely trigger an audit. So if it was a mom-and-pop shop and they were in on it, easy to cook the books and get away with something like you're suggesting. But a chain like the Cactus Stop? Nearly impossible."

"But if it was just one employee, it would be considered small scale?"

"Small if he was having maybe six to ten of these transactions a week."

"So not a dozen or more a day."

"That would create a paper trail at inventory time. In the short term? A sneaky employee could destroy the goods he pretended to sell, and could probably get away with it for a while. But in my experience, people get greedy. They want more, like the mother and daughter Medicaid scammers. And remember, if they're using an EBT card, the employee isn't going to get the money—that goes to the store. So I don't know what his motive would be. Selling drugs for cash behind the counter? That definitely happens a lot more than you might think, and DEB would take lead in that investigation."

"That helps," I said.

"Are you going to share more?"

"I promise, if I learn more, I'll share."

"Fair enough," Jessie said and drained her beer. "Thanks for the beer. I should get going. It was nice to meet you."

"You too," I said and watched her walk out.

I was starving so ordered a plate of Irish sliders. While I ate and finished my beer, I considered what might be happening at the Cactus Stop.

EBT transactions went to the store. So either I was wrong about the scam and nothing was going on at the Cactus Stop, or the staff was selling drugs for cash, or whoever ran the business end of the Cactus Stop was involved.

Elijah must have thought *something* illegal was happening, or why else would he sit outside the store for hours at night taking pictures of people coming and going?

Maybe he was trying to identify the specific person involved, but didn't know where he should focus his attention.

I was at a loss, but I couldn't ignore the photos or what Elijah had been doing in the weeks before he died.

Ramos should be very interested if there was any sort of EBT fraud going on in one of his Cactus Stop locations. But I didn't have proof, and I wouldn't go to him without solid evidence. Still, he was in a better position than me to find answers.

I called Tess. If anyone could dig up dirt on Cactus Stop employees, it was my sister.

But reaching out to Ramos before I had proof? I needed to sleep on that.

chapter twenty-seven

MARGO ANGELHART

Scotty brought over a half pint of Guinness for me.

"You know me so well." I wasn't quite ready to leave as I mulled through all the information I'd learned.

"I'd stay and chat, but it's getting busy," he said. "D-backs might clinch playoffs tonight."

I noticed every seat in the bar was occupied, and most of the tables, chairs turned to the large screen where the pregame show played.

"That'd be awesome," I said. I wasn't as into sports watching as Jack and Luisa—I liked to play, not observe—but I did enjoy going to baseball games. It was relaxing and fun and you could chat with friends and family. Unlike fast-paced basketball where your brother would punch you in the arm if you talked too much. "I'll free up the table in a few."

"Take your time," he said and went back to the bar.

The background chatting and voices of sports announcers didn't bother me. It was actually comforting, reminding me of the two years I'd worked here while building my business, and the people I'd gotten to know, some of whom I'd been able to help in a small way. It was a nice neighborhood pub on the south side of Sunnyslope.

I drained my beer and was about to leave when my phone vibrated. It was Josie. I owed her a lot of groveling for outing her nickname.

"Well, if it isn't my favorite cousin," I said cheerfully.

"If you think flattery is going to save you from my wrath, you are sorely mistaken."

"I'm *really* sorry."

"You won't know the time or the place when I enact my retribution," she said.

"I deserve it."

"I'm *never* going to live this down," Josie moaned. "Anyway, I was held over and am still at the station, but I dug around and have some details about the dead girl."

"Thank you," I said. "I *really* appreciate it."

"Stop kissing up, it's not going to help," Josie muttered. "So, she was identified as Megan Osterman, nineteen, Caucasian, five foot four, ninety pounds."

"Petite," I said.

"Underweight, malnourished, habitual drug user. Died of fentanyl poisoning."

"You have the ME's report?"

"Yep, it's attached to the police report. Showed signs of long-term heroin abuse."

"Heroin, not fentanyl?"

"Over the last several years, dealers have been lacing heroin and other illegal drugs with fentanyl, which is cheap, in order to increase the high and their profit. Almost every drug bought on the street these days has traces of fentanyl, which is increasing accidental overdose deaths."

"Do you have an address for Megan?"

"She lived with her mother, Corinne Osterman. I'll text you the address. Only a few blocks from where she was found. It was pretty cut-and-dried. DEB took the case, Detective Ian Solomon. Don't know him."

"Why would DEB take it? Are they still investigating?"

"No signs of foul play, but let's see . . ." Josie clicked on her keyboard. "Okay . . . yeah. She had a fanny pack with packaged heroin, and tests found it contained a specific fentanyl compound they'd seen before in several OD deaths, so they took the case. Probably as part of a larger investigation. There's a DEA number attached as well, so it's a joint investigation."

"Are they actively investigating her death?"

"No," Josie said. "They took the case because the drugs found on her body may connect with another investigation. You'd have to talk to DEB about that, it's not in this report. Unlike Elijah, Megan is a clear overdose of a known drug addict. Interviews with her mother reveal that she tried to get her into rehab multiple times, going back to high school. Her mother didn't want to kick her out, but also didn't know how to help her. It's a sad story, but unfortunately common."

I didn't know how Megan fit into Elijah's death, but I knew in my gut that somehow she did. Then I had another thought.

"Do you know if she went to Sun Valley?" I asked.

"I don't have that information."

I had the yearbooks in my car; I needed to go through them with a fine-toothed comb. Based on her address, Megan had most likely been a student at Sun Valley. Elijah . . . Megan . . . Lena. One more piece of a puzzle where I still couldn't see the whole picture. But if Megan had been a student at the same time Bradford was dealing, it was the best lead I had—thin as it was.

"I gotta go," I said to Josie.

"Wait! How does this connect to Elijah? Did they know each other?"

"I'm going to find out. Bye." I ended the call before she asked more questions.

I brought my glass up to the counter and put forty dollars

under it. Scotty never charged me for beer—the Flannigans didn't either—but the money would cover the sliders, Jessie's drink, and give him a decent tip.

I went to my car, turned on my dome light, and flipped through the two yearbooks Angie had brought me. Megan Osterman was a junior when Elijah and Angie were freshmen. She looked young and sweet, not a strung-out addict. What had happened in the three years between when she was this kid with a future until she turned into a habitual user who died in an alley?

I wished I'd asked Angie for more yearbooks. I would have liked to have seen what Megan looked like her senior year, after she started using. Would her decline into addiction be obvious, or something she'd been able to hide?

I remembered the anonymous call to Phoenix PD, about how the police believed the call was made by a girl on the softball team. I flipped to the sports section of the yearbook, thinking I'd uncover something big that would connect all these events.

No such luck—Megan Osterman hadn't played softball. Just to be diligent, I picked up the yearbook from Megan's sophomore year, before Elijah and Angie were in high school. I looked at her picture again, younger, smiling, happy. Thinking that she was now dead was damn depressing.

I flipped to the softball page, not expecting to find her; I didn't.

But I found one name I didn't expect.

Bradford, Kayla

What were the chances that Kayla Bradford was Coach Bradford's daughter? She was a freshman the year Megan was a sophomore . . . I flipped to the later yearbook, and there she was, a sophomore when Megan was a junior. There was only one photo of Kayla in the second yearbook—her official school picture. She was no longer on the softball team, likely because she'd been shipped to South Dakota to live with her grandparents in January. She would have graduated high school this past May.

What were the chances that Kayla Bradford didn't mean to say *my coach* but instead almost slipped and said *my dad*?

DON'T SAY A WORD

What if his own daughter turned Bradford in to the authorities?

Why had I jumped the gun and talked to Bradford *today?* I felt like I'd royally screwed up. No way would he speak to me again.

I'd found a trail from Elijah to Coach Bradford when I wasn't even looking for it. Yes, it was thin, and yes, I'd already decided to focus on Elijah's Cactus Stop surveillance, but this was something I hadn't expected.

As I drove home, I came up with a plan. I sent Tess all the names of the girls on the softball team from both years, and asked her to find out where they were now. Most of the girls overlapped: A couple seniors in the first book were not in the second, and there were a few girls in the second who weren't in the first. I'd played softball for years, and there was always a core group that moved through together.

My phone buzzed. It was Harry, from the MVD annex.

"Hi, Harry."

"What do you want?"

Always blunt and to the point.

"A Tesla owner."

He snorted. "Tomorrow," he said. "I was training this idiot today, fucking gave me a headache. There was nothing behind the eyes. Why they hired him I don't know."

I rattled off the number. "Thanks."

"What they do?"

"Don't know yet. I'm investigating a suspicious overdose death. Tesla may be involved, may not be."

"Fucking drugs," Harry said and hung up.

My sentiments exactly.

I called Jack.

"What's up?"

"Where are you?"

"I just dropped Whitney and Austin off and am heading home."

"What? Whitney again?"

"It was open house at Austin's school." Austin went to a Catholic school in Avondale, near where Whitney still lived in the house that they'd bought when they were married.

"Oh." I shifted gears, asked all the right questions about Austin and his teachers. He was in sixth grade now.

"Not one insult about Whitney, I know your heart is not in this conversation," Jack said after a few minutes.

"Sorry. Yeah, I'm preoccupied. I really need to talk to Hitchner."

"I reached out, he hasn't gotten back to me."

"Where can I find him?"

"What's going on?"

"I think—" I hesitated, because as I was about to verbalize my theory I wasn't certain it would make sense.

"I'm not going to shoot you if you're wrong," Jack said.

"It's a theory," I said.

"Continue."

Jack really was the best person to bounce ideas off. "Elijah caught on to illegal activity, likely drug dealing, at the Cactus Stop, probably around the time Megan Osterman—who he'd gone to school with—died of a drug overdose across the street." I told him what Edith Mackey had said. "Maybe Elijah *had* reached out to Silent Witness, or maybe he just thought about doing it. But he lied to his mom about taking community college classes. He took online classes, but she believed he was going to night classes."

"And instead he was surveilling people where he worked."

"Yes. It started the week after Megan Osterman died."

Jack didn't say anything.

"You there?"

"Just thinking. He might have suspected she obtained drugs through the Cactus Stop and wanted to prove it. But two months is a long time—he had how many pictures?"

"Hundreds. All at night, some of the same people."

"But no photos of drug deals or suspicious behavior."

"No. I need to sleep on this. I'll be in the office early in the morning."

"You also have to go to Prescott tomorrow and finish the background check. Logan wants to hire the new groundskeeper ASAP. Or ask Tess to do it, she won't mind."

"I'll do it. I already told Tess I'd take care of it, and I sent her a bunch of names to run since she can do it faster than me. I'll go first thing in the morning, the drive will help me clear my head. I'll be at the office around noon."

"And I'll call Hitch again."

"Thanks, Jack."

I took a shower and lay in bed, but it took me a long, long time before I fell asleep.

chapter twenty-eight

ANGIE WILLIAMS

Angie waited in the student parking lot Thursday morning. She'd hardly slept the night before, replaying her last few conversations with Elijah in her head, searching for something she'd missed.

He'd been quieter, less himself. No jokes, few smiles. In hindsight, the signs were there: He was worried and distracted. She should have pushed him harder to tell her what was going on. Maybe they could have figured it out together. Instead, he'd kept it to himself and now he was dead.

Now Benny worked at the Cactus Stop. Maybe he'd heard something that could help Margo figure out what happened. It was a long shot, but Angie trusted Benny.

While waiting for Benny to show up for school, she reread Chris's messages from the last two days. She'd wanted to call him, but didn't want to be needy. He had college, new friends, a full life.

They'd been friends first, bonded over broken homes—her mom, an addict; his dad, a violent jerk. Lori had never hit Angie, but Chris's dad smacked both his sons, especially when they were younger. She'd never told anyone—not even Gina or Elijah—how bad it really was. It was easier to be angry, to say she hated her mother and whichever dipshit man she had in her bed. But with Chris she told the truth. How she didn't *want* to care about her mom, but she lived in fear that her mom would overdose or bring home the wrong guy. She'd put a dead bolt inside her bedroom and kept a butcher knife in her nightstand, just in case.

Angie didn't want to be a burden to Chris or anyone. She had plans for college, but now everything was uncertain. Elijah was gone. Mrs. Clark was gone. She had no one to help her figure it out.

Benny drove into the lot in the old pickup that Chris used to drive. They'd had a lot of fun in that truck, the three of them, sometimes with Elijah, often just her and Chris.

He parked near the exit even though there were plenty of spaces closer to the classrooms. Chris used to do the same thing, saying he'd rather get out of the lot fast than have a short walk.

Benny didn't look much like his brother. He was taller, skinnier, more awkward, with brown hair that often fell in front of his eyes like a sheepdog. But the smile was identical, and he flashed it when he saw her leaning against the fence.

"Ange! Were you waiting for me?"

"Yeah," she said, smiling. It was impossible to be sullen around Benny. Even with his shit father, he was always happy. "Do you have a couple minutes?"

"Sure. We'll walk slow."

They walked along the fence that separated student parking from the practice field.

"Chris said you're not returning his calls," Benny said.

"I don't want to talk about Chris."

"He misses you."

"*Benny*—" she said in warning.

"Okay, okay," he said, hands up, a half smile on his face. "I get it."

He didn't, but that was okay. "It's about Elijah," she said.

"Oh. Were you, um, seeing him?" Benny glanced at her, but then looked straight ahead, his face red. She wanted to laugh. He was sixteen but still shy talking about relationships.

"No, we were just friends."

"I thought so, but . . ." His voice trailed off.

"He was one of my best friends," she said. "And I'm worried I didn't see everything going on with him." She hesitated. How did she broach the subject? "Have you heard anything?"

"About?"

"Elijah. At work."

He shook his head. "Not really. In fact, no one even talked about him until a PI came in and started asking questions."

"Margo."

"She talk to you?"

"Yeah. Elijah's mom hired her to find out what happened."

"I thought he OD'd."

"No," she said emphatically. "I mean, someone drugged him and he died. He wasn't an addict."

"Oh."

"You don't believe me?"

"I do, but . . ."

"But what?" She stopped walking. "Benny, what do you know?"

"I need the job at the Cactus Stop because I have to pay my insurance on the truck or I can't drive. And they pay well. But . . . it's kind of a weird culture there."

"How so?"

"Tony, the assistant manager, is always high. It's not illegal, I get it, but he shouldn't be stoned when he's working, you know? It's not like he's keeping it a big secret, so Elijah must have known."

"You think Elijah might have turned him in to management or something?" Maybe Tony got a slap on the wrist and took it out on Elijah.

Benny shrugged. "I don't know. I'm not going to. Don't look at me like that."

"I'm not looking at you in any way."

"You are. I don't want to be around it any more than you, but I *need* the job. I'm already looking for something else, but I should stick it out a few months and then maybe find a job at one of the malls over Christmas. If I don't find something that sticks, I have to work for my dad next summer."

Mr. Vallejo owned a small construction company that worked primarily for larger companies on a project-by-project basis. Chris had worked for his dad every summer. He got paid, but it was grueling work, especially in the heat, and Mr. Vallejo was as big a jerk on the job as he was at home. The only benefit, Chris had told her, was that his dad paid well, almost as much as he paid his regular crew.

Angie didn't know what she wanted from Benny. "Just be careful. It's not a great area, and I'm worried that maybe Elijah witnessed a crime or something like that."

"You really don't think he died of an overdose?"

"No, not on purpose."

Except the more she thought about it, the more she wondered if she was projecting. The Elijah *she* knew wouldn't have gotten so high that he curled up and died in a park. But maybe he had changed.

They walked through the courtyard in silence as people talked in pairs or groups, laughing or complaining. When they reached the corridor that separated the new building from the old, Benny stopped and faced her. "After that PI talked to Tony, Desi—the manager—came in and ranted to him. I didn't hear everything she said, but she was mad about something. It seemed weird."

"Weird how?"

He shrugged. "I just do my job and keep my head down. It's what I have to do so I don't have to work for my dad."

He knew something, she realized. But he wasn't going to tell her.

She pulled out Margo's card from her pocket and handed it to Benny. "If you need help, or see something illegal, call her."

He took the card, nodded, but Angie didn't know if he would call.

He gave her a quick hug. "I gotta go, I have chemistry first period."

She watched him leave.

She didn't want to go to class, but she couldn't cut anymore. She slowly headed to her first period class. Gina was with a group of her volleyball friends and waved at her; Angie waved back, but didn't join them. The others weren't her friends, and Angie always felt uncomfortable around them. She was acutely aware that people were nice to her for the last two years because she'd been dating Chris, who was generally liked and didn't care if he wasn't. This year? She might as well have been invisible.

"Angie, we need to talk." Mrs. Webb, the vice principal, looked as stern and unfriendly as usual as she approached Angie.

"I'm going to English."

"I'll walk with you," she said, heading down the corridor without waiting for Angie to agree.

"I've been going through Mrs. Clark's records," Mrs. Webb said. "She erased your absences last week. But I spoke to your teachers and you've only been to a couple of classes for nearly two weeks."

"I know. I'm sorry. It's been fuc—a tough week."

She didn't want this conversation.

"I'm not unsympathetic to the fact that you lost a friend, but you need to focus on *you*. And you didn't go to your classes yesterday afternoon."

Angie didn't say anything.

"Did you leave campus because of the police?"

"They didn't do anything about Elijah's death, but Mrs. Clark is killed and they suddenly care?"

She didn't want to talk to Mrs. Webb, but it just came out.

"Elijah died of a drug overdose. Mrs. Clark was murdered. Two very different things."

Angie wanted to scream at her, but she didn't. She bit her lip, wanting to just disappear.

"If you cut another class," Mrs. Webb said, "I'll have no choice but to give you detention."

"I won't," she mumbled.

"There's a private investigator who has been asking questions on campus. She talked to Mrs. Clark and Mr. Parsons, and I'm sure she'll reach out to you and Elijah's other friends. You don't have to speak with her."

"What if I want to?"

"Do you know where Elijah got the drugs?"

It sounded like an accusation.

"No," she said. "I don't do that stuff."

"Then I don't see how you can help her. However, she's not allowed on campus. If she finds you, you can ask someone to sit in with you. I would be happy to help."

Why? she wanted to ask. Like everyone else, Mrs. Webb believed the worst in Elijah.

"Okay," she said. Sometimes it was easier to agree than argue.

"I would hate to see you go down the same path as your friend."

Angie stopped outside her classroom. "What does that mean?"

Mrs. Webb sighed, rubbed her eyes. "Angie, you're a smart girl who is under a lot of pressure. Mrs. Clark was helping you with your college applications, and it's going to be hard to replace her, but I would be happy to assist you. I know you have a difficult home situation."

Angie reddened. She didn't want to talk about her mother or anything else, especially with Mrs. Webb. How did she even know? Was everything she told Mrs. Clark written in her file? It was humiliating.

"I am here for you if you need me. Okay?"

She nodded and slipped into the classroom. The teacher gave her a look, but noticed Mrs. Webb and didn't give Angie a tardy slip.

Angie sank into her seat and wished she were anyplace but here.

chapter twenty-nine

JACK ANGELHART

Jack came into the office shortly before nine Thursday morning and was surprised to find Tess and his mother in the conference room going over stacks of records. He stepped in and asked, "Did I miss something?"

"Margo has a hunch," Tess said.

Jack picked up one of the sheets. "Who are these kids?"

"Softball players," Ava said. "They played for the coach who was arrested."

He sat down. "How does this connect to Elijah's death?"

"I don't know that it does," Ava said, irritated. "Margo is in Prescott and not answering her phone, so we can't even follow up. She wants to know where all these girls are now and said she'd know it when she saw it."

Jack understood that. Sometimes you didn't know what was important until you had all the facts laid out and could see the bigger picture.

He said, "She wants to talk to the DEB detective who worked the case. I reached out to him, but haven't heard back yet."

"She thinks that Coach Bradford's daughter turned him in to the police," Tess said.

"That would be big."

"It may not be relevant," his mom said. "Margo has good instincts, but I don't like how she had you two running around pulling records, going through archives, running backgrounds, without even a *hint* of what she thinks is going on."

Jack didn't want his mom and Margo at odds, and their different styles were heading them down that path. "Margo thinks Elijah uncovered illegal activity where he worked."

"What kind of illegal activity?"

"I assume drug-related."

Tess pulled a file from near the bottom, handed it to Jack. "Margo got this file from Josie last night. I don't know why she's looking into the OD of a girl who has a long history of drug use—it's not similar to what happened to Elijah. The only connection is that she died near where he worked, and she'd gone to Sun Valley High."

Jack opened the thin file. A nineteen-year-old female, Megan Osterman, was found dead on July 6 across the street from the Cactus Stop.

"She mentioned this," Jack said. "She thinks something happened over the summer that he didn't tell his friends or mom about. Maybe this girl was a friend of his."

Ava leaned back. "This is a lot of work when we don't even know what we're looking for."

Jack didn't think Margo knew what they were looking for either, but he didn't say that. No need to further antagonize their mom.

"I'm getting a headache," Ava mumbled. Her phone vibrated and she picked it up, read the message. "Good news. Margo is done with the interview and Logan is cleared to hire the new groundskeeper. She's on her way back." She rose. "Tess, I'm going to leave this with you and Jack. I'll call Logan, tell him we'll deliver the final report this afternoon, and when Margo returns, we need a sit-down."

She left the room and Tess let out a long sigh.

"That bad?" Jack asked.

"Mom is meticulous. She likes a detailed plan and clear goals."

"We have a clear goal: find out what happened to Elijah the day he died. That's not as easy as it sounds."

"Tell me about it," Tess mumbled as she opened another file and turned to her computer.

"Do you need my help?" Jack asked.

She looked at him with a frown. "It would take me longer to get you up to speed than for me to finish it myself," she said. She slid over a sheet. "However, here is the list of everyone at Sun Valley High School who was part of Coach Bradford's operation and the disposition of their cases—most of them received probation. I've filled in the blanks where I could find them, but there are several people I can't locate. They could be in prison or moved out of state. Lulu is looking out of state, can you check with the Bureau of Prisons?"

"Not a problem," he said and took the list to his office.

Just as he sat down, Mike Hitchner returned his call.

"Sorry it took me so long to get back to you," Hitchner said. "It's been crazy around here."

"I hear you," Jack said. "How you've been?"

They made small talk for a minute, then Hitch said, "Did I get the message right? You're looking into the Coach Bradford case?"

"My firm was hired to investigate the overdose death of a teenager from Sun Valley High School." He gave Hitch the basics about Elijah's situation. "In the course of our background, we may have made a connection to Bradford's old network." Slight exaggeration, Jack thought. "I was hoping my sister Margo and I could have a sit-down and pick your brain about that investigation."

"I don't know how I can help. He took a plea, his wife took a plea, we rounded up everyone involved."

"You caught the supplier? The records indicate Bradford's supplier was never identified."

A long silence. He had pushed and maybe overstepped.

"True," Hitch said after a moment. "The DEA has that end of the case. Do you have leads on that?"

"No, we only know what you know," Jack said. "We theorized that someone may have recreated the Bradford network. A staff member at Sun Valley was killed on campus Monday. She had been talking to us about Elijah Martinez's death, and questioning his friends and classmates."

"And how's that connected to Bradford?"

He didn't have an answer to his question, so instead said, "We'd like to pick your brain on how Bradford's network operated," Jack said. "It could help us figure out where our dead kid got the drugs."

"I don't have any active investigations at Sun Valley."

"He didn't die on school property, and the detective in charge ruled it an accidental overdose."

"I really don't know how I can help," he said again.

Jack knew Hitch wasn't this obtuse. It was like he didn't *want* to help.

"I read the original case reports and we have some follow-up questions that you might be able to answer."

"Look, I don't have the time for this right now, Jack. If you uncover anything *specific* that relates to the Bradford investigation, send it up the chain. But that case is closed, and the investigation into the supplier is one hundred percent under DEA purview. Sorry I can't help you. I gotta go."

He hung up so quickly that Jack just stared at his phone.

That was unusual. Something was definitely up with Hitchner.

He doubted there was another undercover investigation at Sun Valley—it would have come up at some point after Elijah's death or Lena Clark's murder. Maybe Hitch was trying to put something together. That didn't feel right—if DEB had an active Sun Valley investigation, then he would have called Jack immediately to tell him such, and ask him to stand down. He wouldn't have to give any details, and Jack would have put the case aside to leave room for Phoenix PD to do their job.

So what was going on?

He called Margo.

"Hitch called me back."

"I'll meet him anywhere."

"He doesn't want to help."

"Why?"

"He claims he's swamped."

"Claims?" Margo questioned.

"He says there's no active investigation involving Sun Valley, and that the supplier end of the Bradford case is on the DEA's plate."

"But I wanted to ask questions about how he investigated—"

Jack cut her off. "I know, and I pushed and he pulled back even more."

"Why?"

"Maybe it has to do with the DEA investigation. I can't force him to share."

Margo said, "There was a DEA number attached to the Megan Osterman death."

"You're thinking that Osterman's death might circle around back to Bradford's supplier."

"That's exactly what I'm thinking."

"If there is an active investigation," Jack said, "maybe we should slow down."

"Nope. I've been thinking about this on the drive up to Prescott. Elijah started working at the Cactus Stop in March. By all accounts, he loved his job. In July, Megan Osterman died across the street, early Sunday morning. Elijah didn't work weekends but he knew her—and he knew about her death. After her death, he began taking pictures of people coming and going—in the evening, after he got off work. Megan died of an overdose, Elijah died of an overdose."

"Megan was an addict."

"Yes, and her death was probably accidental. But that tells me drugs are involved in whatever crime Elijah had uncovered.

All the pictures he took, maybe he was monitoring drug deals. And yesterday, when I went to talk to Coach Bradford at Eyman Prison—"

"What the hell? You went to Eyman?"

"Uh, yeah." Margo sounded sheepish. "I was going to tell you when I got to the office. It's been a busy couple of days."

"Why talk to him? Do you think he's running a criminal organization from behind bars?" It wasn't unheard of, but Jack didn't think it likely.

"I actually hadn't thought of that," Margo said. "I thought someone else on campus might be running drugs. Everything I have—my theories, interviews—is just conjecture. Nothing I can prove. I *think* Elijah uncovered a crime at work which got him killed, but there's still a lot we don't know. And where does Lena Clark fit in?"

"Maybe she doesn't," Jack said, though he didn't believe it, and neither did Margo.

"Elijah also went to Silent Witness on his computer the day before he died. I don't know if he reached out or was simply looking for information."

"If someone contacts Silent Witness without linking it to an active case, it's hard to follow up. Tips like seeing a drug deal at a known spot doesn't give police enough to act on. But if they provided specific details, like names or locations, someone will follow up."

"Would you be able to find out if he called?"

"No," Jack said. "The program is compartmentalized. Cops are only told information that is relevant to their specific investigations. Most of the time the Silent Witness program is used for current cases that Phoenix asks for someone to step forward anonymously. You could get Elijah's phone records which would show a call, though if he filled out the online form, then that won't help."

"I have most of his records, and Alina is getting the rest from the phone company," Margo said. "After talking to Jessie Oliver yesterday, if there *was* something illegal going on with the Cactus

Stop, the staff would have to know. It's too small a store for them *not* to witness one of their coworkers committing a crime. More, if what I *think* is happening—illegal use of EBT cards—that means someone in the Cactus corporate office must also know what's going on. Maybe we should loop in Manny Ramos. He would be able to get answers faster."

"Be careful," Jack said cautiously. "You're jumping three steps ahead. You have no hard evidence of any crime, barely even circumstantial evidence."

"Fortunately, I'm neither a cop *nor* a lawyer, and I can pursue my theory without worry that I'm going to screw up a conviction. Let's talk to mom about it, okay? She knows Ramos. Hey—I have a call, I'll be there in less than an hour."

She hung up before Jack could say another word.

chapter thirty

MARGO ANGELHART

"Margo Angelhart," I answered.

"I got a call you wanted to talk to me."

A female voice with a slight Mexican accent and sharp edge of anger.

"And you are?"

"Desi, from the Cactus Stop."

"Thanks for calling me back," I said.

"I can't believe you went to Mr. Ramos about me."

"You're not in trouble. I wanted to talk to you about Elijah Martinez."

"I *know* I'm not in trouble, but shit, he's the boss's boss. So what'd'ya want to know?" she said, her voice clipped.

"Do you have time to meet this afternoon?"

Desi sighed dramatically. "Really? I mean, this could have waited until tomorrow when I'm working."

"Would you like to meet in Mr. Ramos's office?" I said, irritated at her attitude. "Because I can make that happen."

"Shit, no, why?"

I needed information, and running in circles with Desi wasn't getting me anywhere, so I changed tactics.

"You worked with Elijah on Friday, correct?"

"Tony already told you that."

I was usually good at dealing with belligerent people, but I hated doing it over the phone.

"Desi," I said in a voice I hoped was calm and nonthreatening. "Elijah's mother hired me to find out where he was the day he died. I have a timeline. I know when he arrived at school, when he left, when he got to work. Now I need to know where he went after work."

"I don't know. I wasn't friends with him. I only worked with him on Fridays."

"He didn't say anything about his plans?"

"Nope. We didn't talk much. He stocked shelves and cleaned, I worked the register. We didn't have anything in common."

"What time did he leave?"

"How the hell am I supposed to remember what happened two weeks ago?" Desi snapped.

"Because he died that night."

"I don't know, probably his usual time, eight, eight thirty." She paused. "You know, now that you talk about it, he left a little early. No big, we weren't busy, and I got a guy who comes in eight to midnight. So I said fine."

"How early?"

"Ten, fifteen minutes?"

"Did he have his backpack with him?"

"I don't know."

"Did you find his backpack in the store after he left?"

She sighed dramatically and was muttering something in a hybrid American-Mexican slang that was supposed to be an insult, I surmised.

"No," she finally said. "It wasn't in the store, so he probably had it with him. I didn't think about it. Are we done? I'm supposed to call Mr. Ramos's admin to let him know that I talked to you."

I ignored her desire to get off the phone. "Did anyone pick him up when he left?"

She sighed dramatically. "I didn't see. I know he didn't have a car, he usually walked home, so I assume that's what he did, okay? You were in the store talking to Tony, right? You can't see shit in the parking lot because the windows are all papered over. So he walked out, that's it. I'm sorry the kid is dead. He was nice, did his job, never bitched."

"Did the police come in and talk to you?"

"Police? What the hell for?"

"About Elijah."

"No. Not me, and not Tony. He would have told me. Are we done?"

She was rushing, but I had one more question. "Did Elijah have problems with any of the customers?"

Another overly dramatic sigh. "He never said anything to me about problems with anyone. Never got into a fight, never yelled at anyone, just did his job. I worked with him a couple hours a week for, like, six months. Maybe you should talk to his friends, you know? They know him, I just worked with him. Okay?"

"Okay for now," I said.

She hung up without saying goodbye. *Piece of work*, I thought. I glanced at my phone and saw I had a missed call from Harry. He would never put in text or email information he couldn't legally give me, so I called him back; it went to voicemail. "Tag, you're it," I said and hit End.

Desi was right about one thing: Elijah's friends should know more. They saw a change in behavior when they returned to school, but he didn't confide in any of them. Over the last few months—possibly since Megan Osterman died and Elijah started his nighttime photographic surveillance—he'd changed. Change in behavior and personality was a big red flag in drug use.

But I didn't think Elijah was using, not then, at any rate. Unless he started using uppers to stay alert while watching the store. Then downers to sleep.

That should be noticeable in the autopsy report. I called my brother Nico.

He answered with a sigh. "You want something."

"Hi, Nico. How's my favorite brother?" I said brightly.

"You call when you want something, text when you don't."

"Testy."

"I'm busy."

"I need you to explain an autopsy report to me."

"You have it?"

"Not with me. You can look it up."

"Now?"

"Two minutes, pretty please?"

He grumbled, but I heard his fingers on the keyboard and grinned. "Name, if you don't have the case number."

"Elijah Martinez. Drug overdose at Mountain View Park in Sunnyslope. Josie was the first responder."

"I remember it," he said, his voice softening. "Tragic."

"Yep."

"What's your interest?"

"His mom hired us. It's complicated. I'll tell you everything at the party tonight."

Nico typed, paused. "Cause of death asphyxiation due to fentanyl poisoning. Likely accidental overdose, not suicide."

"Is there anything in the report that shows whether he had a history of drug use? Wouldn't that be obvious in an autopsy?"

"Habitual drug use would be obvious; occasional drug use not without additional tests."

"And?"

"None of those tests were conducted. There was no need. He wasn't a habitual user—there were no impacted organs, such as the lungs or liver, that indicated he was a regular user."

"Would you be able to tell if he started using sporadically two to three months ago?"

"Where are you going with this, Margo?"

"I'll give you the details tonight. I just want to know if he used drugs at any point from July on."

"I don't know what evidence is logged, and if I don't have hair samples, there's no easy way to determine."

"Please?" I begged.

"I can't get blood from a stone."

"Just see if the stone is there."

"You are the bane of my existence."

"You love me anyway," I said.

"I'll see what we have. No promises." He hung up without a goodbye.

Five minutes later, as I was passing the 101 interchange, Manny Ramos called.

"Margo, I just got word from my assistant that Desi spoke with you. Was she of help?"

Belligerent and bitchy, but I didn't say that. "She didn't know much about Elijah's personal life," I said. "How long has she worked for you?"

"I can't say for certain, but at least two years, maybe longer. I can find out if it's important."

"Who hires into the store? Desi?"

"No, I have a personnel manager who fills openings at all thirteen Cactus Stops, as well as our corporate office. I'm having a small dinner party Friday night. Why don't you join us? And your mother—in fact, I'll reach out to Ava myself. Maybe we can brainstorm together? I would like to know what happened to Elijah and see how else I can help. I've had hundreds of teenagers work for my stores over the years, and nothing like this has happened before."

"You don't need to have us over, I'll call if I have more questions."

I didn't want to spend hours socializing with strangers. My mom would enjoy it.

"I had our accounting office email Elijah's hours worked for the past three months. Did you receive it?"

DON'T SAY A WORD

"Thank you, I'll check when I get to the office."

"Think about dinner, please," he said. "I have a call, but I'm at your disposal."

"Thanks."

Tess had texted me while I was talking to Ramos.

> Eric McMahon's contact info. Home: lives with his mom. Work: restaurant in Scottsdale. Don't be late to mom's party.

She sent pins to both locations, and I sent her two thumbs-up emojis.

I hit his home address and navigated there. The McMahons lived in a well-maintained, tree-lined neighborhood of modest one-story ranch-style homes about half a mile north of where I'd grown up.

I didn't know if Ms. McMahon would be home at noon on Thursday, but I knocked on the door anyway.

A young woman in her mid-twenties answered. She was very pregnant, her hand on the small of her back as she stood there.

"Can I help you?" she asked, sounding exhausted.

"I'm looking for Eric McMahon."

"You are?"

My phone vibrated in my pocket; I ignored it.

I handed her my business card. "Margo Angelhart."

She scowled at my card. "You going to screw with my brother? He's been through hell and back and finally has his life going in the right direction."

"I don't want to screw with Eric."

She snorted as if she didn't believe me, then clutched her stomach. "Settle down in there. Two more weeks." Then she said to me, her face a little softer. "Though I wouldn't complain if this little guy wanted to come out sooner."

"You need to sit down?"

"No. My mom's at work. Why do you want to talk to Eric?"

She eyed me suspiciously, and I felt honesty would be the best approach.

"A student at Sun Valley High School died of a drug overdose, and I was hired by the family after the police closed the case. In the course of my investigation, I have some evidence that the police didn't nab everyone working in Coach Bradford's organization." Okay, not *complete* honesty, but close.

"You tell my mother that, and she will explode. Eric is *not* involved with drugs."

"I don't think it's Eric," I assured her. "I want to pick his brain, go through the list of everyone involved and where they are now. I have no intention of getting him in trouble."

She bit her lip, so I pushed, "Would you please give him my name and number and ask him to call me? I'll meet him anywhere, anytime. His rules."

"I'll give him your information, but that's it."

"I appreciate that. Thank you."

She closed the door without saying goodbye. Fifty-fifty she'd give Eric the info. But it was a start.

When I got back into my Jeep, my phone vibrated again. I had two missed calls from my mom. I didn't want to talk to her . . . but I hit Call Back. She answered on the first ring.

"Margo, I appreciate that you are working to find answers for Mrs. Martinez, but you have Tess and Jack working without any context."

"Mom, I can explain it all when I get there, but—"

"But you're not here. Does this three-year-old closed investigation into Coach Bradford connect to Elijah's death?"

"I think so, but I don't know."

"You need to give all the information you have to the police. We weren't hired to investigate a drug ring, or reinvestigate Bradford."

"I don't have anything specific, it's a gut feeling. Based on some evidence," I added quickly. Jack appreciated intuition; my mom wanted cold hard facts.

"There is an active homicide investigation and if you have any information that may assist Detective King in solving Lena Clark's murder, you have a responsibility to share it."

"I don't, I'm working on it."

"Margo—"

"Mom, trust me."

"I do," she said. "But we need to talk. You're part of a team now, and we're all good sounding boards."

"I know. I'll be there soon."

"Thank you. By the way, I received an email from Manny Ramos inviting us to dinner on Friday."

"You go, I don't need to." Or want to, I thought.

"It would be good for us. Manny said he admires your tenacity in helping Alina. Councilman Borgas will be there—you remember Bill, right?"

Bill Borgas was a longtime friend of Mom and Dad's. "Yeah, so?"

"Think about it. Manny would be a good contact for the agency."

"And you're the best face for the agency," I said. "Not me."

"We'll talk about it later. And please, as soon as you're done in the field, come down here and explain your thought process. To me, this is a lot of work with no goal in sight."

"I'll be there as soon as I can."

I hung up before she could say anything else.

chapter thirty-one

CAL RAFFERTY

Mike Hitchner, Hitch to his friends, walked up to the food truck, ordered, then sat across from Cal at a covered picnic table. Cal had already eaten his street tacos—he loved this place, ate here all the time. It was convenient to both DEA headquarters and Phoenix PD where he spent far too much time working on joint task forces. They were necessary, but frustrating. Cal liked to be in the field. He needed to *do* something, even if doing something was watching a drug house for three days straight.

He and Hitch had been friends and colleagues for nearly a decade, ever since Cal transferred to Phoenix DEA from Texas. It was either transfer or quit, and Cal wasn't a quitter. Here, he had thrived and—mostly—managed to push the bullshit that happened in Texas into the past where it belonged.

So when Hitch called and said he needed a one-on-one, Cal put everything aside and met him for an early lunch.

"You look beat," Cal said.

"Typical bullshit. Closed this fucking miserable case late last night working with CAC on a child endangerment case. Parents had drugs everywhere, addicts going in and out, and two little kids sitting in the middle of it. But parents are in jail and kids are with a relative who seems to be solid."

Cal tipped an imaginary beer toward Hitch. "Cheers."

"But that's not why I wanted to meet."

Hitch's number was called and he went up to grab his basket, then returned to the table. "So," he said after eating one of the street tacos in two bites, "I had a call this morning. A former cop I used to work with reached out about the Bradford case. He's a PI now and wanted a sit-down, his partner and me, to talk about the Bradford case. I shut him down because I think they're fishing and it has nothing to do with the supplier we've been looking for. But if they start stirring the shit, we may never get a handle on this guy."

"A PI? Is the name Angelhart?"

Hitch stopped mid-bite. "He call you too?"

"No." Cal's name wasn't on any of the documents related to the Bradford bust. All credit went to Phoenix PD with an "assist" from the DEA.

"His partner—Margo?"

Hitch nodded. "Margo is Jack's sister."

"She paid a visit to Bradford yesterday."

"Maybe I should have talked to him."

"Not yet. Let me see what I can learn through my sources, then we can make the call. What do you know about the Angelharts?"

"Their mother used to be the county attorney, then went into private practice. Jack was a cop until three years ago. He worked VICE when he first got his gold shield, did a stint in CAC, then Violent Crimes. Good reputation. His grandfather is a retired judge."

"What did they want from you?" Cal asked.

"They're looking into an overdose death of a kid who went to Sun Valley, pulled the Bradford file, wanted to talk to me about the case, pick my brain, he said. I told him it was closed, and he mentioned Bradford's supplier."

"Does he have anything?"

"No. Fishing, like I said. I told him that end of the investigation was all DEA. Didn't mention your name, but it's been cold for three years."

Which was frustrating for both of them.

Hitch continued, "I told him if he had anything actionable to call me."

Cal was thinking. This might be an opportunity in disguise.

"Should I have passed him to you?" Hitch asked.

"No, I want to dig into their firm, see how they operate. Was the sister, this Margo, a cop too? I did a basic run on her and didn't see it."

"She wasn't a cop, but I don't know much about her."

Cal knew a little, and he would find out more.

"Gut feeling. Do you think they might have a line on the supplier we've been hunting for the last three years?"

Hitch finished his last taco and took time before he spoke. "I can tell you that Jack Angelhart was a good cop and has a solid rep. If he gets a whiff of something, he'll follow it."

"Okay. Good. I'm going to do my own recon, but if I need you to set up a meeting with them, could you?"

"Whatever you need, just call."

"Thanks, buddy."

Cal tossed his garbage in the trash and walked to his car.

He needed to know what the Angelharts were up to, and whether he should shut them down—or bring them in.

chapter thirty-two

MARGO ANGELHART

Being a PI means a lot of grunt work. Talking to people who might know something, until you learn they don't. But the work had to be done because you never knew when you'd find that one piece of information that would lead to the truth, that needle in the haystack.

I didn't know if my conversation with Eric McMahon's sister would get me a call back, but it was worth a shot. If I didn't hear from him and I was still stuck, I'd track him down at work.

After leaving McMahon's house, I went to talk to the receptionist at the veterinary clinic that fronted the alley where Megan Osterman died. They were pleasant, but only had internal cameras, so that was a dead end. Next, I went to Mrs. Osterman's house, near where Seventh Avenue dead-ended at North Mountain. The area had few trees and no grass, with small rundown houses—mostly cinder block construction from the 1950s. The yards were either rock or dirt, and even the cacti looked tired. Mrs. Osterman lived on the corner, and an older sedan sat in the carport.

A locked security screen blocked the door, so I rang the bell. A few moments later, a woman answered. She was in her early fifties, wore shorts and a tank top, and looked tired. "Can I help you?" she asked.

"Mrs. Osterman?"

"Yes," she responded warily.

"I'm Margo Angelhart, a private investigator. I'm working for a family to find out what happened to their son, who died of a suspicious drug overdose. I think he may have known your daughter."

"My daughter's dead."

"I know, and I'm sorry. Do you have a few minutes to talk to me?"

"I don't know how I can help."

"Maybe you can't, but I have some questions about your daughter and I think if I find the answers, it will help another grieving family. And maybe give you a bit of closure as well."

"I have closure. I loved Megan, she couldn't stop the drugs, and she died."

Her voice cracked, and I felt for her.

"I'm really sorry."

I waited, and a beat later Mrs. Osterman said, "Fine, come in. I don't work until five, anyway."

She unlocked the screen and I entered her small house. The blinds were drawn to keep the house cool and the air was fresh, filled with a strong hint of lemon. Despite the tired exterior, the interior had been thoughtfully updated, featuring sleek wood floors, textured walls, and modern lighting. The living room flowed seamlessly into the dining area and kitchen, giving the space a more expansive feel than it appeared from the outside. The kitchen was bright and airy, mostly white, with a butcher block island at its center and colorful subway tiles adding a touch of character to the walls.

"I love your kitchen," I said. "I have a little house off fourteenth, built about the same time, and I haven't figured out how to remodel the kitchen."

Mrs. Osterman smiled. "It cost a pretty penny, but I love to cook. We'll sit in there."

I followed her and sat on one of the counter barstools.

"I don't want to take up much of your time," I said, removing a card from my pocket and sliding it over to her. "Especially since you have to go to work in a few hours."

She waved off my comment. "It's fine. Tell me what you know about Megan."

"I am investigating the overdose death of a boy named Elijah Martinez, who went to school with Megan, though he was a few years younger. Did you know him?"

She shook her head. "Megan didn't bring her friends home—most of them were addicts like her. She was my baby. Maybe I babied her too much." She shared that Megan was much younger than her two sons, and when her daughter was eight and her boys were out of the house, her husband was killed in a car accident. It was just her and Megan and they were close—until Megan started high school.

"I couldn't kick her out of the house," Mrs. Osterman said. "I couldn't condemn her to a life on the streets, knowing what happens to girls who are addicts and homeless. Here, she had food, a bed. Eventually, I had to change the locks because she stole from me, but I told her she could live in the room behind the garage. She cleaned it out, made it into a nice little space. I told her I would pay for rehab, but she never went through with it. The last few months of her life were difficult for both of us."

Mrs. Osterman wasn't looking at me, but at the water bottle in her hand. I couldn't imagine the pain of watching your child slowly kill herself and not being able to stop it.

"Three years ago a coach at Sun Valley High School was arrested for running a drug distribution network using kids at the school," I said.

"Yes, I remember it well. I wondered if Megan had been working for him, because it was that year—her junior year—that she started acting different. Before, she had good grades, good hygiene, friends. But sometime early in her junior year, that all changed. I confronted her, she denied it, then ran away. For a week I didn't know where she was. Then she came home and apologized and said she hadn't worked for him, but she knew people who did."

"Did you believe her?"

"Yes. The way she said it, one of her friends was in serious trouble with the police after everything came out, and it scared Megan. She was clean for a while, but then she started smoking pot again and spiraled from there. The marijuana she was getting was tainted with other drugs—that's how I think she became addicted."

"What I'm looking for is anyone who worked for Coach Bradford three years ago, and who might be running a similar operation now, especially if they have a connection to the school."

"I don't think I can help you," she said sadly. "The last few months of Megan's life . . . she didn't talk to me much."

"Who were her closest friends in high school?"

"Before she started using drugs, it was Christina O'Reilly. They were friends forever. Christina is outspoken and extroverted and fun. I loved having her over because she would bring Megan out of her shell—Megan had always been very introverted. I think—Megan never said—that Christina expanded her friend group. She never excluded Megan, but Megan excluded herself."

"Do you know where Christina is now?"

"College. I haven't seen or talked to her since high school graduation. When Megan started using, Christina was outspoken and blunt with her. I thought the honesty would help Megan turn away from hurting herself, but Megan shut Christina out. I asked Christina to keep trying, but she said she was done. Which, I suppose, is partly why I went in the opposite direction. Megan knew I disapproved, but I didn't constantly criticize her. Maybe I should have," she added sadly.

"Did Christina live nearby?"

"Yes, right across the street from Sunnyslope Middle School. I don't remember the number, but it's the only two-story house on the block. She's the oldest of five kids."

"And after Megan started using? Anyone she hung out with regularly?"

"She dated someone for a while, Scott—I don't remember his last name."

"Jimenez?" I prompted.

"That sounds right. I didn't like him, and I didn't like how he would stay all night in her room, even after I told her I wouldn't allow it. He went to prison because of what he did for Coach Bradford. I don't know how this helps."

"Have you seen him since he was released?" I asked. Tess hadn't yet been able to track him down.

"No," she said.

"Have you emptied Megan's room?"

Mrs. Osterman shook her head. "I've only been in there to air it out, clean up some. I found drugs there, called the police. They came to retrieve them."

"Do you remember who?"

"I don't. He said he was in the Drug Enforcement Bureau, and he would first test, then destroy the drugs. He seemed very kind, but he pitied me. He probably sees this all the time."

"Would you mind if I looked through Megan's things?"

"What do you hope to find? It's not going to bring Megan back. It's not going to bring your friend Elijah back."

"It won't bring anyone back, but it helps. I think there's another organized drug operation that may be centered at the school." Or, the Cactus Stop, but I didn't say that. Maybe both. I wouldn't even have thought about the school except for Lena Clark's murder and Bradford. "There might be evidence in Megan's room. Names, her supplier, what she did in the days and weeks leading up to her overdose. The police aren't investigating, but if I can find some evidence, I'll pass it on and they may be able to stop these people."

"All right," she said. "I guess I just feel that no matter what we do, it's not enough."

"Maybe one piece doesn't seem important, but when we put them all together? That makes a difference."

I believed it, though it probably wasn't much consolation to Mrs. Osterman—or Alina Martinez.

I convinced Mrs. Osterman to let me go through Megan's room alone. First, because I could see she was upset with the reminders and memories of Megan's last few years, and second, because the room was very small.

I stood at the door, surveying the room, which had once been a storage space behind the carport. A tiny bathroom tucked behind a pocket door was cramped with a toilet, sink, and a barely functional shower. Despite its size, it was clean and organized—whether because of Megan or Mrs. Osterman, I couldn't tell.

The room itself was small, with a double bed, a narrow dresser, a small wooden desk with a pull-out stool, and a mounted TV. There wasn't much room for anything else, but Megan had made the most of it. A fan hung from the ceiling in the ten-by-eight-foot space, and a small window let in some natural light. The cement floor was covered by an indoor/outdoor rug, and the bed, with a purple comforter and colorful pillows, was set up to comfortably watch TV. Two shelves above the desk displayed neatly arranged books and knickknacks, while tropical beach posters and pale lavender walls added a personal touch. What struck me though was the absence of personal photos. And there were no mirrors in the bedroom or bath.

Megan reminded me that addicts came from all families, all races, all socioeconomic ranges. Addiction didn't discriminate.

I carefully searched the room, though there weren't many places to hide anything. Her clothes were made up of shorts, jeans, and T-shirts; shoes were tucked under her dresser. No jewelry or makeup. Her books were the sort you read for school, with a lot of fantasy mixed in. I flipped through them, nothing fell out, but based on the condition of the spines, they had all been read multiple times.

Maybe there really was nothing here that pointed to who Megan associated with during the last months of her life. Nothing to point to who might have been involved in the drug ring three years ago—and now.

But I hadn't looked *everywhere*.

I had shared a bedroom with my sister Tess my entire life, until Tess went to college the year I was a high school senior. Tess had a diary that I loved to read—mostly to annoy her. She would hide it; I always found it. I was a brat as a kid, I can admit it now, and I eventually grew out of invading her privacy.

Sometimes, Tess found ingenious places to hide her diary—like in the tank of the toilet. She did that until the bag leaked and ruined her book. And I'll admit, that was the one place I had never thought to look because all five of us kids shared one bathroom.

So I checked the tank; nothing. I looked between the mattress and the platform it rested on; nothing. Nothing under or behind the dresser, desk, or drawers. I even looked behind the television—only a little dust.

Maybe Megan didn't have a diary. Maybe she kept a diary on her phone, or her computer, which wasn't here, if she'd even had one. I should ask Mrs. Osterman about Megan's phone—she might have contacts in it, if I could get through the passcode.

Then I started opening DVD boxes, not expecting to find anything except DVDs.

I was wrong.

Megan had the entire collection of *Buffy the Vampire Slayer*, which was one of my favorite series. Nico and I had binge-watched it as teenagers one summer when he was going through a bunch of tests in the hospital that left him tired and grumpy, before he was diagnosed with a rare but curable bone cancer. The series took his mind off not knowing what was wrong with him and immersed him into a new world.

The collection came in a box with a hinged lid, each of the seven seasons in a separate case. When I opened the lid, I noticed that one of the DVD cases protruded a half inch above the others. I took all the cases out and at the bottom was a flash drive.

After searching every other DVD, this was the only oddity I found.

I carefully put everything back, contemplating whether or not to ask Mrs. Osterman's permission to take the flash drive. If she said no, I was screwed. But if there was evidence of a crime on the drive, I would need to turn it over to police and tell them how and where I found it. And at that point, I would have to admit I stole it, which could jeopardize my license.

I was all about bending rules. Hell, I'd broken a few when I had a good reason. But the truth was I didn't *know* if this was important to my investigation, so I didn't have a solid reason to pocket it.

I made sure the room was in the same condition I found it, and went back inside the house. "Mrs. Osterman?" I called, then saw her in the living room. She was sitting on the couch looking through a book. As I came closer, I saw it was a scrapbook from Megan's childhood.

"Megan made this for my fiftieth birthday. She was thirteen. It's all the things we did together. I try to remember the fun years."

She was silently crying, and I really hated that I had reminded this woman of what she'd lost.

"Thank you so much for your time, Mrs. Osterman."

"Did you find anything to help?"

"I might have." I held out the flash drive. "This was hidden in one of the DVD sets. Do you recognize it?"

Mrs. Osterman frowned and shook her head.

"Would you mind if I borrowed it? If it's personal pictures or anything like that, I'll immediately return it. But I think there was a reason she hid this."

She bit her lip, then nodded.

"Did Megan have a cell phone?"

"Of course. The police returned it with her personal effects. I haven't gone through it—I don't know if I want to."

"Would you mind if I looked at it? I only want to look at her contacts to see who else I can talk to."

"It wouldn't be charged."

I also wanted to check her text messages, but didn't say that. Mrs. Osterman hadn't hired me. But I felt strongly that something about Megan's death had prompted Elijah to investigate on his own, which led to his death.

"If you charge it and want to send me her contacts, I would appreciate it. Or, I can do it myself."

She seemed torn, then she nodded. "Give me a minute."

She left the room and I felt like crap. Megan had been dead for less than three months and Mrs. Osterman was still grieving. I'd brought it all back to the surface.

A few minutes later she returned with a small cloth bag. "Her phone and charger. The passcode is 1117."

"Thank you. I'll get it back to you as soon as possible."

Mrs. Osterman opened the front door. "It's been eleven weeks since Megan died. Sometimes, it feels like yesterday. But I really lost her three years ago."

When I left the Osterman house, I was depressed. Megan had had a good life, a mother who loved her, and seemed to have been a happy kid. Until someone introduced her to drugs and she became addicted. Addiction was complicated—some people were more susceptible than others. Some people needed more help to quit. And some people fueled addictions.

Those people made me angry.

I headed downtown toward the office when Harry finally called me back. I was irritated that it had taken him so long. Yes, he was doing me a favor, but it would take him, like, two seconds to look up the plate.

Still, I answered in my sweetest voice. "And how is my favorite veteran today?"

"The idiot I spent two days training? Quit. Didn't come in today and sent a fucking email that the job was too much pressure. I'll show him pressure!"

"Sounds like you're having a worse day than me."

"John Brighton."

"The Tesla?"

Harry rattled off an address and I barely had time to swing to the side of the road and scribble it down on the only piece of paper I could find, the back of a receipt.

"Thanks, Harry."

"I hate people," he said and hung up.

Since I was already pulled over, I looked up Brighton's address. The address was Phoenix, but the zip code was the area bordering Paradise Valley.

I stopped, thumb hovering above my screen. What was familiar about this address?

Then it clicked. Elijah had searched *this address* on Google Maps the day before he died.

I typed it into Maps to see exactly where it was. The road John Brighton lived on led to Piestewa Peak. Older homes, but very pricey because of the view. I itched to drive over there and check it out, but it was midafternoon, and no guarantee he'd be home.

I texted Tess the name and address.

> Can you find info about him? Work, play, whatever. I'm on my way to the office—fifteen minutes tops.

She sent me an angry face emoji, so I followed it up with a kissy face emoji before I pulled into traffic.

Elijah had looked up this address the day before he died. He'd taken photos of the vehicle registered to this address.

What did you find, Elijah?

What did you find that got you killed?

chapter thirty-three

MARGO ANGELHART

It was after two by the time I arrived at the office. I had gotten a lot accomplished since I left my house at five thirty this morning.

"We have a party tonight," Tess said as soon as I walked in. "I wanted to leave by now."

"I'm sorry. I spent too much time at Mrs. Osterman's house, but I might have found something." I held up the flash drive. "Let me see what's on this first, then we'll talk, okay?"

"Five minutes, max. I have information too, and you're going to want to hear it."

Then she turned on her heel and went to the conference room, where Jack and our mom were talking.

First, I plugged Megan's phone into an outlet to charge.

I then put the flash drive into my computer. There were three video files. I clicked on one and . . . it wanted a password. Shit.

I put the drive in my top drawer and as I walked to the conference room, I texted Luisa.

> I need you to get info from a password-protected file. I'll bring it tonight to the party.

Luisa immediately sent a thumbs-up emoji.

Mom said, "Margo, I know you have been working hard to find out what happened to Elijah, but we need to touch bases more often. You have a theory, but haven't shared it with anyone."

"Happy Birthday, Mom," I said.

She blinked, then gave me a little smile. "Thank you, dear. But you're not going to distract me from lecturing you."

"Of course not," I said as I sat down.

I looked at the stacks of paper on the table and three open laptops. They'd all been working as hard as I had.

"I'm really sorry that I didn't explain everything clearly, but I was running on a hunch that I couldn't quite articulate."

"It's fine," Tess said. "But I do want to get to the house, so let us all know what you discovered."

"I'm pretty certain that Elijah uncovered drug-related illegal activity at the Cactus Stop." I told them about Megan Osterman's overdose and how Elijah started taking pictures at night of everyone who came in and out of the store. "Megan's boyfriend was Scott Jimenez, the teen who went to prison for shooting Eric McMahon."

"That gives us a connection to Coach Bradford's former operation," Jack said, "so why are you not focused on the school?"

"Because Elijah was taking pictures of people going in and out of the Cactus Stop, and not people on campus. My primary goal was to retrace his steps Friday night. And I'm stuck, because no one has come forward to say they saw him or were with him. I have no idea where he was after he left work until he died in the park. So going back to the photos—why was he taking them, what was he planning to do? Was he caught taking pictures Friday night, and that person drugged him? Megan Osterman's death was the catalyst, and learning from her mother that she was connected to Coach Bradford through her boyfriend brings us back to Sun Valley High."

"Where does Lena Clark fit in?" Tess asked.

"She's connected to Elijah directly, and indirectly to Coach Bradford because they were colleagues," I said. "Lena was asking questions, so I figure she saw or heard something that made her suspicious, or someone became nervous because of her interest in Elijah's death."

"Conjecture," Mom said. "But go on."

This was one of the problems with bouncing ideas off a lawyer's brain. I wasn't trying a case, I was working through facts and theories. I wanted to talk things through, not have to prove anything yet.

"I shelved Lena's murder," I said, "because I don't have access to the information the police have. However, I want to talk to Parsons, her boyfriend. He might know who she was talking to, maybe she said something to him, something that he doesn't realize is important."

"The police would have asked him the same thing," Jack said.

"No," I countered. "Because the police aren't thinking about Elijah."

"You think he was murdered," Mom said.

"Yes, but I can't prove it," I said. "There're reasons to support this theory. The photos he took. The fact that his phone and backpack are missing. His behavior—yes, different, but not addict different. He was preoccupied and quiet, but not erratic or irresponsible."

My mom didn't interject—score one for me.

"Elijah had taken a picture of a license plate. I asked a friend to look it up, the car is registered to John Brighton. I have the address. But Elijah had the address as well—he looked it up on his computer the night before he died."

"Who's John Brighton?" Jack asked.

I turned to Tess, and she immediately said, "I haven't had time to run him yet."

"Tomorrow's soon enough," I said. "But Elijah had the address. Maybe that's where he went Friday."

Mom said, "I don't know that I would jump to the conclusions you have, but I see where you're going. We'll run Mr. Brighton, but you still don't have evidence that Elijah went to his house."

"I want to ask Brighton."

Mom nodded, though glanced at Jack as if for confirmation. I tried not to let it irritate me.

"A good idea," Jack said. "I'll back you up, Margo. In fact, I'll check out his house first. I won't confront him, just get a lay of the land."

"Thanks," I said, and meant it. There were some definite advantages to working on a team.

Mom said, "Why did you have Tess tracking down more than a dozen softball players from Sun Valley? This is all tedious, time-consuming work that doesn't directly connect to Elijah."

"I'm sorry," I said, and this time I really meant it. "It was a tickle I had when I saw that Coach Bradford's daughter was on the softball team—and my gut tells me she's the one who called in the anonymous tip against him."

"It wasn't that time-consuming," Tess said. "I found most of the girls, so if we need to follow up with them when we can. I also learned that Scott Jimenez was released a year after his arrest, put on probation. But I couldn't find a current address or employer. Scott has an older sister named Desiree Jimenez."

I blinked, then it came into focus. "Desi."

"And she works at the Cactus Stop," Tess said with a smile.

"Small world," I muttered. "I talked to her today."

"Here's her address," Tess said and slid over a printout. "She lost her license because of two DUIs, spent six months in jail for the second. That was four years ago. No drug arrests, and she hasn't had a ding in four years."

"Desi could have known Megan Osterman," I said. "Megan dated her brother for at least a year, maybe longer. Maybe McMahon knows more—I reached out, and I hope his family will give him the message."

"What do you expect to learn?" Mom asked.

"Eric may suspect another teacher or staff member was involved, even if he doesn't have proof."

"What incentive would McMahon have to talk to you?" Jack asked. "He was shot, he probably wants nothing to do with any of those people." He glanced at Tess. "Has he kept his nose clean?"

"Yes," Tess said.

"So he's keeping a low profile."

"I'm still going to ask," I said. "Megan's mom let me take her phone and a flash drive I found hidden in her room. I'll go through those and see what I can learn. Megan's file has a DEA case number attached, so I think there may be a bigger investigation that we know nothing about."

"We don't want to step on the toes of a federal investigation," Mom said.

"Yes, we do," I said. "Elijah is dead because of something that was going on at the Cactus Stop. If there was an investigation, where are they? Why didn't they take over the death investigation? Or talk to his mother? And then Lena Clark—why was she killed? Just a random coincidence ten minutes after she called me? I'm not going to sit back and wait for some lazy ass fed to *maybe* solve the case."

Mom said, "In four days, you have learned a lot of information that *may* point to a criminal enterprise, but very little to give to Mrs. Martinez about what happened to her son that night."

"I know." And I was frustrated. "But I think Elijah's activities after work are directly connected to his death. I need to follow through and see what I can learn."

We all looked at Mom. She nodded. "It's suspicious, and a good avenue of investigation. When do you feel we should tell Manny Ramos what may be going on?"

"When we have something definitive," I said. "Or if we're stuck, maybe we bring it to him. The EBT fraud angle seems weak, based on what I've learned. That would show up in their financials. But if Desi or Tony are involved in some sort of scam, or dealing drugs and Elijah caught on, that would give them motive to kill him."

"Okay," Mom said. "But when you have solid, actionable evidence, we turn it over to the police."

I agreed.

"One more thing to discuss," Mom said. "I met with Madison O'Neill's legal team. I'm inclined to take the case. The arrest was a rush to judgment by the police, and the indictment is weak. I'm not saying she's innocent, but this is the reason I became a lawyer—to maintain the integrity of the justice system. Because I was a prosecutor and then a private defense lawyer, I am uniquely qualified to assess the evidence. If we take it, I need all of us on board. It'll be weeks of work—maybe months. Work that will fund pro bono cases like Elijah Martinez. I'm going to write up what I know, then we will vote."

"Mom," Tess said, "we trust your judgment on this."

Mom was looking at me, and I read between the lines. "We start soon, don't we?"

"I need to give them an answer next week. But it's important that all three of you are on board."

"Do you think she's innocent?" Jack asked.

"She says she is. And I want you all to assess what we have. If any of you are uncomfortable with it, we'll pass on it."

"Fair enough," Jack said.

I didn't need to assess anything—the O'Neill case sounded interesting.

Mom said, "Tess, send me everything you have on the Jimenez family and the Bradford investigation. I'll go through the legal documents, see if anything else jumps out at me."

"It's your birthday, Mom," Tess said.

"And I said I'd take tonight off," she countered. "Besides, you're having the party, I just have to show up, right?"

Tess glared at me. "You'd better help."

"I'll be there at five thirty." I jumped up and made a beeline for the door.

"Where are you going?" Jack asked.

"To talk to a friend of Megan Osterman's. She might know who she was close to before she died."

chapter thirty-four

ANGIE WILLIAMS

Angie sat at the top of the volleyball stands and watched Gina and the team warm up. The next three games were away, and Angie wouldn't be able to go unless she got a ride with Gina's mom.

She'd heard nothing from the PI since she gave her the yearbooks the day before. The police had unsealed Mrs. Clark's office yesterday. Mr. Parsons was still on leave. Detective King hadn't talked to her again. Angie had no idea what was happening, and it was disconcerting.

A teacher had been *murdered on campus* only three days ago, and other than some whispered gossip, everyone was going about their business.

Andy and Peter walked up the stairs to sit with her. "Hey," they said.

"Hi." She glanced at Peter. "Don't you have your internship thing?"

"The guy I apprentice for is going to a wedding in San Diego and took a couple days off." Peter shrugged. "They said come back Monday."

"How's it going?"

"Good," he said, noncommittal. "You still planning on going to U of A?"

She shrugged. "I dunno."

Angie, Elijah, and Andy had all talked about going to U of A. They'd already applied—early applications opened September 1. But Angie didn't know what she wanted to do. Nothing seemed important anymore.

"The PI talked to us yesterday morning," Andy said. "She didn't say much, but I think she was surprised that the police didn't have his backpack."

"Some bum probably stole it," Angie said.

"What do you think happened?" Peter asked.

"I think someone killed him."

"Isn't that weird? That someone killed Elijah, then Mrs. Clark is killed?" Andy said.

It was, and Angie hadn't been able to stop thinking about it. The school office had been quiet Monday afternoon, right before Mrs. Clark died. She'd only seen Mrs. Villines and Mr. Borel.

Angie frowned, thinking back to that afternoon. She'd heard someone talking, and a jingle of bracelets or maybe keys. She'd thought it was Mrs. Clark, because she wore a lot of jewelry, but she'd been talking to someone . . . and it was a familiar voice. But Angie couldn't quite place it.

"Did the PI show you pictures?" Angie asked.

They both shook their heads.

"I think something was going on at the Cactus Stop," Angie said.

"Yeah, me too," Andy said.

"Really?" she asked.

"Elijah was going to quit."

Why hadn't he told her? Angie wondered.

They sat quietly for a moment, until Andy and Peter started

talking about the girls on the team—Andy had a crush on the only sophomore on the varsity team. Angie let her mind drift, thinking about her argument with Mrs. Clark, about what Margo had told her, about Benny and his job.

She was worried about him. She knew why he couldn't quit, but she didn't want anything to happen to him. Did Benny take her seriously this morning? Should she let Chris know that something weird was going on at the Cactus Stop?

She was surprised to see Mr. Parsons walk into the gym. He looked around the stands, and when he saw her, he put up his hand. He wanted to talk to *her*?

"I gotta go," she said to Andy and Peter. "See you later."

She clomped down the bleachers toward a very pale and tired-looking Mr. Parsons. "Did you want to talk to me?"

"Can we step outside?"

She followed him out and they walked across the blacktop toward the football field, but she didn't think he was taking her anywhere specific. She didn't know what to say, but felt like she had to say something.

"Um, I'm really sorry about what happened to Mrs. Clark. I really hate that she thought I was mad at her."

He stopped walking when they reached the benches that ran along chain-link fencing. He sat. She hesitated, then sat next to him.

"Lena understood," he said quietly. "She liked you quite a bit."

That made her feel worse.

"My brain is in a fog," he said. "The police are no closer to finding out who did this."

"How do you know?"

"They talked to me Monday, and then again yesterday. I heard they talked to you as well."

"Same detective who closed Elijah's case. They made it sound as if I had killed her—which I didn't. I wouldn't, I swear."

"You didn't do anything, Angie. They made it sound as if I

killed her too. I think it's just the detective who's running the investigation, turning everyone into a suspect. I talked to the private investigator on Monday, but with everything that has happened, I don't remember her name. Did you ever talk to her?"

"Margo Angelhart," Angie said. "I talked to her a couple of times."

"It doesn't even ring a bell. It's like I blocked everything out on Monday."

"Why didn't you walk back with her from the volleyball game?" Angie said.

"I've thought the exact same thing a hundred times. If I had, she would still be here. I'd left some papers I wanted to grade in my classroom, went to get them and ended up in a conversation with Mrs. Porter. Fifteen minutes. And she was gone." He shook his head. "I'll track down Ms. Angelhart."

"You want to talk to the PI?"

"The police said Lena called her before she was k-killed." He cleared his throat. "But they didn't tell me anything else."

"I have her number." Angie pulled her phone from her pocket and showed it to him.

He put Margo's number into his phone. "Thank you."

He made no move to get up, so she sat there with him. It was weird, and she wanted to go back to the game, but Mr. Parsons looked so sad.

"Um," she said, bit her lip. "Are you okay?"

"I will be. Thank you."

"I'm going back to the game. Do you want to watch it?"

"I'll sit here for a minute."

She got up. "I'll see you tomorrow in class?"

"Yes. I'll be there. I need to get back to work, it might help."

Angie headed toward the gym, but looked back at Mr. Parsons. He was still sitting on the bench, watching the football practice. But she wondered if he could see anything at all.

Instead of going into the gym, she left campus and walked to the Cactus Stop. She had a sudden urge to check in on Benny. She didn't know if he had taken her seriously this morning, and if she had to, she would call Chris and let him know why she was worried. If anyone could convince Benny to quit, it was his brother.

chapter thirty-five

MARGO ANGELHART

I drove to the O'Reilly house and convinced Christina's mother to call her for me. We had a good ten-minute conversation where Christina confirmed everything Megan's mother said, and added more details about Megan's relationship with Scott Jimenez. She was completely attached to him. She visited him every week while he was in jail, and they planned to move in together when he got out.

Christina also remembered seeing Megan near the end of the summer after graduation. She seemed to be doing better, and said she had a part-time job. That was news to me—her mother hadn't mentioned it, and I hadn't seen anything about a job in her room. "Rumor was," Christina said, "Scott was supposed to be released right before Christmas, when he turned nineteen. I heard through the grapevine that he bailed on Megan. She was already on thin ice, and that broke it."

Christina didn't know where Scott was or who I could talk to about him, other than his sister Desiree.

I thanked her for her time and left. Eric McMahon had texted me while I was there and said he was leaving for work at four.

I had fifteen minutes. I texted him that I would be there in five minutes.

I glanced around, noticed an older model black 4Runner I thought I'd seen turn into the neighborhood after me. The driver was still in the car, looking at his phone. I made a mental note, but when I pulled away from the curb, he didn't follow.

It took me five minutes to get to Eric's house.

Eric refused to let me inside. We stood on his porch, him with his arms crossed, glaring at me, even after I explained who I was and what I was doing. He was a lean six feet and would have been attractive if he didn't have a chip on his shoulder a mile wide, and eyes that looked older than his years.

"I can't help you," he said.

"What I'm trying to understand is how Coach Bradford's drug distribution network operated."

"Why do you care?"

"As I told you, an honors student died of a drug overdose, and I don't think it was an accident. I think someone poisoned him."

Eric didn't say anything, just continued to glare.

I said, "I know the basics. You were Bradford's right hand. You recruited others. But you were the only one who knew that Coach Bradford was in charge."

He gave a very small nod.

"When Bradford was caught, Scott Jimenez tried to kill you."

"I remember." He lifted up his sleeve to reveal a scar.

Definitely a bullet wound.

"Bradford swore in his plea agreement that he never told or asked Jimenez to kill you."

"Right. And you believe him?" Eric shook his head.

"It makes more sense to me that he was telling the truth. I'm thinking that someone picked up where Bradford left off. Do you remember a student named Elijah Martinez?"

Eric shook his head. "Should I?"

"He was a freshman at the time."

"If he wasn't a jock, or dealing for me, I didn't know him."

"What about Lena Clark?"

"Of course. She's the guidance counselor."

"Was the guidance counselor," I said. "She was stabbed to death on Monday."

He blanched. "Oh, my God. Who did it?"

"The police don't know, but she was asking questions about Elijah's overdose. And I think Elijah was killed because he was investigating the overdose death of Megan Osterman."

"Megan," he said with a whisper.

"You know her?"

"She died?"

"She had a drug problem for the last three years."

"I thought she cleaned herself up," he said. "Fucking asshole."

"Excuse me?"

"Jimenez. He got her hooked. Megan was a sweetheart, a year younger than us. Always came to our games. Very shy though. Fell hard for Scott. He was obsessive with her, and I thought when Scott went to prison, she'd turn her life around."

"She died the Fourth of July weekend behind the veterinary clinic on Hatcher, across from the Cactus Stop. Scott's sister is the manager there."

He blinked rapidly, but didn't say anything. He knew something.

"Two months later, Elijah Martinez died," I said.

"Drugs kill," he said. "Even when I was dealing, I never touched the stuff."

"Someone poisoned him with fentanyl."

"Like I said, drugs kill."

"Eric, help me. A name. A teacher. An administrator. A student who didn't get caught up in the sting."

"I don't know any specific person," he said, "but yeah, there was someone else. Someone that Coach took orders from. I told that to the police when I agreed to turn state's evidence. If I knew who it was, I would have told them because my immunity deal required it. I suspected, but I had no knowledge. I couldn't even guess who. Just like I didn't know where he got the drugs. All I did was what he told me to do, and I regret every single minute."

I believed him. "Who was Scott close to?"

"You mean, like a teacher?" He thought on it. "Other than Coach? No one. He wasn't a good student, always in trouble, got detention practically every week. I swear he spent more time in the vice principal's office than he did in class. He didn't have friends outside of the football team either. Except Megan."

I handed him my card. "If you think of anyone, call me."

"I don't think you understand who these people are. If I were you, I'd walk away."

"Elijah's mom deserves to know why her son was killed."

"Is the truth worth losing your life?"

"I've been a PI for eight years," I said. "I'll find the truth and turn it over to the police."

"To be honest, I'm glad I didn't know anything more than I did. You know why? They would have sent someone better than Scott to kill me."

"They?" I asked.

"Whoever was in charge. Whoever Coach answered to. I have to go to work. Don't come by here again. I don't know anything else that will help you."

I walked to my Jeep. Eric had turned all the information over to the police—probably Hitchner, the head of the task force. I still wanted to talk to him, but didn't know how to convince him to talk to me.

If there was someone above the coach, it might not be someone at the school. It could be someone he knew in his personal life, his neighborhood, his family, a parent, hell, it could have been a local drug dealer. God knew Phoenix had plenty of them. It would make sense that they would set up a completely new operation. At the school? Maybe. He drove down to Yuma at least once a month, ostensibly to pick up his supply. Hitchner believed his supplier was somewhere along that route . . . and the supplier could have recruited another dealer.

As all this was going through my head, I didn't notice the older model black 4Runner until I pulled away from the curb.

It was the same vehicle I'd seen when I left the O'Reilly house.

Someone was following me.

I pretended I didn't see him as I drove away. The driver was white with dark hair, probably thirties, but it was hard to tell because he was smart enough to park down the street and wear dark sunglasses. When I passed him, he was looking at his phone as if he wasn't following me. Just like he had been doing outside the O'Reilly house.

I didn't believe that for a minute.

I headed toward the Cactus Stop on Hatcher, though I didn't intend to go in. I was just trying to see what Mr. 4Runner would do.

He didn't follow me. Okay, maybe I was paranoid. Maybe there was a reason for him to be outside Sunnyslope Middle School, then the McMahon house.

My phone vibrated, but it was an unknown caller, so I sent it to voicemail. I needed to stay alert in case the 4Runner showed up again.

Maybe I'd gotten on someone's radar. Questions had a way of doing that. I considered Eric's warning, and a chill went down my spine. I needed to stay on alert.

I headed down the side street past Edith Mackey's house, toward Sun Valley High School. A girl up ahead with long dark hair half dyed pink looked just like Angie.

Dammit. She *was* Angie.

I pulled over and honked.

Angie jumped, then recognized me. I motioned for her to get in my car.

"Were you at the Cactus Stop?" I asked as soon as she closed the door.

She hesitated.

"Didn't I tell you to keep a low profile?"

"I just wanted to talk to Benny for a minute."

I hit the steering wheel. "Your friend was killed because of something going on at his work, and you wander in there and ask questions?"

"I'm sorry."

"Who was working there with Benny?" I demanded.

"Um, Tony."

"What was so important that you're willing to risk your life?"

Angie was angry and trying not to cry.

"You didn't tell me what happened yesterday!"

"Because I haven't kept you clued into my investigation, you think it's okay to start asking questions, putting yourself on their radar. I don't fucking believe it."

I was angry as well as worried. I was being followed, Eric was still scared of the people Coach Bradford had worked for, and people were dead in what I believed, but couldn't prove, were two connected murders. And Elijah's murder was because *he* had been investigating Megan Osterman's drug overdose.

"We talked about this," I said, forcing myself to calm down. "I told you to go to school and lay low. I have been making progress. It might not be fast enough for you, but I don't really care."

"The police are doing nothing to find out what happened to Mrs. Clark. No one has been arrested, no one knows *anything*. I talked to Mr. Parsons today and he's depressed—he asked for your name, he couldn't remember it."

"Oh?" I asked, shifting gears. "What did he want to talk to me about?"

She shrugged. "I don't really know. He said he knew that you'd talked to Mrs. Clark right before she died. The police talked to him twice, thought *he* was a suspect, but I guess not anymore. He hasn't been at school until this afternoon. He looks miserable. He said he didn't walk her to her office Monday because he forgot papers to grade in his classroom. It's like he blames himself."

"Survivor's guilt," I said. "I'll talk to him, he'll be okay. Now, what were you doing at the Cactus Stop?"

She sulked, but then said, "This morning I talked to Benny and asked him if he saw anything weird at work."

I wanted to throttle her. Instead, I prompted, "And?"

"He said Tony is a pothead, stoned all the time. Benny's rarely allowed to work the register, and he doesn't like the job at all. He's looking for something else. All day I was thinking, I don't want him there. He's Chris's little brother, and if anything happened to him—well, after losing Elijah, I can't bear to think of anything happening to Benny too. So I went just to see how he was doing. And I told him to call you if he sees anything really weird going on."

I let out a long breath. I had to remember Angie was a teenager, and teenagers weren't generally patient. I know—I'd been one.

"I know you're frustrated," I said. "I'm not lying when I'm telling you I'm getting closer to learning the truth. Being a PI is not what you see on television. It's a lot of legwork. Interviews. Research. I've talked to at least a dozen people who all have a small piece of the puzzle. I'm making progress, but it's slow."

"Maybe I can help?"

I shook my head. "It's too dangerous and I'm not going to be responsible for your safety." But I needed to give her something. "I'll tell you this. Whatever got Elijah killed connects to Coach Bradford's drug distribution network. I think he had a partner—someone affiliated with the school."

"Because Mrs. Clark was killed."

Angie was a smart kid.

"That's part of it. I don't know if they recreated the network, or if they're running it out of the Cactus Stop or the school or both, but Elijah must have seen or heard something that made him suspicious. And I'm worried about Benny too. I don't want him asking questions that might put him in danger. I don't want anything to happen to *you* if someone thinks you're being nosy."

"You're right. I'm really sorry."

"Are you safe at your house?"

"It's fine," she said.

"If you need me, call. If you learn something, whether or not you think it's important, call. I promise to follow up. I want answers as much as you do. But don't ask questions, don't put yourself out there where they might see you as a threat. Drugs are a huge moneymaker that people are willing to kill for."

Angie nodded. "Okay."

I pulled away from the curb and in my side-view mirror noticed a car pulling out of a driveway.

It was the damn 4Runner again. I *knew* I was being followed.

No way could I take Angie home without losing this guy first. If I was alone, I would confront him. With Angie, I couldn't risk a potentially violent confrontation.

"What's wrong?" Angie asked.

I thought I'd masked my concern.

"Someone has been following me." Who the hell was this guy? Where had I picked him up? I thought back . . . I noticed him pulling into the O'Reilly neighborhood, but he could have started following me from my office downtown. I hadn't seen him there, he hadn't been in our small parking lot, but there was ample street parking and only one exit out of our lot, which turned onto a one-way street. It would have been easy to wait until I exited and follow from there. With all the traffic downtown, I wouldn't have immediately seen him.

That made the most sense, which told me he knew who I was. He could have confronted me at least twice before now. Was he just tracking me? Could he be a cop?

Or maybe he was one of the people who'd picked up where Coach Bradford left off.

"What are you going to do?" Angie asked, her voice tight with nervous energy.

"Lose him," I muttered, glancing over to make sure she had her seat belt on. She was gripping the edge of her seat, her eyes flicking nervously to the rearview mirror.

"That black car?"

"Yeah.

I focused on the road ahead, my hands steady on the wheel,

even as the adrenaline started to kick in. The guy tailing us wasn't new to this game—he knew what he was doing. But so did I.

I pushed the gas pedal down, taking the corner on Dunlap with more speed than usual, trying to throw him off. I glanced in the mirror. He copied my move—right turn, just like I'd predicted.

I kept my foot on the gas, heading south, past familiar landmarks, not slowing down. Then, I took a sharp right, onto a narrow side street. He turned sharply as well, a little too eager. He was still on me, but this was where the game got interesting.

If Angie weren't in the car, I would try and trap him, close him in, identify him. But I wouldn't risk her getting hurt, so losing the bastard was the only option.

I swerved right again toward Highway 17, crossing over the freeway through a yellow light like I had nothing to lose. My eyes flicked to the rearview again. He was still there—he must have run a red light to follow me. I was getting a little worried—earlier, I thought he was just following me, trying to figure out where I was going, what I was doing.

Now I wondered if he meant to do me harm.

I took a sharp left onto Twenty-Ninth Avenue, cutting through a narrow neighborhood. The houses here were packed tight, the streets like a labyrinth. Perfect for a ghosting maneuver. I stomped on the gas and made a right onto the first street—sharp and sudden.

He was three cars back, but he could still see me turning onto Twenty-Ninth. He probably thought he had me cornered. But I had one move left.

I threw the wheel hard to the right as soon as I could, disappearing around a bend that curved around the block. He'd lose sight of me for just a few seconds—but it'd be enough.

I looped back, pulling into a small side road and stopping behind a parked car. I held my breath. There was a break in the sound of my engine, the quiet before the storm. I waited, eyes locked on the end of the street, my gun within reach.

There. He came flying down Twenty-Ninth, too fast for the neighborhood, his car bouncing on the uneven pavement. Not even bothering to slow down for the curve. He didn't know I was already gone.

Score one for the PI.

I let him pass, watching him zoom by, oblivious. By now, he must have known he'd lost me, and I couldn't afford to have him backtrack and search the neighborhood. I counted to three after he passed, then hit the gas and merged back onto Twenty-Ninth, heading back the way I'd come. I scanned the rearview mirror for any sign of him. Nothing. I'd lost him.

I crossed back over the freeway, still no sign of him. I kept my speed steady, my Jeep humming.

He was gone.

For now.

"Who was it?" Angie asked.

"Don't know. I'm going to take you home. If you see that 4Runner again, call me, do not engage. Go somewhere safe. A library, a police station, fire station, anyplace where there are people."

She nodded and bit her thumbnail.

"I'll take care of it," I assured her.

Still, I took the long way to her apartment. No other car followed me, and the 4Runner didn't show up again. I dropped Angie off, made her promise not to go to the Cactus Stop again, and left.

I hoped she listened to me.

Arizona didn't require front license plates. I didn't get a good look at the plate when he passed where I was parked because he was too far away, so I couldn't even call Josie and ask her to run it. But if I saw the 4Runner again, I would get a better look.

I called Jack as I drove to Gabriel's house for Mom's party.

"You're late," he said.

"No, I'm not." I looked at my dashboard clock. "A few minutes, but that's just for setup."

"I put Austin to work," Jack said. "But Tess wants everything perfect, and she's stressing."

"I'm on my way. Ten minutes, tops." Maybe fifteen. "I spotted a tail. Had to lose him because Angie was in the car with me."

"Plates?"

"Didn't see them. Older model black 4Runner. Kind of beat-up, white male driver, possibly in his thirties, dark hair, wore shades. I think he picked me up outside our office. I went from the office to Christina O'Reilly's house, where I first spotted him, then I saw him around the corner from Eric McMahon's house."

"Did you learn anything?"

"Yeah. Eric's still scared of these people, but he doesn't have names. I believe him. Still, he said Bradford answered to someone. Christina hadn't spoken to Megan Osterman since they graduated, but she confirmed what we suspected about Scott Jimenez, and also that Scott had an older sister named Desiree."

"Circumstantial."

"Thanks, *Mom*," I said sarcastically.

"I think you're right, Margo, but we don't have proof *anyone* has done anything illegal. We need something tangible."

I was stuck. I didn't know what else to do, who else to talk to, how to retrace Elijah's steps.

"Well, I have a few things to follow up on, and tomorrow I'm going to talk to Desi Jimenez again. Maybe something will shake out. Did you check out Brighton's house?"

"Yep. It's nearly at the end of the road that leads to the preserve. I looked it up on Zillow and it sold for an even mil two years ago, and that was before it was remodeled. Brighton has done a lot of work on the place. Google Earth pictures show that two years ago the backyard was all rocks. Now there's a full outdoor living space with a pool and mature trees, which would have cost a small fortune to bring in."

"And he regularly shops at a Cactus Stop six miles away," I muttered.

"He could work in the area," Jack guessed. "Tess will get his details tomorrow."

"Thanks," I said. "I'll see you in a few."

I ended the call, then listened to the voicemail my unknown caller had left.

"Ms. Angelhart, this is Dwight Parsons, we met on Monday in Lena's office. Have you made any progress in your investigation? I thought maybe we could trade notes. I can't believe that her murder after your visit is a coincidence. I said as much to the police, that maybe it was because Lena was helping you with your investigation into Elijah's death, that she was killed. They listened, but I don't think they believe me. I'm struggling, Ms. Angelhart. I should have been with her. I could have saved her. I can meet anytime."

He ended the call.

I immediately called him back. His phone went to voicemail.

"Hi, Dwight, it's Margo Angelhart. I'm free first thing tomorrow. Text me a time and place and I'll be there, I don't care how early."

Ten minutes later, I received a text.

Your office, perhaps? Is nine a good time?

I responded with: Nine is good. See you then.

chapter thirty-six

MARGO ANGELHART

Gabriel's grand house was bustling with our large extended family. Even most of the uptight Rubios showed up—his two sisters brought their families. I didn't think much of his mother, who I'd only met once at their engagement party. She'd subtly belittled Tess, making my sister uneasy, so I was glad she wasn't here tonight.

Tess outdid herself for mom's birthday. Sure, Uncle Tom—Josie's dad—was in charge of the food, and Tess had hired his staff to help with the event. But the decorations? That was all her. The house was overflowing with flowers in soft whites and pinks—Mom's favorite colors. A single banner hung gracefully, and balloon bouquets in pink, white, and gold adorned every corner, adding a festive touch.

Tess had seamlessly transformed into the epitome of the Elegant Hostess. Gabriel, as always, was the perfect Debonair Host. They really were made for each other.

Mom's fifty-ninth birthday party was everything we could have wanted for her—except that Dad wasn't here.

I helped myself to food—I was starving because I'd skipped

lunch—and stood in the kitchen with Uncle Tom's staff because I wanted to eat before I socialized. A hungry Margo is a grumpy Margo.

Luisa found me mid-bite. "Flash drive?" she asked.

"One sec," I said with my mouth full. I swallowed, reached into my pocket, and handed it to her. "I don't know if what's on there is going to help, but it was hidden and password-protected, so it could be something interesting."

"Shouldn't take me long," Lu said. "You were followed?"

Word got around. "I lost him. If I didn't have a kid in the car with me, I would have called Jack and found a way to trap him. If I see him tomorrow, I'll engage."

"If you need me, let me know. No classes on Friday."

"Will do."

Nico came in. I glanced around for his boyfriend and was grateful Quincy was nowhere in sight. I loved Nico; I didn't love his arrogant FBI boyfriend.

Nico hugged Lu. "I'm late because of you," he said to me.

"So I don't get a hug?"

He kissed my cheek.

"I'm going to hunt down Josie and her new boyfriend," Lu said.

"Give him hell," I told her. "He's in Fire and an only child."

Lu laughed. "Oh, that'll be fun!"

"Josie will kill you," Nico said.

"She already wants to because I accidentally let my nickname for her slip around her partner. But—" I quickly added before Nico could chastise me "—I didn't know he was in the car with her or that she had me on speakerphone."

Nico barely suppressed a grin. "I pulled up Elijah's file. Because the case is fairly recent, I was able to get my hands on hair samples to personally analyze them. There is no sign of long-term drug use."

"I didn't think so," I said. "Does that cover all drugs?"

"No, but almost any long-term drug use will show up in hair.

I might not know what specifically without further testing, but I can see a change. I also read the report in detail and there was no sign of long-term use in the organs. The liver usually takes the brunt of the hit, but depending on the type of drug, the lungs, brain, and stomach can also show signs of prolonged toxicity."

"The detective should have explained that to his mom," I said. I liked Rachel King less and less with each passing day. "King made it sound like Elijah was a statistic in a sea of overdose deaths."

"He could be," Nico said. "It doesn't take repeated use for someone to die."

Nico didn't have to tell me that, but at the same time, knowing Elijah wasn't a habitual user further validated my theory that someone had poisoned him.

"Did you test the cup found in the trash near the body?"

He didn't say anything.

"Nico, it's important."

"No, because there is no evidence that the cup belonged to him, and because the case was—"

"Closed as an accidental overdose, yada yada." I was getting sick and tired of that line. "Can you do it now?"

"No. Even if the detective orders the test, and I could find DNA or prints on the cup, that won't tell you if he was poisoned or if he willingly ingested the fentanyl."

"But he *did* ingest it. I read that in the autopsy."

"That's true." Nico touched my arm. "These cases are always difficult, for cops and for families."

"He was murdered, Nico."

"I don't see how to prove that, not based on the physical evidence."

"If King had done her fucking job, she may have been able to prove it," I snapped, then mumbled an apology. "I don't mean to take my frustration out on you."

"If anyone can find the truth, it's you."

"Thanks for your vote of confidence," I said, "but this time,

I'm stuck. I *know* there's something weird going on, but every time I think I see one small part of the puzzle, I get three more pieces that don't fit at all."

"Don't force them," Nico said. "If there's one thing I've learned in forensics, it's that every piece is a truth, but not all pieces fit in the same puzzle."

"That makes no sense."

"Don't force what you know into a box, Margo. Figure out where each piece goes and proceed from there."

Nico left to find Quincy and I rinsed and stacked my plate with the other used dishes. I grabbed a beer and mingled. Talked to family, friends, and even managed a five-minute conversation with one of Gabriel's sisters. I didn't remember if she was the heart surgeon or the college professor.

Yes, Gabriel's family were all overachievers.

Laura walked in with her two kids. Jack immediately made a beeline to her. I was thrilled he'd finally found someone who made him happy. He deserved it.

Cody ran over to me. "Margo, we can bring you your kitten anytime you want."

"It's not my kitten."

He grinned. "Just call! After four, because that's when we're home from school. There's Austin!" And he was off.

That kid could charm Scrooge.

"What do you think?" Tess asked as she came over to me. "Is everyone having fun?"

"You can't tell?" I looked pointedly around the huge great room at the dozens of people eating, drinking, talking, and laughing. "Yeah, everyone's miserable."

She rolled her eyes. "Okay, it's good. Mom is happy."

"I don't know how we're going to top this for her sixtieth."

"I have an idea—"

"Save it until after you get back from your honeymoon, okay?"

"Oh, I was going to text you, but I got distracted."

"I wonder why," I mused.

She reached into her dress pocket and pulled out a folded note, handed it to me.

"I had a few minutes, so I ran John Brighton for you. He's twenty-five, graduated from ASU with a degree in business economics. And, more importantly, he's the corporate manager for the Cactus Stop. Basically, he oversees the management of all thirteen Stops."

That explained why he was at the store, but it didn't clarify why Elijah had taken his picture or looked up his address. Maybe I was chasing a dead end, but I felt the need to talk to this John Brighton guy. Perhaps he was stealing from the company, and Elijah had caught on. Then again, maybe Elijah had reached out to Brighton about something suspicious he noticed at the Stop, which could explain why he visited the Cactus Stop corporate page the week he died.

"Thanks, Tess."

"I'll be in late tomorrow, but text if you need anything else."

She was summoned by someone I couldn't see, and a headache started scratching behind my eyes. I went to the bar to grab a second beer. Josie introduced me to her boyfriend, Ryan. He didn't seem like a deer caught in the headlights—he looked like he was having a blast. I definitely liked him at first glance. They left early because Ryan's shift started at six in the morning.

I loved family, and I loved catching up, but my heart wasn't completely into the festivities tonight. I didn't want to be a Debbie Downer on Mom's birthday, so I slipped outside into the beautiful evening to unwind.

I had a dark sense of foreboding that I was missing something. I'd asked Christina and Eric all the questions I wanted. Both were forthcoming—even Eric, who hadn't initially wanted to talk. I thought I'd finally convinced Angie that she needed to stay clear of the Cactus Stop, so I worried about her a little less. I was curious about the message from Dwight Parsons, however. It might be nothing—maybe he just wanted to talk about his dead girlfriend. Or maybe he had information that could help me figure out what the hell was going on with Elijah before he died. At least he was an insider at Sun Valley and might be a good person to brainstorm with.

Megan's phone. Dammit, I left it charging in my office. I would swing by on my way home and pick it up. There could be nothing there . . . or the answers to all my questions. I was specifically looking for any relationship with Elijah—romantic or platonic. If there was something going on between them, that would explain why his nighttime activities started after her death.

My apprehension boiled down to being followed today. That told me I was on the right track. Who the hell was that guy? Why me? What had I done to get on his radar—and how could I trap him next time I saw him?

Because there would be a next time.

Uncle Rafe sat down next to me. He was sipping a beer. "Thank you again for the tequila. I'll have you over one evening and cook for you, then we can enjoy a glass."

I grinned. "Make your famous Mexican gumbo?"

"Aw, yes, that would be nice. I haven't made it in nearly a year."

Uncle Rafe had spent two years living in New Orleans before he entered the priesthood. He went as part of a mission group in order to discern his calling, and he loved the food. When he returned to Phoenix, he experimented and came up with some unique dishes—Cajun food with a Mexican flare. His Mexican gumbo was my favorite, but his poblano chilis stuffed with Cajun-spiced shrimp were a very close second. I'd once told him if the priest gig didn't work out, he could open a restaurant.

We sat in silence, looking at the multitude of lights decorating Gabriel's beautiful backyard.

"Ask," I said.

"Just tell me," Uncle Rafe said.

I sighed. I didn't know what to say. "I don't know. I have a theory, but little to support it, and I haven't figured out how to prove it." I hesitated, then said, "I think Elijah was poisoned. Someone put a lethal dose of fentanyl—and it doesn't take a lot—into something he consumed, and I don't see how it's an accident. The reason? That's a little murkier. One of his friends died of a drug overdose this summer, and after that Elijah's behavior changed."

"I don't understand."

I told Uncle Rafe everything I had learned.

"What if I can't prove it?" I said, half to myself.

Rafe didn't say anything for a long minute. He probably thought the same thing. The only way to find out where Elijah had been those five hours was if someone came forward. Yet, the person who knew the truth was most likely the person who had killed him.

Rafe said, "You need to take the night off."

"I can't just shut it off."

"This is your mother's birthday."

"And yours."

"Tomorrow."

Uncle Rafe never wanted to have a party. My mom was the oldest of seven kids. He was the youngest. As long as I've known him, he never wanted to be in the spotlight, yet found one on the altar.

"You can't think clearly because your mind is too full. Clear your head, relax, come at the problem fresh tomorrow."

"Easier said than done," I muttered.

"Alina will understand whatever truth you find," he said.

"I'm afraid I'll never be able to prove he was killed."

"But if you know, that will be enough. Alina will rest easier."

"No, it's not enough. Yes, I believe the killer will receive eternal judgment, so don't tell me God has a plan. I get that. But he needs to be in prison. It's not just Elijah. It's everyone else who may cross him. Once someone gets away with murder, it's easier the second time. And the third."

"Like I said, clear your mind and you'll find the truth."

Sometimes, Rafe's platitudes annoyed me. It wasn't always easy to stop thinking.

Mom approached us, smiled at her younger brother. "We're keeping you out late."

"Father Brian is celebrating the morning Mass. I'm having too much fun. Did Mom and Dad leave?"

"Not yet, but I think they're heading in that direction."

Rafe rose, kissed me, kissed his sister, and said, "I'll go say goodbye."

And with that, he left me with Mom. In the past, it would have been wholly uncomfortable. For the three years we were estranged, Rafe did more than anyone to bring us together. It pained him that we didn't talk, and when we did, we argued. Now, we were better. Not perfect, but better.

She sat in the seat he'd vacated. "Jack told me you were followed today."

"Yep."

"Why didn't you tell me?"

"I told Jack."

"I'm concerned, Margo."

"I have it under control. I know what he looks like, his vehicle, I'm keeping my eyes open."

"Jack said he may have followed you from the office. Which means he knows who you are, where you work, and could know where you live."

"I'm aware."

"You're not taking this seriously."

"I *am*," I assured her. "*Very* seriously. I promise," I added when she didn't look convinced.

"You have always been tenacious."

"I get that from you."

Mom's lips twitched. "Perhaps. But I preferred the safety of the courthouse, the system of justice, checks and balances. You prefer the field. Where things get sticky, and often dangerous."

"So does Jack," I said. "Did you give him the same lecture?"

"Oh, yes. When he joined the police academy I had many sleepless nights. I've prosecuted two cop killers over my years. Just by putting on the uniform, he put himself in harm's way."

"Because you and dad taught us to care about our community and do what we could to help people. Jack's a natural protector."

"So are you."

"Not really."

"You've taken this case personally. Why?"

I wouldn't talk to Mom about Bobby. She knew what happened and what I suspected, but I wasn't sure if she remembered the details after fifteen years, and I didn't want to revisit it. My obsession with Elijah's case was driven by my anger at how someone might get away with murder. It was about Elijah's lost future, the pain in Alina's heart, and Angie's anger at the system that had shelved Elijah's death. Then there was Megan Osterman, the drug addict who died alone in an alley, and her grieving mother. Murder didn't just affect the victim; it rippled out to everyone around them.

Mostly, I couldn't stand it when criminals got away with violent crime.

"Margo," Mom said, "you need to be cautious. We don't know what's going on here, we don't even know where the threat is coming from. Your questions are making someone nervous, and nervous people are unpredictable."

Aunt Rita waved at Mom from across the yard. Mom acknowledged her and rose. "I need to break up the party. It's after ten and no one looks like they want to leave." She hesitated, then said, "I know you saw your dad yesterday, as well as Ben Bradford."

"Jack," I said. It wasn't like I was keeping it a secret, but I hadn't wanted to discuss it.

"Your dad called," Mom said. "Even when you were little, you always jumped first, asked questions later. It's a great trait—if you have someone who can help you up if you fall."

"I know when to ask for help."

Mom nodded. "Usually. We're a team now, Margo. Please don't keep me in the dark."

"Okay," I said, feeling guilty. Mom was right. I should have talked through my idea to interview Bradford. If I'd thought it through better, I might have yielded more information.

"Don't look chastised," Mom said. She gave me a tight hug. "I'm on your side, Margo. Always."

I wanted to believe that. But I couldn't forget three years ago when I wanted to investigate the murder that put dad in prison and she said to let it go.

Still . . . three years was a long time. And Mom had given me a lot of freedom this week to investigate the way I wanted. I think she meant it.

And that meant everything to me.

chapter thirty-seven

CAL RAFFERTY

Cal was both irritated and impressed that Margo Angelhart had slipped his tail. Partly impressed. It was his fault for not being more careful. He should have known she was good. She'd been in the Army and had been a PI for the last eight years.

After her meeting with Bradford down in Eyman, he had assumed she was working a wrongful death case for one of the kids who OD'd during the time Bradford was selling drugs through Sun Valley High, or perhaps a school liability issue. But after meeting with Hitch, he realized it was an active case. Maybe it started with a wrongful death, but she was talking to people who knew Bradford and the kids involved in Bradford's criminal organization.

Was she looking for the supplier? And if so, why? Because a kid died? Had she uncovered something more, something that would lead Cal to the supplier? Maybe she had an informant. If so, why hadn't she passed intel on to the police?

He looked up Elijah Martinez's death investigation—it was an accidental overdose, but he wished they'd bumped it over to DEB. Because of the Bradford case, Hitch was interested in anything associated with Sun Valley High, even though they had no reason to believe they hadn't caught everyone involved on the campus. Cal had been deep cover. It was one of the best covers he'd ever had. And the supplier wasn't part of Sun Valley High.

Yet . . . the guidance counselor was killed on Monday. If that had been the only thing that happened, Cal wouldn't have thought twice about it. Phoenix was a violent city. But the woman was stabbed with her own letter opener, there were no suspects, and that in and of itself seemed odd. He had already reached out to the detective in charge to find out more about the case, but so far he hadn't heard back.

He might need to pull in the big guns to get answers. But he'd start by going through Hitch.

Following Margo around had initially seemed like a waste of time . . . until she'd rolled up in front of Eric McMahon's house—and Eric was waiting for her on the porch.

Eric McMahon was *his* witness. When the DEB couldn't convince him to turn state's evidence, they brought in Cal—and the deal was done.

Why the hell was she talking to McMahon? What did she know?

So now, close to midnight Thursday, he leaned against Eric's beat-up Honda waiting for his shift to end.

At 11:52 p.m., Eric stepped out of the elevator in the parking garage of the Scottsdale Quarter and swore when he saw Cal.

"What the fuck is going on?" Eric said.

It was late, and there wasn't anyone around, but voices carried in the garage. He motioned to his car, which was parked next to Eric's—a basic sedan, one of many vehicles he used, all registered to the DEA—and Eric threw his hands up in the air, then slid into the passenger seat.

Cal got in and said, "What did Margo Angelhart talk to you about?"

"I should have figured you're still watching me."

Cal wasn't, but he didn't tell Eric that. The kid had gotten his life mostly together, but it was easy to fall down the same dirty path. If he thought the DEA was keeping an eye on him, all the better.

"I'm waiting."

"She was asking about how Coach's network operated. I told her to fuck off. She kept pushing, wanted to know if I had an idea of who he was working with at Sun Valley. I said if I had, I'd have told the police, but he wasn't working with anyone there. I told her what I told you three years ago—that he had a supplier, that guy called the shots, and I don't know who it was. Never saw him, never talked to him, wouldn't know him from Adam. But she pushed, said Mrs. Clark was killed, and that surprised me. She also asked about Scott Jimenez." He frowned.

"What aren't you telling me, Eric?"

"I'm telling you everything! I tried to block it out because I don't want to go back there. I nearly died."

Slight exaggeration, but Cal didn't correct him.

"Okay, okay," Eric said, thinking for a second. "She asked if I knew Megan Osterman, said she died of a drug overdose this summer. Around the Fourth of July. I knew Megan, told her that. The PI already knew that Megan had been dating Scott. Then she asked about Scott's sister, Desi, who I barely know. I honestly don't know what she thought I knew, because I swear to God, I told you everything about Coach and his network. I didn't hold out. You *know* that, Cal."

Cal didn't think Eric withheld information on purpose, but he had been working for Bradford for more than two years. He could have forgotten something, or seen something he didn't realize was important.

Why did Margo think there was another player at Sun Valley? Was there something about Lena Clark's murder that had Margo thinking Bradford?

Had Cal and Hitch been so tunnel-focused on Bradford and how he got his drugs that they'd missed something? The supplier had been their key focus, who they believed was the only operative they hadn't caught. They didn't even have a name. The Bradfords stuck to their story of how they bought and packaged the drugs even when confronted with evidence that they were lying. They hadn't budged, and Cal always believed that the supplier held something over them. Because why would they be so loyal to someone who would remain free while they went to prison?

"Okay," Cal said.

"That's it?"

"For now." He slipped him a phone. "Call me if you remember anything else. Call me if you get in trouble. Call me if Angelhart or anyone else talks to you about Bradford or Sun Valley. And answer the phone if it rings. I'm the only one with the number."

Eric reluctantly pocketed the flip phone. "I thought this was over."

"So did I," Cal said.

chapter thirty-eight

MARGO ANGELHART

Luisa and I helped Tess and Uncle Tom clean up after the party and I didn't get home until one in the morning. It wasn't until I woke up at six thirty that I remembered I'd wanted to stop by the office and inspect Megan's phone. I'd have time to do it before my meeting with Dwight Parsons.

I showered and was in the Black Rock Coffee drive-through lane when my phone rang. It was Angie.

"Margo, there's crime scene tape around the high school, cops all over the place. Everyone says that someone was killed, but no one knows who!"

"Where are you?"

"Standing with, like, three hundred people in the parking lot."

"I'll be there in ten minutes," I said.

I was trapped in the line with cars in front of me and behind me, so I called Josie.

She didn't answer. She was probably at the crime scene since she was on duty today. I texted her.

Are you at SVHS? Is there another murder?

She didn't immediately answer, so I called Jack and told him what Angie said. He said he'd find out and get back to me.

I was halfway to the high school when Josie texted me.

I'm on scene. Suicide, teacher. Sometime last night, trying to get more details from the ME who just arrived.

I asked: How do you know it was suicide?

I was already parked in the student lot when Josie finally responded.

Left a note. Parsons, Clark's boyfriend. He confessed.

No way. No fucking way, I thought.

I was about to tell her that Parsons left a message for me yesterday, but I didn't. She might be compelled to put that information into the report, and I needed time to think.

Instead, I texted: Let me know if there is anything weird, as in not a suicide.

She responded with several question marks, but I texted Angie instead of Josie.

Where are you? I'm in the far corner of the student parking lot.

A second later, Angie wrote: coming, and I waited. She slipped into my passenger seat and said, "Everyone is saying it's Mr. Parsons and that he killed himself. I don't believe it."

"It is Mr. Parsons," I said.

Tears welled in her eyes, but she didn't cry. "Fuck. I talked to him yesterday. He wanted to talk to you. He was sad, but . . . he killed himself? No way. Why?"

"Guilt, maybe?"

"For what?"

"Killing his girlfriend."

"No. Absolutely not."

I was having a hard time wrapping my head around it. I had listened to his message twice while waiting for Angie.

Have you made any progress in your investigation? I thought maybe we could trade notes.

He also said he was struggling and that he could have saved her. Why would he want to talk to me and then kill himself before he did so? Why would he tell me he could have saved her, yet confess to her murder?

"Is there someplace safe I can take you?"

She shrugged. "I just want to know what's going on. Mr. Parsons was a great teacher. Do you think he really killed her?"

"No," I said before I caught myself. "Angie, this is important. What exactly did you and he talk about yesterday when you gave him my number?"

Angie thought. "He was upset. He said he should have stayed with her, but he left papers in his classroom to grade and ended up talking to Mrs. Porter. She's across the hall from him. He said the detective made it sound like they thought he was guilty, but said it was just the detective's style, like how she made it sound like she thought I killed her." She paused. "I asked him if he was okay, and he said he would be. He was sad, but he . . . he really wanted to talk to you again."

"He left me a message. I have to talk to Detective King. Dammit."

I didn't want to, but she needed to look at his death as a homicide investigation, not a suicide inquiry. "Can you hang with your friends today?" I asked Angie. "Don't be alone. Okay?"

"Yeah. Gina's over there with Andy and a couple of her friends. School's canceled, but I'll find something to do."

"I'll call you later."

I locked my car, watched Angie head toward her friends, then I texted Josie.

I'm here and I have information directly related to Parsons's death. Can you get me through the line to talk to the detective in charge?

Then I called my mom.

Ten minutes later, Josie brought me through the crime scene tape and into the center courtyard. "King is pissed," she muttered.

"I figured," I said.

Rachel King was talking to the ME when we approached, but her partner, Jerry Chavez, saw us and immediately came over. "Margo, thanks so much for reaching out. Officer Morales, can you make sure the line is secure? We just caught two kids trying to sneak through."

He said it with a smile, clearly trying to play nice.

"No problem," Josie said. She glanced at me, made sure I knew that she would be close. What did she think, that King was going to arrest me?

When Josie stepped back to the crime scene tape, Chavez said, "Seriously, thanks. What can you tell me?"

He was edging me slowly away from King and I wondered if he hadn't told her I was here. But she saw me, said something to the ME as he and his team went into the building, and made a beeline for us.

"Why am I not surprised to find you in the middle of this?" King said with a deep scowl.

"Goodbye," I said and started to leave.

"Hold up," Chavez said. He reached out and held my arm. I looked down at his hand and he immediately removed it. "That came out wrong," he said.

"Don't apologize for your partner."

King said, "You avoided me all day when I wanted to talk to you about Lena Clark, and then an hour after a body is found you're willing to help? What are you in the middle of?"

"I told you. Elijah Martinez's mother hired me to find out where her son was during the time when he left work until he died in the park."

"And have you?" she snapped.

I didn't answer her question. Instead, I said, "Parsons didn't kill himself."

"We have a note, gunshot appears to be self-inflicted, and a half dozen people said he was depressed. Guilt has a way of doing that."

"Wraps up your homicide with a pretty bow," I said.

"You have one minute to explain why you don't think he killed himself, make it good."

I pressed Play on my voicemail. The detectives listened to his message. At the end King said, "That's not evidence of anything."

"After he left the message, I called him back and left my own message, then he texted me and we scheduled a meeting for this morning at my office."

"Not evidence that he didn't kill his girlfriend and then himself out of guilt. A delayed murder-suicide."

"Did he sound like he was in a suicidal mindset?" I said, holding up my phone.

"Send me the message," King said. "I'll consider it once I get the ME's report."

"As long as you keep an open mind," I said.

Though her jaw was clenched, King dipped her head with a nod.

I sent her a copy of the voicemail. "Can I see the note?"

"No."

Chavez bumped King lightly. "Maybe just a look."

She glared at him, then breathed out a long sigh. She pulled up an image on her phone. "Look, don't copy. I mean it."

The photo consisted of a bloody note written on blank white paper, like what might be found in a copier. His hand was partly visible. Parsons—or the killer—had written in block letters with a black Sharpie, the thick ink making handwriting analysis much more difficult.

> **I CAN'T EAT, I CAN'T SLEEP. I KILLED LENA. I DIDN'T MEAN FOR IT TO HAPPEN, BUT SHE BROKE IT OFF AND I LOVE HER SO MUCH. I DON'T EVEN REMEMBER PICKING UP HER LETTER OPENER, BUT I DID. AND I KILLED HER AND I CAN'T LIVE WITH MYSELF. I'M SO SORRY.**

"He found her body. Had blood on his hands because he claimed he was trying to stop the bleeding," King said.

"Which could be true," I said.

"Or he stabbed her and then tried to stop the bleeding to cover it up. We have a very tight window, and Parsons said he didn't see anyone leaving her office, nor did he see anyone in the corridor when he walked in. I think it's because he went in, she broke it off, and he killed her."

"Or whoever killed Lena also killed him, then framed him."

"Very unlikely. Unlike on television, it's not all that easy to fake a suicide."

"You promised you'd keep an open mind," I reminded her.

"We will investigate his death fully," Chavez said. "It's really going to come down to what the ME says."

"And what if it's indeterminate?"

"That's rare," King said. "Like I said, a suicide is hard to fake."

"Don't be so sure of that," I said. "The ME was wrong about Elijah Martinez."

"For shit's sake," King muttered.

"He was murdered," I said. "Someone poisoned him with fentanyl, and if you had followed up and asked questions, maybe you would be as suspicious as I am."

"There was no evidence of foul play," King said, her anger rising. "I've had so much shit over that kid's death."

"When I solve his murder, I'll be sure to let you know."

"Stay out of it—" she began.

"Why? You closed the case."

I walked away before she made me angrier.

I had two missed calls from my mother. I called her back.

"Tell me you did not speak to the detectives without me," Mom said.

"I did. I sent her the voicemail Parsons left for me. She said the determination is up to the ME."

"You sound angry."

"I am," I said as I walked directly to my Jeep. "Told her what I think of her, and you're right, you probably should have been here. But she didn't arrest me so that's a plus."

I was trying to be light, but Mom wasn't happy. "She could file a complaint with the licensing board. She could make your life—all our lives—difficult."

"Not if I solve Elijah's murder," I said. "I'm coming down to the office. See you in a few."

chapter thirty-nine

MARGO ANGELHART

By the time I arrived at the office, I had a headache. Tess was already there, and she practically tackled me as I stepped through the main doors.

"I got something!" She motioned for me to follow her to her office.

"Good morning," I grumbled. I smelled breakfast burritos. I made a detour to the kitchen and noted six wrapped burritos from El Norteno. *Iris*, I thought. I always brought burritos from Orozco's (family first!) but El Norteno was a close second choice. They were known for their machaca and the praise was well-deserved. I grabbed two of the burritos and went to Tess's office, putting one in front of her.

Before I could ask what she'd found, she started talking faster than Lorelai Gilmore.

"You've had me looking for a lot of people—like, dozens and dozens—so I started all the searches, ran backgrounds, everything we can get with our databases, thank *God* Lu helped streamline the system, otherwise it would have taken me *days*."

We subscribed to a bunch of databases that gave us public information about people. People had no idea how much data someone could legally find on them.

"So this morning I downloaded all the reports and was reading them after Gabriel left for the hospital. I should have done it yesterday, sorry, but I was so worried about Mom's party, and making sure everything was okay, and then—"

"No apologies. I get it. You have a life." Did I sound jealous? I wasn't, mostly, and fortunately Tess didn't take it that way.

"But this *is* important. I know that. Anyway, when you told me Bradford's daughter played softball and that she might have been the one who called in the tip about her father, I looked at the softball team thinking one of them might have been hospitalized with a drug overdose or died or something. Nope. But then I did a *broader* news search. I found a girl on a *competitive* softball team who died."

"Drugs," I muttered.

"No. Well, yes, but not what you think. Ginny Nichols played with Kayla Bradford. They were best friends and played on the same team for *years*. Lots of social media pics of the two of them, went to the same middle school but different high schools. The summer before their sophomore year, Ginny's older brother was driving her home after a tournament in Chino Valley. It was at night, just south of Black Canyon City on Highway 17. The brother had gotten gas—and got on the freeway going the wrong way."

"Oh, shit." There were some dangerous on and off ramps where you really had to pay attention to the directional signs, especially at night. Wrong-way drivers were unfortunately too common.

"They were both killed when they collided with a semitruck. The brother was high on oxy. So was Ginny. She had a serious injury the summer before, but her prescription for hydrocodone was for one week. The autopsy found she had been using oxycodone for a year. She didn't get it from a doctor."

"Still doesn't prove why Kayla thought her dad was dealing."

"I also read the Bradford files. The kids who worked for him were almost all teenage boys from broken homes, usually without a dad in the picture. The Nicholses' dad left when the kids were young, and as I dug into social media, it's clear that Ginny's brother was very close to Bradford. He could have been one of his dealers outside of Sun Valley."

I didn't see it. Circumstantially, I could draw lines, but there was nothing solid.

"You wanted me to find someone in Kayla's life who was impacted by drugs," Tess said. "Ginny and Kayla were close. What if Kayla saw something? Maybe she didn't make the connection until the truth came out about the crash. Or she heard her parents talking. I'm speculating, but Ginny was killed only weeks before Kayla made that call. At a minimum, it gives us motive for Kayla calling the police. Maybe she didn't know her mother was involved and thought only her dad would go to prison."

I nodded. Definitely something to mull over. "Did the police investigate the origin of the drugs in the crash?"

"I asked Jack to find out."

"Thanks, Tess, this is all good info." I didn't know quite how I could use it, but every piece helped. "By the way," I said as I stood, "the party was great last night."

"Yeah, it was." Tess beamed.

"You're a natural event planner."

She laughed. "No. I stress too much. But I'm glad everyone had fun."

I went to my office and finished my burrito while going through Megan Osterman's phone.

What I saw was a tragedy.

The texts revealed drug deals and "dates" where she exchanged sex for drugs or money. The photos told a story too—older ones showed family and friends, many with Scott. As I watched the slideshow, I saw her fade over time, the light leaving her eyes. After high school, when her drug use peaked, there were fewer photos or videos. None in the month before her death.

But she and Elijah had texted often, starting a few weeks after he started working at the Cactus Stop. Early messages had Elijah offering help and counseling, but she either ignored them or said she'd think about it. It was clear they'd also met outside the Stop. I didn't sense romance, though it was possible. One message Megan apologized for propositioning Elijah. He told her she was too valuable to sell her body. What I saw was a young man repeatedly trying to help a young woman make better choices.

I nearly jumped out of my chair when I read an exchange the week before Megan died.

Megan: Desi cut me off. I don't know how I'm going to make it.

Elijah: Go to Hope Center. They'll help.

Megan: Please. She won't let me sell for her anymore, she said I took too much. I need it.

Elijah: I'll stay with you. Visit every day. I know it's hard, but you can make it. You're stronger than you think.

Megan: Screw you.

Silence for a day, then:

Megan: I'm sorry.

Elijah: I don't hold grudges. Ready to try?

Megan: I don't know.

Elijah: I'm here.

Megan: I'm scared.

Elijah: Change is scary. But getting clean will save your life. You know that.

Megan: I know.

Two days later, the Friday morning before Megan died:

Elijah: Where are you? I'm here.

Elijah: I'll come to you.

Elijah: Hello?

Elijah: Megan, talk to me.

Elijah: Hello?

Then, the night before Megan died:

Megan: sorry

Elijah: Where are you?

Megan: sorry

Elijah: Are you okay? Where are you?

Megan: tired so so so so tired

Elijah: Megan, you're not answering your phone. Call me.

Elijah: Where are you?

Elijah: I'm worried. Please call.

Then, Sunday, when Megan was already dead.

Elijah: Megan, please let me know you're okay.

There were so many voicemail messages that the storage box was full. I used the AI function on the phone to read the messages. Most were from Elijah or Megan's mom.

An old message she had saved was from Scott Jimenez. He called her the day he got out of prison.

```
Meggie, I'm out. Happy fucking Birthday to
me! I need to see you. We're going to be
fine, I have everything set. God, I miss
you. I'm going to crash with my sister
for a couple of days, then we'll blow this
Popsicle stand with a big fuck you to that
asshole. Call me.
```

I dug into her call history. She had tried calling Scott more than two dozen times after he left the message. She also texted him several times. That all stopped after a month.

He never called her again. Didn't text her.

I crossed over to Tess's office. "Tess, have you found Scott Jimenez yet?"

"No." She clicked on her computer. "Nothing. No employment, his driver's license still has his mother's address on it, but she moved to Colorado after his arrest. Father not in the picture.

I didn't reach out to his mom, but he didn't get a license in Colorado, so I don't think he followed her there."

"Don't bother," I said. "I'm pretty certain he's dead."

And killed within forty-eight hours of getting out of jail.

I needed a face-to-face with Desi Jimenez.

But I was getting a good idea of what was happening at the Cactus Stop and why Elijah was killed.

chapter forty

MARGO ANGELHART

When I pulled into the Cactus Stop parking lot, I saw a text from Angie.

> School's closed, but there's a memorial service for Mrs. Clark on the football field at 3, open to the public.

I responded that I would try to make it, and reminded her to stick close to her friends.

The killer might think he got away with it. Observing those who attended the memorial might be productive.

I hoped King didn't just tie up the murders as a slam dunk murder-suicide, but I honestly didn't expect her to do anything else. Chavez, however, seemed more open-minded to the idea that Parsons was innocent.

Josie told me that preliminary time of death was between eight and midnight. The janitorial staff had finished cleaning the new building, where Parsons had his class, at 7:15 p.m. Thursday evening and locked up; the head of maintenance told police that

Parsons was still in his room. They exchanged a few words, but nothing stood out as odd to the supervisor. They finished the administrative building at nine and didn't see any other staff or students on campus.

Aside from the alleged suicide note, the argument that supported that he'd killed himself was that the campus was locked up tight and no one could get into any of the buildings without a card key. None were used after the cleaning crew left, until 6:20 in the morning when the school secretary came in.

There were ways to thwart the card key system. Someone could have been hiding in the building—you didn't need a card to get out, according to Josie. Could a physical key unlock any of the doors? Or perhaps Parsons let his killer in.

I really hoped Rachel King was asking these same questions.

When I entered the Cactus Stop, only one person was in the store—a heavily made-up twentysomething female with dark hair and no name tag. But she was behind the counter so I made an assumption.

"Desi?"

"Yeah?" she said.

I put my card on the counter. "Margo Angelhart. We spoke on the phone the other day."

The woman blinked. "I remember. I told you everything I know."

"I'm not here about Elijah," I said. "Have you talked to your brother lately?"

"Wh-what?" she stammered. "My brother?"

"Scott Jimenez."

"Why?"

"I talk to my brothers nearly every day, what about you?"

"He doesn't live here anymore. Why do you want to know about my brother?"

Why was she acting so nervous? Did she have something to do with his disappearance? That would really suck. I know, people didn't always love their families, but it would really disturb me if Desi had killed him.

"In the course of my investigation, I learned that Scott dated a girl named Megan Osterman."

Desi rolled her eyes. "She OD'd right over there, across the street," she said with a flip of her wrist vaguely in that direction. "I told Scott she was a no-good addict, but he never listened to me."

"Do you know how I can reach him?"

"Why?"

"Because I'd like to talk to him."

"Look, Scott and I had a falling out, okay? I don't talk to him. Hell, I don't even have his new number. He was in prison for nearly two years, got out, I let him live with me until he could get on his feet. Next day he just took off."

"When was that?"

"Fuck, I don't know. Last year. Before Christmas. Why do you want to talk to my loser brother?"

"His name came up in the course of my investigation," I said.

"What investigation?"

"Elijah Martinez."

She stared at me blankly, so I asked, "Did you know that Elijah was trying to help Megan get into rehab?" I'd looked up Hope Center. It was a thirty-day rehab facility with six Phoenix locations.

She stared at me. "Look," she said in a very calm voice, "I *am* sorry about Elijah. I answered all your questions because my boss told me to. I don't know where my brother is. I don't even think my brother knew Elijah."

"But they both knew Megan."

"So?"

Did she even know her brother was dead? Maybe she suspected, but her attitude didn't even hint at grief. For a split second I considered that she'd helped him skip town with a fake identity. Possible, but not likely.

"So you don't have a number for Scott? Maybe a friend he might have gone to live with?"

"No," she said. The door dinged as a customer entered and Desi looked relieved.

I turned to leave, then said, "Oh, one more thing. Did you know that after his shifts, Elijah sat outside and took pictures of people exiting the store?"

Her face paled. "Why would he do that?"

"I don't know, why would he?"

Her hand was shaking when she picked up the six-pack that the customer put on the counter, but she didn't say anything.

"It's weird," I said. "I'll be back if I have more questions." I walked out. Desi Jimenez was up to something. I called Mom as I walked back to my Jeep.

"Okay, I'll go to dinner with you tonight."

"What changed your mind?"

"I think the staff at the Cactus Stop is involved in something very illegal. Megan Osterman was selling drugs for Desi, and she was fired from that job because she used too much of the product. So, maybe we should bring Manny Ramos into it. He would be in a better position to evaluate the store records." I remembered what Jessie Oliver said about Ramos being tight with law enforcement. "And if they are up to something criminal, he can bring in the police to investigate. That might be the only way we learn what happened to Elijah."

"Manny may not have knowledge of day-to-day operations," Mom said. "Sometimes, less is more—maybe share your observations and leave the rest to him."

I considered. "Okay, I can do that. We'll touch bases beforehand."

"Certainly," Mom said. "Can you pick up Rafe from the rectory?"

"And take him where?"

"Manny invited him to join us tonight, and he has a rare evening free."

"Sure, if he wants to spend the night at a fancy dinner party for his birthday instead of drinking the tequila I got him."

"Even priests want to be treated as human and have a normal conversation."

"I'll bring him. Text me the time and address."

I ended the call and turned the ignition.

Then I saw him. The guy who had followed me yesterday. Only he wasn't driving the old 4Runner. He was sitting behind the wheel of a dark green sedan in front of the vet clinic.

I buckled up and expertly navigated through the narrow lot, thanking both my military training and my brother Jack who taught me how to drive.

I was going to trap him.

I pulled out of the parking lot and sped up. The guy in the sedan saw what I was doing and backed up straight, expertly turned a one-eighty, and merged onto Hatcher, almost hitting a car in the process.

I followed and memorized his license plate.

I said, "Hey, Siri, call Josie Morales."

Siri informed me that she was calling Josie Morales.

The guy was driving way too fast for the street, but with such smooth confidence I was almost impressed. I kept pace, while also looking at the periphery for pedestrians and other dangers.

"Yep?" Josie answered.

"I'm pursuing the guy who followed me yesterday. I have his plate. Shit!"

He plowed through a red light, causing multiple people to honk. I slammed on my brakes to avoid T-boning a minivan. The mother driving flipped me off.

"Are you okay?" Josie asked.

"He ran through the light on Hatcher at Cave Creek. Fuck!" I slammed my palm on my steering wheel.

"What's the plate?" she asked.

I told her. "It's not the same car he was driving yesterday."

"It's coming up that it's owned by an LLC."

"An LLC? Seriously?"

"Yep, and no address."

"That can't be right."

"It's unusual. Tyrell says he's never seen this before. High Force LLC."

"Who the hell?"

"Sounds like a video game company," she said.

The light turned green, but I'd already lost him. "I'll find out exactly who he is," I muttered.

"Are you okay?"

"He's following me, I'm pissed. He didn't try to talk to me, he wants to know where I'm going, what I'm doing. And I think—damn."

"Damn what?"

"I went to Eyman on Wednesday and talked to Ben Bradford."

"What did he say?"

"Not much. But I'll bet he called someone to find out what I knew and who I talked to. Dammit. I need to track down Eric McMahon. If Bradford thinks he knows something, I don't want that kid to get hurt."

I ended the call, turned at the next street, and headed to Eric McMahon's house.

He wasn't happy to see me on his porch.

"What the fuck about leave me alone don't you understand?" he said.

"I'm just giving you a heads-up. Someone's been following me, and they might know I came to talk to you. You need to be careful."

"I am out of that business."

"I believe you, but I talked to Bradford at the prison, and now someone is following me. He could have called one of his people, told them to find out what I'm doing and how much

I know. People are dying, Eric. I don't want you to be one of them."

He looked up and down the street, eyes wide and scared.

"I swear, if anyone in my family gets hurt—"

"Just be careful," I said and left. I'd warned him. There was nothing more I could do.

chapter forty-one

CAL RAFFERTY

Cal hit Highway 51 south, confident he'd lost Margo. Damn, that was close. She'd recognized him, even though he'd changed vehicles. He was lucky she hadn't boxed him in.

He smiled. He was beginning to really like the PI.

His cell phone rang ten minutes later as he pulled into DEA headquarters thinking that Margo had caused him to burn two undercover cars in two days. That might be a record.

He looked at the number. It was the flip phone he'd given to Eric.

"Yep," he answered.

"That PI came here. She says I'm in danger."

"Explain."

"She said someone is following her and might know where I live. Might think that I'm talking to her, that I know something. I don't! I don't know anything and I just want people to leave me alone. My sister is pregnant. God, if anything happens—"

"No one is following her."

"Fuck, Cal, she was adamant. She's not lying about this."

"I was following her."

Silence.

Cal continued. "So don't worry, you're in the clear."

"But—she said she talked to Coach in prison and he called somebody."

"He didn't. The guards called me after her visit and have been monitoring his calls. You're fine, Eric. Lay low and be good. I'll take care of it."

He hung up before Eric could argue with him. Dammit, he didn't want to read Margo into the program yet, but he might not have a choice.

But first? He needed to figure out what was so important about the Cactus Stop. That meant going back to the Bradford file and looking at everything again. Had he missed something the first hundred times he went through it?

Maybe. Probably not. But maybe.

He went up to his office and got to work.

chapter forty-two

MARGO ANGELHART

Jack met me at the high school just before three. I told him it wasn't necessary, but he was worried about the guy he called a *stalker*. Truth was, I was glad to have a second pair of eyes. I gave him a description of the guy and both vehicles.

I was still mad that I'd lost Mr. Sunglasses.

Because classes had been canceled, the student parking lot only had a few dozen cars, but the football stands were beginning to fill up with students, parents, and staff. A decent crowd, I thought, showing up when they didn't have to.

We stood off to the side as the principal, Mr. Borel, began to speak about Lena Clark. He didn't say anything about Dwight Parsons, his suspected suicide, or that Lena had been murdered by a fellow teacher.

The vice principal, Melissa Webb, then spoke about student counseling and a service they were planning at the school after the family had a private funeral. As she spoke, Jack tapped my shoulder and said, "Chavez just walked in through the gate."

I looked; King wasn't with him. Chavez spotted Jack and approached us.

"Late," I muttered.

Chavez didn't say anything.

The student body president spoke and shared a personal story about what Lena meant to her. She was a good speaker, I thought, but it went on seemingly forever, and it was hot.

I looked at the staff, studied each face. I suppose a student could have killed Lena and Dwight, but I thought staff. A teacher. A coach. An administrator. Someone who knew the ins and outs of the school and could get into Dwight's classroom without being detected. Someone Dwight knew and trusted.

Their killer was here. Unfortunately *killer* wasn't stamped on any forehead.

I didn't see Angie until the student body president finally finished her speech and I spotted her, Peter, and Andy heading toward the parking lot. Good, she was sticking close to her friends.

"The autopsy won't be until Monday," Chavez said. He walked with Jack and me toward where we parked.

"And? You came here on the off chance that you'd run into me just to say you have nothing?"

"However," Chavez continued, "we're working the case as a homicide."

"What did you find?" Jack asked.

"No physical evidence, if that's what you mean. The scene looks like a suicide. But two things stand out. First, his message to you. We must have listened to it a dozen times. He was making plans. He also responded to your message with a text, and we confirmed it came from his phone, and his phone only has his prints on it.

"Then, we interviewed the maintenance manager a second time. His story is consistent. He's worked for the district for thirty-two years, and at Sun Valley for more than half that time. Parsons has been here for all those years, so he knows the teacher well. He was grading papers at his desk. The manager asked when he was leaving, and Parsons said he didn't want to be home alone just yet, but he was looking forward to seeing his son, who was flying in Friday night."

"When does his son arrive?" I asked.

"Tonight at nine. I just don't see a man who knows his son is coming home, who sounded happy about the visit, killing himself."

"Playing devil's advocate," Jack said. "What if he killed himself at school so his son wouldn't find his body?"

"Maybe," Chavez said, but didn't sound like he believed that scenario. "Why not in his car? Check into a motel so a student or colleague doesn't find him? Again, we're not ruling out suicide, but all the boxes aren't checked."

We stopped at Jack's truck.

"The other issue we keep running up against is the timing in Lena Clark's murder," Chavez said. "Exact time of death is generally hard to pinpoint, but we have a very short window between her call to you, Margo, and when Parsons called for help at 5:27. He could have walked into her office and immediately stabbed her then called for help. But we know he didn't get there before 5:25. Too many people saw him walking from his classroom to the administrative building."

"The suicide note," I said, seeing what he saw. "It doesn't ring true."

Chavez nodded. "His letter says she broke up with him and he saw the letter opener and stabbed her before he realized what he was doing. She was stabbed four times. One of the wounds nicked her heart. She died in minutes. When did they have time to argue? Did he walk in at 5:25 and she told him, 'It's over,' and he stabbed her and then called for help? The 911 call came in at 5:27. And there's one thing that we've kept out of the media. I'm going to tell you both this, but please don't share the info."

"Of course," Jack said, and I nodded. Who did he think we'd share it with?

"The killer had to stab deeply, but they didn't pull the weapon fully out. Four jabs, essentially widening the hole the first stab wound made. This would minimize blood spatter, especially since the killer left the letter opener in her body. But it went in so deep the killer had to have blood on their hands and likely on their clothing. They had to have left quickly. It's only eight minutes between the end of Lena's call with Margo and when Parsons arrived. Eight minutes to go down the hall to the washroom and clean up."

"You found evidence," Jack said.

He nodded. "The killer must have had something to wrap his hand in to prevent blood from dripping, but he went to the washroom and did a good job cleaning up. Still, we found traces of blood around the sink area and a decent size drop on the floor under the sink that we confirmed is the victim's."

"And Parsons was found next to her body trying to stop the blood flow. He'd have no reason or time to wash up," Jack said.

"Exactly."

"Then why did King give me shit this morning when I said it wasn't a suicide?" I asked.

"Because we had just arrived and were going off the evidence we saw. We only got the forensic report on Clark's homicide late last night, didn't read it until today. Parsons was our first and primary suspect."

"Then why did you interview Angie Williams?" I asked. "King intimidated her."

"I'm sorry about that. The girl got under Rachel's skin."

"I thought cops were better than that," I said. "Don't react, don't take it personal."

Before Chavez could say anything, Jack asked, "How did the killer get into the building? I thought it was on a card key system."

"It is, but there is a master key. A physical key. Maintenance has them because most of the utility rooms use a key."

"Maintenance and who else?"

"That's what we're still trying to determine." Chavez looked from Jack to me and back to Jack. "If you learn anything that can help, please call. We're on the same team."

"Absolutely," Jack said. He hit me and I nodded my agreement, though I was still irritated that King had shelved Elijah's murder and made Angie feel like a suspect in Lena's murder.

Chavez left.

"What do you think?" Jack asked.

"The killer has to be on staff. Killed Lena, washed up in the administrative building, cleaned up after himself. Then had access to the main building after hours without using a card key. Teacher, admin? Someone who knew there was a master key and had access to it, or someone Dwight trusted enough to let into the building." I looked at my watch. It was four. "I need to shower and change for this stupid dinner party."

"I was surprised when Mom said you wanted to go."

"I want to meet with Manny Ramos about what's going on at his store. I don't want to have dinner with a bunch of stuffy people."

Jack laughed. "Better you than me."

"I'll call Mom and she'll make you join us."

"No, you won't, because you love me best." He kissed my forehead and I playfully hit him. "Keep your eyes open for your stalker."

"Roger that."

chapter forty-three

CAL RAFFERTY

Cal's brain hurt. He'd spent the last six hours going through all his notes and records from the Bradford investigation. The conference room was a mess. His boss walked in and said, "You okay?"

"I missed it."

George picked up the transcript from Ben Bradford's plea interview where he gave, under penalty of perjury, all information that he knew in exchange for a reduced sentence. But because he refused to give up the supplier, he got fifteen years minimum.

"You're not the only agent who went over these files, nor the ranking agent," George said. "If anything was missed, we all missed it."

"Okay—bear with me," Cal said. "We ended the investigation with one unknown—the supplier. We knew Bradford had a deal with someone, and we assumed that person was in Yuma because of his travels. We never had a line on him, but we had, between Bradford and Eric McMahon, all the players at Sun Valley High. Everything they gave us confirmed what we had learned. So nothing was off, right?"

"Have you slept in the last two days?"

Cal ignored him.

"So, case closed, supplier on the back burner, I put in all the alerts so if something pops, we get it. Now, three years later, a PI who's investigating an overdose death suddenly is talking to all our people. She talks to Bradford. She talks to Eric. So I'm looking at where she's going, and she's been to the Cactus Stop twice in the last two days. Why?"

"She was thirsty? She wanted smokes? It's a convenience store, Cal."

"Yeah, but she was talking to people. Investigating. I know what it looks like when someone is looking for answers."

George's mouth twitched, but Cal ignored him.

"So I'm going through everything that we have and seeing if the Cactus Stop was mentioned."

Cal pulled out a thin folder. "Reams of paper, and I find this." He handed it to George. "A work permit?"

"For Scott Jimenez. Anyone under fifteen and a half needs a work permit signed by the school. He worked at the Cactus Stop on Hatcher from age fifteen until he was arrested when he was seventeen. He worked there for more than two years. But it was a job, and no one else worked there that we interviewed or arrested, just Scott."

"This is weak, Cal."

Cal ignored the comment. "So I looked up Scott's data, wanting to see where he is, what he's doing, maybe I'd pay him a visit, see what's what. I can't find him."

"Moved out of state?"

"Gone. No sign that he has moved, left the state, got a job, has a phone, gone to prison for another crime, nothing. But get this, I called juvenile detention, thought they might have some info from when he was released, and surprise—two days ago Teresa Angelhart from Angelhart Investigations pulled his file, asked specifically for his last known address."

"That's a little interesting."

"It's more than a *little* interesting. I don't want to work with a PI, but they know something, and I need to know what they know. But that means I'm going to have to give them something, because they're not going to want to share."

"Especially when Margo Angelhart finds out a DEA agent was following her."

Cal winced. "You read my report."

"Thank you for at least writing a report. I got your back, Cal. It needed to be done. Reach out to them."

"I'm going to use Hitchner with Phoenix DEB as a buffer. He knows the Angelharts and can smooth things over."

"Fine. Keep me in the loop. I'm gone for the weekend with the family, so technically, you're in charge. Don't abuse it."

Cal grinned. "No promises."

chapter forty-four

MARGO ANGELHART

Manny Ramos lived in a beautiful house in Paradise Valley built into the southern edge of the Phoenix Mountain Preserve. While it faced mostly south, the slight angle had the setting sun turning the house aglow in golds, reds, and oranges as I drove up the steep drive. Discreet lighting along the edge, interspersed with desert-thriving shrubs and cactus, guided my route to the sprawling two-story mansion that blended beautifully into the rocky terrain.

I parked next to my mother's classy Escalade. My mother wasn't pretentious, but she'd bought the SUV after she went into private practice. After decades of driving either a beat-up Excursion that finally stopped running with 420,000 miles on the odometer a week before Lu graduated from high school, or the subsequent practical Volvo she'd bought used, she wanted what she wanted. Who could blame her? She gave the Volvo to Tess after she graduated from law school, and Tess was still driving it.

I didn't know *exactly* what was going on at the Cactus Stop. I had a tickle of doubt about bringing in Manny Ramos only because of what I had learned about EBT fraud. If it was happening at scale, someone in accounting would know. This wasn't a mom-and-pop shop, this was a thirteen-store chain.

Yet, I could be wrong about the fraud. It could be a simple drug-running operation, which would better explain Megan's messages to Elijah, and his subsequent stakeout of the store. He had been looking for someone specific, or looking to catch someone in the commission of a crime.

"You're quiet," Uncle Rafe said.

"Just thinking everything through."

I quickly assessed the property. There was only one way in and out—the long driveway. Even in an emergency, there would be no scaling up the steep mountainside unless you were an expert climber and had appropriate equipment. The other houses in the area were no less elegant—except for one columned monstrosity at the base of the mountain that was a cross between a Greek palace and antebellum mansion.

It wasn't like I expected the need for a quick escape—this was a dinner party with a lawyer, a priest, and a politician. I almost laughed—was this the beginning of a bad joke?

"Alina truly appreciates your help," he said. "This has been a difficult time for her."

"I think I know what happened," I said. "Proving it isn't going to be easy."

"Sometimes, just knowing the truth can bring peace."

"I want justice."

Uncle Rafe glanced upward and I knew exactly what he was thinking. God would enact His own justice, that it wasn't up to us. That was true, but I wouldn't sleep well knowing Elijah's killer got away with it.

"I want earthly justice," I clarified. "Because if we don't stop these people, more kids are going to die. I'm tired of it, Uncle Rafe. And it only seems to get worse."

He put his hand on mine. He didn't have to say anything for me to regain my calm. Sometimes, I see a halo around Uncle Rafe's head.

We got out of the car and he said, "You look nice."

"Mom made me," I said with a grin.

My mother had sent me a text to not wear jeans. I knew what she meant—wear a dress—but honestly I wasn't a fan. That there was no place to conceal a weapon was only a small issue. The biggest issue was shoes. I don't like heels. I pick shoes solely for comfort. I didn't want to think about my feet, and if my feet were sore or my toes cramped I would be miserable. The low-heeled boots I loved were scuffed and well-worn. So I had slipped on strappy flat black sandals and hoped I didn't have to chase anyone.

I did dress up, but for comfort in a knee-length stretchy black skirt and a loose-fitting white blouse which hid my gun in the holster at the small of my back. The Glock 42 wasn't my favorite sidearm, but it was the smallest Glock on the market and one of the easiest to use and conceal. I'd added a blazer and looked like a butler or a bodyguard, even wearing the small diamond earrings that were a high school graduation present from my parents.

Manny Ramos answered the door.

"It is good to see you again, Margo. Father Rafe."

He shook my hand, then Uncle Rafe's.

"Thank you for having us," Uncle Rafe said. "Your home is as breathtaking as I remember."

The look on my face must have told Rafe I was surprised he'd been here before because he said to me, "Manny is a longtime parishioner."

"Though I have been bad about attending regular Sunday Mass," Ramos said.

If he was looking for Uncle Rafe to tell him it was fine, he was looking at the wrong priest. Rafe just smiled and said, "I hope to see you soon."

"Father, a drink? Ava says it's your birthday, so surely you can enjoy a glass of wine, or perhaps a tequila? I have several to choose from."

He waved his hand toward the interior of the house and we followed.

"Wine would be nice, thank you," Rafe said.

"I'll wait until dinner," I said.

We walked through the stunning home. On one side were towering windows that looked out on a large outdoor living area featuring an infinity pool lit up with purple lights and a breathtaking view of Phoenix.

On the other side of the great room were windows that looked out at the rocky mountainside, the landscape lit with perfectly placed bulbs highlighting plants, desert flowers, and a huge saguaro cactus. A multilayered patio had been created among the rocks, but I couldn't see how to access it. An outdoor fireplace, comfortable chairs, and small waterfall dropping into what I assumed was a pond completed the area.

The furniture was a bit too ornate for my taste, though classy, and the contemporary-style structure complemented the old-world furnishings. It was a unique and comfortable blend of old and new.

We followed Ramos to the bar and I said, "Where's my mom?"

"She and Bill are in the library," Manny said.

Ramos poured Uncle Rafe a glass of red wine in a rounded stemmed glass, and I accepted the offered water.

I heard my mom's laugh and she stepped into the great room with Bill Borgas, the councilmember who had been friends of the family since before I enlisted in the Army.

We made small talk, which would have driven me up a wall except I was too preoccupied trying to figure out how to tell Ramos about the trouble at his business. He was a genuinely interesting guy who—other than the house—didn't seem pretentious.

I asked about the house; how long he'd lived here and if he'd done the work himself.

"I've been here for more than thirty years," he said. "My dearly departed wife and I moved in after we married. It was a much smaller house then, but we loved every inch. Would you like a tour?"

"Yes, thank you."

I followed him through the great room, down a hall past the

dining room—where he said he never ate except when he had company—and into the kitchen.

"My Uncle Tom would kill for this space," I said as we stopped in the middle of a huge kitchen glistening in white and stainless steel. The smell of Mexican spice filled the kitchen. It would have felt sterile, except for the amazing hand-painted tile wall done primarily in turquoise, burnt orange, and yellow. I stared at it.

"My wife commissioned the wall. I thought it a bit extravagant, but she had seen the artist's work and wanted a touch in our home."

"It's amazing."

"It truly is."

He looked sad, and I knew he was a widower, so asked, "How long has she been gone?"

"Seven years in November. I still miss her every day. She was the love of my life."

We walked down a wide corridor. A library. Guest rooms. Downstairs was a family room, a second kitchen and bar, and two more guest rooms. A wall of photos of all different spaces and sizes had been put up rather haphazardly but it worked. "Your family?"

"Extended," he said. "Marisol and I were blessed with only one daughter. She's in college now. But I have a brother and three sisters, they all have many children."

I did a double take when I saw John Brighton in a group picture with a bunch of young men fishing.

"This guy—he works for you." I pointed to Brighton. I didn't want Ramos to know that we had run him—not yet, at any rate. I was surprised to see him on the wall.

"John, yes, my nephew. He started working for me three years ago when he graduated from college. Smart young man. I didn't know you knew him."

"I don't. I just recognized him," I said vaguely and hoped he didn't ask how.

Did this change how I approached Ramos about his Hatcher store? Maybe not. But if his nephew was involved in a crime, would that change the way he handled the situation?

Almost certainly. Damn. I had to walk on eggshells.

And I really wanted to talk to my mom about it. She would have a more diplomatic approach.

We went back upstairs just as Ramos's housekeeper announced that dinner was ready.

Ramos must have known my uncle well, or he also practiced meatless Friday, because dinner was tilapia ancho chili, new potatoes, and an amazing salad with chunks of tomato and mozzarella drizzled with a spicy ranch-style dressing.

We ate, made more small talk, and I kept glancing at my mom. I wanted to get her the information about John Brighton, but we hadn't had time alone.

Wing it, I thought.

My phone buzzed as Ramos suggested we have coffee in the library. I excused myself and went out onto the deck to take the call. It was a lovely evening, and the sunset was spectacular.

"Hello?" I answered the unfamiliar number.

"Um, Margo? The PI?"

Sounded like a teenager. "Yes, that's me."

"This is Benny Vallejo. I'm a friend of Angie's? She gave me your number, she said it was okay?"

"Are *you* okay?" I asked. He sounded awkward and a little stressed.

"Yeah, yeah, I'm fine. I just finished my shift and Angie said if I saw anything weird I should call you. I don't want to lose my job though."

"What did you see?" I pressed.

"I got here at four when my shift starts, and Desi left, told me to run the register. She *never* lets me run the register. I mean, I know how, I've done it, but it's not my job. Three people came in looking for her, all kind of, well, sketchy. I'm not judging, but they were all sort of in my face. Edgy. Jumpy, you know? Suspicious-like. If they hung around longer, I would have called the police because I sort of thought they might rob the place. But then they left."

When he stopped talking, I said, "Go on."

"Um, yeah, and she got back an hour later. She was angry and stomping around, had me restock shelves that she said were sloppy, and they weren't. I just did what she said. Those three people all came back and she rang them up for nothing. I mean, maybe I missed something, but Angie told me to observe, and maybe because they came in one after the other, like they were waiting for her, it made me suspicious."

It clicked. "Benny, did Desi hand these people anything?"

"No."

"She handed them *nothing*?"

"I mean, like what?"

"Anything."

"Well, they didn't buy anything, but she handed them a receipt. They didn't get food or cigarettes, just put in their card and she gave them a receipt."

"A receipt from the register?"

"Yeah, it's rung up like all transactions."

"Do you know if it was a debit card or an EBT card?"

He thought on it. "One was a debit, had a Disney character on it. The other two I think were EBT."

I knew what she was doing. I just didn't know *how* it worked because of the paper trail Jessie Oliver warned me about. These people were paying Desi for drugs . . . maybe to pick up later? Was that what Elijah had figured out, why he was taking pictures? Except he didn't take pictures of an exchange. Just of people leaving.

Maybe he had evidence in his missing backpack.

"You're right to call," I said. "When do you work again?"

"Monday."

"Okay. Stay away until then."

"I can't quit. Angie wants me to quit, but I need this job."

"If you quit, I'll find you something." I had lots of family in the restaurant business—they were always hiring. "Might not pay as much," I told him, "but it'll be safer than where you are."

"I don't go back until after school Monday."

"We'll talk before then," I said.

I pocketed my phone and went back inside. Everyone was having coffee in the library, which seemed to have books for display more than for reading. I accepted a cup from Ramos. "Everything okay?" he asked.

"Yeah, fine. Work." I smiled. I wanted to talk about Brighton, but wasn't certain now was the time to bring up his nephew. Maybe Elijah tried to reach out, but was killed before he could talk to him.

Or maybe Brighton was involved in Desi's scam. If she was ringing up purchases on debit cards and EBT cards, someone in the corporate office had to be involved.

My mom, perhaps sensing my edginess, said, "Manny, we have made some progress in our investigation for Alina."

He smiled sadly, put his hand to his heart. "She will be relieved. I invited her tonight, but she declined. I didn't push. When I lost my wife, I didn't want to leave the house for months. I can imagine how much worse it is to lose a child."

Mom said, "We believe there may be someone at the Cactus Stop who is engaging in illegal activity that Elijah uncovered, which may have resulted in his being poisoned with fentanyl."

Ramos blinked, then his eyes darkened. He was angry. *I would be too*, I thought.

"Who?" he demanded.

Mom straightened her spine at the tone. "We don't have confirmation. It's mostly hearsay."

I said, "A friend of Elijah's died of a drug overdose in July. After, he began taking pictures of people going in and out of the store—he did this in the evenings for about two months. I found text exchanges between Elijah and this friend that implies, but doesn't confirm, that Desiree Jimenez may have been dealing drugs. She may not have been doing it through the store," I said quickly, even though I was positive she was, "but based on Elijah's behavior, he believed she was."

Ramos was quiet. A vein throbbed in his neck.

Mom said, "We wanted to tell you because there is some evidence that Ms. Jimenez and her assistant manager may be using the EBT system or dealing directly behind the counter. We considered going to the police with the information, but again, we have no hard evidence, and this appears to be an isolated situation at the Hatcher store."

"I see," Ramos said. "I'm stunned. Desiree has worked for me for years. Why would she do this?"

"Her brother went to prison for dealing drugs and attempted murder," I said. "She could have been working with him back then, took over his end of the business. I'm not sure yet because I haven't been able to track him down."

I didn't mention that I thought he was dead. That seemed a bit morbid and not on point with what we were discussing.

"I will have my accountant audit the store immediately, and I'll send in my own investigator. I have someone on staff who does this, though he's usually looking for people skimming or stealing, not *dealing*." He squeezed his eyes tight with his thumb and forefinger. "Dear Lord, if that poor boy was killed because of this? Why didn't he come to me?"

"Blame is only on the person who killed him," Mom said firmly.

"Elijah may have been thinking about it," I said. "I found evidence on his computer that he visited the Cactus Stop corporate site multiple times. He may have been trying to figure out who to call about what he observed. But going to the owner? That's jumping over a half dozen people, so he may not have been comfortable."

"I knew the boy," Ramos said. "Not well, but I knew him. And Alina works for me as well."

That was news to me.

"She does?"

"Yes. She started working for my company last year after we terminated the contract with our cleaning company and decided to hire directly. It was more cost-effective to hire two full-time staff than to contract out. She urged Elijah to apply for a clerk position because of my predilection to hire high school students. I remember how hard it was to find a job when I was in high school, and how so many kids turn to petty theft or drugs because they feel they have no future."

Bill said, "You've helped turn things around, Manny. The Sunnyslope youth center is always busy, and with the work programs at the high schools, these kids have options you and I didn't have forty years ago."

My phone was vibrating and I finally looked down at the message. It was from Jack.

Hitch just showed up at the office. You need to be here.

It was eight thirty.

I responded: **I'll leave in five minutes.**

I listened as the conversation shifted to Ramos's philanthropic activities, but it was clear his heart wasn't in it. I'd want to act quickly if I learned one of my managers had abused my trust—and possibly killed one of my employees.

I found an opening in the conversation and said, "I have a very early morning, so I need to go. Uncle Rafe?"

Mom said, "I can take Rafe back." She got up. "Besides, I should leave as well. Last night's party is catching up with me."

Ramos walked the three of us to the door while Bill went to use the bathroom. "It was so good to get to know you better, Margo. I promise, I will get to the bottom of what is going on at my Hatcher store. Thank you so much for letting me know." He reached for my hand, shook it. "If you find anything else, call me, anytime. It'll take a few days to get the audit started, but I will make sure nothing like this happens again." He paused. "Have you told Alina?"

"Not yet," I said. "What I think and what I can prove are two different things. But I plan to tell her that her son was trying to do the right thing by exposing a drug dealer, and that person may have killed him. I won't give her details because again, I can't prove it."

Mom said, "You'll want to go to the police, Manny. Tell them what you suspect, and let them investigate. Margo was followed, so there is at least one other person involved, perhaps working with your manager. He could be more dangerous, someone who won't care if there's collateral damage."

"I will," he said. "Thank you."

We left.

"What's going on?" Mom asked me when we reached our vehicles.

"The DEB cop who has been avoiding Jack and me? He suddenly wants to meet ASAP."

"Well then, Rafe, I hope you have ice cream at the rectory to satisfy my sweet tooth."

Uncle Rafe laughed, put his arm in Mom's. "I can find a scoop or two."

chapter forty-five

MARGO ANGELHART

I walked into Angelhart Investigations two minutes before nine Friday night. Every light was on and three men sat at the conference table eating pizza and drinking energy drinks. Jack, a man I didn't know, and the man who had been following me.

I stood in the doorway, took off my blazer and tossed it across the back of a chair.

I said to Jack, "You didn't tell me you were buddies with the asshole who has been tailing me for two days."

"Just met the asshole tonight," Jack said.

The man jumped up, nearly knocking over his Monster energy drink, and strode over to me, extended his hand. "You're fucking brilliant," he said.

I blinked and took his hand even though I was still really angry that he'd followed me.

"I know," I said automatically.

He grinned. "I'm Cal Rafferty with the DEA. I followed you because you met with Bradford down at Eyman, and I needed to know what you were doing."

"You could have asked."

"Yyyyeah, nope."

"I could have shot you."

He laughed. "I think you're too smart to shoot first, ask questions later."

Who was this guy? I didn't know if I wanted to punch him or have a beer with him.

I did like being called brilliant.

"What's going on?" I asked.

"Mike Hitchner," the other man said and extended his hand. "Call me Hitch."

I shook his hand, glanced at Jack as if to ask *what the hell is going on?*

"They brought the pizza," he said. "Help yourself."

Instead, I grabbed an energy drink. This looked like it would be a long night.

"So did you lie to my brother that you didn't know what was going on when he called you and wanted a sit-down?"

"Not exactly," Hitch said. "I wasn't intentionally avoiding you. Bradford isn't my case anymore. Once he was in prison, everything became Cal's headache."

"Why did you visit Bradford?" Cal asked me.

I didn't answer. I didn't owe him an explanation.

Jack said, "We are investigating the death of a teenager. Police closed the case, but there were some threads they didn't tie off. The kid worked at the Cactus Stop, and over the last week we've come to believe he was tracking illegal activity within the store, and may have been killed because of it, framed as an accidental overdose."

"And Bradford?" Cal pushed.

"One of the teachers at Sun Valley High mentioned him," I said. "Then she was killed. I wanted to figure out if he was still running things at the school, or maybe someone took over for him and Lena Clark was stabbed to death because she had been asking questions that threatened their organization. Elijah attended

Sun Valley, but there was no other connection to Bradford. I was, frankly, fishing. I didn't get anything out of him, but I think he's somehow involved, or may know who is."

"Their operation was fucking brilliant," Cal said.

"More brilliant than me?" I asked with a half smile.

He laughed. "I'd put my money on you. The Bradford operation was simple and straightforward, which is probably why it wasn't on our radar until the anonymous call."

He drained his energy drink, tossed the can in the trash, then grabbed another. This guy was already wired—he didn't need more caffeine, but I didn't say anything.

"They compartmentalized everything," Cal said. "Only Eric McMahon knew that Bradford was in charge—at least of distribution. So when we got him to turn state's evidence, the only thing Eric could give us was Bradford—and by extension his wife—and everyone Eric recruited to deal for him. It was a pyramid. But while we watched for months, we never got the top guy. They were very, very discreet in how they communicated with the supplier. When Scott Jimenez shot Eric, we pulled it. Took everyone we had down and wrapped it up."

"Without knowing who the supplier was," Jack said.

"Yep. Really irked us, but we really didn't have a choice at that point. Then, after following Margo around, I noted she stopped at the Cactus Stop on Hatcher twice. And something in the back of my mind told me I'd missed something. I found it. A work permit for Scott Jimenez. He worked at the Cactus Stop for more than two years. Lightbulb!" Cal flicked his fingers above his head and I couldn't help but smile.

"So I began digging into the Cactus Stop," he said. "Manny Ramos is squeaky clean. No investigations by any agency, not even OSHA. He has a corporation, under which the Cactus Stop holdings are just one business. He started from one store and built it up. Gotta admire the guy. Hires teenagers because they're cheap and it gives them experience. Gives back to the community. Friends with law enforcement. Donates to politicians and the Catholic Church. Everyone likes him."

Jack said, "What are you getting at?"

"I'll tell you everything we have, if you tell me everything you know. Even if you can't prove it. Then maybe we can finally put an end to this operation."

"On one condition," Jack said.

I glanced at him, confused. Jack usually jumped to work with law enforcement.

"Sure, if I can," Cal said.

"Promise me that you'll *never* follow anyone in my family again."

Cal shrugged. "No can do."

Hitch said, "Cal, *come on*."

"Well, I don't know if our cases are going to cross again. I don't want to make promises I can't keep."

I laughed. "I like honesty."

Cal grinned.

"One minute," I said and went to my office.

I'd put up all my notes this morning on my whiteboard, but hadn't really had time to analyze them. I rolled the board into the conference room and turned it to face the three men.

"Whoa," Cal said. "Holy shit."

He stared, taking in everything at once. The notes, the connections, the questions, and the copies of Elijah's photos that I'd taped along the bottom because I had run out of room.

Jack slowly rose and I saw he had narrowed in on one corner. I looked where he was looking—my notes on Lena Clark and Dwight Parsons. He glanced at me and I shrugged.

"They're connected, Jack. I just don't know how."

Hitch looked at the photos. "I know half these people. They're dealers."

"Yeah," Cal said. "This guy—he's been on our radar on and off for a while."

Cal stared at the photo of Megan Osterman, then glanced over at me. "What do you know of Megan?"

"Is that your case?"

"It's in my office as part of a task force with Phoenix. But I refreshed myself this afternoon. She dated Scott Jimenez before he went to prison. We looked at her, interviewed her, scared the bejesus out of her, but she hadn't been involved with Bradford, and we had no evidence she was dealing with Scott."

"We had one of our female detectives try to scare her straight," Hitch said. "I thought it worked, but I guess it didn't."

"She died of a drug overdose on July 6," I said. "Across the street from the Cactus Stop."

Cal squinted at my board, then at me. "You think Scott is dead?"

"Jeez, what gave that away? My starred note *Jimenez killed after release?*"

"Funny," he said.

"My sister can't find him, and if Tess can't find him, he's either completely off the grid or in WITSEC or he's dead. I think dead."

"We'll look into that," Hitch said.

"We couldn't get anything on Desiree," Cal said. "But we interviewed her since she was Scott's sister."

"EBT," Hitchner said. "What do you think is going on there?"

Cal frowned, as if he were thinking.

I said, "Well, I don't have all the pieces, but Desi and her assistant manager, Tony, are running a drug operation out of the Cactus Stop. I *think* it works like this: Someone comes in, either using a debit card or an EBT card, and ostensibly buys something. But they don't take anything from the store. Instead, they're given a receipt and they leave. So I'm wondering if they take the receipt to another place to pick up drugs."

"You *are* brilliant," Cal said. "That's exactly what's happening. Fuck!"

He was excited. And I was pleased that he thought I was brilliant yet again.

"Brilliant," I said to Jack and pointed to my chest. "Me."

"I'll have it engraved on your headstone," he said. I stuck my tongue out at him.

"Damn! Cash?"

"I didn't see cash," I said. "One witness I have said he only saw debit and EBT cards."

"How does this work?" Jack asked. "I never worked white-collar."

"Not my expertise," Cal said, "but I know a lot about laundering drug money. It's why I was so impressed with Cecilia Bradford and *her* laundering operation. If she'd used her brains for good instead of evil, she'd have gone far and not be in prison. These people are dealers." He tapped the pictures Elijah had taken. "Just like Sun Valley, but they're not students. Some look like homeless, some gangbangers, others could be college kids for all I know. They're buying their product at a discount, then setting their own prices. It's fucking brilliant. No drugs on the property, much harder to catch."

"But *how*?" I asked. "They get a receipt and do what with it? Go to the drug emporium down the street?" Then I thought of what Edith Mackey had said, about people walking up and down her quiet street. Maybe I wasn't that far off.

"Pretty much," Cal said. "Go in, run your card for some predetermined amount, get a receipt, take that receipt to pick up your supply, sell it. Where do they go? There has to be a place close by where they bring proof of purchase."

"Same street?" Margo asked. "At least in the neighborhood?"

"Most likely. From the pictures, these people came on foot."

"That's what I also observed."

"So close by. Blocks. And that's why this works. Someone raids the place, they're not going to find anything."

"When I spoke to a financial crimes detective, she said that EBT fraud wouldn't work on a scale like this because the inventory wouldn't match and the corporate office would eventually figure it out. On a small scale, staff could cover it up, but this is a dozen people a day. For what? A hundred, two hundred bucks a pop?"

"It's much bigger than that," Cal said. "We're talking thousands of dollars a day per location. EBT fraud is rampant—people get cards fraudulently, clone cards, steal cards. Find a business that will let them buy alcohol with the card, sell drugs under the table, but *this* operation is far more sophisticated. And it can't be hidden. Your staff can't steal from you. You're getting five thousand dollars in receipts without the corresponding product sales." He closed his eyes. "So, there's roughly 3300 transactions a week in a small convenience store, which is about 450 a day. If the average is twenty dollars—easy math here—that's nine thousand a day in gross sales." He opened his yes, nodded. "Five thousand dollars a day more—that's more than fifty percent increase in sales than a store this size and location should have. It's going to pop for any accountant worth their salt."

I tensed. "You're saying the corporate office is involved." I pointed to the picture of John Brighton. "Like him. Elijah took his picture—he works for the Cactus Stop. He's Manny Ramos's nephew."

"It just takes one person in the right position, someone with access to the accounting system. Fudge the numbers, it won't show up unless there is a full audit—a real audit, not just bookkeeping checks."

"Manny Ramos is going to audit his store next week," I said. "And now, my number one suspect is his nephew." Stealing from family—that really burned me.

I told them that my mom and I filled Manny Ramos in on what we thought Desi was up to at the store.

"Why would you do that?" Hitch snapped. "Why not come to the police with the information."

"Oh, maybe because you were avoiding us?" I snapped back.

"We would have opened an investigation."

Jack put his hand up. "We're working together now," he said. Hitch looked like he wanted to argue, but Cal said, "We're not going to get a warrant without more evidence. Like your witness. You have someone on the inside?" He looked at me hopefully.

"I have a scared kid who doesn't think he can quit, but yeah, he's seen things that are suspicious. But I'm not putting him in danger. One teenager was already killed."

"And two teachers," Jack said. "This also goes back to Sun Valley."

"Who did you miss?" I asked.

"I don't know," Cal said and sat down. He looked glum. "I didn't think we missed anyone at Sun Valley, and the supplier wouldn't be on campus. That wouldn't make sense, because they wouldn't need the middle man in Ben Bradford. Plus his monthly trip to Yuma."

"Which could have been a distraction," Jack said.

Tess and Luisa walked in. "You guys are having a party and didn't tell us?" Tess said.

Jack introduced Hitch and Cal. I stared at my board. Cal had moved a few things around as he spoke, and I saw everything much clearer. Elijah knew Desi was selling drugs, but hadn't understood exactly how it worked. Had he been following the people she sold tickets to? Is that what got him killed? Or had he reached out to the corporate office . . . and someone from there killed him?

"I didn't know you were coming in," Jack said to our sisters.

"We've been working," Tess said, "and I called Mom to let her know what we found, and she said you and Margo were here."

She waited a beat.

"Apparently," I said, "we're working together." I waved hands to include Cal and Hitch. "Did you find something?"

"Yes," Tess said. "I went back to the Bradfords. Went back as far as I could and found that Cecilia Bradford's maiden name is Brighton."

I stared. "Brighton? Same name as the guy in the Tesla? Manny Ramos's nephew?"

"Her parents are William and Sylvia Brighton. Sylvia's maiden name is Torrens. The name sounded familiar, so I went through all my notes. Manny Ramos's wife, who died seven years ago of breast cancer, her maiden name was Torrens. They're sisters."

"Cecilia is Ramos's niece," I said again. "But how does John Brighton fit in? Her brother? He'd be much younger than her."

"Cecilia is an only child," Tess said. "I think John is her son. I can't prove it, but on paper it works. After a lot of digging, I learned Cecilia had a baby in high school. She was sixteen and there were whispers of sexual assault. She never named the father. Her parents went through a nasty divorce around that time, and she moved in with her aunt and uncle—Manny and Marisol Ramos. While living there, she had the baby, then finished school, then left town. Basically, disappeared. At least until the wedding announcement for Cecilia Torrens and Ben Bradford eight years later."

"Why did she use her mother's maiden name?" I asked.

Tess shrugged. "Don't know. But while it's not widely known, there is ample evidence that Manny Ramos raised his *nephew*, John Brighton."

Cal walked over to the whiteboard. He'd moved some of my notes around and added additional information.

I saw the truth.

"Shit," I said softly. "Can we prove this?"

He had laid out what was essentially a pyramid scheme where dealers bought drugs from the Cactus Stop through a ticketing system, then ran their own little mini operations. Like the Bradford operation, it compartmentalized the organization, so if one person was caught, it wouldn't take down the entire network. It all ran around the Cactus Stop on Hatcher Street.

Cal said, "It would take a huge multi-agency task force, including the FBI, to come in and audit the books. We have more than enough to launch the investigation, but we can't shut them down overnight."

"Unless we can prove murder," I said. The final piece clicked into place for me. "Manny Ramos hired Elijah's mother last year to his janitorial staff. She got Elijah the job at the Cactus Stop. Based on Megan's text messages to Elijah, he knew that Desi was running a drug operation. Maybe he ignored it because of his mom, or because he didn't know who to go to, but when Megan died, he couldn't ignore it any longer."

It fit. It fit how he was protective of his mother, how he became preoccupied, and why he was being discreet taking the pictures. He wanted to have evidence before he turned anything over to the police.

Could he have gone to the wrong person? Like John Brighton, which would explain why Elijah had his address. Maybe he went to his house to tell him his suspicions . . . and that was the wrong person to confide in.

Would John Brighton have done this on his own? He'd been raised by his uncle—could he have betrayed him so deeply? Or . . .

"Did Ramos know about this?" I asked the group.

Cal shrugged. "It's his business. I'd think so, but not necessarily, especially if he's hands-off."

"I tipped him off," I said and clenched my fists. "Dammit!"

"He owns the company, he has no record, and he's a philanthropist," Cal said. "He may not work day-to-day in that business. But Brighton? He's now my target. Because he works for the company, he lives very well, and he has a connection to the Bradfords. He could have picked up where they left off. He could be the conduit to the supplier. And you show right here—" he tapped my board "—that Elijah looked up his address and photographed his vehicle."

"I think I can help here," Luisa said. "I broke the security on the thumb drive." She walked over to the television in the corner and plugged the thumb drive into the side.

"I didn't even know the TV had a USB port," I muttered to Jack.

"Neither did I," he admitted.

Luisa used the remote to quickly navigate to an app on the television, then launched the flash drive. "Jack, lights?"

Jack pressed a couple of buttons on the table and the lights dimmed. On the television, the first video played.

"Where is that?" Cal asked.

Lu shrugged. "A residence. Look at the angle, the camera is on the ground, I think under a couch." She pointed to the top of the screen. "It's tilted slightly so we can see the people when they sit down, but not when they're standing."

Scott Jimenez was the first to come clearly into view when he sat down on a chair to the left of the camera. He looked almost directly at the camera.

"He knows it's there," Cal and I said at the same time.

A male voice said, "Are you in?"

"Yeah," Scott said. "This really sucks."

"Eric burned us."

The voice stepped into the frame—he could be seen chest down. He reached into his pocket and took out a gun. He wore gloves. As he bent to put the gun on the table, his profile came into view.

"Brighton," Cal said. "I'll be damned."

"What if I get caught?" Scott asked.

"We'll take care of you," John said. "Buddy, you're a minor. You're not going to do serious time. If you're caught, plead down, you'll be out by the time you're nineteen. I suppose I can have Desi do it . . ."

"No, no, I'll do it. She's too volatile."

"If anything goes wrong, you know who hired you."

"Prick of a coach who didn't realize he promoted the wrong person."

John leaned down and clamped a hand on Scott's shoulder. His full face came into view. He was a handsome young man, I thought. What a waste. "Just remember, don't say a word beyond what we agreed to, understand?"

"I'm good. Thank you for trusting me with this. I won't let you down."

"You never have," John said.

John left and a minute later Scott got up, bent down, and retrieved the camera. The video shut off.

"That's why they killed him," I said. "He tried to blackmail Brighton when he got out of jail."

Lu started the second video, which was better quality. The feed was stationary, showing people going in and out of the Cactus Stop on Hatcher. We watched for five minutes before someone came in, used their EBT card, and received a receipt. Desi was behind the counter. Elijah came into view once as he stocked shelves.

Lu stopped the video and said, "This goes on for hours, showing fourteen people using their EBT card or their debit card and getting a receipt."

Which confirmed Cal's theory.

"A solid piece of circumstantial evidence," Hitch said. "With these pictures—" he waved at the photos Elijah took "—we can rattle them. Someone will talk."

"Will they?" I asked. "Ben and Cecilia didn't."

"I think," Cal said slowly as he sat back down, "that Cecilia was trying to protect her son. That's why she didn't turn him in."

I could buy that. "What's Ben Bradford's motive?"

"He loved his wife?" he suggested.

Maybe, I thought. Or he remained silent to protect his family.

"What's the third video, Lu?" Jack asked.

Lu said, "I found the date stamp code for each video. The first was taken the day before Eric was shot. The second longer video was taken on June 3 of this year. This last video was taken July 5." She played it.

It was Megan Osterman, sitting on her bed in the tiny room behind the garage. She looked sick, hollow and drained. She had been crying.

July 5. The day before she died.

"My name is Megan Osterman. I miss Scott so much and I think they killed him." She breathed in deeply. "On this flash drive is a video and that's why Scott is dead." She scratched her face, drawing attention to an open wound on the side of her head. From drug use, like a large open zit.

"Okay, from the beginning. I am Megan Osterman. I'm going to rehab tomorrow. I think. I'll try. Scott gave me this flash drive before he went to jail. He told me to hide it, to not say a word. I kept my promise. And then he got out of jail and said to bring it to him, so I did, but he wasn't there and he never came back. I hid it again, because I thought he would call. Then I forgot. And I found it today. I never watched it until today, and they had him killed like they wanted Eric killed, and they'll kill me. I saved the video Elijah gave me for evidence. Eli says he needs it later and to keep it in a safe place, and this is a safe place."

She looked at a spot beyond the camera for a long minute, periodically scratching her face. She started talking without looking at the camera, but it was clear no one else was in the room. "Eli found a place for me and said if I really, really, really want to be clean, I have to go. I do. But I'm scared. I don't have a life anymore and Scott is gone and I know he's dead because he wouldn't leave me. I asked Desi where is he? Where did he go? And she said he left because I'm an addict. And no!" She pounded her fists on her bed. "I'll get better. I'll get better!"

She looked back at the camera, straightened up, and said, "Eli said I need to go to rehab to keep me safe because he's going to the police with this video. And if I'm clean, I can tell the police how everything works because I know things. I used to be a dealer for Desi. Until I took too much."

She lit a joint and took a deep drag. Her eyes got glassy, but she spoke clearer. "I've been wondering lately if Desi killed her own brother. Scott worshipped her, because their parents were shit. Dad left, mom a drunk, Desi basically raised him. Treated him like shit too, but Scott doesn't listen to me about her." Another drag. "I'm sorry, Mom. You are a great mom, really, and I'm going to get clean, for me, and for you. I didn't realize how good a mom you were until I saw how shitty other moms are. Anyway, I want to look back on this so I know how far I've come. When I'm clean." Another drag. "I go in Monday. Maybe Tuesday. Fuck. I'm scared." She smiled, but it was a sad, sad, smile. The video ended.

No one said anything for a minute.

Cal kicked a chair and walked out. I didn't see that coming.

"His older sister died of an overdose when they were in high school," Hitch said quietly. "It sometimes hits too close."

Hitch turned to Lu and motioned to the flash drive. "Can I have that?" he asked. "We're going to put the wheels in motion. Major investigation into the Cactus Stop. It'll take time, but we'll shut them down."

Lu tossed it to him. "It's a copy," she said when Jack and I both scowled.

Hitch said, "We could go in undercover, run through the scam, build a background, but it'll take a lot of time. Maybe now, we won't have to, but getting a warrant even with this drive might be difficult. We'll run it up the chain."

Cal walked back in. "I'm sorry," he said. "I'll take this to my boss first thing Monday morning, but we'll get a warrant on the first video alone. I don't want to wait until Ramos does his audit. Family complicates everything, and we have a clear case of John Brighton giving a gun to the man who attempted to kill a government witness and instructing him to blame Bradford."

I asked, "Did you know that Kayla Bradford was the anonymous caller?"

Silence.

Jack smiled. "You did say my sister was brilliant."

"No proof," I said, "but I'm positive."

"She turned in her own father," Cal said, almost in awe. "I'll say, I've seen it before. A family member coming to us. But I didn't expect this."

"We might not be able to prove it," I said, "but the recording fits."

"She might know more," Cal said.

"You could also put her in danger," Jack said.

"Consider her feelings," Tess added. "She might not have thought it through. The anonymous call, then finding out her mother was just as involved as her father. Maybe she doesn't even know about her half brother. You could destroy her."

"More than her parents did?" Cal said quietly. "I'll table it for now, listen to the recording again. It won't be my call, has to come from on high."

My phone rang. It had to be family—who else called at quarter to midnight? But I didn't recognize the number.

"This is Margo," I answered.

"Margo Angelhart? This is Edith Ann Mackey. I think something bad is happening across the street."

"Edith, call 911. I'm on my way."

I ran out, the three men on my heels.

chapter forty-six

ANGIE WILLIAMS

Angie stood frozen outside the back door of the Cactus Stop, her pulse pounding in her ears. The night air was suffocating. Or was that just in her mind? She rolled her shoulders, trying to loosen the tension, then she heard something.

She glanced around, scanning every corner of the alley, every shadow, as if she could feel eyes on her, watching her, watching everything she did.

She saw no one. Every instinct screamed that she wasn't alone, even though no one was there.

Yeah, she was scared—hell, she was *terrified*. Benny's text had promised something big, said he knew what happened to Elijah and she had to come to the store when he got off at midnight. But now that she was here, dread crawled up her spine with each passing second. She was early, her mind racing with dark thoughts she couldn't shake.

The promise she'd made to Margo hung heavy on her soul like a lead weight. She wasn't supposed to be here—out in the open, in plain sight, at the Cactus Stop. Margo told her to stay away . . .

that someone might get suspicious . . . but Benny needed her. She couldn't let Benny die like Elijah.

She pulled out her phone, fingers trembling, and shot him a message:

I'm here, out back, I'm not coming in.

Her heart skipped a beat when his response came too quickly.

What? You're in my backyard?

Angie scanned the parking lot again, but Benny's truck was nowhere in sight. Her breath caught in her throat. This didn't make sense. Her gut churned with the sinking certainty that something was terribly wrong.

Did you text me an hour ago and ask me to come to the Stop tonight?

She stared at the screen, waiting for him to respond. But her skin prickled, every fiber of her being screaming for her to run—*right now*. The seconds stretched. Her pulse thumped, waiting.

One, two, three, four . . .
Then, finally—

I got off at 8. Where are you? I'll pick you up.

No. No. No! She immediately texted back, her fingers shaking:

I'm leaving. I'll call in a bit.

A muffled *pop! Pop! Pop!* Came from the store.
It sounded like gunfire.
Again, another deafening crack echoed from inside the store,

followed by a fifth shot, closer this time, too close. The sharp, hollow sound sliced through the night, and her body surged into motion before her brain even caught up. She didn't stop to think, didn't wait to see who or what was inside.

Run, run, run.

The mantra propelled her legs to move faster, every step carrying her farther from the danger, but she wasn't fast enough. The back door of the Cactus Stop slammed open, blinding light spilling out behind her. She heard the unmistakable click of a gun being cocked—another shot fired, this one louder. The bullet grazed the pavement just inches from her heels.

The weight of terror pushed her forward. The world blurred as she sprinted, her lungs burning, the sound of another gunshot ringing in her ears. How could she outrun a bullet?

But she didn't want to die, so she ran.

chapter forty-seven

MARGO ANGELHART

I didn't know how I got stuck with the fed in my Jeep, but at least he didn't complain about my driving as I floored it all the way up Central and prayed that I didn't get pulled over.

I didn't drive down Hatcher, but turned up the side street from Dunlap and parked in front of Edith's home.

Two patrol cars were in the Cactus Stop parking lot, blue and red lights going around and around.

Edith was on her porch. Cal and I approached her.

"Edith, are you okay?" I asked.

"I was sitting out here smoking like I do. And—oh, Lordy."

I reached out for her. She was shaking.

"You need to sit."

Edith sat in her chair and lit a cigarette. "Three men. Masks. I called you when I saw them because you were asking about odd things, and this was odd. I thought they were being robbed. I was on the phone with 911 when I heard gunfire. So many shots. I lost count."

"Are you okay?" I asked again.

She nodded. "Go. Find out. So much violence," she whispered.

I looked at Cal. He had pulled his badge out and put it around his neck. "You with me?" he asked.

"Sure," I said.

Jack and Hitch pulled up behind my Jeep and the four of us walked over to the parking lot. Immediately, an officer tried to stop us, then he recognized Hitch.

"Detective, we haven't even called it in."

"I heard on the wire. This is one of my cases. What happened?"

I was beginning to like Hitch. He certainly commanded authority.

"We just got here, cleared the place. Three bodies, all deceased."

Hitch nodded to Cal, and they both went inside, leaving Jack and me just inside the crime scene tape.

"They're cleaning house," I said to Jack.

"It could be a robbery."

"You don't believe that. Not after tonight." I thought back. Lena Clark was asking questions—then she was murdered. Dwight Parsons wanted to talk to me—then he was murdered. I told Manny Ramos what I thought Desi Jimenez was doing—and now she was likely dead. It was Friday, her regular night. Cleaning house because he feared she'd talk? Once he launched the audit—*no*, I thought. Once the police investigated, she would talk.

John Brighton wasn't the man in charge. He wasn't even at the house tonight. Ramos called the shots. He may have called his nephew to clean up the problem. Brighton may have pulled the trigger.

But I knew in my heart and my head that Manny Ramos ordered these murders.

Maybe Desi didn't know her brother had been killed, maybe she did. Maybe she knew Ramos was in charge, maybe she didn't. But Manny Ramos wouldn't want his favored nephew, the boy he raised as his own, to go to prison.

"Manny fucking Ramos is running the whole thing," I said. "I told him about Desi. Either he ordered this hit, or he told Brighton who ordered the hit. He's dirty."

Jack didn't say anything.

"I know, I know, we can't prove it—yet."

Cal came out. "Hitch is talking to the cops. Three bodies. One woman, two men. A bloody mess. The woman is Desi Jimenez. One of the men is a customer, in a janitor's outfit, shot and killed next to the beer cooler. The other guy I don't know, his head was near blown off. The back door was open and there's evidence one of the gunmen ran out that way. Maybe someone got away, or he was clearing the alley, I don't know. Cameras, destroyed. Cash register, busted. It wasn't a robbery—it was a hit."

My phone vibrated.

I glanced down, not intending to answer anyone this late, when I saw the message.

They used Benny's phone to set me up. I ran. Help.

I immediately hit Call and headed toward my car. "Angie, where are you?"

She was sobbing and panting, clearly out of breath. "I—I—I'm running. The canal trail. They followed me, but I lost them. I think. I don't want to die!"

"I'm coming for you. Where?"

"I—I passed. Nineteenth. I'm stupid!"

"Listen, Angie—listen to me. Take the path up to Twenty-Fifth, near Rose Mofford Park. I'll be there. I'm coming."

I got into my car and Cal climbed into the passenger seat.

"Out," I said as I turned the ignition.

"Backup."

I looked out the window at Jack as if to say, *Why aren't you coming?* But he just motioned me to leave.

"Well, shit," I said and made a U-turn since the police had blocked off Hatcher.

"Trust me," Cal said.

"Like hell," I said. "You were stalking me."

"Not stalking. That's a crime. I was following you in the course of a legitimate investigation. Is this the Angie you told me about?"

"Yes. I told her to stay away from here."

I wove through the neighborhood until I hit Seventh Avenue, then turned west on Dunlap and floored it until I hit Twenty-Fifth, turned north too fast, my tires squealing as we crossed over the canal. There was a jogging trail along the north side of the canal. I didn't see Angie, so parked the car and jumped out.

I heard a gunshot from down in the canal and ran toward it. Cal was right behind me. Then he passed me. I sped up.

I saw a body lying on the path and wanted to scream.

"Freeze! Federal Agent!" Cal shouted and that was when I saw a man in black running toward the fallen figure, his gun raised to fire.

The shooter turned his gun toward us, and Cal fired with a calm, cool efficiency that I didn't have time to admire.

The shooter went down, and Cal ran over to him, fifty yards down the path, as I knelt next to Angie.

"Angie, talk to me! Are you hit? Are you hurt?"

Angie sat up and started crying. She clung to me tightly, tears streaming down her face, her body convulsing.

"Are you bleeding?" I asked as I held her.

"N-n-n-o. I fell. My ankle. B-broke. I thought—oh, God, Benny."

"Benny wasn't there. He wasn't at the Cactus Stop."

"He texted me, told me to meet him there, but he wasn't there. I don't know why! He said he didn't text me." Her hands were shaking as she handed me her phone. I read the exchange between her and Benny.

"They spoofed his phone or used a VPN." I sounded smart, but I wasn't. It was something I heard Luisa talking about.

I sat with Angie, her head buried in my lap, and watched Cal handcuff the suspect, who looked dead to me. But I guess it was protocol to restrain dead guys. Cal got on his phone, walked back over to me. He ended the call and said, "Police are on their way. You okay?" he said to Angie, but was looking at me.

"She doesn't appear to be hit."

"I looked over my shoulder," Angie said. She was still shaking, but her voice was calmer. "When I saw him, I tripped and fell and my ankle snapped. Then I heard the gun and I thought he was going to kill me."

"Your broken ankle saved your life," I said. "Angie, you should have called me when Benny texted you."

"I'm sorry."

I handed her phone to Cal. "Someone spoofed Benny's phone to lure Angie to the Cactus Stop," I told him.

I caught Cal's eye. His face had hardened, but when he squatted and spoke to Angie, his voice was kind. "You're a tough kid. I hope you'll let me sign your cast."

"I don't know you."

"Smart kid too," I said.

"I'm DEA Agent Cal Rafferty. And I think you know something that will send all of these people to prison."

"I don't know anything."

"You do. Otherwise, they wouldn't want to kill you."

I frowned at him. "Kick the puppy while she's down," I muttered. But I did appreciate his bluntness. It's what I would have said, if I hadn't thought she'd been shot. My heart was still racing.

I nodded toward the shooter. "Dead?"

"Unfortunately," he said.

"Sorry—probably a headache for you."

"That, but mostly, dead men don't talk."

"I don't know anything," Angie insisted.

"Well, how about if you go to the hospital, get that ankle

looked at, and we can have a chat. See what you think you don't know."

"Only if Margo's there," Angie said. Then she looked at me and seemed so small. "Please?"

"I'll be there," I said.

chapter forty-eight

MARGO ANGELHART

Cal was not a person people said no to—even nurses, which was pretty damn impressive. My dad had been a doctor my entire life, and good nurses ran the floor. Cal sweet-talked or threatened, whatever the situation called for, to ensure that Angie had a security guard until the police detail arrived.

After Angie returned from X-Ray, I sat with her. "It's totally broken," she said. "Clean break, like *snap*. They wanted to give me drugs for the pain and I said no."

"You know, sometimes drugs actually do what they're supposed to and help."

"It's not that bad," she said. She looked at the ceiling. "You know, my mom got oxycodone after a slip and fall where she worked. That's how she started smoking pot every night. And drinking. The first thing she does when she gets home from work is pour vodka and whatever she has around. When she's not working, the clock strikes noon, she pours a drink. I don't want my life to be all about work and getting stoned every fucking day. I want to *do* something."

I touched her hand. "You are doing something. Do you know how many people see what's going on around them and just ignore it? Pretend it doesn't exist? You *see*. That puts you ahead of the game."

Cal came in. At first, his expression was angry and tired, then like a switch it was gone. "Hey, kiddo, I hear you're getting an actual cast. Don't forget to let me sign it. I get to be first."

"Kiddo? I'm seventeen."

He shrugged. "My baby sister is twenty-nine and I call her kiddo all the time. Among other things."

He pulled the other chair up and sat next to me. "So, because you're a minor, Officer Morales—you remember her, right?"

"Yeah," Angie said cautiously.

"She went to your house. Talked to your mom. Long story short, she won't be coming by for a while, but lucky me, I'm authorized to sign off on any procedures."

"She's wasted, isn't she?"

He nodded. "By the time she comes down, you'll be outta here. And if you need a place to crash—not a group home or any bullshit like that, those places suck—I know someone who can put you up for a few days."

The unspoken words were clear. Angie had a choice.

"Oh. Thanks. I can stay with my best friend, Gina Martinelli, and her family, they're really nice, but I don't want to bring anything bad to them."

"I hear you loud and clear. And I'm hoping we wrap up this entire operation in the next couple of days—with your help. And I arranged it so you can stay here for another day or two if we need it. Just telling you, the option is out there, and the people I'd put you with are one-hundred percent safe."

She sighed. "I can't help. I didn't see his face. They didn't say anything, just started shooting. But they knew I was coming."

"They spoofed or cloned your friend Benny's phone. They might have seen the messages you sent him, so they knew you were out back. I won't know for certain until we finish processing the dead guy."

Angie took a deep breath, then let it out. She winced.

"So, I heard you don't want painkillers," Cal said. "I don't blame you, I refused them even when I was shot."

"You were shot?" she asked, eyes wide.

"Not today, a few years ago. Can't show you the scar, it would be indecent," he added with a glance in my direction, and a wink. "But pain really sucks. You can get the mildest oxycodone out there—"

"No," she said.

"Or they have prescription strength Tylenol. I told them to bring you some. You don't have to take it, but I strongly recommend it. It won't numb the pain, but it'll take the edge off and it's not addictive."

She nodded. "Okay," she said.

I watched Cal. He worked the nurses, Angie, even me. He was charismatic. It was subtle, but it was undeniable. The guy who stalked me—okay *tailed* me—was extremely affable.

Probably charmed everyone he met. A regular Mr. Prince Charming.

I couldn't help but wonder exactly where his scar was.

"So, that'll take them awhile—in the meantime, I'd like to pick your brain," Cal said.

Angie looked at me.

"You're not in any trouble," I told her. "Right, Cal?"

"Not at all. I mean, if you were *my* kid, I might lock you in your room until you turned twenty-one for sneaking out of the house in the middle of the night, but I did worse." He grinned again, an easy smile that, this time, reached his deep blue eyes.

Cal continued. "You know something. You don't know you know it. Between Margo here and Officer Morales—Josie—I think I know what's been going on. One of the reasons my bosses love me even when I drive them crazy is because I see patterns. I see how things fit together—or don't—and that solves cases."

I thought back to how he tweaked the information on my

board at the office and how everything became so much clearer when he moved a few connections around.

"And I've gone over everything that happened in the last few weeks. Plus, Margo came up with the one thing I missed three years ago."

"The work permit?" I asked, thinking about Scott Jimenez.

He frowned at me. "Okay, I missed *two* things. The big one? Coach Bradford wasn't the only adult involved at Sun Valley High School. Margo thinks that Lena Clark was killed because of something she learned, because she was asking questions about Elijah Martinez and maybe she got a sense that something was wrong. Maybe someone lied. Maybe someone looked at her the wrong way. Maybe she asked the wrong question to the wrong person."

"I'd like you to relax, close your eyes, and go back to Monday," Cal said to Angie in a hypnotic voice. "You went to the volleyball game and Mrs. Clark came to talk to you."

Angie took a deep breath and closed her eyes. She was tense and trying to relax. I'm sure the pain didn't help. "She saw me coming out of the bathroom," Angie said. "I wasn't supposed to be there. I'd cut school."

"A witness said that you were arguing."

"Yeah. I felt bad for cutting school because Mrs. Clark had always been so nice to me, but I didn't think anyone cared about what happened to Elijah. And—it was more than that."

"How?"

"I was mad at myself for not making Elijah tell me what was going on. I knew something was off with him. But he was so prideful, he didn't want to ask for help. Not from me, not even from Andy who was his best friend since they were little. Like me and Gina."

"Okay," Cal said, "you argued. What did Mrs. Clark say?"

"I don't remember. Really, I don't. Except that Elijah's mom had hired a private investigator to find out what happened that night. How he got to the park, who he was with, that stuff. She wanted me to sit down with her and the PI, but right then I knew I wanted to talk to her—you—" she glanced at me "—alone. I didn't want Mrs. Clark there as a buffer where I couldn't say what I wanted. So I went to her office and took the card."

"You told the police that Mr. Borel saw you leaving the office," Cal said. "I read the report," he added when I glanced at him. Then he smiled again. "I told you, I see connections, but that's only because I read fast."

I almost laughed. He was both supremely self-confident and humble at the same time. It was almost endearing.

"Yeah, I got out of there fast."

"Did you see anyone else?"

"No." She paused. "Yes. Not really."

"What do you mean by no, yes, not really?"

"I was leaving and I was going to go out the closest door because I didn't want to talk to anyone, but I heard two people coming in, talking. One was I think Mrs. Clark. Because of her jewelry."

I nodded, said, "Lena Clark wore a lot of necklaces."

"Yeah, but—" Angie paused.

"What did you remember?" Cal asked.

"It wasn't jewelry, or not just jewelry. It was a jangle of keys. But . . ."

"Don't stop. Spill it. You're safe here," Cal repeated.

"Mrs. Webb always has keys around her wrist. She's the vice principal. Mr Borel didn't give me shit when he saw me, but she would have. But I didn't really think about it when I heard it, it was like . . . I don't know, I just knew it was her but didn't consciously think about it until now."

"You heard her. Did you see her?"

"No."

"Do you remember what she said?"

"I don't . . ." Angie paused, squeezed her eyes shut. "Give me five minutes."

"She was talking to someone and said, 'Give me five minutes'?"

"Yeah." Angie opened her eyes. "Then I heard heels coming down the hall . . . Oh, my God!"

I knew it almost before she said it.

"Mrs. Clark! She wears heels, they were her heels. I heard her walking down the hall toward her office as I left."

"So Mrs. Webb, who you recognized by the keys jangling around her wrist, and maybe her voice, came into the building with Mrs. Clark, they parted ways, and Mrs. Webb said to give her five minutes."

As if she would be meeting her in five minutes.

Which gave Lena enough time to call me before Melissa Webb came back to kill her.

After Cal called in a protection detail for Angie, we leaned against the wall outside her room as we waited for her bodyguard to arrive.

"It's all set," he said to me. "I'll hang until they arrive. Shouldn't be more than an hour."

"You did great with Angie," I said.

"She's a great kid. A little too smart and sassy for her own good, but who doesn't love a smart-ass?"

"Most parents."

He laughed. "Well, I'm not a parent."

We stood there in silence and it wasn't uncomfortable. "What's your story?" I finally asked him.

"What do you mean?"

"Well, we're waiting here for a guard for who knows how long. Why DEA?"

"Why not?"

It was a flip answer, and I didn't believe him. "Your sister?"

"Hitch blabbed."

I didn't respond.

"In part," Cal said, and that was it. For now.

"Where you from?" I asked.

"All over." He glanced at me and raised his eyebrows. "Army brat."

I laughed. "You looked me up, didn't you?"

"Of course I did. Have to know who I'm *tailing*."

"And you didn't want to enlist?"

"Nope. We moved a lot, and Mom was responsible for all of us—me and my three sisters. My dad was a good dad, but he worked a lot and deployments were really hard on my mom especially." He paused. "He died overseas."

"I'm sorry to hear that."

"I was eighteen. I miss him. My mom never really recovered. Maybe because it was only a couple years after my sister died. Or maybe it was like she expected the worst their entire marriage and when the worst happened, she couldn't deal with it."

There was more to the story, but I didn't push. This wasn't the time or place.

"So, three sisters. Where do you fall?"

"Middle."

"Middle of four?"

"I have a twin sister. She's only two minutes older than me."

I laughed. "Well, I am an *actual* middle child. I have an older brother and sister, and a younger brother and sister."

"All the baggage we middle children have," he teased.

"Where do we go from here?" I asked.

"Well, I was hoping I could take you for dinner sometime this week."

My stomach did a little flip when I realized he was flirting with me. "I meant our cases. Mine, yours."

"I knew what you meant."

But he didn't answer my question.

"Well?"

"You first. Dinner?"

"Really?"

"I can think of a lot of things we can do, places we can go, but we still have to eat at some point. I like eating."

"I'll think about it. But I don't want to be shut out of this case."

"I wouldn't think of it."

"Okay. How are *we* going to take down Manny Ramos and Melissa Webb and John Brighton before they hurt anyone else?"

"Well, funny you should mention that, because I have a plan."

He told me his plan and I smiled.

I was really beginning to like this guy.

chapter forty-nine

MARGO ANGELHART

No one else liked the plan, but Cal sold them.

I was impressed.

We were briefing in the DEA conference room Sunday afternoon. A surprising feat considering Cal and his boss were the only federal agents involved right now.

Cal had gotten five Phoenix PD detectives and cops in the room: Hitch, King, Chavez, Josie, and her partner Tyrell. I could have done without King—I still didn't like her. But she was onboard, especially since we did all the work to prove Melissa Webb was in the building when Lena was killed.

Apparently, she had lied in her statement. She claimed to have left right after the volleyball game. And since no one saw her in the building, they had no one that contradicted her alibi.

Except Angie. I wondered if Webb had seen Angie and Parsons talking Thursday afternoon and worried that Angie *had* seen her. Or maybe Parsons had doubts based on some knowledge he had.

He *had* wanted to talk to me. *Trade notes*, he'd said. He could very well have had something big to trade. And we'd probably never know. Unless Cal could charm Melissa Webb into turning state's evidence. If anyone could, it was Cal Rafferty. He'd already started.

I enjoyed listening to him go through how he spent his Saturday: A deep dive into Melissa Webb and—surprise, surprise—she had millions of dollars in an off-shore account.

I liked how Cal took over the room. He had an easy confidence and was very nice to look at. He ran through Webb's finances, injecting humor here and there, then came up with information that I hadn't known until he spoke.

"John Brighton graduated from Sun Valley High School," Cal said. "He was a freshman the year that Melissa Webb was hired from a school in Los Angeles. The year after she started, she brought Coach Bradford in. Probably at the request of Manny Ramos. Going through publicly available archives, Melissa Webb has been to many of Ramos's charity events over the years so it's safe to say they have known each other for some time.

"After Bradford went to prison, they changed their recruitment process. Melissa Webb took over the work-study program and referred students to Ramos. She appears to have focused on young men with no father figure at home, who were easy to manipulate and had no support structure. Once we arrest her, we can depose staff and ask for records and may give us a clearer picture."

Then Cal called me up to help him lay out the plan. It was Cal's plan; I'd just improved on it.

"Any questions about Operation Saguaro?" Cal said and I laughed at the tongue-in-cheek label he'd given our plan. He winked at me. I hope no one else saw it.

There were questions, which we answered as best we could. When there were no more questions, we had a little time before we began.

I stepped outside because I needed air. Jack followed me.

"That happened fast," he said.

For a split second, I thought he had noticed Cal flirting with me . . . and how I didn't shut him down.

But he was talking about the plan.

"Yep," I agreed.

"You did good," Jack said.

"*We* did good," I corrected. "I couldn't have found what Tess did about Manny Ramos and the Bradfords—she really dug in. And without that file you got from your contacts at Phoenix PD, there's no way we would have had so many details about the Bradford arrest."

"You're good in the field," Jack said. "I'm really glad you're working with us."

"So you've said."

"I mean it, Margo."

"Why so serious?"

He didn't answer me right away. Then he said, "I loved being a cop. But then three years ago—well, you know."

I knew. With Dad in prison and Jack going through a divorce, his life had been thrown into upheaval.

"I like being a PI, and I couldn't go back to the force, not after having so much freedom from arbitrary rules and the intense scrutiny by politicians, the media, the brass. It was exhausting and depressing. But after seeing that bloodbath last night? I wanted back in. I wanted to have a badge and bring those killers to justice. They shot that janitor in the back. He was just coming in for a six-pack after work and they killed him. But while I miss parts of the job, I'm happy where we are now. Working with my family. Helping people like Alina and Angie. I don't know if I like Cal's style, but I can't argue with the results. Be careful tomorrow."

"I will."

I looked down at my phone. I had a message from Rick.

Sam's team made it to the final championship game of the tourney. It starts at 4 if you can make it.

An olive branch.
But there was no going back.
I responded.

I'm working. Sorry.

I *was* sorry because I missed Sam and would have enjoyed watching her play. And sometimes, I missed Rick.

But even if I went, it didn't mean anything. Because nothing had fundamentally changed between Rick and me.

Well, maybe something had shifted. Maybe we could be friends now. It wouldn't be easy, but lunch the other day hadn't been awkward. We had history, but we were friends before we were lovers.

Rick responded.

Ok.

And maybe we were.

chapter fifty

MARGO ANGELHART

Operation Saguaro commenced early Monday. The joint DEA and Phoenix PD operation had obtained all the necessary warrants and seemed to be working together smoothly. It was nice when agencies got along.

After seven in the morning, I went in wired to talk to Melissa Webb.

There had been intense discussion over the weekend about whether Detective King and Chavez should interview her, and Cal listened to their arguments. But in the end, he'd said it would take too much time. If it was a formal interview, Webb could delay long enough for Manny Ramos to shut down and leave the country. Already, the DEA had learned that John Brighton used his passport to fly to Mexico City on Friday night, before the Cactus Stop shooting. That meant Ramos had likely sent him south to give him an alibi, before the hit on Desi and Tony—who was the third victim of the Cactus Stop shooting.

Connecting Ramos to the criminal enterprise was going to be difficult because there was no sign the drug operation was being run out of any other Cactus Stop location. Ramos could claim it was just Hatcher Street. That Desi and Tony were responsible, that whoever they worked with had killed them. He could throw his nephew John Brighton under the bus because John worked in the corporate office. Ramos had money and a stellar reputation. He would be nearly impossible to indict.

Unless someone turned state's evidence.

No one wanted to let Webb walk on murder. But a reduced sentence? Federal prison? Some enticements to come clean? All on the table.

There was no evidence that Webb killed Lena Clark, and Angie's testimony wouldn't be enough to get a conviction. It *was* enough to get a warrant for Webb's house, which was being executed as soon as she left for work Monday morning.

I wasn't wearing the wire to catch Webb in a lie. The feds probably couldn't use anything she said because of potential entrapment accusations, though I was pretty certain they would try since Arizona was a one-person recording state. The wire was for my protection, in case Webb reacted violently to what I said.

Cal had insisted.

I walked into the administration building five minutes after Cal confirmed Webb had entered, at 7:10 in the morning. I told the secretary I was a PI investigating Elijah Martinez's death and had information for Mrs. Webb about a student who may have given him the drugs, and I wanted to tell her before I told the police.

Melissa Webb came out to greet me and take me into her office. The keys that Angie had heard were wrapped around her wrist. They jingled as she walked. It was a distinctive sound because of a large metal shamrock in the middle of the ring of keys.

She opened her door and motioned for me to sit in the chair across from her desk before she sat behind it. "Normally, I would refer you to the district, but I hope we can handle this situation before it gets out of hand."

"Me too," I said.

"Who was it? I'll call them in first thing."

"John Brighton."

Webb froze. Every cell in her body seemed to go still. Then she said, "Excuse me?"

"He was a student here, and while I'm not positive that he gave Elijah the drugs, he was privy to the conspiracy. But that's not the main reason I'm here. Your plan to have Angie killed failed. She wasn't at the Cactus Stop when the hired guns came in and killed three people: Desi Jimenez, the assistant manager Tony, and an innocent bystander."

"You need to leave."

"Angie heard you and Lena entering the building. She heard you tell Lena 'five minutes.' Angie left in the opposite direction because she didn't want to talk to Lena. Lena then called me from her office, and a few minutes later you came in and stabbed her."

"You are crazy," Webb said in an übercalm voice.

"Two things. Police reports are public information. And you told the police that you left directly from the volleyball game. Which is a lie, because you came into the building with Lena. You told the police you didn't see Lena after the volleyball game, but Angie heard you talking to Lena in the corridor." Slight fib—Angie heard the keys and thought she might have recognized the voice, but I didn't have to say that.

"You were concerned when you found out that Angie was talking to me, but it wasn't until you saw Angie and Dwight Parsons talking on Thursday that you feared they would put information together. So you figured you'd kill him, write a fake suicide note, and he'd get the blame for Lena's murder. What you didn't factor is that the police generally do a good job investigating homicides. They found Lena's blood in the administrative bathroom. Dwight didn't have time to clean up—nor have any reason to clean up because he called 911 from Lena's office and was found putting pressure on her wounds. He had her blood all over him."

"I didn't kill her."

Webb's voice was flat, her eyes calculating.

"Good luck with that," I said. "We have a witness, and the police have evidence." Some, not enough. I needed her to break.

She sounded calm, but she was shaking.

"You were Manny Ramos's mole here," I continued. "Bradford didn't even know you were part of his own operation. He thought he was the head honcho, working for his *uncle-in-law*. He remained silent to protect his wife's son, the boy raised by his uncle, the boy who was the light of his uncle's eyes because he never had a son of his own. Manny Ramos didn't want John to go to prison, and Ben would do anything to stay in Manny's good graces—and to make his wife happy."

Webb paled. "You can't prove anything. Manny Ramos is a pillar of society."

"Angie will testify that she heard you entering the administration building with Lena Clark. Circumstantial? Sure. But my guess is there is a lot more evidence as soon as the police start looking. And they will, when I turn over all my notes to them."

"What do you want? Money? I have plenty. I'll wire you a million dollars today." She snapped her fingers.

"Tempting, but no. I want Manny Ramos."

She laughed, but she sounded scared. "You'll never get him."

"You're going to give him to me on a silver platter."

"I don't have a death wish."

"Then you'll spend the rest of your life in prison."

"You have no idea who you're going up against."

"Manny Ramos thinks he's a god. He sits in his big house on the mountain and looks down on the city of Phoenix and thinks he owns it. He doesn't. You recruited teenagers for Ramos, kids with no dad in the picture, kids with a troubled home life." I remembered then what Eric McMahon told me, that Scott Jimenez spent a lot of time in the vice principal's office. "You recruited Scott Jimenez, didn't you?" Webb didn't respond. "Elijah knew what was going on, but when his friend died of a drug overdose, he needed proof. Maybe he came to you, said something that had your instincts humming. And you warned Ramos that Elijah was a problem."

"No." But her voice was quiet, too quiet.

"Who killed Elijah? Who poisoned him with fentanyl?"

"You're playing a dangerous game, Ms. Angelhart."

"My favorite kind," I said.

We were at a standoff, and I needed something to knock her over the ledge. And the only thing I could do was show most of my cards. Or lie.

Or a little of both.

"Okay."

She looked at me quizzically.

"Not talking to you," I said and put my finger to my ear where there wasn't an ear bud, but she couldn't see that with my hair down. "Just got word that the warrant on your house is being executed. They already know about the off-shore account."

She blanched, reached for her phone.

"Don't pick up that phone. I mean it."

"Who's going through my house?" Her voice ended on a squeak.

"Who killed Elijah?" I countered.

"I don't know! I told John he was asking the wrong questions and two days later I heard he was dead. Kids make bad choices."

"Sometimes they do."

"I didn't know until Monday that Elijah was dead."

As if that made her innocent.

The door opened, and Webb looked like a deer caught in the headlights. Cliché, but in this case very true.

Detectives King and Chavez entered. "Melissa Webb, you are under arrest for the murders of Lena Clark and Dwight Parsons."

She turned from them to me. "I didn't! I—I didn't." Her voice trailed off.

Chavez read Webb her rights.

"I thought you had a search warrant," Webb said, looking at me. "You lied about that?"

"No," I said. "I just didn't say who was executing the warrant. I think it was the feds."

I, unfortunately, couldn't participate in Melissa Webb's interrogation, but Cal was in there with King and Chavez and came out an hour later grinning ear to ear.

"She spilled everything and all we had to do was reduce her sentence to twenty years for second-degree murder and promise a federal penitentiary as far from Arizona as she can get."

"And?"

"I have a list of all the drug houses, a statement of how the operation worked—you were right about that—and all the players she knows, including John Brighton. It's a multimillion-dollar operation. Plus the kicker—Webb has Elijah's backpack. John Brighton gave it to her and told her to put it in a locker. She did, in the gym, since there are no other lockers on campus. No one thought to look in it, not even the coaches, because the lock was standard for the school. Your cousin Josie and her partner are getting it now and will transport it to the crime lab for processing."

"What now?"

"The FBI is going to raid the corporate offices, Phoenix PD and DEA are going to raid the drug houses, and I'm going to serve the warrant on Manny Ramos at his house. I'd love for you to come with me, because you've earned it, but I can't."

"I don't need to be there," I said. "Just get him—and be careful."

He smiled. "This is why I love my job."

While Cal was having all the fun serving the warrant on Manny Ramos, I went back to the office to clean up the mess we'd left in the conference room on Friday night. I was surprised that it was already clean.

My mom was in her office, her reading glasses on the edge of her nose as she was reviewing a file. She looked up when I came in and smiled. "Adventurous weekend, wasn't it?"

I sat down. "You didn't have to clean up."

"It wasn't me—I would have made you and Jack do it, just like when you were kids. But Iris has a soft spot for you both."

"I'll get her those flowers she likes, the mums."

Mom nodded her approval.

"So. The Madison O'Neill defense. Are Jack and Tess on board?"

"Reluctantly," she said.

"Why?"

"Because Tess is a romantic at heart and Madison is accused of killing her husband, and Jack doesn't want to work for anyone who might be guilty. But they also both agree that everyone, even the guilty, deserve a fair trial and proper defense. A good investigator is crucial to a proper defense."

"Do you think she's guilty?"

Mom didn't say anything for a long minute. "To be honest, if I thought she was guilty, I wouldn't have taken the case."

"So you think she's innocent?"

"No."

"Mom," I whined.

"I honestly don't know. That's what makes this case so interesting. Are my instincts failing me? Can I no longer discern fact from fiction? I'm fifty-nine, I'm not old, but maybe I'm getting there."

I laughed. "Hardly."

"I want the truth. I can't help it. I told the lawyers that we would be their investigators of record. There's a lot to unpack, and the Scottsdale Police really messed up the crime scene. So we have to recreate exactly what happened, and determine if Madison's version of the story is accurate, and if we can help prove it, or if she's lying. And if she's lying, what is her motivation? It's not money—she had plenty of money going into the marriage."

"Maybe she wanted more."

Mom sighed. "Maybe she did."

"I'm all in."

Mom smiled. "Like me, you can't stand an unsolved mystery."

A ding sounded in the office, telling us the door had opened. Mom looked up and immediately frowned. She reached under her desk where I knew she had a panic button.

I turned and saw Manny Ramos. He had a gun on Tess.

I jumped up.

"Slowly, Margo," he called across the office. "Hands where I can see them."

Peter—Elijah's friend—came in behind them. I mentally hit myself. Peter was another fatherless kid, given a great work-study job at the Cactus Stop headquarters. How could I have forgotten that fact while everything went down over the weekend? Peter could keep tabs on Elijah and anyone else on campus because he was so normal, so very average.

I'd asked questions—they got back to Ramos. Angie talked to Peter, texted him, and it got back to Ramos.

Angie probably texted Andy and Peter about her conversation Thursday with Parsons, and it got back to Webb—through Ramos.

Damn, I'd missed it.

Because you weren't looking at his friends, you were looking at his coworkers.

"Peter, get her gun, tie her up, tie up Ava. Ava, dear, please stay seated."

Peter complied. He had no expression on his face, as if he had no emotions at all.

I didn't attempt to convince him to turn on Ramos. Peter had my gun. Even if I could get him to listen to reason, I doubted I could do it quickly.

"Why are you here?" I asked.

Peter used zip ties on my hands, but I was confident that I could get out of them when necessary.

But not while Ramos had a gun on Tess.

"It seems my partner was arrested today, and I heard you had something to do with it."

Did he have a mole in Phoenix PD? Or was it Peter? Or someone on campus who saw Webb being escorted out in handcuffs?

"Then why haven't you left the country? Ticktock, Manny," I said.

"You have something I want. Teresa, darling, please."

He pushed Tess into her office. What did we have? I was tied up in the middle of the office, Mom was tied in her office, and now Tess was in her office with Ramos.

What information did we have that he wanted?

My phone vibrated in my pocket. Peter pulled it out and looked at it. "Mr. Manny? Someone named CR is calling her."

Cal.

Ramos said, "Just watch her, we won't be long. Now, Teresa, I am tech-savvy. So no tricks. Download the files—every file—you have on me."

"We have backups," Tess said, her voice cracking. "We have—"

"I don't care, I want them, you don't need to ask questions."

We had something he didn't have. Did he think someone other than Webb ratted him out? Or was he looking for someone else?

I thought back to everything we'd learned over the last week, about Elijah and the Bradfords and John Brighton and the Webb/Ramos network.

The Bradfords. Did Ramos think we knew who made the anonymous call? Did he think that's how we were clued in to his operation? Or that we knew about a mole in his organization?

If he heard Kayla's voice, he would know it was his niece. Would he hurt family?

Yes, he would. He would because she hurt him. John was the "good" son. But Kayla had taken down his operation with one phone call.

My phone vibrated again. Peter called out, "Now someone named Jack is calling."

After Mom pressed the panic button, the security company would first try her phone, then Jack's. If neither answered, the police would be called.

Our office was on a busy corner, set back from both streets by a narrow strip of grass and trees. But there were windows in every office, and the conference room looked out to the parking lot in the back. If the police showed up, Ramos would see them.

Jack would know that. Jack would keep it under control, stage outside of any line of sight.

But what if Ramos took my sister as a hostage?

He couldn't get on a plane, but he could drive. The border was three hours south. They could monitor it, but he could slip through. Or drive anywhere in the country. He had resources. Even if the feds managed to shut down his network here, he likely had accounts they didn't yet know about.

"You should have stayed put and took your chances with the legal system," I called out to him. "It could be years before the police prove anything."

Ramos ignored me. "Good, thank you, Teresa, this is what I need. No, no, don't get up."

He tapped on the keyboard.

Kayla's voice came out of Tess's computer.

Ramos's face reddened.

The ding on the door alerted all of us that someone was coming in. I turned. It was Cal, dressed in tactical pants and a polo shirt. He didn't quite look like a cop, but close enough. He probably hadn't had time to change. At least he didn't wear an obvious gun and his badge was nowhere to be seen.

"Hey, Margo, wanna get an early dinner—"

Ramos stepped out of the office with Tess in tow, gun still on her. "Hands up," he told Cal.

Ramos didn't appear to recognize Cal, but if Cal served the warrant when Ramos wasn't there, he would have no reason to know that he was a federal agent.

Cal's eyes widened and his hands went way up over his head. "Hey, hey! I didn't mean to—"

"Shut up, sit down."

Cal walked toward me. He looked at me and gave me the faintest of smiles, just one side of his lips curving up.

Outside, I saw some movement, then it was gone. Under the windows—a tactical team? Or just Jack?

"I said *sit*," Ramos ordered, moving the barrel of his gun from Tess's side to Cal's chest.

Cal moved fast and shouted, *"Down!"* to Tess.

I broke the zip ties as Cal ran like a bull toward Ramos. *What the hell?* He was going to get himself killed.

But Ramos turned the gun toward Tess, as if startled more by her dropping to the floor than by Cal's charge.

Then he swung the gun toward Cal.

I disarmed Peter, elbowed him in the gut and kneed him in the balls. He went down to his knees. At the same time, Cal leaped toward Ramos. He kicked Ramos in the chest with both feet, before Cal smoothly dropped, rolled on the ground, and ended in a kneeling position while simultaneously pulling a gun from the small of his back.

I was very impressed.

Jack ran into the office with Hitch and two Phoenix PD officers behind them.

Ramos was reaching for the gun that had fallen from his grasp.

I stepped on his wrist. Hard. I heard the bone crack and he screamed in pain.

I pressed harder.

Cal got up, retrieved Ramos's gun, and grinned at me. "That was fun," he said. "So, that dinner you promised me is going to have to wait a bit longer."

"I didn't say yes."

He laughed and read Ramos his rights.

chapter fifty-one

MARGO ANGELHART

On Tuesday I told Uncle Rafe everything, and he agreed to come with me to tell Alina. Of course he did. Because my uncle was one of the best people I knew, and he would want to be there for Alina when she learned the truth.

"Elijah was recruited by Mrs. Webb to work at the Cactus Stop," I said. "They primarily target young men without fathers. I don't think he knew what was going on at first, but he figured it out. Because you worked for Ramos's corporate office, he didn't say anything, but he was collecting evidence, copying security recordings, maybe taking notes. When his friend Megan died of a drug overdose, he started surveilling the Cactus Stop at night. He wanted to do the right thing, Alina."

Alina was crying. Had I said too much? Should I have lied? I looked to Uncle Rafe for help.

Uncle Rafe said, "Alina, Elijah made a wrong decision for the right reasons. But his conscience was strong, and he ended up doing the right thing."

"Why? Why didn't he tell me? Tell you? Go to the police?"

"He planned to," I said. "He was building a case. But I think he was scared. I want you to know that the evidence he found is crucial to the federal case against Ramos and his nephew. Because of Elijah, they will go away to prison for a long time."

Uncle Rafe let her cry on his shoulder. "You have a job at the rectory."

"No, I can't take charity from the church."

"It's not charity. The church secretary is having surgery in two weeks. She'll be out for two months after, then part-time for a while. Father Diaz and I were going to try and make do, but we have the approval of the diocese to bring in someone temporarily. I want you. It's not charity, you will work. And it's not permanent, but will get you through the New Year until you find something else."

Alina nodded and cried at the same time.

I caught Uncle Rafe's eye. He didn't need to say anything else. *Thank you*, I mouthed, and then I left.

Angie was in her apartment. The place reeked of pot and stale beer. Her bedroom was clean and the window was open. I sat in her desk chair.

"So, you didn't want to take Cal up on his offer of a place to live?"

"This is fine," Angie said.

"You're sure you're okay?"

Angie nodded. "My mom is an addict—I know it. But I can't force her to quit, and she hasn't gone so far off the rails that she can't pay the rent. Bruce is a jerk, but they're okay together. He's better than a lot of the men my mom brought home. And honestly, when I go to college, I'm not coming back. I don't think she'll notice."

My upbringing was so different from Angie's.

"You can always call me if you need a break. I don't live far from here. We can go get pizza or something."

"Maybe. I have friends. I can hang out at Gina's anytime I want. Mrs. Martinelli said that as long as our grades don't drop, I can even stay over on school nights."

"She sounds great."

"They all are." Angie shifted on her bed. "I'm going back to school tomorrow. Gina is going to pick me up until I get this cast off and can walk again."

"You two going to college together?"

Angie shrugged. "I doubt it. Gina has a volleyball scholarship to U of A. I don't know if I'll get enough financial aid and grants and scholarships to pay for it, and I don't have any money. Mrs. Clark said she would help put it together, but . . ."

"You'd be surprised. My parents and my sister all graduated from U of A."

"Not you?"

"Nope. I didn't go to college. It wasn't for me. But if it's right for you, then I want to help."

"I'm not taking any money from you."

"I'm not offering," I said, then laughed. "What I'm offering is my little sister, Luisa. She's a computer whiz, and the smartest in the family. She'll help you find every scholarship, grant, and financial aid package out there so that you won't have to pay a dime."

"Really? Why would she do that?"

"Because I'll ask her to. She's my sister, and she'd like you."

Angie seemed surprised that someone would help without strings. She shrugged.

"Well, maybe. But I don't know what I want to do with my life."

"That's okay. At seventeen I didn't either."

"How'd you know being a private investigator was right for you?"

"By doing it. When I solved my first case, I just knew. And I've never looked back."

"So going to the Army was a waste of time?"

"Absolutely not. It helped me figure out who I was here." I tapped my chest. "I know who I am, I'm happy with who I am. I love what I do. I didn't like when I thought you were shot, and I hated that I couldn't stop Manny Ramos before people died." I'd thought I'd failed her. I didn't want to feel that way again.

"I was scared," Angie admitted. "I did some stupid things."

"You sure did. And thank God you lived through it so hopefully you learned something."

Angie looked at her phone. She blushed.

"Have to go?"

"Chris and Benny are here. They shouldn't be."

"Because?"

"Chris has classes. At ASU."

"Maybe his brother needs him. Maybe you do too."

"Benny said you got him a job."

"Not really. I just asked my Uncle Tom if he had an opening in one of his restaurants for a good kid who's a hard worker. If Benny slacks off, Uncle Tom will fire him."

"Well, anyway, it was nice of you. And I'll talk to your sister, thanks."

"Great." I texted her Luisa's phone number. "She's expecting your call."

"I'll walk you out," Angie said.

She got up, grabbed her crutches, and we left.

Lori and Bruce were sitting on the couch watching television and barely noticed when we walked out.

Angie had a spine of steel. She had been dealt a shitty hand, and she was going to make something of herself. If I could help in even a small way, I'd do it.

Even just by offering up my brilliant sister's time and talent.

I walked Angie to Benny's truck. A kid I presumed was Chris got out and hugged her tightly. Angie introduced us, then got into the truck, sitting between the two brothers. They left.

Yes, she was going to be okay.

I got home late Tuesday night. I read an email from my mother about the Madison O'Neill case, though I didn't have to start right away. Mom had a bunch of legal issues to discuss with the defense attorney first.

Take a couple days and relax, Mom wrote in her message. I wanted to laugh. Me, relax?

Well . . . maybe I would go to the gun range and let off some steam. That always made me feel better. There was a movie Josie and I were talking about seeing. We could see a matinee and get drunk. I hadn't been drunk in a long, long time.

I felt out of sorts. I'd figured out what happened to Elijah and why, and justice would be served, but too many people were dead.

Too many *young* people. Kids with a future that had been cut short. Murder or drugs, they both left holes in the heart of someone who loved them. Two teachers who had done a good job helping teens navigate their lives as they entered adulthood—gone. Because of the selfish plans of violent criminals.

Sure, I'd take a couple days off—*not*. What would I do but think about all the bullshit that had happened? Better to start the next case and put this last week firmly in the past.

I was about to email my mom and tell her I'd be in the office tomorrow when my doorbell rang.

I got up, looked through the peephole.

Cal.

I opened the door.

He stood there wearing tactical pants, a black polo shirt, a sidearm, and carrying a pizza from Bianco's along with a six-pack of my favorite Church Mouse IPA.

"How did you know that's my favorite beer?" And my favorite wood-fired pizza—maybe my favorite pizza ever.

"I asked your brother." He smiled. "Can I come in?"

I waved him inside, then closed the door.

He looked around, turned left into the kitchen, put the beer in the refrigerator, and opened the pizza. "I hope you're hungry."

"I didn't say yes to a date."

"You didn't say no."

He found my plates, pulled out two, and put two slices on each one.

He was making himself at home. Searched two drawers before finding my bottle openers, cracked two beers, then brought everything to my small dining table. I couldn't help but follow him.

He sat down and took a bite. "What a couple of days," he said. "You okay?"

I shrugged, took a bite myself. It was still hot. "Angie is good. Talking to Alina Martinez was tough."

"The FBI is extraditing John Brighton from Mexico. He's already in custody."

"They knew we were getting close," I said. "Ramos was trying to save his enterprise and ended up destroying it."

"Pretty much." Cal took a sip of beer.

"What about the shooters?"

"We know who they are. The dead guy is a known thug, runs with a gang of known thugs. They were smart, but not as smart as they thought, and we caught their vehicle on camera on Dunlap. Now they're wanted and we'll find them. Plus, evidence at the scene—they destroyed the cameras, but didn't police their brass. Fingerprints on all of it."

"Did you get Bradford to talk?"

"I'm going to work on him tomorrow. Fifty-fifty he will. The FBI is going to have a sit-down with Kayla Bradford. She's in college in Tennessee, but may be able to fill in some gaps. Even if she doesn't help, we have a solid case against Brighton and Ramos. But if Ramos gets out, watch yourself. He blames you."

"Great," I said sarcastically and drank some beer.

"I'm serious."

And he was.

"I'm okay," I said, and meant it.

He looked at me for a beat too long. Cal wasn't like most of the guys I'd dated. He was cute, sure, with his short-cropped hair a little too long on top and bright blue eyes. He looked like the boy next door. He was talkative—I usually dated the strong silent types—and he was supremely confident. I liked confident men, but Cal had this arrogance that could be off-putting, but wasn't because he was so damn cute.

He listened. He wasn't so cocky that he didn't listen to everyone's opinion, then make an informed decision.

And he said I was brilliant. That was a big plus in his favor.

We ate, chatted about the case. They'd shut down the house where the dealers picked up their drugs—down the street from Mrs. Mackey. Cal's team was processing it, but he was focusing on Ramos himself. "We're pushing for no bail," he said, "and your mom is pretty amazing. Did you know there are cameras in your office? When she pushed the panic button, they turned on. The entire thing is on video—with sound."

"I didn't know that." *Good to know*, I thought.

"So we might get him in lock-up until trial. But still, be careful if he manages to get out on bail."

"Peter?"

"Don't know. He's not my concern, but that kid has no emotions. I think he's a budding sociopath."

"Terrific, we need more sociopaths," I said with thick sarcasm.

"Hitch is working him, so maybe we'll get something more. He'll be in juvie for a while at a minimum. Oh, I think we found Scott Jimenez's body."

"That was fast."

"Not really. He's a John Doe found in the middle of nowhere out past Buckeye. Near skeleton. But the timing works for when he disappeared, so they'll run some comparisons and see if they can confirm ID. Age, gender, and height all match." He looked at his watch. "Damn, I gotta go."

"Okay."

"I don't want to, but I have to be up before dawn for another case I'm working."

He cleared the plates and stacked them neatly in the sink. He was definitely trying to get on my good side.

I walked him to the door.

"I don't count this as a date," he said.

"Oh?"

"I have to re-qualify with my gun on Friday—quarterly range time. Want to go to the gun range on Thursday to practice?"

Now my stomach really did flip. "I'd love to."

"Then dinner afterward."

"Now you're pushing it," I said with a grin.

"Then maybe dessert," he said and took a step toward me.

I stood my ground.

Cal leaned over and kissed me. I tried to act casual, like every day I had a man bring me pizza and beer and kiss me good-night.

But I didn't.

I kissed him back. And then our bodies were against each other, my back was against the wall, and I moaned as a thrill shot through me.

A lust I hadn't felt in a long, long time.

"Damn," Cal whispered, his forehead against mine.

"Don't like the way I kiss?" I said lightly, but ended on a little squeak.

"Nothing could be further from the truth. But if I don't leave now, I'm not going to want to leave. And Margo? I don't want to rush. I really like you."

He kissed me again, quick and hard, his hand on the back of my neck.

Then he walked out with a wave, leaving me with half a pizza and a crooked grin.

I closed the door and leaned against it.

Had I seen that coming? Maybe. Yeah, I did. There was a hint of it when we worked together this weekend, a little spark.

I just didn't expect it to feel so good.

★ ★ ★ ★ ★

ACKNOWLEDGMENTS

So many people help me with research when I'm writing. For this book, my daughter Mary, a teacher, was a great sounding board with all things related to education—she also listened to my ideas and helped me discard what didn't work. My daughter Katie, a Phoenix PD officer, helped with details to make this story as authentic as possible. It was her true story about EBT fraud that was the nugget from which this story grew. If I got anything wrong about schools or crime, it's definitely not their fault!

Thanks also to Tim Matteson with Sunnyslope High School, who answered my questions quickly—I appreciate it! Once again, Crime Scene Writers is my go to source for all things murder and mayhem. A huge shout-out to Doug Lyle, doctor and writer, who helped me understand what fentanyl does to the human body.

As always, my editors April Osborn and Dina Davis are fantastic. A special shout-out to Dina, who really helped me turn a story I struggled with into a story I'm proud of. The art department once again knocked the cover out of the park. And last but never least, my agent, Dan Conaway at Writers House, who keeps me on task with this and all my stories.